MW01615035

BREATHE AGAIN

ROBERT F BARKER

By Robert F Barker

The DCI JAMIE CARVER SERIES

LAST GASP (The Worshipper Trilogy Book #1)

The last time Jamie Carver let a would-be victim as bait for a serial killer, it ended badly. Now they want him to do it again, only this time the 'victim' is a dominatrix.

FINAL BREATH (The Worshipper Trilogy Book #2)

A monstrous killer, safe behind bars, but just how safe is 'safe'? An archive of debauchery and murder, poised to ruin reputations, carers, lives. A detective, running out of time to find what he seeks

OUT OF AIR (The Worshipper Trilogy Book #3)

One City; Paris. Two killers, one in hiding, the other stalking the streets. An innocent young couple, bewitched into the deadliest danger. The detective who must find them before the worst happens.

FAMILY REUNION

How do you save a family from slaughter when you don't know who they are, and you're not allowed to find out? A killer is coming, and Jamie Carver has to to stop him. But how?

DEATH IN MIND

"Five minutes before she killed herself, Sarah Brooke had never had a suicidal thought in her life."
A mind-bending psychological thriller with a terrific twist. 'A treat for all Derren Brown fans.'

BREATHE AGAIN

Grainy photographs showing a woman whose features recall someone who died two years ago. A murder in upstate New York bearing signatures with which Jamie Carver is all too familiar. Dare he even ask the question…??

OTHER TITLES

MIDNIGHT'S DOOR

A novel of nightclub bouncers, Russian mobsters, and serial killing. Introducing Danny Norton, the man who runs the door at Midnight's, the hottest nightspot around. When it all kicks off, you'll want him by your side.

A KILLING PLACE IN THE SUN

His 'Place In The Sun' is simply a house. But to this Englishman, it's his castle, and he wants it back. "An action-packed international thriller that grips from the start, and ends with a gut-punch that pulls at the heart."

FREE DOWNLOAD

Get the inside story on what started it all...

To teenagers everywhere, in recognition of the confusions they face trying to figure stuff out.

Prologue

TWO HOURS HAVE passed since Curtis Whittingham first realised the extent of his miscalculation, and that in all likelihood it is going to cost him his life.

In that time, the rope around his neck has bitten ever deeper, making it harder by degrees to draw breath. Now, he is at the point where he is gulping for air, swallowing it down in mouthfuls to force it through his narrowing windpipe. He knows that without some intervention, or a change of heart on the part of his captor, what remains of his life can be counted in minutes, rather than the years that, less than four hours before, he would have assumed was his due.

When it began, of course, the arrogance that had long been one of Curtis's more defining characteristics, led him to assume that whilst the peril in his predicament was clear, the path to escape was relatively simple. All he had to do was deploy those techniques that were his stock-in-trade to demonstrate to his would-be killer that taking his life was, (a) unnecessary; (b) counter-productive; (c) dangerous; (d) a grievous mistake; the consequences of which any person of intelligence would immediately see as something to avoid, at all costs.

For close to forty minutes, such oratory as he has been able to manage with a slowly tightening hemp rope around his throat was, by turns explanatory, persuasive, and financially tempting, before turning threatening then - humiliatingly - pleading, topped off with plain old begging - something that is as alien to Curtis as cutting a deal capable of being seen as, 'fair to both sides'.

When, after that time, the response to his final, desperate appeal - '*Please* don't kill me. I'm begging you.

Just let me go' - resulted in no more than the same silence that greeted all that had come before, realisation dawned. The situation he is in is not intended as a warning, aimed at dissuading him or anyone else from following the path that has led him here. It has but one purpose. To bring about his death, and in such a way that his captor may derive some personal pleasure from it, both now and, probably, in its recalling in days to come.

In the beginning, he had sufficient strength in his upper body he was able to draw himself upright every few seconds, relieving the pressure on his windpipe caused by the rope around his neck. But on his knees, with his hands tied in front and with a second rope pulling him forward and down, he is fighting a losing battle against that most intransigent of foes - the force of gravity. If the rope continues to tighten, he will die. Not for the first time, he curses his own stupidity. He knows of others before him who attempted a similar betrayal. Some at least ended up paying for it with their lives. He wonders now what disordered reasoning ever made him think he might succeed where they failed?

The answer, of course, is simple.

Arrogance.

Throughout his sixty-four years it has been the weakness that always carried the potential to bring him down. The over-confidence that comes with thinking you are cleverer than those who oppose you. That even if you are exposed, your gift for negotiation - backed by a wealth of damning intelligence about your enemies - means a safe route out of the swamp seeking to suck you down will be found.

Not this time. The silent response to his pleadings testify to that. All it accomplished he now realises, was to confirm in the mind of his captor that he is indeed both a threat, and a liability. And that when a choice has to be made between risking one's own future safety, or removing the source of that threat… Well, it is no choice at all really, is it?

A lifelong agnostic, Curtis now finds himself contemplating theology. *Is this what this is? Some sort of divine retribution?* An act of mortal penance, intended to wipe out a debt accrued during a life lived according to a moral code many would consider deeply flawed? Only a believer in some sort of afterlife, overseen by some guiding deity could ever believe such a reading of his situation. And though he is not minded, consciously, to reverse his lifelong lack of belief, as he momentarily loses his balance and leans forward into the noose, triggering a panic that this may, finally be it, he finds himself praying to a God who, from the age of eight or thereabouts, he has never believed in.

'Please God, help me. Do something God, anything. But please, please, please, do not let me die. Not here. Not like this. *Please* God.'

'He cannot hear you,' a voice says.

Still fighting to regain the balance that may buy him further precious minutes, the words register enough that his eyes swivel left, then right, trying to glimpse if the speaker is within his peripheral vision, or still hanging back, somewhere behind. If the former, and he might catch a glance, he may yet, he hopes, convince his tormentor to a change of heart. But when, having explored the limits of his vision and seen no one, he realises. It is just the arrogance again, toying with him now, the way he has toyed with others over the years.

But his latest attempt to communicate with the God he doesn't believe in, has brought about a change. The rope is even tighter around his throat now. His attempts to twist round must have caused the noose's knot to slip further. Suddenly, the only way he can breathe is by grabbing at a mouthful of air, then swallowing, hard, to force it down and into his lungs. Once again, the panic he has already fought off several times returns, only this time his attempts to counter it lack the certainty of before.

He knows he cannot breathe this way for long. Already, he can feel the strength ebbing out of his stomach, legs, thighs and arms. If he rocks forward too far, he may not have the strength to right himself. His full bodyweight, all two-hundred-and-thirty odd pounds of it, will press against his windpipe. It will become even harder to breathe and he will weaken further. It will become a vicious circle, in which there can only be one outcome.

'*PLEEEEASE,*' He makes one last try.

It is the last word Curtis Whittingham ever speaks.

PART I

THE WOMAN ACROSS THE STREET

CHAPTER 1

IT'S ONLY NOW, looking back, I realise how my life changed that late summer. I didn't at the time because I was too young - just closing on fourteen. I probably assumed that what I saw, learned and experienced over that period was all just part of 'growing up'. In many ways I guess it was, just not the sort of growing up most parents would wish for their only son.

A lot of it, of course, was to do with us moving from Brooklyn, where I was born and grew up, to the sleepy, upstate New York town of Brackers Lake. This was in the July, during school summer recess. The first three weeks, I hated every minute of it. Not surprising really. Any teenager forced to abandon everything and everyone they know, and transported to somewhere as alien as the surface of the moon would probably feel the same.

It was around this time I gave serious thought to running back to Brooklyn. Fuck family, college and the career in medicine my parents kept telling me was my future. I would get a job at Denny's and live with my Aunt Katherine and Uncle Hector. They have a big old brownstone over in Park Slope. It's a nice area. Lots of interesting people live around there. Katherine and Hector aren't my 'real' aunt and uncle, but they've been close to our family for years. My mom and Aunt

6

Katherine went through nursing college together.

I spent most of those early weeks wondering what sort of people these 'Lakers', as they like to call themselves, are. People say New York can be an unfriendly place. I always thought it anything-but. Growing up, I knew and got on with everyone in our neighbourhood, apart from the Hirsches, but then they never got on with anyone. But those 'Lakers', well... I don't know whether it's just how they are, or simply a case of not trusting 'foreigners', as they label anyone who moves in from elsewhere. But in my book, anyone who can't be bothered to return a simple, 'Good Morning', is just plain rude.

They weren't all like that. Around the end of the third week, my father volunteered my services to help clear the yard for the woman who lived on her own across the street. It was soon after this my thoughts about running away went on hold. They didn't come back.

At this point it may help if I describe myself. People say I'm tall for my age and, as my Mom used to like to joke, 'pretty well set' for someone my age. I'd been blessed - Mom's word - with broad shoulders, and my hair was thick and black, unlike hers - blond - and my father's - brown going on grey. Growing up, I sometimes used to hear people - Aunt Katherine and Uncle Hector among them - joshing with my Mom about who my father was. My appearance wasn't something I was particularly conscious of at the time. That would come later.

It's also fair to say that when it all started, I'd already learned how being around girls triggered feelings I didn't yet fully understand. Most of what I *was* familiar with, I'd picked up from my friends, or learned about during school break-times. Like most high schools, SE - Sex Education - was on the East Williamsburg Latin School curriculum from the start, though in fact it begins long before that these days - as early as sixth grade for some. But I never did get the reasoning behind a programme of learning that includes using a condom and the benefits of 'abstinence', yet fails to properly explain what a hard-on is, and/or just how wide the range of triggers is that can cause one. And the effects I'm talking about weren't just to do with girls at school. I've always played Saturday morning soccer. Some of my teammates' Moms - I believe the term is 'Soccer Mom' - have a similar effect.

When my father first mentioned about me helping clear her yard, I'd seen Miriam Cole - as I heard my Father call her - a half-dozen times or so. Mostly it was when she was picking up from the mailbox at the bottom of her driveway. I noticed she walked with a slight limp, sometimes using a stick to help her back up the slope. Twice, I'd seen her coming home in her black convertible, a smart-looking Mercedes. She had the top down both occasions, and as she slowed to turn up the drive, I remember thinking how the wrap-around sunglasses and blond hair blowing in the wind gave her something of a movie-star look.

We'd even exchanged words. Rather, in my case, *word*.

It happened in Albertsons one Saturday afternoon. I was there looking for a new charger cable for my cell phone when I came across her, grocery shopping. 'Came across', isn't entirely accurate. I actually saw her come in and hung around a bit, watching to see what she was buying. I realised later she must have spotted me following her - probably when I looked away too quickly to check out the salamis when she turned round - because when she turned left up an aisle out of sight and I sprinted to catch up, just as I reached the turn I met her coming back after she must have made a quick reverse. We both stopped, looking straight at each other, and as she stood there, staring at me with a strange half-smile on her face, I could feel the redness spreading upwards from my neck. I realised at once that I'd been 'made', and froze. Just for a second, I thought I was in trouble, but she must have taken pity on me because the look in her face changed from, '*Gotcha,*' to one close to sympathy.

'Hello.' She said it cheerfully, like we knew each other. Before I could get my mind in gear, she continued. 'Aren't you the young man who lives on Henry Street, across from my house?'

The first time I'd heard her speak, I noticed her accent at once, a kind of mix of French, a bit of what sounded like British, and good old American. My first thought on hearing it was *Canadian*. Surprised by her friendly openness, I managed to blurt, 'Yes', before my legs started working enough to turn me round and march me straight out of the store. I even forgot to pick up the cable I'd come in for.

And it was that one-off, embarrassing, cringe-worthy encounter that was uppermost in my mind that Saturday morning as my father walked me across for the purpose of introducing me to the woman he'd already set me up to work for for the rest of the summer break. His, 'She's nice. You'll like her,' was my only preparation for what was to follow.

And as we stood on her porch and I heard her coming down the stairs to answer her door in response to my father's bell-pressing, I could feel butterflies dancing in my stomach, and my heart thumping in my chest.

The door opened. And for the second time in my life I found myself face to face with Miriam Cole.

CHAPTER 2

AS I WAITED for my father to introduce me, officially, my big fear was that she would mention our previous meeting. If she did, the embarrassment I felt on that occasion would be as nothing to having my father learn about it right then, with her looking on to witness my humiliation.

But when I lifted my head to find her gaze waiting, I was relieved to see no sign of recognition, just a friendly smile and a detached look of curiosity.

'Good morning, Mrs Cole,' I heard my father say. 'And how are you this fine morning?' It was the greeting I had heard him use a thousand times. Most of his life my father worked in sales.

She cocked her head to one side, acknowledging his enquiry. 'I am very well indeed, Foster,' she said. 'Thank you for asking.' The accent was as I remembered, and the formality in her reply made me wonder if she was maybe a teacher. She turned her face to me, and as she said the words, 'And who would *this* be?' I felt the redness returning.

'This, Mrs Cole, is Brandon. Brandon, say hello to Mrs Cole.'

'Hi Ma'am,' I said. 'Pleased to meet you.'

Growing up, my parents had taught me the importance of making a good first impression - the legacy of my father's occupation no doubt. Nevertheless,

I was conscious that my greeting was probably more restrained than it may otherwise have been in such circumstances. Even so, I still managed the polite smile that was required. And as I saw the hand hovering in the air in front of me, I remembered to take it.

Her touch was light, her skin soft, and warm. In that moment I noticed a distinctive fragrance in the air - wafting through on the draught from inside her house. Then I realised, it was coming from her. She was wearing *perfume*. The fact caught me by surprise. My Mom and Aunt Katherine sometimes wear perfume, but never on a Saturday morning, or any other day so early.

For what must only have been seconds, but seemed like an hour, we stood there, staring at each other as we held hands. I have no idea what sort of expression was on my face during those few moments - 'Goofy' I suspect. But hers was quite open, the sort of interested look adults sometimes wear when meeting a friend's children for the first time. It was right then I first wondered about how long she and my father had been acquainted. To that point, I had assumed they had met only since we arrived in Brackers Lake. But that wasn't the sense I got as I realised they seemed to be taking an undue interest in how I was reacting to meeting her for what was supposed to be the first time.

Finally, she let go my hand. 'And I'm very pleased to meet you too, Brandon.'

The smile that came with it was one I will always remember. It wasn't particularly wide, or beaming or anything, but for some reason it struck me as containing a good deal of warmth - affection even - though there could be no reason for it. To my youthful mind it contained 'hidden depths'.

She followed it up with a flick of her hand, which was when I noticed all her rings. 'But *please*. Don't ever call me, "Ma'am" again. It makes me feel so *old*. Miriam, will do fine. If that is alright with your father?'

I glanced at him to check that such informality would not cut across the fairly strict guidelines I had been brought up to believe governed interactions with grown ups who were not part of our family. I was surprised to see he had taken a step back and was just standing there, staring at me, arms folded across his chest. I was even more surprised to see he was wearing a smile similar to the sort he might wear if he had just learned I had passed some examination, or witnessed me winning a race in the school swimming gala, or scoring the winning goal in a Junior Soccer League match. Catching my glance, he gave a quick nod.

Turning back to her, I tried to engage in a way that might help dispel the embarrassment I was still feeling. 'If you say so, Mrs- *Miriam.*'

Formalities over, she stood back and threw open her front door.

'Please,' she said. 'Come through and let me show you what you are here for.' Then she let out a low chuckle that, to me sounded almost like a giggle. 'At least, I *hope* it is what you are here for. Welcome to my home.'

She ushered us down through the hall towards the back. As I followed my father - he seemed to know where he was going - I noticed that Miriam Cole's house was quite a bit bigger than ours. But while it seemed spotlessly clean, there didn't seem a lot in the way of furniture. A sofa and chair in a living area off to the left - no TV as far as I could see - and a square table with chairs in a dining area on the right. At the back of the house, next to the open kitchen, was another large living area - again just one huge sofa with deep cushions - with folding glass doors opening out onto what I saw was not just a yard, but a real garden full of trees, shrubs, flowers and grassy areas. Before stepping outside, I noticed that the kitchen looked as bare as the rest of the house. None of the domestic clutter I was used to seeing in our family kitchen. But then, so far, I had seen nothing to suggest there *was* any 'family'.

As we trooped through and out onto a wide deck that ran the full width of the back of the house, I got my first indication of the scale of the task she and my father must, at some point, have mapped out for me.

To describe Miriam Cole's garden as 'overgrown', would be an understatement. The several bushes dotted around, which I could not then have named, had expanded so that in several places they blended into solid walls of shrubbery. Long tendrils, heavy with leaf and flowers, hung, like vines in a rain forest over the outlines of what looked like hidden paths, weaving through the undergrowth. Over to the right, a roughly rectangular area that must once have been a lawn was covered by grasses and weeds a good three feet high. Over in the far corner, was a mound of what looked like part garden waste, and random household junk. Amongst old tree branches and decaying vegetation I could see a child's bicycle frame and an old stroller, lying on its side, evidence that a family must once have lived there. The garden was surrounded by a six-foot fence, which you couldn't see from the front of the house. Once white, it was now sun-bleached, blistered and, for the most part, bare of paint. Several of the fence-boards hung at odd angles and there were gaps where some were missing altogether. I imagined them lying, discarded and rotting somewhere in the grass, under the overhanging bushes.

The whole thing spoke of months, if not years, of neglect that was in stark contrast to the house's interior. It was then I first realised. Like ourselves, Miriam Cole must be a relative newcomer to Bracker's Lake. Whether she owned the house or was renting, it was clear she could not have been there more than a few months longer than us. From what I had seen, I could not imagine her putting up with the jungle/scrap yard that was her back garden for any longer than circumstances demanded. In fact I was surprised she had not moved to do something about it earlier. Surely there had to be plenty of able-bodied gardener-labourer types in a place like Brackers Lake she could have employed before now? It made me wonder if she been waiting for someone specific to come along.

'So what do you think Brandon?' I heard her say. 'It's not going to be too much for you is it?'

Turning, I saw a trace of what looked like anxiety in her pretty face that made me feel like I wanted to reassure her. *No trouble Miriam. I'll have it sorted in no time.* But before I could say anything, my father got there first.

'He's a fit young man, Mrs Cole. And he's not afraid of hard work, are you son?' Before I could answer, he continued. 'Give him a few weekends and he'll have it looking like a show-garden.'

Listening to my father extolling my virtues, and seeing her, looking at me while still waiting for my response, I began to wonder what was going on. For some reason I was beginning to feel like I was on show - like the ponies I remembered being led around the ring the time Aunt Katherine and Uncle Hector took me to that Horse and Pony Show out at Martha's Vineyard. But I could also see that for all my father's enthusiasm and reassurances, Miriam was waiting to hear from me. It made me feel like a grown up, rather than a fourteen year old.

I looked out, surveying the 'jungle' one last time before turning to face her. 'It shouldn't be a problem Miriam. I'll be happy to help you get it looking the way it should be.'

'There, you see?' my father said. 'Like I told you. He's a fine young man.'

And when I saw her smiling at me and heard her say, 'Yes, I can see that for myself,' I have to say, it made me feel like a million dollars.

'Right,' she said. She turned suddenly serious. 'We need to agree terms. I understand you are due to start back at your new school the week after next, but if you work at it on Saturday mornings and maybe an evening through the week, it should not interfere with your studies. Is that alright with you?'

Once again I was caught a bit off guard. I wasn't used to being consulted on such matters. My parents have a fairly 'traditional' attitude towards parenting. They decide how things will be, I go along - most times. And if we'd still been in Brooklyn, I may have been more careful about committing my Saturday mornings away. But right now, my social diary was pretty much empty, and if I was going to earn myself some 'pocket money', I could think of worse arrangements than toiling away under Miriam Cole's supervision for a few hours each week.

'That should work okay,' I said. I have to admit, I was getting a bit of a buzz from 'agreeing terms' with a nice-looking lady who seemed quite different to most women I knew.

'Now,' she continued. 'About payment.'

Before I could say anything, my father raised a hand. 'Why don't we just wait and see how things-'

'No, Foster,' she interrupted. 'I'd much rather have these things agreed right at the start. And I'm sure Brandon would as well, wouldn't you Brandon?'

I looked from her to my father. I'd never negotiated wages before. Even when I delivered newspapers back in Brooklyn, the rate was fixed at what it had always been. 'Well, I don't know-'

'What about twenty dollars an hour?'

'*Twenty dollars?*' my father said. 'That's far too generous for a bit of labouring, Mrs Cole. I was thinking more-'

'*I'm saying,* twenty dollars, Foster.'

The way she said, *"I'm saying,"* and the effect it had on my father took me by surprise. Rather than come back at her, he fell suddenly silent. He dipped his head, almost like it was a bow. I wondered what had just happened. In truth, even I thought twenty an hour was way higher than it needed to be. But having witnessed the exchange, I wasn't about to speak up. Seeing my father give way like that was a new experience for me. At home, his word is pretty much law on most things.

In the silence that followed, I suddenly realised, she was waiting for my response.

'YES,' I said, louder than I'd intended. I felt I wanted her to know that I was eager to please her. 'Yes,' I said again. 'Twenty dollars is fine. Thank you. *Miriam.*'

I glanced at my father again. He was staying silent.

'Well that's settled then,' she said. 'When can you start?'

I looked to my father, but he seemed to have decided he should play no further part in the conversation.

'Er, I can start this morning, right now, if you'd like?'

'That would be excellent. But I'm not sure what sort of tools there are in my cellar.' She turned to my father, 'I take it you have gardening tools Brandon can use, Foster?'

Whatever spell he was in, he came out of it. 'Yes. Of course. Lots of tools.'

'Good. Well then, why don't you go and fetch whatever you think you'll need to make a start, and I'll rustle up a pitcher of iced lemonade. I think it's going to be a warm one this morning.'

As I walked back across to our house, my father next

to me, I'd never been so conscious that for once, he seemed to have nothing to say.

And as I rooted in our cellar and the utility room at the back for the spades, cutters, pitchforks and other odds and ends I thought I might need, I found myself quite looking forward to the rest of that morning.

That was how it all started.

CHAPTER 3

DETECTIVE CHIEF SUPERINTENDENT Stella Rigby flicked an offending fleck off of her seal-grey, Hugo Boss skirt, before re-crossing her legs, clasping her hands over the tablet in her lap, and resuming her wait. The other side of the desk, the man whose job she had her eye on when he moved on and up in around twelve months' time, was still reading. Sitting there, she was conscious of the image she presented. Poised, professional, prepared, it was the look she'd worked hard at perfecting over the course of her twenty-plus years service. So far, it was working. She was also musing on what Assistant Chief Constable David Moody's failure to read through the report before their meeting, said about his time-management skills - lack of them more likely. It was something else she needed to bear in mind as she worked her way towards the goal that was never far from her thoughts through her working day - a Chief's job.

Stella had already noted that Moody had printed the report off - all twelve pages of it - rather than read it on-screen, as stipulated under the force's recently re-vamped Environmental Awareness Policy. But she saw it for what it was, rather than a deliberate breach. It is not unusual for Chief Officers to effect a 'quirk' that sets them apart from their peers. Moody's was his professed impatience with technology, and having to, 'stare at screens all day'. Stella's position as the force's Head Of CID meant that the pair met together most days. She was still waiting to discover if his particular quirk also extended to porn.

At that moment Moody gave out a loud, 'Tch,' shook his head, and dropped the sheaf of papers in front of him. Looking up, he fixed her with what she had come to recognise as his, 'let's get down to business' face.

'God,' he exclaimed, drawing the word out. 'He does drone on. Give me the potted version. I'm meeting with the Chief in ten minutes.'

Stella managed to hide the smirk that may have given away her thoughts. Lifting her tablet she touched the screen. At the top of the page, the name alongside 'Report from…' read Detective Chief Inspector J Carver. Beneath it, the Report Subject Title - "Intelligence Re HM Prison Escaper, Megan Crane CRO 10798473/17."

Taking a deep breath, she began.

'It boils down to the fact that someone - we don't know who - sent him documents, photographs and some sort of surgical diagram that purport to show the Crane woman may be alive and living somewhere in the USA, possibly around the upstate New York area. One of the photos appears to have been taken in someone's garden, the other in some bar somewhere. Both show a woman who *could* be her, but isn't clear. Whoever sent them wrote "It's her" on the back of one and "She's here" on the other. The diagram looks like some cosmetic surgeon's plan for reconstructive facial surgery for injuries like those she sustained before she supposedly died. Carver managed to pin the garden down to somewhere in upstate New York. Now he's heard from a local Sheriff who has an outstanding murder on his books that bears her signatures. He's asking for permission to go over, liaise, and investigate.'

'Right,' Moody said. 'Like he did in France. That went well.'

Stella kept her face straight. 'But he did find her, and helped the French police solve their 'Pension Killer' case at the same time.'

Moody nodded, slowly, though the doubtful look stayed. 'What happened to the theory that she couldn't have survived a seventy-foot fall into water with a knife sticking out of her ribs?'

'That's his point. It was only ever a theory. No body.'

'Hmph.' Moody leaned back in his chair. 'So what's your assessment?'

Stella paused, gathering her thoughts. She needed to get the balance right.

'Looking at the photographs, there's no getting away from the fact it could be her. The Forensic report says-'

'I don't mean the intell,' Moody interrupted. 'I mean him. Carver. You've met him. What're your thoughts? How well do you know him?'

Stella picked her words. 'I've only met him twice. One was a weekend conference. The other was when we worked together on the Stanley Cheeseman murder in Wilmslow. That was a good few years ago.'

'And?' Moody waited.

'There are two trains of thought,' Stella said.

'Go on.'

'The first is, he's an ill-disciplined, authority-hating self-serving narcissist with significant personality defects who likes to claim credit for other people's efforts but who also has a knack for manipulating the media so he always come out smelling of roses.'

Moody nodded. She wondered if he recognised the profile.

'And the other?' Moody cocked an eyebrow.

'He's a bloody good detective who gets results even if his methods aren't always by the book. Yes, he has some hang-ups, but his instincts are usually bang-on, and he does seem to inspire loyalty in those who work with him.'

Moody looked askance. 'Hmm... I must say, I performance-reviewed Jess Greylake a couple of weeks ago. Carver's name came up. I got the impression she thinks the sun shines out of his arse.'

Stella smiled. 'Considering what they've been through the past couple of years, that's probably not surprising.'

Moody continued. 'I got half an impression he may have a bit of an obsession over this Crane woman. The fact she's a dominatrix makes me wonder if-'

'With all respect,' Stella jumped in. 'I'm not sure it's useful to speculate about that. She did try to kill him. And his girlfriend. Something like that isn't exactly easy to forget.'

As Moody stared at her, Stella felt his scrutiny. She hoped she hadn't overplayed it. And she was relieved when he moved on.

'So where do you sit? Which is the real Jamie Carver?'

'I'm strictly on the fence on that one,' Stella said. 'I can recognise both sides. If I've a difficult job on, he's the first Senior Investigating Officer I'd look for. On the other hand...'

'What?'

'I'd hate to have to manage him. I once heard The Duke say that trying to control him is like plaiting fog. Nothing to get hold of.'

Moody rested his cheek in his hand. 'Fair enough. So what about the actual intelligence then? Does it justify sending someone all that way? Since COVID, the flights alone would put a dent in our Special Ops budget.'

Stella looked down at her tablet, scrolled down, checking out the photographs again. The report's appendix contained several. Two showed a blond woman, the rest, a murder scene.

She lifted her head. And when she looked at him, she made sure she looked him straight in the eye. She needed to make him believe what she was about to say.

Ten minutes later, back in her office, door closed against the hubbub that is the HQ Operations Suite, Stella settled herself in her chair, took out her mobile and brought up the number she had forgotten was there until it popped up as a 'missed call' two weeks before.

Seeing it again, memories stirred. A weekend-long Serious Crime Management conference in a posh hotel just outside Oxford. Two days free from the pressures of running serious crime enquiries. A chance to let hair down. Two nights of madness - they were both married at the time, though not for long as things turned out for both of them. It was curiosity, as much as anything that drove her. That and the need that had always been part of her. The desire to demonstrate that she was her own woman. That she could take the lead in such things as much as any man. She remembered the room. Well appointed, clean, comfortable. The bed soft, the way she liked it. Contrary to her expectation, he had proved gentle, considerate, until towards the end at least. But then, she didn't mind that.

They never spoke of it again. He didn't even mention it when he took the fall for her 'mistake' over the Stanley Cheeseman thing. By rights, she should have gone down for what she did. Career over. Prison even, if it had all come out. Thank God he was experienced enough to know how to play it. He took flak of course. But he seemed to know it would only go so far. And he was right. In time it blew over. And the success that came to him soon after meant people lost interest in digging deeper. Just as well, for her. Nor did he mention it during their conversation when she rang him back having seen his number. 'Hello Stella,' he said, softly, the way she remembered. He was even polite enough to spend a few minutes catching up, before getting to the point. 'I'm wondering how you'd feel about helping me out?'

A knock at the door broke her out of her reverie.

'TWO MINUTES,' she shouted. 'I'M ON A CALL,'

She shook her head, reprimanding herself. 'Get a grip, Stella.' She pressed 'call'. It barely rang out before he answered.

'Hi,' she said. 'He went for it. Get packing.'

CHAPTER 4

CHANGED INTO MY working clothes - cargoes, sweatshirt, boots - and armed with my father's gardening tools, I set-to on my arrival back at Miriam Cole's house, cutting back some of the overhangs and shrubbery that were making it difficult to see what needed doing. The cut-offs went onto the mound at the back. Before coming away, my father had suggested getting a dumpster delivered to the end of her driveway to take all the rubbish I would be generating. Miriam agreed it was a good idea. 'I'll leave that to you to organise, Foster,' she said.

I'd been at it some thirty minutes and was working my way towards the back, when I heard her call. 'Come and have a drink, Brandon. You need to stay hydrated.'

I joined her on the deck and she handed me a tall glass of iced lemon. As I supped it down, I thought it was one of the sweetest-tasting drinks I'd ever had.

'You've a sweat on already, I see,' she said.

I nodded, conscious of the damp patches already showing through my shirt. As she'd predicted, the day was already warming up. I thought about taking my shirt off, but decided against, wary in case my father called to check on progress and found me bare-chested.

When she opened the door to us that morning, she'd been wearing a flowery summer dress, all pinks and yellows. Since then she had changed and was now dressed in a white top and pair of black jeans which seemed quite snug on her. She was also wearing jewellery - necklace, bracelet, earrings - and had done something with her hair. I asked if she was going out somewhere.

She smiled, like I'd said something funny, and shook her head, which made her hair 'bounce' in a way I quite liked.

'No,' she said. 'This is what I normally wear. Besides, it would be rude of me to leave you on your own during your first morning. You may need me for something.'

We chatted as I drank the lemon. She asked me what kinds of things I enjoyed and I told her. Basketball, soccer, Fortnite as well of course, though it's a bit old-hat now and I don't play for too long at a stretch. Something else my Mom and Dad are quite strict on - screens! She seemed interested, and was easy to talk to. At one stage I managed to slip in a reference to, 'Mr Cole.'

'There isn't a Mr Cole,' she said, simply, and moved on.

Standing there on her deck, in the warm sunshine, drinking sweet-tasting iced lemon and talking to a lady who seemed as nice as any I had met to that point, I was already looking forward to what the next few Saturday mornings may bring.

I swigged another glass down before picking up the gloves I'd taken off to avoid dirtying it. 'Better get back to it.' I imagined it the sort of thing a real gardener might say. As I made my way back into the undergrowth, I had the feeling she was watching me, though I didn't turn to check.

Late in the morning, my father showed up to see how I was doing. He seemed impressed with the work I had done, and how much I had managed to clear in just a couple of hours. Leaving me to it, he went and joined Miriam on the deck where they chatted. I couldn't hear what was being said, but the repeated nods and looks in my direction left me in no doubt that I featured in their conversation, several times.

That first day, I ended up working through into the afternoon. There was more lemon, and plenty of iced water. Around midday, Miriam appeared with a plate on which was a doorstep-size salami, cheese and tomato with mayo on rye, which was delicious.

I finished up around three-thirty. The mound had grown considerably by then, and to be honest, I was beginning to feel the effects of my labors. Apart from sweating all over, my arms were aching and I could feel the beginnings of a twinge in my back. I've always kept pretty fit, but that's mainly through basketball and soccer. As I was discovering, gardening uses a whole different set of muscles. But as I stood on the deck, watching her casting an approving eye over my early accomplishments, I made no mention of my aches and pains.

'That's a good start, Brandon,' she said. 'It's looking a lot better already.' Turning, she looked at me in a way I can only describe as strange - head lowered, peering at me through her eyelashes, a wry smile showing. 'If this is an example of what I can expect from you, I may have to think about how else I might make use of you.'

I was glad she approved of what I'd done. In fact her words of praise gave me a little buzz. About to leave, she handed me an envelope. 'Thank you,' she said. 'You've earned this.'

I was tempted to look in it, but then worried it may seem rude so decided to wait until I got home. However she dispelled my curiosity by saying, 'There's a hundred and twenty dollars in there. As it's your first day I've added a little bonus. And just so you know, as far as I'm concerned, what I give you is between you and myself. What you tell your parents is entirely up to you.'

Just for a second, I wondered if I ought to make a show of protesting she was being too generous. But then I remembered her response to my father when he tried it, so I settled for a simple, 'Right. Thank you. Miriam.'

'One more thing. I'd like you to have this.'

She had something in her hand which she handed to me. I was surprised to realise it was a black-handled lock knife. Heavy in my hand, it looked barely used.

'A gardener needs a good knife. This was my father's. It's actually a throwing knife but I'm sure you'll find a use for it.'

'Wow,' I said, though I was a little uncertain. 'Are you sure?' I once bought a lock-knife off a kid in school. I only had it two weeks. My Mom found it when cleaning my bedroom. She went ballistic.

'Of course I'm sure,' Miriam said. 'I'll never use it and it needs a good home. Look after it, but I'm relying on you to treat it with respect. It's not a toy.'

'I will Miriam, thank you.' I pressed the catch and the polished-steel blade sprang out. I looked it over. Beautifully made and well-balanced, it already felt good in my hand. After spending a few moments admiring it, I closed it up and slipped it into my pocket, already thinking about where I might sneak off to later to try it out.

Before we said our goodbyes, we agreed that I would return that coming Wednesday evening, dependent on any plans my parents may have for the coming week. As I headed back across to my house, my fervent hope was that they had not made and would not be making, any such plans. Arriving home, I found my parents were out so I spent an hour in the garden, trying out my new knife against a tree. After a bit of practice, I was getting it to stick two out of three throws. Not a bad start, I thought.

Later, alone in my bedroom, showered, changed,

and fortified by cola and chips, I reflected on my first day working for Miriam Cole. Without going into detail, I decided it had been a pleasurable experience. There was just one small incident, that seemed out of sync with the rest of it.

Sometime during the morning, working away in the undergrowth, I heard a raised voice. Looking back at the house, I could see Miriam, talking on her cell. She was in the living room adjoining the kitchen, pacing up and down. The folding window-doors were closed-to, so I couldn't make out details, but from the expression on her face I could see she was having what looked like a 'serious' conversation. Up to that point, all I had seen of Miriam was warmth, friendliness, and good humour. But as I watched her, it was like she was a different person. Her face was stern, and there was fire in her eyes. She seemed to be giving instructions to someone - a pointed finger emphasising her words - but I had the impression that whoever she was talking to was either not listening, or arguing back. As she paced, she shook her head in a clear gesture of disagreement. Suddenly she stopped. Her hand came up and I heard her give a very clear, and loud, 'NO.' Her next words were delivered slowly, clearly and loud enough for me to hear. 'LISTEN TO ME. You will NOT do any such thing, under ANY circumstances. And if you do, you will answer to me. Is that clear?' There was a pause, then, 'GOOD.' Ending the call, she tossed her cell onto the sofa. As she turned, hand on hips now, to face out into the garden, I just managed to turn away in time that it would not be obvious that I had witnessed the exchange - I hoped. When, several moments later, I risked a glance back through the branches I was hacking away at, there was no sign of her.

The next time I saw her - when she brought out some more iced lemon - she was her normal self again, which encouraged me to let the incident sink in my memory. The time would come however, when it would resurface, when its significance would become clear.

CHAPTER 5

DETECTIVE CHIEF INSPECTOR Jamie Carver stood looking down at the array of folders laid out, grid fashion, across the surface of his desk. His arms were folded, one hand up to his mouth, finger and thumb pulling at his top lip. Every now and then, he shook his head, the movement so slight, a casual observer might miss it.

Like most detectives, Carver had learned to not dwell too long or too deeply on past cases. To do so invites pain and risks the sort of downward spiral that can lead to dark places. A premature end to a career. A ruined relationship. Depression. Suicide even, in a couple he had known. But whilst he was adept at keeping most, though not all the details of his priors filed away somewhere deep but accessible, their overall impact was always with him.

The dozen or so folders now spread out before him represented only a fraction of those cases. But they covered a period in his life which, when the time came to look back on it, he would remember more for its bleakness, than anything else. Amongst it all, one in particular stood out.

Even now, he still wasn't entirely sure if what existed between him and Angie fitted with any definition of what people call 'love'. Whatever it was, it was certainly full of passion, maybe even more than what he and Rosanna now enjoyed. Memories of their times together were never far from his mind. But barely a day went by when her brutal murder at the hands of, *The Woman,* didn't, in some way, cast its shadow.

That wasn't to say there weren't some highs over that period. Getting to finally meet and spend time with Jason, being the stand-out, though even that was tempered by the knowledge that, four years on, the boy's longer-term future still remained unclear. For now, he was just glad that the eight-year old was enjoying living with his grandmother. It meant that most of the time he remained free to continue searching for the closure that may one day allow him to assume the responsibilities he might have taken on long ago, had other matters not intervened.

Then there was Jess. Bringing her onto the team and training her up had proved one of his better decisions - maybe the best. Working with her and watching her grow to where she was today had brought both satisfaction, and a sense of pride. Apart from her personal life which, he kept having to remind himself, was nothing to do with him.

Despite everything he, they, had been through these past years, he did still enjoy his work. The challenge, the excitement, the satisfaction that comes with seeing a case through to something as close to justice as one can hope for in these days of human rights and ultra-cautious equality-for-all. The fact that he'd had a personal hand in curtailing the activities of some who would have gone on to further their killing careers, was something else he should, he knew, be proud of. Because of him, people were going about their lives who may otherwise be dead. Unfortunately, and as his conscience never let him forget, the converse was also true. And no matter how many times those closest told him it was not the case - that detectives don't have crystal balls, that it is in the nature of psycho serial killers to be devious and unpredictable - he would always see it that way.

Right now, looking down on the folders, he wasn't so much dwelling on the events they covered and which still wakened feelings of loss, grief, and guilt now and then. Rather, he was thinking about the specific documents that lurked within the folders themselves. Photographs, statements, reports, diagrams, Anacapa-flowcharts, and the rest. Space alone meant there was only so much he could take with him on his forthcoming trip. And though just about all of it was stored in digital format in his new notebook, or capable of being accessed remotely with only minimal delay, his traditional detective's distrust of technology meant he leaned towards a belt-and-braces approach. Carver's view, forged over time, was, Sod's Law dictates that the time you need to retrieve some photograph, or the details contained within a witness statement, that will be the time the technology fails, or there's no signal, or something. So backups are always good. The trouble was, which of the hundreds of documents before him should he pick?

Reaching down, he flicked idly at some of the covers, allowing himself glimpses of some of the contents, as if to remind himself of their variety - not that he needed to. As even Nazir Hassam, Chief Crown Prosecutor for The Northern Area himself commented on the last time they met, when they fell to discussing the weight of evidence against The Woman in respect of those murders for which, thanks to her escape, she was yet to face charges. After thirty minutes spent bombarding Carver with questions - many over points of quite fine detail - Hassam dropped his pen on his yellow notepad, fell back in his red, leather chair, and shook his head.

'Bloody Hell, Jamie. Do you spend all your spare time studying this stuff, or have you got a photographic memory?'

'Neither,' Carver had said. 'But when you know that one vehicle sighting, one minor scene detail or some witness observation that seemed unimportant at the time may make the difference between a guilty, and a not-guilty verdict, you tend to focus on the small stuff.'

Some documents he knew right-off he would be taking with him. The first his fingers alighted on - no great surprise - was the photograph contained within the scarred and dog-eared buff folder with 'Megan Crane' scrawled across in red felt-pen. It was the one that had featured, prominently, during the original 'Worshipper Killer' enquiry. It showed her professionally made up, with her coal-black hair beautifully coiffured, and wearing the outfit that defined her for what, who, she was - a 'lifestyle dominatrix'. She once told him it was taken by a young, but attentive, studio photographer for what she described as, 'promotional purposes', whatever that meant. But Carver had not picked it out for the aesthetic value he knew many ascribed to it. Or so he told himself. Rather, it was the one image of her in his possession that came close to conveying the raw power that lay within her, and which she was so capable of wielding. Only fair, he thought, that those he may meet be fully informed about who - and what - they may be up against.

Then there were some of the scene photographs. Video serves its purpose, but when it comes to focusing on detail that may be crucial in making evidential assessments, photographs remain the best medium, often, strangely enough, the monochrome prints. Carver considered for a moment, before reaching down and singling out the folder bearing the name, "Corinne Anderson". As much as any, her horrific death, executed in her own Chester mews-house cellar, contained all the classic, 'Worshipper' elements. Post, rope, positioning of the body, ribbon, super-glued hands, as well as all the ancillary scene 'dressing' - home-dungeon environment, lingerie, moody lighting, and so on. It would certainly help give a clear impression during briefings, if he ever got that far.

So too, some of the Anacapa charts. He didn't know for certain yet, but he would be surprised if what they now knew about her history, her associations with Edmund Hart - especially the time they spent together in the US - would not prove useful. So far, his mission was being spoken of in 'scouting', rather than full on 'search and find' terms, unlike Paris, two years before. On that occasion there was hard intelligence attesting to the fact she was hiding there. This time all he had were two grainy photographs, a couple of cryptic notes that could easily be a hoax, and a murder scene that could just as easily fall into the category of, 'copycat'. But if things went in a particular direction, and speculation moved towards suspicion, it would be useful to be able to share with others the extent of the web she had woven over the years, the linkages that existed, the network of which she was the centre. And though much of the material he had used to chart his analyses was no longer available - destroyed in the fire that was intended to prevent her associations with that network coming to light - enough remained as might give detectives in several countries good reason to look at some prominent figures in a new light, and wonder if maybe they ought to be taking a closer look at what they get up to in their 'private' lives. New York City, Carver knew, was of particular interest in this regard. And it wasn't so far from Brackers Lake. The Sheriff he had heard from, this Matt Lynch, may well be more familiar with some of the names than Carver was.

And if he had any sort of nose for investigation, it may just help convince him that further enquiry, beyond County jurisdiction at least - may prove productive.

But even as Carver reached for the bulky folder containing the printed out versions of the charts - all folded concertina-style to allow for easier access and display - the opening bars to Tina Turner's classic 'Simply The Best', with its heavy, rising beat, broke through the silence.

'I call you, I need you, my heart's on fire...'

He knew who it was at once.

CHAPTER 6

SEARCHING FOR HIS MOBILE, Carver spotted it over the other side of the room, on top of the bookcase, its flashing light bouncing off the ceiling.

'Tch.'

He crossed to retrieve it.

She had set the punning, personal ring-tone herself after sneaking his phone during a boozy, post-trial-and-conviction celebration at The Ring O'Bells a couple of months before - she knew his lock-code of course. He only discovered the fact days later, and he stopped enquiring if someone on the team could show him how to get rid of it when he realised that the several variations on, 'Sorry boss, mine's an iPhone,' or 'Never worked out how to do that,' did not evidence so much his team's lack of mobile savvy, as the fact that opportunities to get one over on the man who was known to have done the same to certain out-of-depth Chief Officers in his time, were as rare as a quiet duty-cover weekend. Weeks later, he still wanted rid of the embarrassing noise. It had just stopped being a priority.

'HELLO,' he said, loud enough she would know he was busy.

'How's it going?' Jess Greylake said. 'Are you there yet?'

'Nearly. Just sorting some last minute bits and pieces.'

'Still?' She sounded surprised. 'You'd better get a

shake on. You're flying tomorrow.'

'I know, I know,' he said, wearily. 'I'm almost there.'

She paused before saying, 'Are you taking the photograph?'

'Which photograph?'

'You know which photograph. The one-'

'I don't know. I haven't thought about it.'

Another pause. 'Right.' A single word, she somehow managed to load it with doubt.

'Have you got your new notebook? Did Alec set it up for you?'

Casting his eye around, he spotted it over on the chair next to the door. Neatly stowed in its shiny, black leather case where Alec had left it, earlier that afternoon. Detective Sergeant Alec Duncan was the longest-serving of the Special Murder Investigation Unit's cadre of six DSs. A detective of the 'old school' his tech skills were, nonetheless, a match for any of the tousle-haired youngsters the Regional Joint IT Support Unit kept sending over. Alec had assured him that everything in the folders, was now accessible either via the hard drive or on-line.

'It's here,' Carver said.

'Did he give you the log-in and password?'

Carver experienced a moment's panic, before remembering the slip of paper Alex had given him and which he then stowed in his wallet as Alec watched, shaking his head in despair. 'Yes,' he said.

'Good. Don't lose them.'

Carver sighed. Realising it could go on all night, he said, 'How about you? Are you set up yet?'

'Almost,' Jess said. 'They've not finished data entry on two of the six yet. Monday, they're telling us. Then we should be good to go.'

'Good luck with it,' Carver said. 'I'm sorry I'm

running out on you.'

'Don't worry,' She said. 'It'll all still be here when you get back. I'm not expecting anything dramatic.'

'You never know. Stranger things happen.'

In truth, Carver thought, she was probably right. Right now, there was nothing to show that any of the six, seemingly random and, in almost every significant respect, unique, outstanding murders spread over a twelve year period, were even connected, never mind the work of a single killer, as Jess's 'Six' theory proposed. The likelihood of an early breakthrough during the enquiry's first couple of weeks was remote - though not to the extent suggested by those who tried to block the enquiry in the first place on the grounds it was, 'too theoretical,' or 'too costly.' Thankfully, Jess's hard research - with support from The Duke, Carver himself and one or two others - had seen them all off. Now, staffed up and budgeted for, the enquiry had been given six weeks to come up with something concrete enough to justify its continuance. Connections between at least two of the murders needed to be found, assuming they existed.

'How's Kradesh shaping up?' he said. 'Is he behaving himself?'

'He's fine,' Jess said. 'A bit up himself, but fine.'

Carver gave a wry smile. Jonathan Kradesh was Visiting Professor in Cognitive Studies at Bristol University. He was also former head of its Centre for Criminal Justice Studies. Too self-aggrandising for Carver's tastes, he nevertheless had to acknowledge that the man's expertise in subliminals and associated areas of what he referred to as 'psychological influencing behaviours', had proved crucial in securing the conviction of the 'Mind-Control Killer', Aaron Lockwood. One of a handful of media 'go to' experts on profiling and related subjects, and an author of several popular books around similar themes, Carver had long ago conceded that, for all his doubts about Kradesh, Jess and The Duke signing him up as consultant to the enquiry on such matters had been a shrewd move. And Kradesh's high profile had certainly helped sell 'The Six Enquiry' to SMIU's overseeing Joint Chief Officers Board when they went looking for financial backing.

'Keep an eye on him, Jess. I'm still not sure about him.'

'Don't worry I will. I know you regard him more as a publicity-hound than an expert with a social conscience, but don't forget, some have said the same about you in the past.'

Ouch. But she was right. 'Touché, Inspector Greylake.'

'Sorry, I didn't mean-'

'Don't worry about it. I'm a big boy.' He switched tack. 'What about The Duke. Have you seen anything new lately?'

'Hmm... Nothing particularly alarming. Could it not just be age? He's not getting any younger you know?'

Carver became pointed. 'This is The Duke we're talking about, Jess. And he's only in his mid-fifties. For him not to remember my name... And twice? I've got to be honest. I'm worried.'

'I know,' Jess said, but sounding less dismissive. 'I must say, that day he froze in the middle of the Cargill briefing... That was scary. Did you get to speak with his daughter?'

'I'm going to wait until I get back. It might just be something as simple as exhaustion. Since Grace died, he's never stopped working. Could be he just needs a break. And I don't want to alarm Jennifer unnecessarily. Just let me know if you see anything worrying.'

'I will. And give me a ring when you get there. I want

39

to know what this Sheriff is like.'

'How about I run him through a Pinnacle Inventory? That'll tell you all you need to know.'

'That'd be nice.' But when she next spoke, she sounded serious. 'So, how're you feeling? About going I mean? Bringing it all back?'

'Honestly? I'd rather not. But it's got to be done. If there's the slightest chance... Well, you know.'

'I do. And if you need me over there-'

'Thanks. I hope I won't. But believe me, if things turn bad, I'll shout.'

After ringing off - no questions about Rosanna, thank God - Carver fell to reflecting. For all that was happening, The Duke's episodic bouts of apparent sudden memory loss, had been on his mind as much as anything the past few weeks. Carver's Uncle Norman - not a blood relative but married to Carver's aunt - had suffered with early-onset Alzheimer's when he was in his forties. Carver was around twenty at the time. His memories of that time were vague, and back then his attendance record at family gatherings - weddings, funerals, birthdays - wasn't the best. But his hope was that the similarities between what he saw in Uncle Norman then, and The Duke now, was more imagined than real.

Shrugging the dark thoughts away, Carver turned back to his desk. But Jess's call had interrupted his train of thought. He checked the time. Coming on eight o'clock. Rosanna was waiting. Maybe for the last time.

'Fuck it.'

Rifling through the folders, he pulled out the items his instincts told him may prove useful, transferred them into the wallet he had ready, then stuffed it into his satchel, along with his notebook, and headed for the door.

Setting off, his thoughts were around how he owed it

to Rosanna to make sure their last evening together before his trip was what it ought to be - relaxing, enjoyable, fun and later maybe, even arousing. Providing he didn't overdo the wine that would accompany the 'special meal' he suspected he would find waiting. But as the miles slipped by, the clouds he thought he'd managed to escape seemed to follow him down the A55.

For most working detectives, trips such as the one he was about to embark upon were rare. Something to look forward to. An opportunity to escape the day-to-day pressures, the routines, the paperwork. He always found experiencing policing beyond British shores interesting and, usually, invigorating - even if only because it reinforced what he'd always believed. That for all its faults, the British system of policing remained pretty much the best in the world, though he knew some would argue the point. But on this occasion, any enthusiasm for his USA trip was dampened by a feeling of wariness - conscious that once over there, he may discover things that would revive the past in ways that could prove 'difficult'. He still wasn't sure whether he was looking forward to going or not. Thoughts of The Duke and his troubles didn't help.

By the time he parked up at the back of the house, he was feeling no better than when he ended his call with Jess. And when he walked in the kitchen door and smelled the aromas that immediately got his juices going, then came through and saw Rosanna waiting on the sofa, wearing something that set juices of another kind flowing, he had to work as hard as he had done in a long time to stitch a wide smile to his face and greet her in the way he knew she was expecting.

CHAPTER 7

ON THE WEDNESDAY evening, after an early supper, I returned to Miriam's when I put in another couple of hours chopping branches and clearing scrub. I did the same the following Saturday morning. Both times, the experience was pretty much similar to the week before. She was pleasant, considerate, and I enjoyed showing her how hard I could work. There was plenty of iced lemon, cookies and, on the Saturday, a slab of a type of black-bread that was a little sweet, almost like a cake, and which she told me was from Germany, though how she came by it in Brackers Lake I had no idea. Towards the back of the garden, partially shielded from view by undergrowth, was a tall silver birch. On each visit I took a bit of time to practise my knife throwing. It would come to be a regular part of my visits and I looked forward to the time I might impress Miriam with my skills.

Half-way through the Saturday morning session, I set about re-fixing some of the fence boards that had come loose on the section between Miriam's house and next door. I was pulling out old nails with my father's claw-hammer when I looked up to find Miriam's neighbour watching me from the middle of her manicured lawn. Elderly, gray-haired, frail looking but with the kind of face that suggests she didn't miss much, her beady eyes were following my every move.

'Good morning,' I said.

Her head jerked upwards in acknowledgement, but she didn't say anything. Nevertheless she took a few hesitating steps towards me. I carried on pulling nails. When I looked next, she was standing close to her border, within a few feet of me.

'She got you working for her now?' she said.

A wizened croak was how I'd describe her voice. The way she'd spoken, I could imagine some telling her to mind her business. Instead I said, 'Just Saturdays and Wednesdays. I'm Brandon.'

If she heard, she gave no sign. She peered through the gap, as if checking Miriam wasn't around. 'You be careful young man,' she said.

I assumed she was referring to my work so I replied, 'It's okay. It's just a bit of digging and chopping. Nothing too heavy.'

She shook her head, like she thought I was some kind of idiot. 'Tch, I don't mean that. I'm talking about getting involved in things you didn't oughta be getting involved in. Remember, cats are beautiful, until they scratch.'

It was a strange thing to say and I was about to ask her what she meant when she turned and shuffled away back to her house. I was glad. She didn't strike me as the sort you could have an easy conversation with. I went back to my nails.

But while I'd looked forward to both sessions, and was enjoying getting to know a lady who seemed very different - sophisticated, mysterious - from most women her age, the greater part of my attention was focused on another matter.

The following Monday marked the end of the summer recess and I was due to start attending at the William Deacon High School. As my first day neared, my thoughts had turned more and more to how it would go, what further changes to my life a new school may bring.

I've always liked school. Having no brothers and sisters, I enjoy the company of other kids, learning how they live their lives, comparing theirs with mine. Up to a couple of years ago, I used to think that my life experience to that point was 'different' and that I was in some way, 'unusual'. But since learning how some other kids live, I've come to realise that maybe I'm not so different after all. Many, perhaps most, families have their problems, some more than others. But while my relationship with my parents was not always as close as some of my friends seemed to enjoy, I never disrespected them. My mother was as loving and caring as I guess most mothers are, and my father was what I believe my grandparents. generation used to call, a 'good provider' with a strong work ethic. Sad to say, not all the kids I knew in Brooklyn could say the same.

I know that changing schools, especially in your teenage years, can be traumatic, but whilst I'd been sad to leave Brooklyn - I was especially missing Afrid - the thought of starting out at a new school didn't bother me particularly. Looking back, I think I probably thought that coming from Brooklyn, the other kids might see me as some sort of 'big city celebrity', and that they - the girls at any rate - would fall over themselves to get to know me. As it turned out, I couldn't have been more wrong. Of course, I wasn't to know that as I made my way through the gates that first Monday morning, my father having dropped me off, and headed towards the steps leading up to the tall glass doors that formed the main entrance.

Though it was my first day, I was happy enough to make my own way inside, having visited the school twice before. The first time was with both my parents when we met with the Principal, a gentleman by the name of Mr Riollo. He welcomed us to Brackers Lake, spoke of how pleased he was that my parents had chosen his school for my education - by happy coincidence it just happened to be the nearest - then talked at some length about what a wonderful time I would have there, and how he and his staff would do 'everything and anything they could' to prepare me for the exciting life I could expect following my graduation. When he eventually got round to asking me if I had any questions, I thought about mentioning the investigation, ten years before, into allegations of sexual abuse levelled against one of his predecessors, a Mr Hickory, which I'd read about on Wikipedia, but could find no reference to any outcome. In the end I said, 'No Sir. I'm just looking forward to joining you all here and getting back to my studies.'

My second visit was during 'freshers' week when I was put into the hands of a tenth grader by the name of Harris, who was supposed to give me a morning tour of the school and answer any questions I may have. Harris was pleasant enough, at first, and spoke highly of the school. But it took him less than thirty seconds to mention that his father was a senior member of the school's board of governors. And another thirty to make clear that here at the William Deacon High School, 'foreigners' like me could expect to have to earn the trust of their fellow students, rather than claim it by right. It took me less than thirty seconds to realise that Harris was some sort of asshole, and that he had no more interest in making me feel welcome than I did in hearing about his achievements as captain of the school soccer team - this after I made the mistake of dropping a mention of my interest in the sport. After managing to somehow become separated from my guide before the morning was halfway through, I caught the bus home. Before I did so however, Harris told me that on the first day of the new term I would be allocated a 'fresher buddy' whose job it would be to show me the ropes and help me through my first few days at WD. He seemed to enjoy being all mysterious about who my 'buddy' might be - like I say, he was an asshole - saying only that his name was 'Kit', and that I would, 'discover the rest when you meet.'

Even though I made sure to arrive promptly that first morning, I quickly realised that attitudes amongst upstate New York students towards school, may prove different to those in the city. The bell wasn't due to ring for another forty minutes, but already large numbers of students - in pairs, groups or singly - were streaming through the gates and towards the entrance. For the most part engrossed in conversation with their friends, none seemed minded to pay me any heed, which was fine by me. Apart from one.

As I headed towards the steps, I spotted a boy off to the left. He was sitting all on his own on the second step, leaning back on his elbows on the step above. When I first saw him he was already looking in my direction, and as I approached his gaze stayed on me. If he knew any of the other students who swung around and passed him to ascend the steps - I assumed he had to - he didn't go out of his way to show it, and other than the odd glance in his direction as they passed, they did the same. As I neared, I judged him to be around the same age as myself, though more slightly built. His light brown hair was cropped fairly short, but not as close as a buzz cut. He kept watching me all the way until I stopped right in front of him at the bottom of the steps. Close enough now to take in facial details, I was just beginning to notice the slightly turned up nose and softer-than-first-glanced features when he opened his mouth and spoke.

'You must be Brooklyn.' The voice was higher than I'd expected, a little softer.

'Actually, it's Brandon,' I said.

46

'I know that. I like Brooklyn.'

Another time I may have mentioned an English soccer player and that my surname was Sawyer, not Beckham, but I didn't want to come across as a smartass from the get-go. 'Whatever,' I said. 'I take it you're... Kit?'

The 'boy' started to rise, and as I watched him stoop to retrieve his bag then heft it over a shoulder, I started to realise my mistake.

'That's me,' Kit said. 'I'm your buddy.'

I stared at the 'youth' before me. 'Kit,' I repeated.

For a few seconds, we just stared at each other. Eventually Kit said, 'Actually it's Katherine, but I prefer Kit. Is that a problem?'

'Fine by me,' I said. 'So long as you remember it's Brandon.'

At that moment she - Kit - hesitated. Right then it could have gone either way, but then she gave a wry, half-smile. 'Fair enough. Come on, I'll show you in.'

As we fell into step together, ascending towards the glass doors at the top of the steps, Kit turned to me. 'And before you ask. No, I'm not trans, or anything. I just hate, "Katherine".'

'Understood,' I said. 'But just so you know? I wouldn't have asked.'

She stopped. We were at the top of the steps. I turned to her. She was looking straight at me, her eyes narrowed, like she was trying to weigh me. I wondered what was going through her mind. After a few seconds she nodded and I saw the wry half-smile again.

'You'll do,' she said.

I wasn't sure what she meant, but I had the feeling I'd just passed some sort of test. 'Do for what?' I said.

'Nothing,' she replied. 'Come on. Let's get you in early for your first day.'

Turning, she began marching towards the doors. As I watched her walking away, a little flat-footed - it wasn't girl's walk at all - I remember thinking that if it hadn't been for her comment about not being trans, I could have remained uncertain about her gender. Suddenly she stopped, and turned back to me.

'Yeah, I know,' she said. 'You're confused. Don't worry about it. Like I said, you'll do.' She started marching again, calling back over her shoulder, 'Come on Brooklyn-Brandon-Sawyer. We've much to do.'

Hefting my own bag, I trotted after her to catch up. And as I fell into step alongside her, I knew.

We were going to get along fine.

CHAPTER 8

CARVER HAD ALWAYS enjoyed combing his fingers through Rosanna's thick, auburn tresses. It was one of the things about her - her voice also played a part, of course - that first grabbed his attention that night he chanced upon her in Lisbon's Barco Negro's smoky depths all those years ago, singing a lamenting ballad in a style he had never heard before. Now, a few bars of *Povo Que Lavas No Rio* - a Fado classic - was enough to transport him back to that signature moment.

For Carver - both of them in fact - the act of combing was as sensuous as it was therapeutic. Over time, it had become a late-evening ritual that was often a precursor to other things. Now, propped on pillows with her head resting on his chest, listening to the steady breathing that told him she was, finally, asleep - *thank God* - he was conscious how much he'd missed the simple pleasure. Now close to one o'clock, their lovemaking had begun sometime after dinner and continued, more or less uninterrupted, since - apart from him having to pad downstairs to refill glasses; red for him, white for her; *and* the brief periods of recovery he couldn't remember needing during their early years.

Given how things had been of late, it was a remarkable session, even by Rosanna's standards. By turns wild, loving, gentle, intense - sometimes frighteningly so - the absence of conversation marked it as different to the cavortings of times past. It made him wonder what it meant, especially considering the doubts he knew she was still harbouring over his impending trip.

Fair enough, the past week she had stopped questioning his reasons for going. Certainly, he had not heard her using the 'O' word, though deep within him, he suspected that his inability to accept The Woman's death as fact rather than possibility, probably *did* amount to obsession. But it was only tonight, sensing the *anger* in her - even drawing blood when she bit his lip - he realised just how big a wedge his obsession had driven between them. And that no amount of explanation was going to dislodge it.

It probably accounted for the vehemence in her reaction when he shared with her first the notes and photographs that had come to him, anonymously, through the post, then the details of the case still under investigation by the New York State County Sheriffs Department. Unable, or unwilling to read in it what seemed to him clear - not even the possibilities - she had reverted to anger, abuse even. It culminating in the devastating, hurtful, but perhaps telling, accusation, 'You *want* it to be her. You *want* her to be alive. Go on, admit it.'

As he lay there, the echo of her words came to him, as they had several times since. And just as they had then, they triggered in him the fear he barely dared acknowledge. Could she be right? Could it be he *did* want it to be her? That he *did* want her to be alive? If so, why? She had once tried to kill him for God's sake. Rosanna as well. Why *would* he wish such a thing? *How* could he?

As he combed, a possible answer came. It may have been a trick of the light - the room was dim - but just for a second, the locks that were previously long and auburn-red, seemed suddenly coal-black, and not so long. And just for a brief second he imagined that the woman whose head rested on his chest was not Rosanna, but someone else entirely. And in that moment, he realised why Rosanna was so opposed to him going.

Resting his head back on the pillows, he gazed up at the ceiling, barely discernible in the semi-dark.

'*Ahh, fuck,*' he whispered.

CHAPTER 9

MY FIRST DAY at William Deacon High was a roller coaster of introductions, explanations and explorations. It was Kit's first day as a full high school student as well, though she had been a WD Junior, which meant she knew her way around and was already familiar with names and faces. Most of the morning we spent in class while our tutor - a young mixed-race woman by the name of Ginny Washington - talked us through everything freshers need to know. There was a lot. The school curriculum. How we were expected to behave and conduct ourselves. Safety protocols - fire, COVID, terrorist attack. Stuff like that.

Ms Washington was shortish - around five feet - and close to barrel-shaped. She was also welcoming, jolly, and generally pleasant. She made a special point of welcoming, 'our new student from the big city,' inviting me to come out front and introduce myself to the class, which I did. I only spoke for a couple of minutes during which time I began to get a feel for what I could expect from my fellow students. Most of the girls - the class was about fifty-fifty - paid attention, more or less, regarding me with the sort of interest girls tend to show in a 'boy from out of town.' I wondered on whether it would have been the same if I'd looked goofier and my acne was a lot worse than it is. The boys, on the other hand - all of them far as I could make out - regarded me with undisguised suspicion. Their expressions ranged from smirky amusement, through to something close to surly contempt. It didn't bother me, and as I returned to my desk, the clicks, snickers and low whistles told me what I could expect the coming days. It wasn't a problem. I'd done it before. What I did come to realise as the day progressed however, was the special status that Kit seemed to enjoy.

It was clear from the moment we entered through the main doors there was something 'different' about her. I first saw it in the way the other students reacted to her. Being the first day, there was a good deal of hugging, air-kissing, high-fiving and fist bumping going on. When it came to Kit however, everything was turned down a couple of notches - quieter, more restrained.

Of course, her appearance alone marked her as different from most other girls. My first impressions that day were that WD's female student population was as obsessed with appearance, at least as much as they are in Brooklyn. Hair was, for the most part, long and glossy, or styled and blow-dried to perfection. Teeth were uniformly white and straight - except for those wearing braces, who tended not to say much. It wasn't that anyone was outright rude or hostile towards Kit - least not as far as I could see. But there was definitely some sort of distancing going on - from both sides. As the day wore on, I came to realise that while she was on nodding terms with just about everyone, she didn't seem to have close friends. Nor was she part of a gang, the way most kids are. There were a few she was clearly wary of, and she pointed them out to me. She didn't say why, just the occasional, 'Stay away from him/her/them', or 'Don't get involved with...' etcetera. The more I became aware of all this, the more I wondered as to the reasons behind it.

All became clear at home time.

At some point in the day I'd mentioned that as my parents were tied up with work stuff, I would be riding the school bus home.

'You live out at Norwood don't you?' she said. I nodded. 'My dad picks me up. We go through Norwood. We can drop you off, if you'd like?

I was happy to accept her offer. I've never gone a bunch on school buses.

As we descended the steps that afternoon, surrounded by all the excitement you would expect at the end of 'first day' - 'Did you see...?' 'Have you heard about...?' - I wondered which among the many cars lined up in the car park opposite the school gates - nearly all SUVs - would prove to be her dad's. Several parents - mostly Moms - were already gathered outside the gates, eager to meet their offspring and begin the debriefing process. I scanned the faces of the couple of Dads amongst them, but none fitted with the blurry mental image I'd formed as to what a 'Kit's dad'-type might look like. But as we approached the gates and I saw the way Kit was paying the throng little heed, it was clear she wasn't expecting to see him there. Through the gates, I was about to swing right, towards the crossing point that would see us 'safely' across the road, as we had been instructed, but Kit grabbed my arm and pulled me left. 'This way,' she said.

William Deacon High School sits about mid-way along the avenue of the same name. The man himself - an eighteenth century fur trader - is especially revered amongst the group of early settlers to whom Brackers Lake owes its existence. As you exit the gates, right takes you south into the downtown area. Left takes traffic north and west towards and beyond the clutch of mainly residential communities - Norwood is one - where a sizable proportion of 'Lakers' have their homes. Tree-lined and grass-verged, William Deacon Avenue is a pleasant thoroughfare of the sort some would say typifies 'small-town America.' Many of the houses even have white picket fences. But as I went with Kit's pull and fell into step alongside her, wondering where we were headed if not the car park, my confusion must have shown.

'Here,' Kit said, pointing ahead of us.

Following her indication, my confusion only grew. While traffic was flowing freely along the road in both directions, the only parking area was the one opposite. The road ahead of us was yellow-lined in both directions and was, with one exception, conspicuously clear of parked vehicles, testimony, I thought, to the law-abiding nature of the locals, and something you'd never see in Brooklyn. Then again, I thought, it probably had something to do with the single vehicle - another SUV - that was the exception I mention. Parked facing against traffic so we were approaching it from the rear, and with its offside wheels up on the sidewalk, the message it was sending out wasn't, I thought, a particularly good one. This was because it was a cop car. Liveried in dark blue and white, with lights atop and "SHERIFF" stencilled above the back plate, my first assumption was that its owner was there to carry out some after-school, traffic-control related activity. But as we neared and I saw the figure in the driver's seat crane to check out the rear-view mirror then, on seeing us, move to open the door and step out, the cogs finally began to fall into place.

'Hiya Kit,' the man in the khaki and green uniform of the County Sheriff's Department called as he turned to us. 'Who's your friend?'

'Hi Pop,' Kit said. 'This is Brandon.'

We stopped in front of him. The silver star on his chest bore the title, "SHERIFF". The name badge underneath read, "Matt Lynch." Kit continued.

'Brandon lives out at Norwood. I said we'd give him a drop, if that's okay?'

There was the slightest hesitation before he replied. 'I gotta call at the Whittingham house. I'm dropping some... things, off.' As I wondered over the reasons for his hesitancy, he stroked his chin, regarding me, as if trying to decide if I was a problem. Kit saw it.

'He's okay Pop. He's from Brooklyn. We'll be quiet.'

He gave us one last look. 'We-ll..' Then, 'Aw, Hell with it. Get in, but you'll have to keep your head down. They might not like me mixing official duties with the school run.'

'I understand Pop. Don't worry, we will.'

So far, the conversation meant nothing to me, other than that Kit's dad obviously had some duty to perform and wasn't sure if my presence made it doubly inappropriate. To that point I'd never heard the name 'Whittingham'. I would do so a lot in the days to come.

He yanked the back door open. 'Jump in.' As I crossed in front of him he put his hand out. 'Nice to meet you, Brandon. I heard we had some incomers. Good. The town needs new blood.'

As we shook I said, 'Thank you, Sir,' I said. 'Nice to meet you too.'

'There's a box on the back seat. Just push it across.'

We piled in, and as I pushed the box over and shuffled across to make room for Kit I turned to her. She was wearing an amused expression, knowing what was coming.

SHERIFF? I mouthed at her. I shook my head. I couldn't believe she hadn't told me. She simply grinned. I wondered how many times she had pulled the same trick.

From the front seat, her father turned to look back, pulling at his shirt to show me his name badge. 'It says Matt, but the rule is, when I'm working, and to you

56

youngsters, it's "Sheriff". You got that?'

'Absolutely Mr- *SHERIFF*.'

Next to me, Kit rolled her eyes. 'Don't
said, so he would hear. 'He's the same with me
a chorus that was clearly rehearsed, they said
'Kids gotta learn to show respect for the law.' I ͜anced
up to see him looking at me through the mirror. His face
was stern but his eyes were smiling.

'Welcome to Brackers Lake, Brandon.'

'Thank you, *Sheriff*.'

As he started the engine, he called back, 'Buckle up
back there. We're the cops, remember.'

As I grappled for my seat belt, I heard Kit sigh.
Glancing at her, I saw her shaking her head. My thought
then was, whatever they had between them, I liked it.

And as we jolted down off the sidewalk to head off
to wherever Sheriff Matt Lynch needed to go to perform
whatever duty he had to perform, my thoughts turned to
how all I had seen that day concerning Kit and her
interactions with her fellow students was now explained.

However irrational, kids are always wary of those
whose parents carry a badge.

CHAPTER 10

TWO MILES NOW from the forest highway turn-off, the pick-up bounces and jostles along the rough road that over the last ten minutes has become little more than a track. As the tyres slew in and out of the deepening ruts, testing the vehicle's suspension, the driver wrestles the wheel to keep the vehicle straight.

The further he travels, the more the trees encroach, narrowing the track and making navigation even more difficult. With the light fading rapidly, the driver is glad when he emerges into a clearing. Across the other side stands a cabin.

Parking on the area of hard-standing to the right, he gets out. As he does so, he is reassured to hear the chug-chug of the generator, and spot the chink of light escaping through one of the boards, low down on the cabin's side wall. They tell him things are working normally and that inside, he should find everything as it should be.

Mounting the steps to the door, he spends a couple of minutes turning keys in locks, removing chains, releasing bolts, before stepping through into the dark. The gaz-lamp is on the table where he left it. It lights easily and, raising it to eye level, he sweeps it round, checking for anything out of place. Seeing everything as he left it, he hoists the bags into the small kitchen area and unpacks some of the essentials - mainly canned food, but batteries and medicines also - and charges and lights the stove before turning to his next and most important check.

Sliding the table back against the wall, he sweeps back the square of carpet. The boarded floor looks unbroken, but reaching down, he removes the short piece of loose-fitting board, revealing the iron ring-handle set into the joist below. Taking firm hold, he pulls open the yard-square 'hatch' that is constructed so that the boards around its outer edges fall, naturally into place alongside those of the surrounding floor, making it invisible to all but the closest scrutiny. Stepping to the edge he begins his descent into the darkness, using the lamp to guide his first few steps down the wooden staircase that is so steep it is almost a ladder. At the bottom, he reaches out into the darkness, feeling for the post to his right and the plastic fitting attached to it. He flicks the switch and the low-wattage strip light suspended from the boards above comes on, throwing out enough of a light to just reach the basement's extremities. The area to his right, roughly twelve feet square, is bare and empty, except for the large travelling trunk - about the size of a small closet - standing against the far wall. To his left, a boarded wall runs the length of the floor. Two doors, a few feet apart, are bolted, chained and padlocked, much like the one above. Approaching the nearest, he takes out another set of keys, removes the chains, and unlocks the door.

As it swings back, a pungent odour, sharp and bitter, hits the back of his throat. He knows at once that before he comes to leave, he will need to attend to the drains again. The single bulb hanging from the ceiling is lit, as it is most of the time, and he steps through. The room is square, and simply furnished. A table and an old, wooden chair. A bed, consisting of a metal frame and single mattress is topped with a pillow and grey, woollen blankets, loosely piled, higgledy-piggledy in the centre. Across the room, mounted on the wall facing the bed is a run of cupboards. The door of one hangs open, displaying its only remaining contents - two, lonely cans of beans. Over in the corner is a plumbed-in sink, another small table next to it. On it is a dish with a bar of soap and a small glass - plastic actually - containing a single toothbrush. In the wall to his right, a door-sized opening leads into blackness. Crossing to it, he flicks the light switch to another low-light bulb. The 'room', such as it is, contains a toilet, and two bulging, black-plastic waste sacks, tied at the top. Checking the bowl, he sees it is blocked, the water level higher than it is supposed to be. Stooping to look behind, he sees that the grey-metal box - a macerator - into which the soil pipe runs, is leaking again. Dark brown liquid - the source of the pungent odour - is oozing out onto the floor. More maintenance. His 'to do' list is growing already.

Returning to the other room, he crosses to the run of cupboards. He has brought the holdall with him. From it he begins to remove cans and boxes of foodstuffs, placing them on the now empty shelves. The bag is nearing half-empty when a noise - something between a whine and a whimper sounds behind him. Checking over his shoulder, he sees movement amongst the pile of blankets. A sly half-smile forms.

Interrupting his shelf-stacking, he crosses to sit on the mattress next to the pile. As he does so, there is more movement, a series of jerks, from within. Reaching out, he takes hold of the corner of one of the blankets, pulling at it slowly, as if peeling a piece of fruit. As he pulls it down, there comes another whimper. A mop of straggly, dark hair starts to emerge. Another few inches, and from behind a spray of bangs he just makes out in the dim light a pair of eyes, wide open, fearful - and glistening.

They are the eyes of a young girl.

'Hello,' he says, smiling.

CHAPTER 11

I'D RIDDEN A black and white just once before in my life. When I was eleven, Louis Suarez talked Tommy Picket and I into joining him and some of his pals in a downtown shop-thieving expedition. At the time, I had just met Afrid and was looking for ways to demonstrate how cool I was. I guess I thought that joining Louis's gang would show her there was another side to the Brandon Sawyer everyone knew. Suffice to say, my 'Louis infatuation' lasted as long as it took us all to be picked up on Macy's cameras and hauled into a back room by a scowling security guard. There, he made us empty our pockets of all the candies and trinkets we had secreted when we thought we weren't being watched. As it happened, the police would never have got involved had Louis not been so high on the crack he'd stolen off his brother that morning that he decided, stupidly, to stage a mass break-out, starting by kicking the security guard in the balls. We learned later that the night before he'd binge-watched the old classics, Fast And Furious 1, 2, and 3, on streaming.

In the end, the store decided that a 'short sharp shock' may do more good than pressing charges. They were right. When I arrived home in the black and white driven by the security guard's Police Officer-sister, my parents' reaction - and the subsequent fall-out - was enough to make me resolve to never attempt anything so stupid again. Leastways, not with the likes of Louis Suarez.

I never forgot that long drive home. Until then, I'd always imagined the inside of a cop car would match its gleaming, rather cool-looking exterior. Wrong. The thinly-upholstered back seat, the hard plastic door-skins, the absence of door and window controls and the metal grill separating front and rear - not to mention the smell of disinfectant - was as close to being in a prison cell as I ever cared to imagine. And it was an experience I was never in any hurry to repeat.

Sheriff Lynch's County Sheriff Department SUV on the other hand, I was pleased to discover, was somewhat better appointed than those of the NYPD. The spec was still basic, but the seats had proper cushions, *and* there was no grille, so riding it didn't make me feel like I was under arrest. There was even a window button.

We'd been travelling a couple of minutes when I turned to find Kit regarding me with a smirk on her face. She obviously found my reaction to the shock of discovering who her father was, and then finding myself in his work car, amusing. I gave her a look, and shook my head.

Kit's father called back over his shoulder. 'How you liking Brackers Lake then Brandon? You all settling in?'

'Yes sir,' I said. 'I'm liking it fine.'

'Bit different to Brooklyn, though, eh?'

'Just a bit.'

He chuckled, checking me out in the mirror.

'Sorry they've landed you with Kit as your babysitter. Pay no attention to whatever she tells you, you'll be fine.'

'DAD,' Kit called.

'SHERIFF,' he returned.

As Kit shook her head, he caught me in the mirror again, sent me a wink. I'd never met a real live sheriff before. But right there, I decided I liked him. And while I'd always imagined Sheriffs as tending towards being on the, 'slow' side, like in most movies, Matt Lynch was a talker.

'So what you been up to today, Kit? Things any different? Are they still distancing?'

'Not really. That's all just about finished. The signs are still there, but everything seems pretty normal.'

'Good. Did you see Doug Mason at all? How is he?'

I remembered one of the science teachers being called Mr, Mason.

'He didn't look too bad. Lost a lot of weight, though.'

'Yeah? Well maybe that's no bad thing. He needed to.'

As Kit and her father chatted about whatever condition Mr Mason had that had caused him to lose weight, I checked out the box beside me. Made of stiff cardboard, and a muddy-brown colour, it looked 'official', rather than something made to carry groceries. The lid was loose and, peeking inside, I saw an assortment of envelopes and plastic bags with labels and writing on them. My thoughts turned to all the CSI episodes I'd seen. On the seat next to the box was a folded copy of The Lake Observer - the county daily. The headline read, "Whittingham Slaying - 'Investigation Making Slow Progress' says Sheriff." A memory stirred. I wasn't sure if maybe I had heard the name, Whittingham, somewhere after all.

As we drove along the Norwood road, I stared out the window, taking in the neat clapper-board houses that reminded me of the sort you see in horror films set in small American towns where everything starts off normal, but there's a monster lurking in the drains.

After a few minutes, we turned right off the road, through a 'gateway' consisting of two tall, sandstone posts supporting stone blocks on which was chiselled, 'Clayton Park'. As we drove into the development, I saw that the houses were newer, bigger and finer than those along the road we'd just turned off, brick-built rather than board-faced, with large garages and expansive, sloping, front lawns. A minute later, we pulled up outside of one on our right. Cutting the engine, Sheriff Lynch turned to look back at us.

'I need you to stay here and be quiet. I'll just be a few minutes.' He remained that way, staring at us until we realised he was waiting for some acknowledgement.

'Okay Dad,' Kit said.

'Yessir,' I followed.

He got out and came around to my side. Opening the door, he grabbed the box off the seat, swung the door shut with his knee, then turned and headed up the path that cut through the greenest lawn I'd ever seen to the front door.

As I watched him ring the bell, Kit's head appeared in my line of vision to lean across me, observing.

'You know whose house that is, don't you?'

'No,' I replied, as in, *How could I?*

'It's Councilman Whittingham's house.'

I turned to her. 'Who's Councilman Whittingham?'

Her eyes widened. 'You've never heard of Councilman Whittingham?'

'No,' I said, still not sure if I had or not. 'Should I?'

'The guy from out in the forest?'

I looked at her, blankly.

'The forest murder?' Her eyes widened even more.

I shook my head. 'What forest murder?'

'Oh my God. You don't know about the murder in the forest?' My silence told her. 'It's only the biggest thing that's happened in Brackers Lake in, like, fifty years. How can you not- wait.' She gripped my arm, staring up at the house. 'That's her.'

I turned to follow her gaze. A woman was standing at the open front door, talking to Kit's dad. She was tall and slim, with pure white, shoulder-length hair. She was wearing a loose fitting top over black cut-offs. Older than my Mom - or maybe the same but tired - my thought was that without the sad look, she would probably look quite nice.

'Who is she?'

'That's the Councilman's wife, Betty.' As Kit spoke, she leaned forward, drinking in every detail of the scene we were witnessing. 'Jeez, she looks awful.'

At that moment, the sheriff stepped up and into the house, the door closing behind him.

I turned to Kit. 'So tell me about this murder. What happened?'

Kit looked back up at the house, as if gauging how long she might have before her father reappeared. 'Some hunters came across his body in the forest a couple of months ago, way out past the lake, towards the Cicero Hills. He'd been strung up and strangled.'

'That's horrible. Did they catch who did it?'

Kit shook her head. 'Not yet. The police are still investigating.'

'When you say 'police', I take it you mean your Dad?'

'Well… He's in charge of the case, but he's getting help from the City detectives.'

I shook my head. I'd lived in Brackers Lake for a little over three weeks. That it was the scene of a gruesome murder didn't exactly fit with the impressions I'd built up over that time. 'Do they know why he was killed?'

Kit smiled. 'Look at you. Brandon Sawyer, boy detective.' She about say something, when she stiffened. Turning, I saw her father coming out the front door. She grabbed my arm. 'If you want to know more, you'll have to come to my house.' She thought a moment. 'Tomorrow's Tuesday. Come tomorrow night.'

'Why tomorrow?' I said.

'Because Tuesdays are usually quiet, so my Dad takes the night off, but usually works from home.'

I was about to ask why that mattered, but the driver's door opening signalled her father returning so I said nothing and clamped my mouth shut.

Ten minutes later, I waved Kit and her Dad off after they dropped me off outside my house. I waited until they were well down the road, then went straight inside and up to my bedroom. There I woke the laptop I use for my school work from its sleep and searched 'Brackers Lake Murder' - In the few minutes following, the picture of Brackers Lake I'd spent the past few weeks building up in my mind underwent a radical overhaul.

And by the time I went to bed, I was itching for tomorrow night to come so I could visit Kit at her home, wherever that was, and discover more.

CHAPTER 12

MY SECOND DAY at school went pretty much the same as the first. More briefings, explanations, and introductions. More warnings from Kit about individuals I either met, or whom she pointed out to me. Not just students. Teaching staff as well. One in particular stood out.

Halfway through the morning we assembled in the gymnasium for a talk by WD's Fitness and Sports Coach. Mr Blackwell. He was tall and slim, and had a buzz cut so short he was almost bald. To me, he looked like he had foreign blood in him. Italian or Greek maybe. As he ran us through all the safety protocols about what to do and not do when using the gym equipment, I got the impression he liked the sound of his own voice. And the way he kept throwing smiles around - especially at the girls - I wondered how many times a day he practised in front of a mirror. A few minutes into his speech, Kit and I exchanged glances. The look on her face - a combination of boredom and disdain - told me all I needed to know about Mr Blackwell.

During lunchtime, Kit told me that her Dad had messaged to say he was going to be tied up with something and could not pick her up so she would have to take the bus home. We rode it together, sat at the back. For some reason the seats in front and either side stayed empty. Before we parted she pinged me directions to her house - 'Within cycling distance,' according to her - and threw me a conspiratorial smile as I rose to get off, like we were about to do something ever-so-slightly illegal.

'See you later,' she sang.

As I stood at the stop, watching the bus depart on its route, she didn't look back but raised a hand in the air, a sort of wave-gesture that made me wonder how she knew I was watching.

Supper that evening was a fairly hasty affair. The night before, I'd primed my parents about me visiting Kit's home - 'for a school project', I lied - so they kept their second-day de-brief short, though I got the impression they were dying to pump me, particularly about Kit. The previous night, when my Mom asked who, 'this Kit,' was and what I knew about her, there was a sudden silence when I mentioned her father being County Sheriff. When I looked up, my parents were staring at each other in a strange way. I had no idea why.

After supper, as I went out the back door to collect my bike to head over to Kit's, my father asked, 'Will you be working at Mrs Cole's tomorrow evening?' to which I replied, 'Sure.'

In truth, at that moment my mind was more on what I was going to learn from Kit, than my gardening work and part-time employer, though thoughts of it and her were never too far away.

It was a twenty-minute cycle ride to where Kit lived. The location she'd sent me took me to it no problem. Her house was one of several dotted around the southern shores of the lake that gives its name to the town. Surrounded by trees and the beginnings of the forest that becomes increasingly dense as you head north, it lay at the end of a spur off the highway that follows the lake's contours. A two-storey affair, constructed entirely of timber, it had something of a 'cabin-in-the-woods' vibe about it - though it was a lot bigger than a cabin. Inside, it seemed little different to any other home, except for the fact that everything - and I mean everything; stairs, floors, walls, even ceilings in some rooms - was made of wood.

Kit greeted me at the door and led me up to her room. As we passed what I took to be a bedroom on my left, I saw her dad sitting at a desk in the corner, working on his PC. He didn't turn or look away from the screen but threw a friendly, 'Hey, Brandon. How you doing?' over his shoulder.

'Good, thank you, Sheriff Lynch,' I said.

'Matt,' he called back. 'Off-duty, remember.'

Kit's room was at the front of the house. Twice the size of mine, it would have passed as some kind of repair shop, rather than a girl's bedroom. Instead of makeup, hair brushes, and what-not, a dresser, computer-style work station and student desk were littered with computer parts and stripped down mechanical instruments. Instead of posters showing boy-bands or pop divas, shelves full of paraphernalia, technical books and journals hung on the walls.

'*Fuuuuck*,' I said, imagining her tinkering away into the early hours every night. ' What are you? Some sort of super-hacker?'

She gave a shrug. 'I just like taking shit apart and putting it back together.'

After returning downstairs to fetch me a Pepper, she closed the door and slid the lock switch, though quietly. When she turned to me, her face had turned suddenly serious. 'You sure you want to do this?' During the course of the day I'd tried pumping her for bits about the murder, but each time she blanked me with variations on, 'Tonight, if you're still up for it.'

'Hell yes,' I answered her now. I was wondering what she was so nervous about. I was soon to find out.

Crossing to her bed, she opened up her laptop. As I joined her, she angled the screen - still blank at this stage - so I could see.

She turned to me and looked me square in the face. 'Have you ever seen a dead body?'

My first thought was, *Of course*. Like most my age, I'd seen hundreds, if not thousands on a screen of one sort or another. I also thought about my grandmother lying in her coffin in her front room, and the guy who got hit by a truck on the street right outside our house in Brooklyn that time.

'I'm talking about an actual, real dead body. Like a murder victim.'

'Uhh- I guess not,' I said.

She nodded. 'Okay. So get ready, and if you think you're going to barf, let me know, I don't want you throwing up all over my bed. That'd take some explaining.'

I watched as she woke the device, opened a folder, and clicked icons. The screen changed to show some sort of text document. Words were being added at the bottom, though she wasn't using the keyboard. She turned to me.

'When my Dad works from home, he logs into the County Sheriff Department's computer system. He's not at all techie, so doesn't realise that because he's using our home network, it means I can see what he's doing. I've got a cloning app on my laptop that allows me to access the system independently, even while he's logged into it.' She turned back to the screen and together, we read what was being typed. It looked like a report of some kind. There was mention of budgets, staffing levels, resources, stuff like that. I got the impression Sheriff Lynch was making out a case for more deputies.

'This is just boring crap,' she said. 'Let me show you

the interesting stuff. I just need to divert his attention for a second. Go out into the hall, and as you pass his office just ask him which room is the John.'

'Why?'

'I'm not sure if anything shows on his screen when I log into the system. I just need him to take his eyes off it a few seconds.'

'Okay,' I said.

I followed her instructions. He actually rose and came to the door in response to my query.

'That door there,' he pointed.

Her scheme must have worked because when I returned to Kit's room, her screen was showing some sort of entry portal, with impressive looking logos and badges laid out in a grid. I was reading the labels under them - Command And Control, Operational Resources, Administration, when she clicked on one labelled, "Case-File Management". It brought up a further set of folders, listed down the left-hand side of the screen. She clicked on one that read, 'Active Investigations', which brought up more folders, each individually named along with an alpha-numerical reference, presumably some sort of case number. She hovered the cursor over one labelled, "Homicide: Curtis Whittingham: HM67/21."

'This is the one,' Kit said, clicking on it.

The screen filled with more folders and icons. She clicked on one that read, "Investigation Log'. Another text document opened which I quickly realised was a dated and timed log of activities and events.

'Just read the top couple of entries,' Kit said. 'You'll get the gist of it.'

As I angled the laptop screen towards me, I had no idea that what I was about to see would come to have a serious impact on the quality of my sleep, and remain with me for the rest of my life.

CHAPTER 13

THE ON-SCREEN log was formatted into three columns. Column one showed the date, column two the time, and column three the details corresponding to the timed entry. The log started at 10.47 on May 25 with a 911 call received in the 'ECS' - Emergency Communications Centre. The details column recorded three hunters reporting finding the body of a white male on the southern slopes of the Cicero Hills, which I knew was some sixty miles or so to the north and west of Brackers Lake. There was reference to the hunters reporting signs of possible violence - asphyxia - but the rest of the log entry related to passing the information on to the County Sheriff Dispatch Centre, with a good deal of jargonese - "SOC", "SOP", "LEEN" - I couldn't work out.

The next several log entries detailed the various communications between the Sheriff's Department, the Coroner's Office, various detective/police units and the County Crime Lab as they coordinated their efforts to get a team of detectives and crime scene officers helicoptered out to the location. A log entry timed at 14.43 recorded confirmation from Sheriff Lynch they were 'on scene'. The next entry showed a link to a witness statement of a Deputy Arlan Taylor of the County Sheriff's Department, of which there was an extract embedded in the log itself. It read:-

"Together with Sheriff Lynch, I entered the clearing using Designated Scene Entry Point 01, (Scene Lcation Plan, Ref AT/01), and approached the deceased from the South East. As I approached the body, I was able to visually confirm that of a mature, white male, appearing late forties-fifties. Body was located in a grassy area, next to a hawthorn tree, and on its western side. The deceased was naked below the waist apart from a pair of black, men's briefs that appeared made of a rubber/latex type material. Above the waist, he was wearing a woman's corset-type garment, fully fastened at the rear with ties made of thin black ribbon material. A further ribbon was tied around the victim's throat. A test showed it was not so tight as likely to constrict breathing.

The body was resting on its knees, leaning forward at an angle of approximately 35 degrees. It was supported in that position by two ropes. Rope One was around the neck in the form of a noose, extending directly vertically upwards, and tied to to an overhanging branch. The second rope was wound several times around both wrists which were extended out in front of the body. The other end of this rope was tied in a lower position around the trunk of the tree so that the arms appeared to be being pulled forward and down.

From my observation, I assessed that from the angle of the body vis-à-vis the ropes, during the period preceding death, the greater proportion of the deceased's body weight would have been borne by the rope around the neck, with the rope pulling the arms forward and down adding to that pressure. Characteristics visible in the face - protruding tongue, darkened skin colouring - and the neck - heavy abrasions and chafing, corresponding with the position of the rope - appeared, in my judgement, to support this assessment.

On examination, I noted that the palms of both hands appeared to be flat and closed together, in a manner similar to an attitude of Christian prayer. A wooden post - square; 4" x 4" - was sunk into the ground directly behind the body so that it rested *up against and between the buttocks. I later measured it as rising 4'.5" from ground level. The deceased's ankles were roped and tied together behind the post, with the left ankle crossing over the right. The presence of fecal matter on the ground directly below the buttocks and associated soiling indicated that at some stage, the deceased's bowel had evacuated. Similarly, residual dampness on the ground in front of and below the groin area, presented possible evidence of urination having also occurred, voluntary or involuntary.*

At this time I observed no other visible signs of violence to the body. There were no items within the vicinity of the body that could have been used as weapons, or which might have played some part in bringing about death."

'You okay?'

I jumped as Kit's voice jolted me out of my absorbed state.

I said nothing, but nodded. At that moment, the image conjured up by Deputy Taylor's account was so vivid, I was probably incapable of replying, even had I wanted to. And whilst I would have imagined that, given all the things I had either read, or seen on TV or some other screen in my life, a written description of a dead body would never have been capable of affecting me in such a way, the stark matter-of-factness of the deputy's words was having a profound impact. I was conscious of a nauseous feeling, growing as the minutes passed, that seemed to be affecting not just my gut, but my whole body. It was unlike anything I had ever encountered before. At the same time and for some reason, I kept remembering Councilman Whittingham's wife, Betty, as I had seen her at her front door talking to Kit's father. This was her *husband* I had just read about, shitting and pissing himself as he died. A real, live, dead person.

If Kit was aware of how I was feeling - *had she felt the*

75

same the first time she read it? - she gave no sign.

'The rest of it is mainly procedural,' she said. 'Nothing too interesting. Not much has been added the past few weeks. But last week I checked to see if there had been any updates, and saw this.'

I watched, still numb, as she scrolled down, scores, maybe hundreds of log entries rising to disappear off the top of the screen. Eventually she reached the final few entries dating from August 20th. I read on. The first message was timed at 20.47 that day.

Sheriff M Lynch reports contact from a British Police Officer. Detective Chief Inspector James Carver, attached to Special Murder Investigation Unit, (Location Nr Manchester). Detective Carver investigated a series of homicides in the UK which share aspects of the modus operandi characteristics in this case. Perp. was arrested and convicted, but later escaped prison custody - since assumed deceased. Arrangements made for further liaison and information sharing.

Three days later, a further log entry read;

Call from DCI Carver confirming sufficient interest in Whittingham case and possible connection with outstanding British investigations to warrant direct liaison on the ground. He is making arrangements to visit NYS and will contact further.

A final entry, dated just a few days before read;

Confirming information received this date from DCI Carver. He will arrive at JFK during week commencing 09/06 - details to be confirmed with Sheriff M Lynch direct.

'Jeez,' I said. Reading the last few entries, my nausea had abated enough to let some excitement in. 'There may be a connection with similar cases in England? And the 'tec from there is coming here? That's like... amazing.'

I turned to look at Kit. The self-satisfied look told me she had been anticipating just such a reaction.

'And it says-' I turned back to the screen to confirm, re-read the final entry. 'He's arriving this week some time?'

Kit nodded, knowingly, like she was enjoying demonstrating her insider knowledge.

'I heard my dad on the phone to someone earlier tonight. I think it was the English guy. He mentioned something about seeing him in a couple of days.

'Wow,' I said. 'That'll be so interesting. Will you get to meet him?'

'Dunno,' Kit said. 'Maybe. Probably. I did the last time an out-of-town cop visited. I think Dad thinks it's good for my-' She mimed quotation marks - '"development", to meet people from other places.'

I shook my head, still taking it all in. 'This is all just so... so...' My vocabulary seemed to have gone missing in action. '-*Cool*'

'Yeah. I know.'

For several seconds there was only silence in the room. I realised later that Kit was giving me time to let it all settle. Eventually I turned to her. 'What else is there? You must have looked through all the folders.' A thought came to me. 'What about photographs, videos? Like they take on CSI?'

She bit her lip. Answer enough.

'Show me.'

She looked torn, hesitated. 'I'm not sure-'

'Come on,' I urged. 'Show me.'

She looked at the door, as if expecting that her father may suddenly burst in and catch us hacking. 'If I show you, you must never, ever, tell anyone. If you do, I'll end up in jail.'

'I won't. I swear.'

She showed me.

To this day, I wish to God she hadn't.

CHAPTER 14

CARVER HAD NEVER flown Virgin Atlantic before and had no idea what to expect by way of coffee. As it turned out, he was pleasantly surprised. There was even a Columbian option. *Kudos, Richard Branson.* After ordering up a second cup via the chatty crew member whose camp safety-drill performance had ensured everyone paid attention, he pulled out his notebook. He had close to eight hours in which to attend to the 'bit of work' he had set himself. But something told him that if he put it off, it wouldn't happen. He'd already spotted one or two films on the programme he hadn't seen yet, and he'd picked up a couple of magazines at the airport. The middle seat next to him had stayed empty - his was the 'window' - and the young woman in the 'aisle' had taken herself off somewhere soon after take off. It meant he could get on with doing what he needed to do free from worry someone might see something they shouldn't.

Booting up, he navigated to the folder containing the remnants of Megan Crane's fire-bombed archive. His intention was to refresh his memory regarding her US connections. When the time came to share information with Sheriff Matt Lynch, it would not do to be 'hazy' over details.

The archive material he had managed to get through before the fire pointed to her US involvements being as extensive, and potentially explosive as those at home - his priority at the time. For that reason, anything to do with America went into a folder marked, "USA", which was subsequently lost. Fortunately there was still enough embedded in what remained or which Carver managed to salvage, that a partial glimpse of the wider US picture was still possible. Names were few and details sparse, nevertheless his hope was that if Lynch's investigation was as stymied as it sounded during their phone conversations, there may just be something there that would help. Two and half hours later, the "Critical Battery Warning" showed his 'quick refresh' had turned into something else. It was a brief reference in a diary entry he had not read since the early days that sparked it.

Back then he assumed, he probably interpreted her note dated 12th May - "CW coming over next week" - as referring to someone relatively local, visiting her Cheshire home. And while his Anacapa chart showed that particular 'CW' remained unidentified - like many initials - that was before he knew of someone called Curtis Whittingham. The "coming over" could as easily mean 'crossing the Atlantic', as a visit from a neighbouring town or village. It led him to wonder further. If her US connections were so strong that someone like Whittingham made personal visits, then what else may now bear some reinterpretation? In particular, he remembered a hand-written journal entry that, while obtuse, at the time triggered a thought so outlandish, he immediately dismissed it as too fanciful - further confirmation, were any needed, of his over-active imagination. The original document was one of several that were scanned before they burned. And everything digital had been backed up to an off-site server, thank goodness. He pulled it up now.

Dated a couple of years before he arrested Edmund Hart, it read.

"Tel call tonight from AK," - *Alistair Kenworthy?* - "Says WH may be a possibility after all. He will be in W for a meeting with ZR when we there in Sept. Says Z reckons P is very keen to meet and would love to arrange priv. meet. VERY excited. Not told Edmund yet. May leave him out. Too risky."

At the time, Carver assumed "W" referred to Westminster, and the rest of the initials to other, unidentified high-ups who shared Kenworthy's interests and propensity for risk-taking. Carver had met plenty who worked or lived within the 'Westminster Bubble'. There was no shortage of candidates. Now however, his imagination took him back to where the cryptic initials led him the first time. Back then, he didn't dig far looking for possible meaning as he was still prioritising UK connections. Apart from referencing a possible meeting - of which there were many - there was nothing to mark it any more worthy of investigation than any of the dozens, maybe hundreds, of similar references. But now... He went searching through the archive, which was when his 'quick refresh' turned into a deep trawl.

It took over an hour - and several coffees. He found what he was looking for not in a diary entry - it would have been too obvious, and besides she was always careful about giving away her movements - but a photograph.

It was one of hundreds she kept in a box in the bottom drawer of her cabinet and which he later got someone from IT Support to scan and add to the digital record before they also burned. Most were innocuous, mainly showing her in social settings with members of her circle, either individually or in groups. They came in useful when Carver had to set about matching faces with initials, particularly those in the public eye. Some were taken at Josephine's or similar venues, showing the range of interests catered for in such establishments, though she was always careful not to appear in them herself. Others showed her with Edmund Hart, and Carver had to bite back the rage that surfaced whenever he viewed them. But Hart was never as careful as she was when it came to documenting their travels. Several images were 'holiday-type' snaps, showing places they visited, and Carver recognised some. Paris, Rome, maybe Greece - and Sorrento, Mount Vesuvius looming large in the background. But the one he stumbled across while idly searching and which might - just might - support his outlandish theory, showed, on the face of it, very little.

Taken on a sunny day, it showed her and Hart together, beaming smiles, in front of some sort of inland lake. What drew him to look closer, was the fact that while Hart was wearing a tee-shirt and jeans, she was dressed formally and, for her, quite soberly - matching dark jacket, skirt, and white blouse. She could have just come from a business meeting - or meeting someone in a position of authority. The photograph had been taken at an upward angle making it difficult to spot. Carver had to zoom in to see it clearly. It was in the far background, just above where their heads were touching. Some sort of pointed structure, like the top of an obelisk. Whoever scanned it had also scanned the back of the photo so they stood together. The writing on the back showed what looked like a date, "18/09". Which could well fit with the reference in the original entry to them being there, "in Sept."

He had never been there himself, so he couldn't be certain. But he had seen enough photographs to ponder the possibility that the structure in the background could be the Washington Monument. And if Megan Crane had indeed been in Washington that September, then references to, "WH" and being "EXCITED" at the thought of meeting someone for whom only one initial - "P" - was sufficient, could render the scenario he had laughingly dismissed some years before as not so outlandish after all.

Carver didn't move, but stayed staring at the image even as the screen darkened and, eventually, died. By then his thoughts were around who she might have met with that day? And who amongst them - if she *were* still alive - she might still be in contact with? In which case, where might his visit to share information with a County Sheriff investigating a local councilman's brutal murder now take him?

Eventually, cramp in his right leg and stiffness elsewhere moved him to stir. Stretching in his seat, he looked about him, marking the faces of those closest, as if they might have glimpsed the photo and - by some impossible means - read what was in his mind. Eventually, satisfied nothing of the sort could have occurred, he turned to settle back in his seat. Lifting one hand to pull at his bottom lip, he stared at the rear of the seat in front.

"Bugger me," he said.

CHAPTER 15

I DIDN'T SLEEP well that night. Each time I closed my eyes, I kept seeing Councilman Whittingham. I never knew CSIs take so many pictures and videos at a murder scene. There can't have been an angle, or aspect, that wasn't covered. I've seen plenty of 'torture-porn' stuff in movies and on some of the more extreme sites. It never bothered me, particularly. Some on-line games are far worse. But the fact the pictures showed a 'real' person, whose wife I had seen, *and* that it occurred within reach of where we lived, put it in a different category to all that stuff.

Two things especially were freaking me out. One, was the corset-thing he was wearing. Apart from everything else, it lent the whole scene an extra layer of weirdness that I just couldn't get my head around. The second was the way he had died. Kit told me that somewhere in the log it talked about the councilman slowly strangling to death over the space of somewhere between two to three hours. I couldn't stop imagining what that would have been like for him, hanging there, knowing he was going to die, and no-one was coming to save him. Every now and then, I found myself shivering at the thought so much I had to force myself to think about something else - Kit, Miriam, Star Wars - anything that might stop the images coming.

Eventually I woke up - late. I barely had time to

shower and had to gobble my breakfast down to get to school on time.

The moment Kit saw me she was full of, 'Are you okay?' 'God, you look awful.' 'I knew I shouldn't have shown you that stuff.'

I tried shrugging it off, telling her it was no big deal, but she saw through that in a second.

I spent the whole of the day in what I guess must have been some sort of trance. I could hear what people were saying, and knew what was going on around me, but very little of it stuck. I lost count of the number of times I felt Kit's tug on my sleeve, pulling me out of wherever I was to ask, 'You okay?' To this day, I believe the only thing that stopped me flipping right out, was the knowledge I was due to return to my gardening work after school. I'm pretty sure the thought I'd be seeing Miriam again helped keep me sane.

At home time, Kit offered me a ride off her dad again, but I declined. I didn't trust myself to be in his company and not blurt out something that would have given something away. As I parted from Kit in the main corridor - the school buses leave from the back of the school - she was still wearing the worried expression she'd had all day.

After a quick bite of the early supper my Mom had waiting, I made my way across to Miriam's. I used the side gate to head around the back, as she'd instructed me to the previous Saturday - 'In case I'm indisposed when you ring the bell.' I found her sitting out on her deck with a pitcher of iced-lemon and slices of the black bread-cake waiting. She seemed eager to know how I'd got on at my new school, if I was enjoying it, if I'd made any new friends. I spent the next twenty minutes talking her through everything. When I told her I'd met a girl called Kit, she said, 'Ahh, that's nice. Who is she?' And when I mentioned about her dad being Sheriff, her eyebrows arched upwards, though for some reason I had half an impression she wasn't quite as surprised as she was making out.

'Really?' 'she said. 'How interesting. Have you met him?'

I told her I had, and then thought to add - I'm not sure why - that he was investigating the murder of a man whose body was found out in the forest.

'I heard about that,' she said. 'It sounded horrible. Have they caught anyone yet?'

'No, but-' I hesitated, suddenly remembering how I'd come by the information.

She leaned forward. 'But what?'

For a moment, I struggled over what to do. I was still getting to know her, but from what I'd seen she didn't seem the gossipy sort. Right from the first time we met properly that first Saturday morning, I felt she was someone I could trust.

'The police are looking at whether it might be connected with something that happened in England. Some English detective has contacted Sheriff Lynch. I think he's coming over to look into it.'

I drank some of my iced lemon. As I did so, I was conscious Miriam was staring at me, eyes even wider than normal, mouth slightly open. There was a short silence during which I wondered if I'd said something I shouldn't.

'When?' she said.

'When what?' I said.

'When is he coming here? This English detective.'

I cast my mind back. 'I'm not sure. I think it may be this week sometime.'

There was another short silence. 'What's his name?'

The question took me by surprise. 'Who? The

detective?' She nodded. 'I don't know.' I tried to remember. 'It might be… Clark? Or Carter maybe. I'm not sure. It began with a 'C' I think. Why?'

She waved it away, pinned her smile back on. 'Oh, nothing. It's just I met an English policeman once. But I suppose that's like asking a New Yorker if they know someone you know lives in the city.'

'Yeah… Well whoever he is, he'll be here soon.'

She nodded, before turning away to stare out over the garden.

I waited a moment, before rising out of my chair. 'Better get on, before the light starts going.'

She nodded again, slowly, saying nothing.

As I stepped down off the deck, pulling on my gloves, a thought came. I turned back to her.

'Erm…'

Her head swivelled, slowly, in my direction until she was staring right at me again. 'Yes?' She seemed distracted.

'I'm… not sure I should be telling people what Kit told me. Maybe you could-'

Her hand came up. 'Don't worry, I won't repeat anything you've said to anyone.'

I nodded. 'Great. Thank-'

She leaned forward in her chair. 'After all, I'd hate for you to get in any trouble… or Kit, for that matter.'

I nodded again, and was about to turn away when Kit's words of warning the night before about not telling anyone came to me. …*If you do, I'll end up in jail.* A sudden panic gripped me. If Kit found out I'd told Miriam, she would never- I stopped, watching Miriam's lips form into a mischievous smile.

'But there's no need to worry, Brandon. It'll just be our little secret.' And as if that wasn't enough, as she spoke the words, the look in her eyes seemed to say, *'You*

87

are safe with me.'

The panic subsided as quickly as it arose. I returned her smile. In that moment I was so relieved, I felt like stepping back up and giving her a big hug. But I just said, 'Right. Our little secret. Thank you Miriam.'

I turned to head off to begin work, conscious that at that moment, something was going on in my stomach, like butterflies dancing. And as I set to with my cutters and saws, I was surprised to discover that considering the day I'd had, and how I'd hardly slept the night before, I wasn't short of energy.

CHAPTER 16

CARVER REMAINED DISTRACTED all through landing, disembarking and retrieving his suitcase. Waiting in line at immigration, he was still musing on how much he would share with Sheriff Lynch when they met. It wasn't until he exited into arrivals and picked out the tall, black man in uniform and holding a board reading, "J Carver, England" he focused.

As Carver approached, the man lowered the board. 'You look just like your picture. Pleasure to meet you, Mr Carver.' He stuck out a hand. 'Arlan Taylor. I'm Sheriff Lynch's number one deputy.'

The chuckle that came with it told Carver all he needed to know, for now, about Deputy Taylor. He would ask which picture he'd seen another time. He hoped not the one from the Sunday Times Magazine.

'The name's Jamie, Arlan,' he said as they shook. 'Thanks for being here.'

Taylor pointed at Carver's bag. 'Just the one?' Carver nodded. Before he could say anything, the deputy took it, turned, and started wheeling it away. 'This way Mr Carver. It's a couple of hours' drive and rush-hour's about to hit so we best not hang around.'

Carver followed his greeter as they followed a convoluted route through the airport, up and down stairs and escalators and through doors marked, 'Staff - No Public Access' which Taylor unlocked using the card on the lanyard round his neck. Eventually they emerged through another marked door into an underground service area. Across an access road, a County Sheriff Department SUV stood waiting in a hatch-marked parking bay. Ten minutes later, as they headed north on 1-678 and away from the airport, Taylor turned to him.

'If you want to close your eyes a spell Mr Carver, feel free. My guess is you've had a long day and there's not much to see this stretch. I'll holler when we hit the county line. The recline button is down on your right."

Up since four that morning, Carver didn't hesitate. 'I might just do that.' Feeling for the button, he closed his eyes and went with the seat-back as it tipped. It was a nice feeling.

But traffic was heavy, and a snarl-up as they headed towards the Grand Central Parkway Interchange stretched what should have been two hours, into nearer three. What sleep Carver managed - more of a doze - was filled with visions of Megan Crane with prominent Washington figures, triggering questions that kept rousing him. Some were around what it would do to Britain and America's so-called 'special relationship - and his career - if he uncovered a scandal of the sort that might have erupted back home, had the note written on notepaper bearing a royal crest not also become 'lost' in the fire.

By the time Deputy Taylor saw Carver into his hotel - a colourful Best Western built in the colonial style on the outskirts of Brackers Lake - Carver felt sufficiently drained to pass when Taylor relayed his boss's offer of a late supper, in favour of meeting early next morning.

Carver went straight to his room where he messaged Rosanna confirming his safe arrival - it was after one back home - before crashing into a deep and, for once, dreamless sleep.

CHAPTER 17

FINISHED SCRUBBING, THE man straightens, pausing to check out the results of his labours of the past hour. The room, especially the toilet, is clean again now, the smell of disinfectant and air-fresh displacing the aromas that hung when he began.

Turning, he drops the brush back in the bucket, then bends to pick it up along with the black waste-sack containing the bedding. Leaving, he does not bother to close the door - no need now - but goes straight to the steps which he ascends carefully, burdened as he is with his load.

The room above is empty, but crossing to the window he peers out, spying the muddy shovel and boots on the porch that point to the other half of the morning's work having also been completed. He gives a satisfied nod. Digging was never his thing. Not that he can't, or is too old for such work - far from it. But no point having a dog and barking yourself.

Crossing to the stove, he pours himself a coffee, then returns to the window. Somewhere, out amongst the trees, the sound of chopping echos. He allows himself a half-smile. Maintaining the wood pile around back is another job he is happy to delegate. And besides, Jasper was always better suited than himself for such work.

Staring out, conscious of how the chopping noises seem to blend, almost naturally with those of the wind,

91

the whispering forest, the occasional bird call, he allows himself a few moments' quiet reflection. It is times such as this he revels most in the sense of satisfaction - and achievement - his work brings. The tranquillity of the surroundings and the sheer rugged beauty of nature in all its glory help of course. Not for the first time he congratulates himself on his decision to relocate his base of operations. It was never like this in the city.

It reminds him.

Soon, he will leave here to return to his other life, the one that provides him with what he needs to sustain this one. And while he enjoys that side of his life, he knows it will not be long before the urges that drive him will lead him to seek out his next 'project'. He has no particular thoughts yet as to what it will be, the form it will take. But the pot from which he sups is deep. There is never a shortage of options - another advantage of his dual, urban-rural lifestyle.

But he must not get ahead of himself. He knows from experience that a lack of self-discipline leads to over-indulgence which can have a blunting effect. Far better to savour the periods of denial, to let them add to the anticipation. That way, when it happens, he will be able to make the most of it.

Too much of a good thing…

Turning from the window, he surveys the room. There is still some clearing up to do before they leave. But the heavy work is done. Another hour should see it finished, then they can be on their way. He feels a little sad at the thought. But he knows it won't be too long before he is back. And now that he thinks about it, maybe there is one possible option on the horizon that could be worth looking at.

The trouble is, if he were to go in that direction, he may have to overcome strong resistance from certain quarters. He smiles, wryly, at the thought. Even when he 'loses' - which is, of course, most of the time - he always enjoys their 'tussles'. And he is sure she feels the same.

CHAPTER 18

NOTHING HAPPENED ON the Thursday, other than Kit told me the English detective had arrived and was due to meet her Dad some time that day. On Friday, she confirmed they had met, but her Dad was giving nothing away other than, 'Seems a nice guy. You'd love his accent.'

Heading across to Miriam's on the Saturday morning, it wasn't in my head to mention it, but after enquiring about how school was going, her next question was, 'Did you hear any more about that English police detective coming here?' She said it in a matter-of-fact way, like it was no big deal.

Remembering our conversation on the Wednesday, I nodded. 'He arrived Thursday, I believe.' Then a thought came. 'If you like, I can ask-'

'NO,' she rounded on me.

The sharpness of her response took me by surprise. But she must have realised because she softened, immediately.

'I meant... there's no need to mention it. Just making conversation.' She moved straight on. 'What's your plan this morning?'

I pointed at the tall birch, back left, I'd started on last time, stating my intention to take down a couple more of the lower overhanging branches shading that part of the garden

'Good idea,' she said. 'That part of the garden is

looking so much better already.' As I pulled on my gloves she added, 'I knew I could rely on you. We obviously think alike.'

As I headed down the garden, I imagined her eyes, following me. I liked that she felt she could rely on me.

I worked on the birch through to my mid-morning break. Today there was a slab of some delicious fruit cake full of cherries, which I love, to go with the iced lemon. After the 'break-time chat' that was now our routine - she seemed to enjoy hearing all about my growing up in Brooklyn, my friends, people we were close to as family - I went back to work wondering about the treats she kept serving up. Try as I might, I couldn't imagine her in an apron and up to her elbows in flour and baking ingredients.

I was still wondering on it when I received an unexpected, and unwelcome, reminder that my twice-weekly visits were only a small part of Miriam Cole's life, and that I knew next to nothing about that life other than, like me, she was no 'Laker' - *and* the fact she knew a good baker. I was using the loppers with the extending handles to bring down the last couple of overhangs, when I became aware of voices from the house. Miriam had a *visitor*. Even as I stopped to listen, the voices became louder, rising in pitch. Then I realised, they were arguing. The doors out onto the deck were closed, and the way the voices echoed inside, I could make out little of what was being said, though I could tell it was a man - especially when he started shouting.

I dropped the loppers and was about to scoot up onto the deck - what my next move would have been I had no idea - when I saw movement inside so I stopped. The next thing I saw Miriam, striding across her living room before turning to take up a position facing a figure opposite her. I couldn't see him because of the way the light was reflecting on the glass between us.

Miriam's arms were folded, tight, across her chest and she was standing with one leg forward in a way that reminded me of my mother when she used to argue with my father about Uncle Hector and Aunt Katherine being around so much. The thought came that Miriam had put herself where I could see her, which made me wonder if she had done so in case she needed help. At that moment, the man was still several feet away, and showing no signs of moving closer. Nor did he seem to be behaving in a way that seemed threatening in any way. They were just talking across at each other, loudly. The direction the man was facing and my position in the undergrowth, meant it was unlikely he could see me, unless I made my presence known, so I did.

Reaching down, I grabbed an armful of loppings, then made my way forward to deposit them at the base of the deck steps. As I did so, the voices stopped. Looking up, I saw Miriam staring at me. And though I still could not see the man's face properly, I could see he was now turned towards me. For several seconds there was only silence as the three of us stood there, me looking at Miriam, waiting for any signal that would decide my next action, the two of them staring out at me. Finally the man moved, turning back towards Miriam, and this time I heard, quite clearly, the, 'Who the *fuck* is he?'

Miriam made a calming gesture and started to address him in a quieter manner than before. And though he turned it down a couple of notches, I still picked up a few phrases.

'...I don't care. What's he doing here?'....

'...you've got to be kidding me...'

'You must be out of your fucking mind...'

Eventually, presumably conscious of my presence, they withdrew back into the kitchen and away from my view. The talking continued, but quieter now. At that point I judged that the crisis - if it was a crisis - had passed, so I returned to my work, though keeping an eye on the house and listening out for anything that might signal trouble.

Over the next half-hour or so, I stayed visible, making a point of taking stuff out to the dumpster at the bottom of the drive. I assumed that the gleaming bronze pickup - A Ram 1500 - was his, and made a mental note of the number. It was a New York plate.

Half an hour passed during which things stayed quiet and I focused more on the garden and less on the house. But then a smell I'd never encountered during my visits to Miriam's made me look up. The man was there, out on the deck, smoking a cigarette. Seeing me mark him, he beckoned me over with a gesture and a, 'Hey, kid. C'meer.'

His voice sounded a bit 'city', and though I hated the way he'd addressed me - like I was a child who should jump to his command - I hesitated only briefly before responding.

As I approached, I got my first good look at him. I wasn't sure if he looked familiar. White, but ruddy-faced, he appeared a little older than my father - and Miriam for that matter - and about the same height, but heavier. He carried himself with his chest puffed out, like he was used to getting his own way. His sandy hair was peppered with grey and slicked back, but I could see it was long enough to curl over his collar at the back. He was wearing a shiny, mid-blue suit over an open-collar white shirt. I also noticed how the jacket's sleeves were tight around his bulging biceps. Whoever he was, he looked like he worked out a bit. My overall impression was of someone who liked to be noticed. I wondered what his business was with Miriam. I hoped he wasn't some sort of friend.

As I stopped in front of him, I could see him eyeing me up and down. His lips were drawn in what I couldn't tell was a smile or a sneer, though his first words gave it away.

'So you're the Sawyer, boy.'

He knows my parents? I nodded, saying nothing.

'Miriam tells me you're a good worker.'

'I do my best.'

The way he looked at me, I wondered if he was waiting for the, *'Sir.'* When it didn't come, he nodded, slowly. 'How old are you? Fifteen? Sixteen?'

'Fourteen, just.'

'*Fourteen?* Fuck, what do they feed you? Three steaks a day?'

I shrugged, but gave no answer. I could see him checking me out again, revising whatever opinions he'd formed the first time.

'You like working for Miriam?'

I shrugged again. 'Sure.'

He cast his gaze about, waving an arm over my efforts. 'I hope she's paying you fair for all this hard work?'

I took my time answering. 'I don't think I should discuss things like that with people I don't know.'

As he drew himself up and his face started to redden more than it was already, I got my first sense of how he could have fallen into arguing with someone as easy going as Miriam. But if he'd been about to explode, he managed to stamp on it. He breathed long and deep, then smiled, a real one this time.

'You've got balls, kid. I'll give you that. And you're right. You don't know me.' He stuck out a hand, reaching down. 'I'm Za-'

'NO.'

We both turned. Miriam was at the door out onto the

deck. The look on her face was like nothing I'd ever seen before - a mix of shock, fear and anger. Whatever she'd been doing, I got the impression she wasn't expecting to return to find us together. And she clearly wasn't happy about it. The glare she threw at the man as she strode forward, purposeful and almost, to my mind, threatening, confirmed it.

'I *told* you....'

She said it in a way and with a glaring stare that conveyed a lot more than the words themselves. Then she stood back and held out a hand in such a way it was a clear invitation - or instruction - that he should return back inside.

Having turned to witness her approach, his back was to me and his position was such I lost sight of her for a few moments. Whatever passed between them during that time, I didn't get to see, but when he turned back to me the smirk was there again.

He gave a 'Humph,' then followed it up with, 'See ya again kid,' before turning to head back into the house. As he did so, I saw Miriam regarding me the way a mother does who knows her child has just had a narrow escape. Then she turned and followed him inside. The door shut firmly, and I heard the lock click.

It was an hour later and I was getting ready to finish clearing up for the day when she finally reappeared. I'd heard his truck leave thirty minutes or so earlier. She seemed her normal self again. Surveying the results of my morning's efforts, she said, 'That's another excellent day's work Brandon. Thank you,' and handed me the by-then customary envelope.

But as I pulled my gloves off to accept it, she surprised me by suddenly reaching out to take my hand. Her grip was fierce and, I thought, surprisingly strong. She leaned forward so her face was close to mine. I could smell her perfume.

'One thing,' she said, her dark eyes burning into mine. 'If you ever see that man again, you must tell me. Understand?'

'Yes Miriam,' I said.

'And if you do see him, stay away from him. Do you understand me?'

I had met the man only once, and knew nothing about him other than he drove a Ram 500 pickup and his name began 'Za-' something. But as I stared into the eyes that seemed somehow darker than I'd ever noticed, and remembered the events of that morning, I felt that somewhere deep down inside, I understood, fully.

'Yes, Miriam,' I said.

CHAPTER 19

I DIDN'T MENTION anything to my parents about Miriam's visitor when I got home that Saturday. They were both busy and I was still trying to get my head around what I'd seen, what it meant. I didn't like the idea of Miriam being shouted at by a man like that. I was thinking about it right through dinner and all that evening, but if my parents noticed, they didn't say anything. They were preoccupied over something that was happening in the next couple of weeks. I kept hearing mention of days and dates, but I wasn't paying much attention and didn't pick up on what it was about.

Next morning, the incident wasn't on my mind so much and I turned my attention to other things - the weekend soccer results, homework - Fortnite. My parents seemed similarly more at ease, and I heard no further mention of the matter they had been discussing. It was over Sunday dinner my mother sought to catch up on how my work at Miriam's was progressing. I talked her through what I was doing and what little I knew of Miriam's plans for the garden when all the clearing was finished. My mother enjoys gardening, though the one we had in Brooklyn was tiny - little more than raised borders around a flagged square. Now she was spending a fair bit of time in her new one, molding it into what she wanted it to be. She talked about possible options and ideas for Miriam's, like I might want to pass them on to her. It was as I was finishing my report that I must have mentioned something about Miriam having had a visitor. My mother was on it like a shot.

'Visitor? What sort of visitor?' My father lowered his paper.

I helped myself to another piece of fruit pie. 'Just some guy. I don't know who he was.' I decided I wasn't going to mention about them arguing. That was private, between me and Miriam.

'Did you see him, speak to him?'

'Only a few words. He was in the house, mainly.'

It went quiet for a bit. I ate pie.

Eventually, my father said, 'What did he look like, this visitor?'

Looking up, I saw them both watching me. I'm not sure why. They know I like my mom's pie.

'Nothing special,' I said. 'He was a biggish guy, wearing a suit. A bit older than you maybe Pa, about your height? He could have done with a haircut.'

'Did you make his car?'

I nodded, still shovelling pie. 'It was cool. A real nice pickup. One of those Ram 1500s? Must have cost a wad.'

It went quiet again. I finished my pie.

My father said, 'Any idea why he was there?'

They were still watching me. I started to wonder about their interest. I shook my head. 'No. But he seemed like a dick.'

'That's not nice,' my mom said. 'In what way was he a dick?'

'Oh, just…' *Done it again*, I thought.

'Just what?' my father said.

'I dunno. He wasn't being very nice to Miriam. They seemed to be having some sort of argument.'

The quiet returned. They were both looking at me. I wondered what was going on. My father put his paper down.

'Did you hear what they were arguing about?' I shook my head, staring at him. He turned to look at my mother.

After a while my mother rose from the table. 'You can hep me with the dishes, Brandon.' I was about to fish for an excuse when she added, 'Your father's got something he needs to do.'

As I helped my mom clear the table and carry dishes through to the kitchen, my father disappeared off somewhere. I don't know where. Normally after Sunday dinner, he likes to read his paper and catches up on the sport on TV. After helping my mom I went up to my room. When I came down again a couple of hours later, my father was there, watching TV.

Miriam's visitor wasn't mentioned again.

CHAPTER 20

CARVER EASED HIS chair back from the table, patted his stomach.

'That was an excellent meal, Matt. Thanks for inviting me.'

Rising to clear the empty plates, Matt Lynch smiled an acknowledgement. 'Our pleasure, Jamie. We don't often get to share Sunday dinners these days. We're just glad you made it.' Turning to the girl seated between them at the head of the table he added, 'Ain't that right. Kit?'

Straightening in her chair, Kit Lynch put on a solemn look that brought a smile to Carver's face. 'Yes, Pa.'

'And if you want to thank someone,' her father continued, 'you'd best thank the cook.' As he headed to the kitchen, he cocked his head in his daughter's direction.

Carver turned to the young girl who reminded him of one only a little older who once saved his life. Like Kayleigh Lee, Kit's manner seemed to belie her age. 'In that case, young lady, thank *you*. You bake a mean pot-roast.'

Half turning, she called to her father in the kitchen. 'You hear that Pa? Jamie thinks I'm a, "young lady". And he likes my pot-roast.'

'Yeah?' Lynch's voice echoed. 'Well he's only just met you. And we should thank your mother for the pot-roast. She taught you.'

Bringing her palms together in front of her chest,

she called up at the ceiling. 'THANK YOU MA.'

Carver gave a whimsical smile. The day before, he and Lynch had driven out to the forest where Lynch showed him the Curtis Whittingham murder scene. On the way back, conversation shifted into 'getting to know each other' mode. Lynch mentioned how his wife had passed from cancer of the liver, three years before.

Kit's round of thanks completed, she rounded on Carver, still curious. 'So you *never* carry a weapon?' Carver shook his head. 'Not even when you arrest a suspect?'

'Never,' Carver said. 'Like I told you, if we think a suspect may be armed, we either run a special operation, or call up an Armed Response Unit.'

Kit shook her head, amazed. '*Jeez*, that just seems so… dangerous. And it must waste a helluva lot of time.'

Returning to the table, her father picked up the thread. 'You gotta understand honey. In England, perps don't normally carry guns. It's not like here. The cops there don't face the same risks. I'm right aren't I Jamie? Guns are still pretty rare?' Before Carver could answer, Lynch pointed a finger at his daughter. 'And we don't need to hear you blaspheme, *'Young Lady'*. Your Ma taught you that as well.'

'Sorry Pa.' She looked up again, adding, 'And you Ma.'

Witnessing their to-and-fro, Carver sensed the bond between them. He tried to imagine what it must be like for a girl like her, being brought up by one parent, who also happens to be town Sheriff. He wondered how she fared at school. He tuned back in.

'Your Pa's right, Kit, though things are changing from how they used to be. Every year we see more and more guns on the streets, but like here, mainly within the gangs. Even so, we've still got a way to go before it gets anything like as bad as say, New York.'

Kit nodded, pondering it. She turned to her father. 'We need to go to England sometime, Pa. It sounds nice. Maybe you could get a Sheriff's job there?'

The two men chuckled. Carver said, 'I'm afraid we don't have Sheriffs in England, Kit. Not like your father anyway.'

'What about the Sheriff of Nottingham? He's a Sheriff isn't he?'

Carver nodded. 'In Robin Hood's day. Nowadays our Sheriffs aren't law enforcers. Their duties are mainly ceremonial.'

'Ceremonial? Like how?'

Carver thought a moment. 'Well… like, if Royalty came to visit the city, the Sheriff might be the one who would welcome them, dressed up in all his finery.'

Kit's eyes widened and she turned on her father. 'PA. We *gotta* go to England. You'll get to meet the Queen.'

It triggered further amusement, which only served to remind Carver how much he missed the sparring that was always an accompaniment to Rosanna's carefully prepared feasts on his days off. *What happened to that?* he thought.

Talk continued over coffee and a batch of Kit's 'homemade cookies'. Her thirst for information about everything and anything English seemed unquenchable, though she was disappointed to hear Carver had no personal connections to the Royal Family.

'None at all?'

'Sorry.'

Eventually, Lynch made to draw a line under it. 'I think it's that time honey. School tomorrow, and don't you have homework to finish?'

Kit tried to resist - 'I can finish it in the morning,' and 'I want to hear more about England,' - but Carver guessed it was for show. From what he'd witnessed, he suspected that in the Lynch household, respect for the law was all.

Eventually, resigned, Kit bade him 'Goodnight Jamie. Nice to have met you,' planted a kiss on her father's cheek, and trooped out.

Carver waited until her steps faded up the stairs. He turned to his host.

'That's a lovely daughter you've got there, Matt. Bright, intelligent, fun. You must be proud.'

Lynch gave a slow nod, and cast a glance at his wife's photograph on the wall. 'We are. Trouble is, she can be too damn bright, you know? Into everything?'

'I can imagine. She's… what, fourteen?'

'Going on forty.'

Carver smiled. 'I've a niece just a bit younger. She's the same.' It reminded him he was overdue a call to his wayward sister, Sally. He'd missed her both times he'd rung before coming away. He needed to know how her new job was going.

Lynch rose to cross to the bureau. Turning, he held up a bottle of Jack Daniel's Green Label.

Carver nodded, and made to look impressed. The GL wasn't his favourite - that was Old No 7 - but it was close enough.

Minutes later, whiskies in hand, they sat across from each other out on the porch. As warm a night as any since his arrival, Carver made a mental note to source some lighter trousers as soon as the opportunity arose. Leaning forwards in their chairs, they chinked glasses.

'I know you'll be going through it all tomorrow,' Lynch said. 'But maybe you could give me a preview. I never know what Monday mornings will bring. What do I need to know?'

Carver sipped his whiskey. Lynch's request came as no surprise. They next morning they were due to meet with the Whittingham Homicide Lead Investigators. It was natural Lynch would want to get a jump on them. Were the roles reversed, Carver would be the same. To date, their contacts had been mainly via email, backed up by a couple of telephone calls. Carver had waited until they met in person before deciding how much of the detail he would be prepared to share. Now, having met Lynch, he felt reasonably safe.

As always, he began with Edmund Hart, and The Escort Murders.

Over the next twenty or so minutes, Carver gave Lynch what he considered the potted version. He would get the rest tomorrow. Nevertheless, he told enough for Lynch to get a sense of the important bits. It included how, for Carver, The Worshipper Enquiry was not just 'one from his casebook.' From its beginnings in The Escort Killings and the Hart investigation, through the whole 'Worshipper' thing, Paris, and what happened in the Chateau de la Roque, high above the Lac du Crescent, it was all, deeply, personal. Lynch needed to know that, to understand it. His account included an introduction to Megan Crane. Not everything, that could take all night, but again, enough that Lynch might begin to understand what he, they, may be up against - unless her bones really were feeding the fishes in the Lac. He was nearing the end when Lynch suddenly lifted a hand. *Stop.*

Carver waited.

Lynch leaned forward in his chair. He appeared to be listening - to or for what, Carver had no idea. Rising, slowly, he stepped down off the porch, took a couple of steps, turned and looked up. At the same time there came a sound from above, like a door - or window - slamming closed.

Shaking his head, he returned to his chair. 'That damned girl.' He shook his head some more. 'I told you. Too damn bright.'

'Would she have heard?' Carver said, looking out into the dark, gauging. 'We weren't talking loud, were we?'

'No. But sound carries at night. And she has ears like a bat.' With a final shake of his head he said, 'Ah, what the hell. Anything she may have picked up, she would probably get to hear or would find out about anyway. I sometimes think she has a spy in my office. She has a knack of finding out things that aren't even in the public domain. God knows where she gets it.'

Over another JD, Carver finished what he felt he needed to cover. He kept his voice lower than before, not that it mattered. If Kit had been listening, as was likely, she'd already heard most of it.

On the way back to his hotel in the black and white Lynch called to pick him up, Carver thought on whether anything Kit may have heard could cause a problem if she were to repeat it to anyone. Lynch had said he would talk to her in the morning and warn her against sharing information she was not supposed to hear in the first place. But she'd seemed sensible, not the sort given to gossip or spreading rumours. Lynch had told how she didn't have many friends, having little time for most of her fellow school students, whom she regarded as 'shallow' and 'boring', except for one, it seemed. A few weeks before, a new family had moved into Brackers Lake. She had taken the son of the family under her wing. So far she was tolerating him more than any she had known for some time. But being new, he wouldn't know many people either, so again any potential danger from accidental spillage was minimal.

By the time he got into bed, having messaged Rosanna, Jess, and left a voice-mail for Sally, he was of a mind that whatever Kit may have overheard, it probably didn't matter.

He was wrong.

CHAPTER 21

SINCE THAT FIRST school day, Kit and I had fallen to picking each other up around the locker area, just inside the main entrance. But this Monday, she was sitting on the steps again, waiting for me. Something must have happened. She couldn't wait to tell me.

'I've met him.'

'Who?', though I had some idea.

'The English detective. He came for dinner yesterday.'

'Yeah? What's he like?'

'He's cool. Did you know English cops don't carry guns?'

'I think I did.'

'I didn't. He was interesting. And a great accent. Wait 'til you meet him.'

'Will I meet him?'

'Why wouldn't you?'

'I dunno, why *would* I?'

'He's an English cop, here in Brackers Lake, investigating a homicide. That's amazing, right?'

She was clearly excited. I didn't want to be a grouch. 'I guess it is. Did you find out any more about what he's doing here?'

As the first bell sounded, she grabbed my arm, started pulling me up the steps. 'Some. I'll tell you about it.'

As I let her pull me along, I wasn't too sure if I was all that interested in hearing what she was obviously dying to tell me. But I also knew I would have no choice in the matter. I resigned myself to a morning of listening, and pretending to be as excited as she was. As it happened, I didn't have to do that much pretending.

One thing became clear to me over the course of that Monday morning. Whoever this English detective was, whatever he was here for, he had impressed Kit - a lot. Between lessons and over the break, she kept returning to 'Jamie' and his visit to her home. She described his manner - 'Cool'; his accent - 'A bit like Paul McCartney,'. Ran me through their dinner table conversation - 'He knows everything about everything. And he's been everywhere. Even Paris.'

As the morning wore on, I began to wonder if she had some sort of English obsession. That said, some if it must have rubbed off as I began to think that maybe it would be interesting to meet this 'Jamie' after all. It was during lunch break, as we were sitting out on the grass behind school and she reached the part where she described overhearing 'Jamie' and her father talking out on the porch, things turned, for me, more interesting.

Before she met him, all Kit's dad told her about, 'the English cop', was that he was investigating a possible connection between some old case of his and the areas around New York. And while she knew from her father's files he was investigating similarities between Councilman Whittingham's murder and one in England, she also knew that any attempt to interrogate him over dinner would earn her a reprimand. Her dad's work was always off-limits at the dinner table, especially when they had visitors. But when Kit took herself off upstairs, they went out onto the porch to talk. Kit's bedroom was at the front of her house. The window was open. She didn't intend to eavesdrop. All she had to do was sit by the window, and listen. The porch roof got in the way of some of it. But she heard enough.

'Jamie' had started talking about an old case - maybe more than one. The porch meant there were times she lost the thread and ended up confused over which case he was talking about. He didn't talk about the details - Kit thought her father seemed to already know - but it clearly involved several 'murders'.

'The English use "murder" rather than 'homicide,' Kit explained, 'But it's the same thing.' She said it like I should be impressed with her grasp of things.

Whatever was involved, it sounded pretty bad. He talked a lot about victims, and suspects. Some of it had involved 'escorts', which she thought meant prostitutes. Later, he started using a term Kit's tongue kept tripping over. 'Dom... ixes, dom-tixes,' she tried.

'Dominatrixes?' I said.

'That's it. Say it again?'

'Dominatrixes.'

'Right. Domina-trixes. How do you know? What are they?"

I told her about Louis Suarez and the occasional gatherings we used to have on the Rodney Playground basketball court on the corner of Rodney and South-Third Street. Back then, those of us whose parents let us have cells had only limited on-line access due to the locks and protections they insisted on putting in place. Louis's parents never bothered with all that stuff. A good many Brooklyn kids my age learned a lot from Louis's cell over that period. One day Louis was full of himself, showing us all some pics of a woman he said was a 'dominatrix,' though he wasn't too clear what that meant.

'I think they're another type of prostitute,' I told Kit. 'They wear leather, and boots with spiky heels, and usually carry whips.'

'Really?' Kit said. 'My mom had some leather pants once, and boots. But I don't think she ever had a whip.'

'Yeah, well I'm pretty certain your Mom wasn't a prostitute.'

'I hope not,' she said, giggling.

Kit didn't pick up where the dominatrix fitted in to it all, though as the conversation went on, Jamie talked more and more about 'her' and 'she'. Whoever 'she' was, she sounded important, to the point Kit wondered if the felon Jamie was looking for had some sort of connection with this dominatrix. I asked if she had ever heard of prostitutes in Brackers Lake. She lowered her voice.

'There's a family called Cullen, live out on the trailer park out past Bushwood. I hear my Dad talking about them sometimes. The Mom is called Mary-Ellen. They say she turns tricks. That's what prostitutes do isn't it?'

I nodded, remembering what the other girls used to say about Conscience Driscoll from tenth grade back in East Williamsburg. Conscience was real pretty. Boys buzzed around her like bees round honey. What the girls used to say about her was probably just bitching.

Kit described how 'Jamie' went on to talk about something that happened in Paris. Again, it involved several murders. She also heard him talk about something that had happened to him and a woman called Rosanna.

'Who's Rosanna?' I said.

'I *think* she's his wife, or girlfriend,' Kit said. 'I'm sure he mentioned her during dinner. Something about her being a singer.'

'He sure seems to have been involved in a lot of murders,' I said.

'That's what I thought,' she said.

We talked more about what 'Jamie' intended doing while he was here, but nothing Kit heard helped in that respect. I asked if he'd mentioned any names of anyone he was planning to see.

'I heard plenty of names, but apart from Councilman Whittingham, none that meant anything to me. I think they were mainly victims.' She paused a moment, thinking. 'There was one name I heard a few times, but I couldn't work out who it belonged to. I *think* it was Megan, or something close.'

I started. 'Like in Meghan Markle?'

She nodded. 'But she's the only Meghan I've ever heard of.' A moment later she said, 'You've gone quiet. What're you thinking about?'

I looked up, gave a quick smile. 'Oh, nothing, it's just-'

'Just what?'

'It's just… coincidence is all.'

'What coincidence?'

'Well… I remember once hearing the name Megan, but it was a long, long time ago.'

'Where? When?'

'At home, when I was a kid. I'm talking like when I was eight, or nine maybe. I'm sure I remember my parents used to talk about someone called Megan. I never met her. I always assumed she was a friend of theirs, or some distant relative.'

'What happened to her?'

'I've no idea. I've not heard them mention her for years, if that was her name. She could be dead for all I know.'

At that moment the bell rang marking the end of break. Kit stood up. 'Yeah, well Jamie's from England, so whichever Megan your parents knew, she can't be anything to do with the one he talked about.'

I looked up at her. 'I'm sure you're right.'

She put out a hand. I took it. 'C'mon,' she said. 'It's

soccer practice this afternoon. We gotta get changed. '
She pulled me up.

'Great,' I said.

But as we made our way back to the lockers to pick up our kit, it wasn't thoughts of my favourite sport that was on my mind. Rather, it was back in Brooklyn, remembering the days when Uncle Hector and Aunt Katherine used to be regular visitors to our house. My parents used to have lots of friends back then, not like now. And they used to go out a lot themselves as well, visiting friends, going to parties. I smiled as memories of Dolly came. Dolly was the girl from next door who used to 'sit me Saturday nights when my parents were out. She had big teeth and huge breasts. It was around this time I used to hear occasional mention of someone called Megan.

I'm also pretty sure it was around that time - though it may have been when I was a bit older - I first heard the word, "dominatrix."

CHAPTER 22

ALONG WITH SHERIFF Lynch, three others made up the Whittingham Homicide Lead Investigation Team. Senior Detective Eric Kerchner, was a brash but amiable enough New Yorker, with a hooked nose and engaging smile. His manner and accent was everything Carver may have imagined in a "Noo Yoik" detective. Eduardo Varas, a more studious Hispanic, was the county's head of CSI - Crime Scene Investigation - Services. His deep-set eyes and hooded lids gave the impression he was suspicious of everything and everyone, including Carver. The fourth 'lead' was Harah Venkatraman from the District Attorney's Office. Her job was to watch over and advise on the legalities. With wavy black hair hanging to her waist and makeup that looked like it had been applied by a professional, Carver thought she could have just stepped off the set of one of those glossy TV legal dramas where lawyers spend all their time trying to get one over on their work partners, while cheating on those at home. She seemed on the young side for such a role, Carver thought. Then again, that could just be his old-school-CID prejudices kicking in.

They met in Lynch's office at ten o'clock that Monday morning. As it happened it had been a relatively quiet weekend, which meant Lynch was there from the start. He began by introducing Carver as 'Britain's, Number One Detective.' He meant it as a joke, clearly - at least Carver *hoped* that was the case. Even so, Carver saw the look that passed between Detective Kerchner and the Assistant DA that made him wish Lynch hadn't said it.

Carver's 'presentation' lasted just short of ninety minutes. He made little use of the snazzy slide-show Jess and Colin from IT had put together. Okay for lectures, he found it too confining for operational briefings, though he did make use of the photographs and videos embedded in it, throwing the images up onto the TV on the wall facing Lynch's desk. On several occasions, what appeared on screen drew winces from his audience, or caused them to shift, uncomfortably, in their chairs. And while it wasn't easy, he got through it without having to break-off too many times to sip from the water bottle, on the table behind him while he gathered himself.

The night before, he'd mentioned to Lynch how parts of the story still affected him. Some were to do with aspects most detectives experience from time to time. Distressing, sometimes horrifying, crime scenes. Dealing with victims' traumatised families. The pressures to make an arrest. Others would stay with him for the rest of his life. What Angie suffered, first at Hart's, then Megan Crane's hands. What happened to Rosanna, Carissa Lavergne, even poor, Gary Shepherd, his misguided former colleague. During these moments, as Carver turned to his bottle, the audience waited in silence. They either understood, having maybe experienced similar themselves, or Lynch had said something to them before the meeting. Either way, Carver was grateful.

He focused mainly on the strands that could support the contention that Curtis Whittingham's homicide might link in some way to Megan Crane were she, somehow, still alive.

The first strand covered her US connections. Apart from the cryptic diary entry that had so consumed his time on the flight over, he could still recall some of what went into the "US" folder. In particular he remembered documents pointed to her visiting the US regularly during the period leading up to Hart embarking on his murderous crusade. Sometimes she visited there with Hart, sometimes without. Following Megan's 'death', Carver had discovered that Hart had actually lived in New York for several years. He may even have been living there when he and Megan Crane first got together. She definitely accompanied him back there several times after they became lovers. Details of who they spent time with, what they got up to during that period weren't known. But given their proclivities and interests, he doubted their visits consisted only of sightseeing and shopping. Two sets of initials kept recurring. HB and FS. Both featured to the point that Carver suspected that however Megan and Hart spent their time, a good deal of it involved 'HB' and/or 'FS'. He had pondered long and hard over who the initials might refer to, but in the absence of further intelligence, it was pointless speculating. There were any number of potential candidates amongst well know sports stars, celebrities and politicians who could fit the bill. On the other hand, the initials could as easily belong to someone with no public profile whatsoever. Beyond the fact that Megan Crane had strong connections with the areas in and around New York, he knew no more.

Carver had hoped that by now Jess would have tracked down Megan's one-time live in house-slave, Tracy. He was pretty sure she would be able to fill in at least some of the blanks left by the fire, but so far, her whereabouts remained unknown. Neither he, nor Jess, were particularly alarmed by the fact. Her rather unusual and highly specific needs - emotional, psychological, *and* sexual - had resulted in her disappearing 'off grid' before. Sometimes she was gone for weeks. On a couple of occasions it had run to months. Given she was a barrister, Carver still found it astounding that, despite all she knew, all she had experienced, she remained willing to engage with the fantasy world she and Megan had once visited regularly. He had voiced his fears to Jess on more than one occasion.

'One day some psycho is going to decide she's going to remain their personal sex-slave indefinitely, when she'll disappear altogether. Either that or we'll find ourselves looking at her body on some mortuary slab.'

Jess concurred.

The second strand of Carver's presentation was more straightforward. It covered the similarities between Whittingham's murder, and what Megan Crane once practised on her victims. For the most part they were obvious. The post to which the victims were bound. The rope-work, even down to the type of knots used to bind the victim. Gluing the victim's palms into the pose that gave rise to the hideous, 'Worshipper' tag that still caused The Duke apoplexy. One difference was, Whittingham had died by hanging, while Megan Crane dispatched her victims using a black-ribbon garrotte. Carver didn't see it as necessarily significant. For Megan, ropes, nooses and ribbons were merely variations on a theme. He and Rosanna could testify to that. As could poor Scott Weston, the young American who, along with his fiancee, Tory Martinez, fell into her hands in Paris. Tory had lived. Scott, alas, was not so lucky.

The third strand however, was more ambiguous. They all leaned forward as he threw up the photographs that had come to him, anonymously, via old-fashioned snail-mail over the course of the past months. The first showed four people enjoying drinks in some garden setting. The face of one, a blond haired woman, was ringed in ink. On the back of the photograph, in the same ink, the words, "IT'S HER". The second was taken in some sort of nightclub, bar, or social club. The same woman - circled again - in company with several others. On the back, "SHE'S HERE". The third showed three drawn images of a female face in diagrammatic form, left and right profile, and forward facing. Marked with dotted lines, arrows and symbols about the cheeks, jaw-line and neck, it looked the sort of thing a cosmetic surgeon might use to plan a procedure. The spaces next to "Name" and "Date" were blacked out, showing the details had been redacted.

Carver described how his partner, Jess Greylake, had managed to get one of Megan Crane's former 'associates', Sir Richard Hayhurst, a once-eminent Harley Street physician, specialising in cosmetic and reconstructive surgery, to reveal his guarded, yet seemingly genuine belief that time would show that Megan Crane's 'death' was not as clear cut as the official record showed. Carver did not reveal the circumstances by which Jess obtained the information. Too much of a distraction, he thought.

He also passed around copies of a witness statement from one Clinton Patterson. Patterson worked at the New York Botanical Gardens where he was renowned as a world expert on native species and their origins. In his statement, Patterson identified every species of flora visible in the 'garden' photograph. All were known to grow in the Northeastern United States. One, a species called Viburnum Lantanoiedes - more commonly known as the 'Hobblebush' plant - was particularly native to an area within an approximate radius of fifty miles, centred on upstate New York. His statement concluded with an 'informed opinion' postulating that the garden in the photograph was, most likely, situated somewhere in New York State.

As Carver knew it would, it was this final strand that

promoted most debate. The discussion that followed was, by turns, sceptical, challenging, and questioning. They each spent several minutes scrutinising the blond woman in the photographs and comparing her with Megan Crane. Carver confirmed that the most effective Face Recognition Technology presently in use - that used by Scotland Yard's Anti Terrorism Unit - had returned an 'Indeterminate' result - which was no great surprise if she *had* undergone cosmetic surgery, *and* considering the relative poor quality of the images. Finally, as it became clear that nothing Carver had said could be ruled out, the discussion turned more accepting, albeit grudgingly, in Kerchner's and Harah Venkatraman's cases.

'It would never stand up in court,' the DA lawyer said.

'Doesn't need to,' Lynch said. 'No one's on trial here. We're dealing with intelligence, not evidence.'

Turning back to Carver, she looked at him, hard and long. Eventually, she nodded, slowly. 'Okay.'

But Kerchner had one further question. 'If by some remote chance she is alive, why would she risk drawing attention to herself by using the same MO she is famous for? It doesn't make sense.'

Carver had his answer ready. 'I've asked myself the same question Eric. And you are right, it doesn't. But that's assuming she killed Curtis Whittingham, which we don't know is the case yet. Even if she did, she would probably never imagine I would get to hear about it. Don't forget, I'm only here because someone sent me the photographs.'

'Which suggests, again assuming she's here, someone wants her caught.'

'Correct. But don't ask me why. That's a question for another time.'

For the time being satisfied - it seemed - Kerchner

lapsed into thoughtful silence.

Carver's input concluded, the investigators took their turn. A good deal of what they shared, Carver already knew. Some lengthy email exchanges backed up with a couple of late-into-the-night telephone conversations with Lynch had covered much of it. Nevertheless he gave them his full attention as they walked him through their investigation to date, from the discovery of the body by a hunting party, through the trawling through Whittingham's personal, political and business affairs looking for a possible suspect, to the most recent enquiries looking at known offenders and previously reported sex-crimes across the Eastern sea-board, now expanding further west. By the time Kerchner finished detailing his officers' enquiries as far west as Minnesota, there was broad acceptance within the group that, right now, the investigation was going nowhere. Pouring himself his third coffee of the morning, Lynch summarised.

'I guess what we're saying here is, we've nothing to lose by taking a closer look at what Jamie has brought us. Agreed?' He checked faces. Everyone nodded. He turned to Carver. 'Where do you think you'd like to start, Jamie?'

Carver didn't hesitate.

'I'd like to run Betty Whittingham through a Pinnacle Inventory.'

Kerchner glanced around at his colleagues before turning back to Carver.

'What the fuck's a pinnacle inventory?'

CHAPTER 23

THE EARLY PART of that week, I saw further signs my parents were planning some sort of night out - possibly a party at someone's house - in the coming days. If so, it would be their first since we'd moved to Brackers Lake.

There was a time they used to go out quite often, mainly weekends, but sometimes mid-week as well. They had lots of friends when we lived in Brooklyn, but that all stopped a while ago. I don't know what happened, exactly. My parents were never great sharers. In fact, they were pretty secretive about a lot of things. Best I could make out from the bits I overheard or the occasional reveal - usually after Mom had had a drink - it was something to do with one of those friends. A falling out, or something. Whatever it was, it had a big effect on them. For a long while they both seemed on edge, like they were really worried about something. I got shouted at quite a bit over this period, something I'd never really experienced before. I know it upset my Mom as I caught her crying a few times when I came home from school. The only other times I ever saw her cry was when Grandpa died, and when we lost Scooter, our raggedy spaniel-cross. We never got another dog. Eventually, after several weeks, whatever the problem was must have gone away as things went back to pretty much normal - apart from all the going out and parties stopped. For a long while, even Uncle Hector and Aunt Katherine stopped coming round. They did eventually, but nothing like they used to.

On the Monday night, I came down from my room to the kitchen and heard my parents in the living room talking about 'outfits' and 'what to wear'. I heard my mom saying something about putting on weight and not being able to get into something, to which my dad said, 'There's time. If you order online, it'll get here.' I was surprised as my mom hates buying clothes online. But then I remembered. Brackers Lake doesn't have the range of shops like in Brooklyn, so I guess it made sense.

Something similar happened on the Tuesday evening, but this time they were talking about what time they should go to wherever it was they were going. 'Around six, I think,' my dad was saying as I went into the kitchen. 'You'd better check,' my mom replied. 'We don't want to be too early.' I thought about asking them what they were talking about, but to be honest, it was no big deal and I would find out in due course anyway, so it didn't really matter. I would learn how wrong I was.

The next day - Wednesday - something strange happened as I was arriving home on the school bus. The bus drops off a little way down Henry Street from our house. As it neared the stop and began to slow, I leaned out of my seat to look ahead and gauge when to stand up. Some way in front, on the left, a car pulled out of one of the driveways to turn right towards us. I couldn't say if it came from the driveway to our house, or one of our neighbours, but as the bus pulled up and I joined the line to get off, it came past on my left. It was a bronze-coloured pickup that looked a lot like a Ram 1500. I didn't get a look at the driver, but it looked the same model as the one I'd seen at Miriam's on the Saturday.

When I got in, my mom was acting real weird. She was in the kitchen, trying to call someone on her cell and

124

didn't see me come through the door. I have a strong sense of smell and I picked up what I thought were traces of cigarettes and aftershave. Mom gave up smoking years ago. My father only wears aftershave on a night out. Mom seemed agitated, almost panicking, though as far as I could see, everything else seemed normal. She kept putting her phone to her ear, looking at the screen, trying again. 'Come on,' she kept muttering. 'Pick up.'

'Everything alright Mom?' I must have made her jump as she whirled round, a look of alarm on her face. 'You okay?' I said. 'Is Dad okay?'

'Yes-yes,' she said. 'Everything's fine. I'm just trying to call your father now, but he's not answering.'

As I poured myself some milk and checked the cooler for something to eat, she took herself off through to the living room, still trying to make the call. He must have answered because a minute later I heard them talking. I couldn't hear what she was saying as she kept her voice low, but from her tone, it sounded pretty urgent. When she returned to the kitchen a few minutes later, she was calmer, though she still needed a couple of long, deep breaths before she was able to ask me about school. As she went back to cutting up vegetables for supper, I walked her through my day, though I had the impression her mind was elsewhere. Before I headed up to my room, I thought I'd better ask.

'Has something happened? Are you and Dad okay?'

She threw me a wary look. 'We're fine. Why do you ask?'

'You seemed wired when I came in. A bit like when we heard about Grandpa.'

For several moments, she stared at me in a way that made me wonder if she was about to cry. Then, putting down the peeler, she crossed the room, wrapped her arms around me and gave me a long, tight hug. 'Everything is fine. Your Dad and I are fine. There's nothing you need to worry about.' She kissed my cheek. 'How are you doing? Are you okay? Do you feel you are settling in?'

'I'm all good,' I said. 'And I'm settling in fine. I like it here.' I didn't add, *'since starting working for Miriam.'*

'Good,' Mom said. 'Nobody hassling you? Nobody giving you a hard time?'

I shook my head. 'Some of the kids at school are air-heads. They like to make stupid jokes about me being David Beckham's son, but mostly they're all fine. Better than I expected actually.'

She looked puzzled. 'David Beckham's son? Why would they say that?'

I rolled my eyes. 'His son, *you know*?' No lights yet. 'BROOKLYN?'

It registered. 'Ahh…' she said. '*Brooklyn*. I get it.' Sorry to say, my Mom was never the sharpest. But she recovered. 'But I wasn't talking about school friends. I was thinking more about adults, grown ups, you know?'

I couldn't think who she was talking about. 'Like teachers you mean?'

'We-ll, maybe teachers. But I was more just thinking adults in general.'

'Like who?'

'Like… anyone you've met since we got here.'

I said it again. 'Like who?'

'I don't know… Like… *anybody.*' I worried in case she was about to get worked up again. 'Like that man you saw at Miriam's? The one you saw her arguing with. Have you seen anymore of him?'

I thought about the bronze pickup. *Is that what this is about?* 'No,' I said. 'I haven't seen him.' Before I could say, *have you?* she said, 'Good. You will tell me if you see him again, won't you?'

'Sure. Can I go now?'

She smiled, gave me another hug - 'Go on, scoot' - and clipped my backside. As I was leaving, she called, 'You going over to Miriam's today?'

'I guess, if it's okay?

'Fine by me. You just be careful, hear?'

As I headed up to my room, I was wondering what I needed to be careful of, and about Mom's strange behavior. I could barely remember the last time she hugged me like that, like I was something, *precious*.

Half an hour later, as I was coming down to get my boots on and get ready to head over to Miriam's, my father arrived home, much earlier than usual. He and Mom disappeared upstairs where I heard them talking, but not enough to tell what it was about. My thought was it had to be about whatever had alarmed her before I arrived home.

I was about to call up that I was leaving, when they both came down. My dad made an effort to look 'normal', though Mom seemed worried again.

'You heading over to Miriam's?' my dad said.

'Just about to.'

'Right.' He looked about him, glanced at Mom. I had the feeling there was something they wanted to tell me. I waited.

He took a breath, hesitated, then said,' 'Before you go, there's something we should mention.'

'Yeah?'

'We, er... Your Mom and I..' I wondered what the heck was coming. 'Miriam has invited your Mom and I to join her and some friends over at hers on Saturday night. Just a bit of a social. A sort of, 'welcome to Brackers Lake'-type thing.'

'Cool,' I said. 'Am I invited?'

They looked at each other, embarrassed. 'Er, no.

That's why we're mentioning it. It's just adults. Us and some of Miriam's friends. As we're out, we thought you might like to invite this friend of yours, Kit, over for company that night'

It went someway to counter the disappointment I'd felt as soon as I heard the, "no". 'Okay, I'll ask her.'

But my father's awkward manner stayed. 'I don't know if Miriam will mention it or not. If she does, you can tell her we've told you. If not, you don't have to mention it.'

'Okay.'

As I made my way across the street, half my mind was taken up with wondering about why all the fuss over a simple night out, why they were acting so weird about it, and what might have happened to make them that way. The other half was excited at the thought that my parents were becoming friendly with Miriam, and what that might mean in the future.

Unlike my parents, Miriam seemed entirely normal when I arrived. Relaxed, pleased to see me, and looking and smelling nice. She had my pre-work refreshment ready and waiting on the deck and as I ate and drank, we talked about my plan for that evening - starting on digging out a large root-ball I'd discovered over in the corner. As I stepped down from the deck, pulling on my gloves, Miriam called out.

'Have your parents mentioned I've invited them over here on Saturday? Just a little social?' She said it in such a matter-of-fact way, it made me wonder again about their strange behavior.

'Yes,' I said, determined to show no disappointment. 'They mentioned it just before I came over.'

'Oh,' she said, surprised. 'Only just? I'd thought they might have mentioned it sooner. Ah well… But I'm sorry I can't ask you over as well, Brandon. I've some friends coming who won't be expecting any youngsters.'

'Hey, that's okay, Miriam,' I said. 'I understand.' *Bastards.*

But I promise, I'll be having another little party soon, and you'll definitely come to that one. In fact, you'll be guest of honour.'

'Really?' I said. 'Why me?'

'Why, to show off all your hard work to my friends of course, and to thank you for being my knight in shining armor. Will that be alright?'

'Sure, that'd be great.' Though far as I was concerned, I wasn't particularly bothered about her friends being there - especially if they were anything like the guy with the bronze Ram.

As I set-to on the root ball that late afternoon, I was thinking about how long I might have to wait for my 'party', what I would wear, and what I'd done to make Miriam think of me as her knight in shining armor.

CHAPTER 24

CARVER THOUGHT THAT in her time, Betty Whittingham would have been a good-looking woman. Even now, and despite what she had been through, she was still taking pride in her appearance. Her shoulder-length, silver-white hair was coiffured and groomed, makeup carefully applied. Her clothes - grey jacket over a cream top and black trousers - were classically fashionable for a woman her age. And she carried herself with the confidence many women in their sixties acquire when they know they are financially secure and living a life that, her husband's death apart, is largely fulfilled.

It was only the blue-green eyes that spoke to the reality behind the facade. There, Carver could see the sadness she carried within her - along with whatever questions the manner of her husband's death must have raised in her mind, as well as the minds of those who knew him.

Prior to his death, Carver knew, Curtis Whittingham had been regarded as the stereotypical, 'pillar of his community'. A successful lawyer, family man, and eight-year-served councilman, Curtis had supported all the right causes and fought as his constituents expected he should to address the issues that impact on a community such as Brackers Lake. That he died wearing a woman's corset, and in circumstances that even his most ardent supporters would have to agree were 'strange', raised questions that threatened to tarnish that image and remained to be answered. Now, as Carver nursed his coffee and waited for Lynch to finish laying the ground for what was to follow, he wondered how many of those questions may get answered over the course of the next couple of hours - provided Betty cooperated, of course.

So far, the wind seemed set fair. When Lynch telephoned to arrange their visit, mentioning a visiting detective who was investigating a possible connection with matters that had occurred 'elsewhere', she was, Lynch reported, politely agreeable, almost to the point of sounding enthusiastic. 'By all means,' she said. 'Come tomorrow morning. I'll have coffee waiting.' Even when Lynch introduced Carver and it became clear 'elsewhere' meant England, she managed a smile and a, 'Welcome to Brackers Lake Mr Carver,' that belied the grim nature of the matters they were there to discuss. If a possible connection with England caused her any great surprise, she managed not to show it. Given the questions he would shortly be posing, Carver wondered how long her equable manner would last. Of the twenty or so times he had run his Pinnacle Inventory using members of a victim's family, he could remember only two when the process had not brought on distress, anguish, tears. In once case, the 'subject' had hated her victim-husband and knew enough about his 'other interests' that none of the questions came as any great surprise. The other actually turned out to be the murderer, so that hardly counted.

In Betty Whittingham's case, all Carver knew was that through the several interviews she had given since the discovery of her husband's body - to Lynch, Detective Kerchner, the Coroner at the inquest - she had remained steadfast in her conviction that she knew nothing that could explain how he had come to meet his death in the way he did. All she knew was, he went out

131

that day to meet with some fellow councillors concerning a routine business planning application - enquiries had showed that the meeting took place; he was there - and he did not return. When his body was found, two weeks later, the best she could offer, from the depths of her shock and grief, was that her husband must have been the victim of a random abduction by some crazed killer. There could be no other explanation for it.

Lynch's introduction included updating Betty as to recent developments in the investigation - not there were any that meant much. Having done so, he turned to Carver. 'Jamie will explain what it is he would like to do. Jamie?"

Carver started with a heart-felt offer of condolences, and stating how he understood everything Betty Whittingham was going through. 'That's not a platitude,' he said by way of explanation. 'I've experienced it myself,' though he didn't expand.

Unzipping his document case, he took out the questionnaire he had finalised and printed off the previous day, having decided that inputting her responses directly into his notebook would smack of some sales agent, ticking boxes. He needed her to know he was paying full attention to her answers, not just filling in data fields. He showed it to her.

'It's called a Pinnacle Inventory. I'll explain what it does, how we use it and why it's important.'

Over the next few minutes, Betty Whittingham paid polite attention as Carver ran her through as much as he thought she needed to know about what was now designated, officially, as 'The Carver Pinnacle Inventory'.

An invention of his own devising following his early successes in Series-Crime Investigation, the CPI was, essentially, a two-hundred-and-fifty-plus questionnaire. The first hundred or so 'core' questions covered a victim's life, habits, interests and movements during the period leading up to the crime under investigation. The length of that period changed according to the circumstances. In Curtis Whittingham's case, and given the possible connections Carver was investigating, he had opted to keep it fairly open ended. In some cases questions reached back years, even before he and Betty met, if Betty had that information. The inventory's purpose was simple. To shine a light on aspects of a subject's life, motivations and movements that may have a bearing on how and why they became a victim, but which normal investigatory processes may overlook. In reality - though Carver did not explain this to Betty - he had designed it for use in 'series' crimes, the idea being that it was the aggregation of subject data - showing up similarities and patterns of behaviour - that gave it its force. Nevertheless, he had found that even with just a single subject, it was capable of identifying new and potentially fruitful avenues of investigation not previously known to investigators. Whether that would prove to be the case here, Carver could not say. Or so he told her. In reality, he thought there was a fair chance it might.

When Carver explained that the process could prove lengthy, and that Betty may like to take a break while she prepared herself, mentally, she waved it away. 'I'm not a wuss Mr Carver. My life hasn't always been as comfortable as it appears now. Let's get on with it.' Though she did re-charge their coffees, and set biscuits - 'cookies', he remembered - on a plate.

Over the course of the next two hours, Carver took her through the inventory, beginning as always with the 'general background' questions before moving on, stage by stage, to those that probed ever deeper into those aspects of her husband's life that only she might know. The questions ranged, extensively. Amongst other things they covered his work as a councilman, their home life, family relationships, relationships outside the home; hobbies and interests; regular routines - daily, weekly, monthly; likes and dislikes; personal preferences - food, drink, cultural pursuits; personal habits -including his, then their, sex life. Some of the questions clearly caught her by surprise in their searching detail, as Carver knew they would. Others caused her to squirm in embarrassment before she settled to answer. Through it all, Betty Whittingham maintained a quiet dignity, answering in a studied, polite manner that evidenced no resentment at the intrusion into their private affairs. Even Carver's, 'Do you know if Curtis masturbated?' drew no more than a thoughtful, 'No more than most men his age, I believe.' The inevitable follow up 'Do you know what he masturbated to?' elicited only, 'The usual, I guess. Pretty girls. Some of the presenters you see on TV. I know he had a thing for Lucy Lu. And women in hose and heels. I know he liked to look at pictures of women in hose and heels But then most men do, don't they?' Even the most potentially embarrassing and mine-laden field of all - their sex life, caused only a slight hesitation and a deep breath, before ploughing on.

'A couple of times a month, maybe?'

'After supper usually.'

'Fairly conventional by todays standards. Nothing kinky, if that's what you mean?'

'He liked me to wear perfume and nice lingerie.'

'No I've never used those sort of toys. I never needed to.'

As Carver worked through the questions, Lynch sat off to one side, watching and listening. He did not interrupt. Around the two hour mark, the increasing brevity of Betty's answers told Carver she was beginning to flag. Experience had taught him the importance of gathering as much quality information as possible on the first pass. Follow-up interviews rarely produce anything meaningful. Once respondents reflect on their experience, they usually become more guarded.

'There's only another twenty-or-so questions, Betty, but let's take a break. I'd love another coffee if that's okay?'

The speed she rose and reached for his mug confirmed his instincts. Nodding to Lynch to 'stay put', he followed her out to the kitchen.

'You've a lovely home, Betty. I imagine you and Curtis were very happy here.'

Spooning coffee grounds into a press, she gave a sad smile. 'We were, Mr Carver. Very happy. Curtis was always proud of the life we made together.'

Carver nodded out the window. 'And the garden?'

She looked out, shook her head. 'He loved his DIY, but he was no gardener. That's my domain.'

'I'm not a gardener either,' Carver said. 'But my girlfriend is. Would you mind if I take a look?'

'Feel free,' she said. She pointed to the back door.

Two minutes later, Carver was putting his mobile away when Betty appeared at his shoulder. She handed him his drink.

'Congratulations,' he said. 'I can see you've put a lot of work in over the years.'

'Thank you, yes, just a few hours, here and there.'

Carver pointed to a tall shrub backing the patio area. 'That's an unusual one. I don't think I've ever seen it before, not in England anyway.'

'I'm not sure you will. It's native to this part of the country, I believe. It's called a Hobblebush.'

Returning inside, Carver resumed his questioning. As he neared the end, he made sure to keep his growing tension hidden.

135

'Just one final question,' he said.

'Thank goodness,' Betty said. 'I was beginning to think I might have to offer you dinner.'

'Can you say if you, or Curtis, ever knew someone called, 'Megan'?'

She looked thoughtful as she lifted a hand to rub at her chin.

'I don't recall hearing the name,' she said. 'Should I?'

Carver smiled, gave a non-committal waft of a hand. 'Just a question I have to ask. Thank you for your time, Betty. I hope it wasn't too much. And I'm sorry if you found it intrusive.'

'Not at all Mr Carver. You've been very kind. I just hope it helps, and that you find what you are looking for.'

Ten minutes later, heading back into town, Carver was staring out the passenger window when Lynch interrupted his thoughts.

'Okay, you've had your ten minutes. What're you thinking? Did you get what you wanted?'

Carver turned in his seat, regarded the Sheriff squarely.

'What?' Lynch said, eyes flicking from the road, to Carver and back again.

Carver hesitated. 'Let me ask you. How do you think it went?'

Lynch shrugged, shook his head. 'I can't say I heard anything different to anything I've heard before. She seemed open and honest in her answers, which doesn't surprise me. That's the way she's been all along. I don't know about you, and I'm sorry if it's been a waste of your and my time, but I'm not sure it takes us any further as far as Curtis is concerned.'

Carver turned back to the view outside his window. He nodded, long and slow. Then he said, 'That's what I thought you'd say. You're wrong. She wasn't open and honest in her answers. Far from it. She was lying.'

Lynch did a double-take, struggling to keep his eyes on the road.

'*Lying?* About what?'

'Everything,' Carver said.

CHAPTER 25

HEADING THROUGH TO his office with Carver trailing, Lynch paused to speak to a middle aged woman dressed in a crisp white blouse and blue skirt working at her desk. 'Hold any calls,' he told her, before moving on inside.

Paula Gale was the County Sheriff's Department Office Manager and the nearest thing Lynch had to a PA. Since arriving, Carver had picked up a couple of things about the late- forties divorcée and Lynch. Past or present, he was yet to discover, but seeing the look on her face as he passed - she was not impressed with Lynch's curt instruction - he guessed that if 'present', she may have words for him later.

Lynch waited at the door to let Carver enter, before shutting it, firmly, behind him. Saying nothing, he removed his belt and holster as he rounded the desk. But rather than lock it up in the metal cupboard, as Carver had seen him do previously, he let it fall onto one of the chairs to the side. He motioned Carver to the other, then took his own, pulling it in, close. He allowed himself one quick sweep of his desk - nothing new - before fixing Carver with a stare.

'Tell me. What makes you think Betty is lying?'

Carver half-expected him to add, *'and it better be good'.* When he didn't, Carver guessed he'd decided to hear him out, before telling him what he thought about a limey cop threatening to up-end his investigation.

All the rest of the way back from Betty's, following his stark assertion she had lied, Carver had sensed Lynch keeping himself in check. Straining to stop himself demanding that Carver tell him - *right now* - how and why, over the course of a single interview, he had come by his conclusion.

Carver understood his impatience. No detective likes to hear that the bedrock upon which he'd laid the foundations of an enquiry may be cracked - and badly. And while Lynch was not a detective, Carver had seen enough to know he was as keen to run an efficient investigation as any SIO. Not that Carver was intending to accuse anyone of missing anything. He'd acted as Review Officer on enough major investigations to know how easy it is for an outsider to spot a line of enquiry that may not have been pursued with as much rigour as it merited. He'd even experienced it himself, which was why, whenever he found himself appointed Senior Investigating Officer, he encouraged his team to constantly challenge assumptions - about anything. Besides, in Betty Whittingham's case, Carver had an advantage.

Carver had designed his Pinnacle Inventory with help from Andy Karadia, the College of Policing Crime Faculty's Senior Data Analyst at Ryton-on-Dunsmore. It was Andy who had taught him all about using Confirmatory Questions to cross-check for consistency and honesty in subject responses. The process is simple. It involves targeting selected topics covered by the inventory several times over, but using questions framed sufficiently differently as to render the repetition invisible. Inconsistent answers across the different sets of questions indicate a subject who may not be answering to the best of their ability. Markedly different responses point to one who is either lying, or seeking to 'game' the inventory, which is what Carver realised Betty Whittingham was doing more or less from the off.

'Show me,' Lynch said, gruffly, after Carver finished explaining the mechanics. Referring to Betty's inventory, he led the sheriff through it. It took him a while, and to begin with Lynch was sceptical, which Carver put down to his sympathy for all Betty Whittingham had been through. But over time, his challenging questions gave way to thoughtful listening.

Carver had picked out two key areas to test Betty's responses. One was how much, or how little, she knew about Curtis's movements and how he spent his time in the weeks leading up to his murder. The other was his sex life and interests in that direction. At different points through the inventory, Betty's responses varied from her insisting she always knew what Curtis was doing with his time - *We were always very close, always together. If he'd been up to something I'd have known*', through being largely ignorant about his work as a councilman - *It wasn't something I took a great deal of interest in* - to having only Curtis's word that his bi-weekly trips to the Yankee Stadium with a group of old friends and former lawyers, were just that, and not a cover for something else. *We never really spoke much about the game after. I'm not a baseball fan.* She even went so far as to admit '*I sometimes wondered what they got up to*' during their days away. Regarding his sexual interests and sex life, she initially described her husband as, '*Entirely conventional. Almost boring*', but later spoke of him having '*quite an imagination when he was in the mood*'. Her early insistence that Curtis would never have been unfaithful in their marriage, and that he '*never looked at another woman in his life*' didn't fit with her later descriptions of a man who '*had a thing about Lucy Lu,*' and '*Likes a woman in hose and heels*'.

When Lynch suggested such inconsistencies may be

normal in someone who had suffered a trauma like Betty, and that many partners think they know more than they do about their spouses, Carver moved on to the inventory's other key aspect - its administration. Carver designed the inventory intending it only ever be administered by someone trained in, or at the very least with some knowledge of, Kinesics - the scientific term for observing body language, particularly in the context of identifying dishonesty and/or deception. Rooted in Professor Maureen O'Sullivan's work on lie detection in the seventies and eighties, kinesics covers the whole range of behaviours that give away people's inner thoughts and feelings. In the context of crime investigation, it focuses, particularly, on the micro-behaviours - facial tics, eye movements, vocal shifts, postural changes - that show someone trying to deceive. It was why the guidance that comes with the inventory insists that it never be administered remotely, or via a computer. The 'inquisitor' must be present to read the respondent's body language, as well as record their answers to questions. It is only when the two elements - kinesics and responses - are brought together, a trained inquisitor will spot when a subject is 'diverting' - lying, in layman's language.

Carver didn't spend too long detailing his observations of Betty's 'give-aways'. He didn't need to. Like many law-enforcers, Lynch had enough of an instinct for the subject to recognise what Carver was talking about. And whilst he had not paid Betty as much attention as Carver, he remembered some of the behaviours Carver described. The 'eye-slides'. The leg-crossing. The hand-to-face gestures; itching, chin rubbing, mouth covering. When matched with the areas covered by Carver's 'consistency testing' - the pattern that emerged was clear enough - Lynch had no grounds to argue. Whenever the inventory touched upon an area that might conflict with her husband's reputation as a 'fine upstanding family man' and a 'pillar of the community' Betty had 'diverted'. Whether it amounted to actual lying, Carver still wasn't sure. But it was enough to convince him that Betty Whittingham's story bore further investigation.

For Carver, one response above all others, was key. It was to his last question, when he asked if Curtis had known someone called 'Megan'. The slight hesitation before she answered, together with the look-away and raising her hand to her face to rub at her chin. On their own, they may not have amounted to much. But occurring together, as they did, they spoke of someone at that moment experiencing great discomfort. She had heard the name 'Megan' before. Carver was convinced of it. Finally, there was the clincher.

'What clincher?' Lynch said.

Carver reached into his document case and brought out one of the photographs that had come to him months before. Taking out his mobile, he brought up the picture he'd taken in the garden before he'd returned back inside with Betty. He showed them to Lynch. There could be no argument, it was that obvious. The foliage, the patio area, the garden table and chairs. The hobblebush in the background. The garden in the photograph sent to Carver months before was, undoubtedly, Whittingham's.

Lynch stared at the two images. 'Fuck,' he said. Carver thought it was the first expletive he'd heard the God-fearing Sheriff utter. Lynch leaned in, peering at the first picture. 'But it doesn't show Curtis, or Betty.'

Carver nodded. 'Which suggests they either weren't there, or Curtis took the picture.'

Lynch stared at him, mouth half-open. 'You thinking *he* sent you the picture?'

Carver shrugged, shook his head. 'It's possible. The

question is, why would he?'

It was Lynch's turn to shrug, 'Maybe she found out about it, and killed him to stop him doing anything else that may give her away.'

Carver nodded. 'Again, a possibility.'

For several moments, Lynch remaining staring at the images on the desk in front of him. Eventually, he looked up. 'So where does this leave us? I assume you'll want to go back and put Betty through the wringer?'

'We will,' Carver said, 'But when we do, we'll need ammunition we can use to shoot down any resistance she puts up.'

'What sort of ammunition?'

Carver reached over to retrieve his mobile. 'Hopefully, this sort.'

Lynch looked puzzled as Carver brought up the SMS that had pinged in his mobile as he took the snap of Betty's garden, and which he finished reading just as Betty bought him his coffee. Lifting it, he showed Lynch the screen.

'Who's it from?' Lynch said.

'My DI- My partner, Jess,' he said. 'She's worked this case with me since the beginning.'

'What's she say?'

'She's been trying to trace a woman Megan once kept as her house-slave. Her name is Tracy. We're hoping she might be able to tell us something about Megan's US connections.'

'And?' Lynch said.

Carver read him the message. *Tracy is back. Just called me. Seeing her Saturday. Will let you know how I get on.*

'Will this Tracy cooperate?'

'Maybe. Probably.'

'Why so sure?'

'Two reasons. First, she's no loyalty to Megan. Megan

143

tried to set Tracy up for the murders she herself committed. Her plan was to kill Tracy and make it look like suicide.'

Lynch nodded. 'The other reason?'

Carver gave a wry smile. 'If you knew Jess Greylake, you'd know. She can be pretty persuasive when she wants to be.'

CHAPTER 26

HEADING ACROSS TO Miriam's that Saturday morning, I was even more nervous than usual, the reason, Kit was with me.

When I first mentioned to her about my parents going out on Saturday night and that she could come and hang out if she wanted, she was enthusiastic. 'Hey, that'd be cool.' But when she continued, 'My Dad works Saturday. We can make a day of it if you like?', I felt bad having to remind her about me working at Miriam's.

'Oh yeah, I forgot about that,' she said.

Seeing her disappointment - she didn't seem to have many what you would call close friends - I thought on it. I was pretty sure Miriam wouldn't mind. The times I'd mentioned Kit to her, she always showed interest.

'If you don't mind getting your hands dirty, you can come and give me a hand? I'll get through it quicker, then we can hang out. And I'd split what she pays me with you.'

Kit chuckled. 'You going to pay for my company now Brandon Sawyer? Like one of those prostitutes?'

Blushing, I said, 'That's not what I meant. I just meant-'

'I'm joshing. I know what you meant. And yeah, I'd enjoy helping out. Besides, it's time I met this Miriam you are always talking about.'

'Great,' I said. 'Let's do it.' But my thought was, *Do I*

talk about her that much?

Just to be safe, that evening I checked with my Dad if he thought Miriam would mind.

'I can't think she would. Give her a call and ask.'

I had Miriam's number in my contacts. It was the first time I'd used it and I remember feeling nervous as I waited for her to answer.

'Brandon,' she said, brightly. 'What can I do for you?'

I told her about Kit and asked if she'd mind her helping me out.

'Not at all. I'll look forward to meeting her. It's about time I met this girl you talk so much about.'

I learned a valuable lesson that day. Women notice when you talk about other women.

Kit biked over early on the Saturday. Mom fixed us ham and eggs while my father poured her juice and generally interrogated her the way parents do the first time they meet their kids' friends.

After breakfast we made our way across to Miriam's. We used the side gate and made our way round the back. She must have heard us coming, as she came out onto the deck as we rounded the corner. She made a big fuss about meeting Kit, which I was pleased about. After arranging it, I'd worried in case Miriam might not take to her. I needn't have. Miriam was welcoming and full of smiles. Over more juice and bread-cake that made me wish I'd gone easy on the ham and eggs, they bounced off each other the way I've seen girls do. Miriam even talked with her as if she and Kit were the same age. A lot of it went towards jokes about me, which I didn't mind, and talking to each other in a way that reminded me of the times I used to watch Mom and Aunt Katherine talking about my father - like he wasn't there.

'I believe your father is the town Sheriff,' Miriam said. 'I imagine that makes life interesting.'

'It does,' Kit' said. 'But I sometimes wish he had a normal job, like an office or up at the plant.' She meant the wood plant up in the hills.

Miriam seemed to understand. 'It's not easy living with a policeman.'

'Tell me about it,' Kit said.

We were making ready to start work when Miriam said, 'Brandon tells me your father is investigating that awful death out in the forest?'

Kit nodded. 'Councilman Whittingham.'

'Has he found out what happened yet?'

Kit went quiet. 'Not yet...' She seemed embarrassed. 'I'm sorry Miriam, but my father tells me I mustn't talk about his work, so I-'

'That perfectly fine, Kit. And he's quite right. I fully understand. I shouldn't have mentioned it.'

At that point I slipped inside to use the bathroom. When I came out they were still talking, but the subject had moved on. Miriam turned to me.

'Oh, there you are, Brandon. Kit was just telling me about this English detective you mentioned the other day. He's working with her father apparently.'

'Yeah,' I said, pulling on my gloves. 'She had him over to dinner last Sunday, didn't you Kit?'

'Did you indeed?' Miriam said, turning to her. 'How interesting. You must tell me all about him later. I love everything about the English. They are so polite.'

'Yeah,' I said. 'And don't forget the accent. Kit loves the accent.'

Miriam grinned at her. 'Me too.' They both giggled.

Kit finished her drink then joined me in the garden as Miriam took the tray of refreshments back inside.

'She's nice,' she said. 'And funny. I like her.'

I was relieved, though I'd never thought of Miriam as funny, just... nice. 'I'm glad you like her,' I said. 'I think the feeling's mutual.'

As we set-to attacking the root ball I was half-way through digging out, Miriam was inside, busy preparing for the gathering she was hosting that evening. She'd mentioned it briefly, as we'd spoken, but hadn't gone into detail. When I popped inside, I'd seen boxes of drink and bags of foodstuffs in the kitchen, and I imagined her getting everything ready the way I used to see my Mom doing when they had their friends around. Most times when that happened, I was sent off to spend the night with my grandparents over in Queens. My grandparents were great, but I was never happy about it. I'd have preferred to stay and listen to what went on from my bedroom. I tried asking if I could stay, several times, but they always made out I wasn't missing anything. They said it just involved grownups sitting round, drinking and jawing. From what I used to come across sometimes after I returned home - including a lingering sweet smell in the air - I always suspected it involved a lot more than that. In fact, it was more than suspicion.

I have this faded memory from when I was around five. I was asleep in my room one night, when a man and woman I didn't know burst in and woke me up. At the time I thought they were playing some game. They were giggling, and missing clothes. The man was bare-chested and the woman was wearing some sort of underwear. It took them a minute or so to realise I was there. When they did, they were out of there like a shot. Next thing, my Mom was going nuclear. I heard her screaming and my Dad shouting and telling everyone to get out. Eventually it all went quiet, and I went back to sleep. It was after this they started sending me to stay with my grandparents whenever they were having people round. I never heard the incident mentioned again. Years later, I was looking at Louis Alverez's cell one time, when I realised that the memory of what I saw during the minute the couple were in my room must still be there, though buried, deep.

When Miriam brought out our mid-morning refreshments, the three of us talked some more and I asked about her 'party', how many were coming?

'Just a few people I know,' she said, which wasn't really an answer. 'And I wouldn't describe it as a *party* Brandon. It's just a little gathering to welcome your parents to Brackers Lake.' The way she was playing it down, I thought about asking why then all the booze and food I'd seen in the kitchen, but didn't want to sound brash.

We returned to work, but later on that morning Miriam called to me from the deck. 'Brandon? Can I borrow you a minute please? I just need a hand with something.'

'Shall I come as well?' Kit said.

'No, it's alright Kit. I'm sure Brandon can manage it.'

I went inside, when she asked me to take off my boots and follow her upstairs, which I did. I've never forgotten that short ascent. To this day, I can remember what she was wearing. Jeans and red heels. On the upstairs landing, opposite the door to what looked like her bedroom, which was ajar, she pointed up at the hatch to the loft-space, where the pole-hook was hanging down from the eyelet.

'The hatch seems to be stuck. It needs a good pull, and I'm not as strong as I used to be. Can you manage it?'

'No problem,' I said.

Making sure to keep my eyes away from her bedroom door, I took hold of the pole and gave it a pull. I thought it would give easily, but it didn't, though the wood around the hatch let out a few creaks.

'I think the wood is swollen. I need to get up there

and release it.' I was using some steps out in the garden. I told her to wait while I went and got them.

'No need,' she said, turning away. 'There's another set in here.' She disappeared into another bedroom, where I heard her moving stuff around.

As I waited, I thought about going to see if she needed my help with the steps, but I couldn't resist peering through the gap into her bedroom. In the window bay, I could see a dressing table full of women's things. Backing the dresser was a large mirror through which I had a good view of the rest of the room, including the bed. It looked stylish and elegant, all blacks, pinks and greys. It reminded me of the sort of thing you see in films, or a department store bedroom display. As I took it in - *her bedroom* -my heart thumped in my chest.

'Here you are.'

I turned to find her setting up the steps. If she'd seen me leering into her bedroom, she didn't let on.

Hoping my face wasn't as red as it felt, I mounted the steps until I was able to get my shoulder under the hatch, and push. There came another creak, louder this time, then it gave and I felt it release. I did it a couple of times to make sure it was free. As I came down the steps, I realised I could see over the top of her bedroom door. I couldn't stop myself. Peering over, I saw a long black dress with some sort of gold trim hanging in front of a mirrored closet. The way it was out on display, I guessed it was her outfit for the evening.

At the bottom, I moved the steps aside, grabbed the pole and gave another sharp pull. This time the hatch came down, releasing the built-in steps that unfolded with several metallic clicks to reach the floor.

'Oh, well done Brandon,' she said. 'Just what was needed. A good strong pair of arms.'

'Would you like me to fetch something down for

you?' I said.

My hope was she would say 'Yes', which might mean more trips up and down - and more glimpses into the bedroom. But she said, 'No it's fine, thank you. I'm just going to go up and get a few things. I know where they are.'

'Do you need me to hold the steps while you go up?'

Just for a second, I caught a glimpse of a smile, then she said. 'No, I've done it before, I can manage. You better go and make sure Kit is okay. We don't want her to think we've abandoned her, do we?'

'No, I, er… guess not.' Turning away, I headed back downstairs. As I descended I couldn't stop myself throwing one last glance at her bedroom door. My eyes were level with her waist and my last glimpse was of her jeans and red shoes.

'Thank you, Brandon,' she called. 'You are *such* a help.'

Back in the garden, Kit was waiting.

'What've *you* been up to?' You look flushed.'

'Her loft-space hatch was stuck. She needed help to open it.'

'Hard work was it?' she said.

'No. What do you mean?'

'You're all red, like you've been running.'

I didn't answer, but just went back to my root-ball. A moment later, as I levered my shovel under it, I glanced over at Kit, also now digging. She was smiling.

We finished work around three. Miriam came out with one last pitcher of lemon and a plate of cake which we enjoyed, sitting up on the deck, surveying the results of our labors - we'd finally got the root-ball out - like we were royalty. Miriam had showered since we last saw her and she was wearing a long, white robe, with her hair wrapped in a towel, like my Mom sometimes does. She smelled all fresh and clean. A fair bit of the time since I'd helped her upstairs, I'd been imagining what she would look like in the black dress. Now, seeing her like this, and knowing she would be returning to her bedroom after we'd gone to change and make herself ready for her guests, my imagination started working again.

Before we left, Miriam handed me my envelope, and gave another to Kit. When Kit realised what it was, she tried to refuse it, but Miriam would have none of it.

'You've worked as hard as Brandon. You deserve it. And it was lovely to meet you. Please, come again, I still want to hear all about your English detective.'

Returning across to my house, Kit was full of what a nice lady Miriam was, and how she'd enjoyed working in her garden, and, 'I'd be happy to do it again, but only if you'd like me to, of course.'

My replies were mainly grunts, 'Uh-huh's and nods. To be honest, right then, I was struggling to think of anything apart from the idea that had come as I sat on Miriam's deck, drinking my lemon and looking at her, fresh out of the shower.

CHAPTER 27

JESS GREYLAKE HAD no idea what Tracy Redmond had been doing during her weeks 'off-grid', but whatever it was, she looked none-the-worse for it. In fact, as she padded about her kitchen in her bare feet, rustling them up coffee, Jess thought she looked better than she had in a long time. The blond hair was longer and glossier than last time, her skin glowing, and there was a calmness about her that was a long way from the fractured, addicted mess she became following her narrow escape from Megan Crane's clutches. It was only the chafing on her right wrist and which Jess spotted when Tracy handed her coffee, that pointed to her absence being something other than a 'quiet, relaxing holiday'. Then again, Jess thought, maybe for Tracy, it was exactly that.

'The Netherlands,' Tracy answered when Jess probed. 'Staying with a Dutch couple I met at Josephine's one time. They're in their sixties, but they're nice and very kind.' Seeing Jess check her wrists, she added. 'It's not as bad as it looks. They're very experienced'.

'Glad to hear it,' Jess said. But she was determined to not get drawn into discussing Tracy's lifestyle. She had tried that before, and got nowhere. Tracy knew the dangers. If she chose to fulfil her submissive fantasies every so often, that was up to her.

And to be fair, right now, watching her settle onto her day-couch, legs tucked under, nursing her coffee in both hands, Jess thought she looked about as far from the person she first met chained up in Megan's play room that time, as she could imagine. A successful, independent professional whose work-life balance was, on the surface at least, back where it should be. It didn't take Jess long to find the crack in the veneer. After they had settled and dispensed with the preliminaries, she said, 'I need to talk to you about America.'

Tracy stopped her mug an inch from her mouth, a wary look came.

'What about America?'

'I need to know what she got up to there, where she went, who she met.'

'Why?'

Jess took a breath. 'There was an... incident over there. A man died. The circumstances recall some of what she did here. Jamie's there now, looking into it. We need to know if there's any connection.'

'Connection? With what? She's dead. How can there be a connection?'

Jess paused, drank her coffee, letting silence do its work. Tracy stared at her.

'What are you saying?' The wariness turned to realisation. 'Don't tell me... Oh my God. You do. You think she may still be alive?'

Jess held her gaze. 'I'm not saying that. We're just trying to work out if this man's death is anything to do with what she did there, or anyone she knew.'

Tracy reached forward to place her cup on the coffee table.

'I'm a barrister, Jess. I know something about how these things work. If Jamie is in America, that suggests he's looking *for* something, not *at* something. Otherwise the American investigators would have come *here* to see *him*. So tell me. Why is he there?'

Jess sighed. She had half-expected it would go this way. Barristers don't get paid for being slow on the uptake. The trick was always going to be, *how much* to share? As far as Jess knew, Tracy's well of loyalty to the woman she once served had dried a long time ago. The truth was, Megan's death had set her free. Any suggestion she may still be alive would fill her with fear. Even if Tracy had any ideas about how to contact her, it was highly unlikely she would try to do so. But then, the relationship between a sub like Tracy and her dom probably doesn't follow normal rules. If Jess wanted Tracy to talk, she was going to have to take a risk.

She described the circumstances of Curtis Whittingham's death. She told about her 'meetings' with Sir Richard Hayhurst, the former Harley Street cosmetic surgeon who knew Megan, the hints he had dropped about maybe seeing her again, one day. She didn't mention Jamie's photographs. Until Jamie found out who sent them, that would be a stretch too far. As Jess talked and Tracy wound herself, tighter and tighter, into a ball, her deepening apprehension told Jess what she needed to know. She wasn't faking. Eventually Jess said, 'The truth is Tracy, if there's any possibility at all she may be alive, we need to dig into it, and deep. Anything you can tell us about her US connections may help in that regard.'

For long seconds, Tracy remained still, eyes closed, digesting what she had heard. Eventually she moved. Uncoiling herself, she rose from the couch and went through to the kitchen. Opening the door to her freezer, she took out a bottle of Smirnoff. After showing it to Jess - she shook her head - she poured some into a glass and knocked it back. As she did so, her long tresses shimmered under the kitchen spots. She poured another, then returned to the couch where she curled herself up again. As she nursed her glass in both hands, Jess could see she was shaking. Taking a deep breath, she began.

Jess was aware that before Edmund Hart ever met Megan Crane, he lived and worked between the US and UK, switching between the two as his work for a multi-national investment brokerage demanded. She also knew that during this time, he and Tracy were regular 'play' partners, but when Megan came onto the scene, she took over in Hart's affections, leaving Tracy to fall to being shared between them. Jess first learned all this during the run-up to Megan's trial, where Tracy was a key prosecution witness. As Tracy told her at the time, she wasn't bitter over being 'usurped' by Megan. In fact, it suited her, having become increasingly worried about the directions Hart's developing tastes for deviancy were taking him. Besides, being bi-sexual, Tracy soon developed a bond with Megan that led to her spending increasingly lengthy periods as her live-in submissive.

Now, Jess listened in still silence - with her mobile's recorder app running - as Tracy began to fill in some of the blanks that, until the first photograph landed on Jamie's desk, neither she nor Jamie ever felt the need to pursue.

During the period leading up to Megan's arrival on the scene, Tracy had used to fly to New York every few months to visit Hart at his Greenwich Village apartment. Around that time he used to host regular 'munches' where fellow enthusiasts would come together to socialise, swap experiences and occasionally partners, and generally spend time with like-minded people. When Megan arrived on the scene, Tracy's involvement lessened, with Megan stepping in to take her place. With her looks and her charisma, Megan quickly became the centre of attention at Hart's gatherings, with members of their circle falling over each other to spend time in the dominatrix's company, whether public or private. It was only later, as Hart's more extreme interests took greater hold, that Tracy's US trips stopped. Soon after, Hart started waging his deranged crusade against high class escorts around northern England - with occasional aid, Jamie had come to suspect, from Megan.

'Tell me about these "munches",' Jess said. 'You must have got to know some of those who were there.

Tracy hesitated, bit her lip, but nodded. 'I did, but it was all a long time ago. I'm not sure how much I remember. They were professional types, you know? Lawyers, doctors, teachers. And mainly couples. Most of them were very nice. Back then it was still a long way from where Edmund and Megan eventually ended up.'

'What about names?' Jess said. 'You must remember some of them.'

Tracy's gaze slid left. She shrugged. 'I'm not sure… This man who died. You said his name was Curtis?'

Jess nodded. 'Curtis Whittingham.'

'There was a guy called Curtis… Was he a lawyer of some kind?'

Jess nodded again. 'What can you remember about him?'

'Nothing special. He was just one of the crowd. I remember he used to sit in the corner, watching rather than getting involved, if you see what I mean?'

'Was he with someone? Wife, girlfriend, partner?'

Tracy thought on it. 'I'm not sure. He may have had a partner, but I couldn't say.'

'Who else do you remember?'

Over the space of the next half-hour, and with Jess's encouragement, Tracy recalled the names of those she could remember - 'Vincent.' 'Stephanie.' 'Miles.' Among them were several couples. 'Sophie and George.' 'Hector and Cathy.' 'Ola and Francine.' 'Annie and Foster.' Digging deeper into her memory, she recalled small details of some she mentioned.

'He was an artist of some kind.'

'They lived upstate somewhere.'

'She had a vile temper. Treated him like shit.'

Jess asked, 'Were Edmund and Megan close to any of them?'

'Not particularly. Cathy and Hector were there quite a lot. And Annie and Foster maybe. But I can't remember much about them. I think Cathy and Annie may have been nurses, or doctors, or something.'

'Anyone else?'

Tracy hesitated, glanced up, looked away again, quickly. 'I don't think so-'

But Jess had caught it. 'Don't hold out on me, Tracy. If you remember something you must tell me.'

Tracy bit her lip again. Harder this time. The shaking that had eased as she talked started up again. She took a deep breath.

'There was, is, one guy...'

Jess waited. The shaking increased. Jess reached across, put her hand over Tracy's. 'It's alright Tracy. You've nothing to be scared of. It's all in the past. Whoever you are thinking about, he can't hurt you now.'

She shook her head, vigorously. "You're wrong. You don't understand. It's not all in the past. Not all of it.'

Jess stared at her. *What's she remembering?* She needed a push. 'What's his name, this guy?'

Slowly, her head came up. Her eyes locked with Jess's.

'He called himself, Charles.'

Jess read between it. 'But that wasn't his real name?'

'No.'

'Do you know his real name?'

'I do now.'

'Why? How?'

158

There was more hesitation, then she said, 'Because I sometimes watch CNN.'

CHAPTER 28

IT HAD BEEN quite a while since I last saw my parents dressed up for a night out. I remember from their partying days how my Mom always used to spend hours doing her hair and makeup. She was real pretty back then, still is I guess, she just doesn't get the chance to show it off much any more. I remember my grandma looking at her one time while she was baking in the kitchen and welling up, saying. 'If you're not the prettiest woman in Brooklyn Annie Sawyer, I don't know who is.' My Father's not bad-looking either I suppose, though he's put on a few pounds since he had to give up the running on account of his knees.

As they left to head across to Miriam's that evening, my Mom was wearing this red dress that had no shoulders, or back and showed off more of her front than those she usually wore. My father was wearing one of his smart 'party' shirts - white with yellow and blue motifs, along with black trousers and his best shoes. The smell of perfume and cologne followed them out the door.

'Have fun you two,' my Mom called back just before she closed it.

'We will Mom,' I answered.

'And don't try waiting up for us. We'll probably be late.'

'Okay Mom.'

'Your Mom's a babe,' Kit said after they had gone.

'*What?*' I said.

'And your Dad's not bad either.'

'Do you mind?' I said. 'They're my *parents*.'

'So what?' Kit said. 'They're still *hot.*'

I groaned, shook my head, turned to head back upstairs. 'Bring your drink,' I said. 'We'll have another game before... you know.' I checked the door, just to make sure they weren't about to return and catch us talking about our plan.

'You still want to?' Kit said.

'Hell, yeah. Don't you?'

'I guess,' she shrugged. But if we get caught, it's all your idea. I'm just along for the ride.'

'We won't get caught,' I said. 'And even if we do, so what? What is it the English say? 'It's just *"larks"*?'

'Firstly,' Kit said. 'I've never heard that expression before in my life and have no idea what it means. Secondly, don't ever say it like that again. It sounded *weird.*' She pushed me to one side as she headed up the stairs. 'Come on. It's time for my revenge.'

Kit was wearing jeans. As she headed up in front of me, I found myself remembering following Miriam earlier in the day.

I'd first mentioned my idea to Kit that afternoon when we were both back in my room after showering and changing out of our work-clothes. As we dug into the potato chips and cola my Mom had brought up to see us through to the supper she was going to leave out, I turned to Kit, still drying her hair. I think I've mentioned Kit wears her hair short, not like most girls I know. Afrid's is long and black and quite beautiful. Even so, as I watched her leaning forward to towel it dry, I thought she looked more like a 'real' girl than I had noticed before.

'I've an idea.' I said.

'About what?' she said, still rubbing.

'Why don't we wait until it's fully dark, then slip across the road, sneak into Miriam's back yard and see what's going on with her party and stuff?'

Kit stopped towelling to give me this strange look. 'Isn't that a bit, like, creepy?'

I gave a shrug. 'You never spied on your folks before?'

She thought about it. 'Not that I remember.'

'Yeah, well it's probably not the sort of thing you do when your Dad's Sheriff.

'What's that got to do with anything? It still sounds creepy. And there's other people there not just your folks.'

'They won't mind.'

'How do you know? You don't even know them.'

'I know Miriam. I'm sure she won't mind. If we get caught, she'll just think it's funny.'

'You think so?'

'I'm sure of it. You saw how she is. She's not like most women her age.'

She gave me a long look. I wondered what she was thinking. She gave a kind of sly smile.

'You've got a thing for her, haven't you?'

I turned to reach for my cola on the desk behind me. 'What do you mean? No I haven't. Don't be stupid.'

When I turned back, the smile was still there. She gave a little giggle, stifled it with the back of her hand. 'Brandon Sawyer. You should be ashamed of yourself, like my Mother used to say.'

'*What?*' I said. 'I haven't *done* anything?'

'No,' she said. 'You just want to go spy on her. My Dad arrests people for doing that you know? "Toms" he calls them. He arrested Herb Wincroft for-'

'HEY,' I said. 'If you don't want to, if you're scared we might get in trouble, that's fine. It was only an idea.'

'I'm not scared,' she said. 'I'm just surprised you would think of it is all.'

'Well there's not much else to do round here right now, is there? It's not like Brackers Lake is party central. Not like Brooklyn was. But like I say, I wouldn't want you to be worrying in case your Dad found out.'

'It's not that, it's just... And anyways, my Dad would never know, *would he?*'

I saw my chance. 'How could he? We'd just sneak in the back of her yard, take a few peeks, then come away. No one will *ever* know.'

For a few seconds, she looked uncertain, but then she caved. 'Okay. It's your house, your rules. If you want to go snooping we will. But just one quick recce okay? I'm not sure how I'd feel, standing in her bushes watching them all partying. It'll be a bit like the beginning of Scream, or one of those old Halloween slasher-movies.'

I smiled at her. 'Just one snoop, then we'll come back and do some more Fortnite. There probably won't be that much to see anyway. Just a bunch of grown-ups standing around boozing and jawing.'

As I rebooted the X-Box I had to work to calm myself. For a few moments, I'd worried she would hold out, in which case I wouldn't get to see Miriam wearing her black dress after all.

As for just watching grown-ups boozing and jawing, I couldn't have been more wrong.

CHAPTER 29

WE WAITED ANOTHER hour after darkness fell before leaving to embark on our little adventure. We were in no rush, and I wanted to give Miriam's party/social/whatever, a couple of hours to get going before taking a look. Besides, I'd finally found something I was better at than Kit - Fortnite - which was a nice change. As we stepped out onto my front porch, I remember thinking how quiet it was. No traffic noise. No sirens in the distance. No sounds of music, partying, kids playing. Just the whisper of a warm summer evening. Not like Brooklyn.

I didn't head straight across to Miriam's. That would mean having to use the side gate and we'd be bound to be seen. Instead I led Kit up a side-street and half-round the block to where the narrow service access path runs straight down between the back yards either side of Miriam's block. I'd used it a few times when repairing her fence and was familiar with the layout. As we approached, I saw a line of cars parked close to where the access joins with the sidewalk. A car was parked across it, but not so much as to block it. As we turned to head down towards Miriam's, I noted the car was some bright, metallic colour, but as the only light was from a street lamp further along the sidewalk, everything was shades of grey. I remember thinking a couple of the cars might even belong to some of Miriam's guests, parked there rather than block the road in front.

As we headed down the path, I used the pencil-flashlight I'd brought with me, but kept it pointed low. I didn't want any of Miriam's neighbors making 'prowler' calls. Miriam's fence started about fifty yards down, on the right. When we got there, I went straight to the mid-section where, that first Saturday, I'd 'fixed' some of the boards that had fallen off. I knew a couple were still loose enough I could easily pry them off the lower cross-batten, and swing them aside to give access. As it happened, when we got there I discovered they had already come loose on their own. One was off altogether, lying in the bushes in the garden. I made a mental note to make a better job of it next time - even if I did decide to still leave the bottom attachments not fully secured.

Stuffing the light away in my pocket, I whispered to Kit. 'Through here. But stay quiet.'

I held one of the boards aside for Kit to squeeze through, then followed after, taking care not to dislodge any more into the bushes. If someone on the deck heard, they would wonder what all the thrashing was.

Through the fence, we found ourselves right at the back of the garden, still screened from the house and deck by the trees and shrubs I hadn't got around to hacking back yet. Slowly, I led the way forward, taking care to point out to Kit the several trip hazards along the way. But as the shrubbery thinned and I started to get my first proper glimpses of the house and the deck, my stomach sank.

I had assumed all along that on a warm evening like tonight, Miriam and her guests would be out on the deck. I'd imagined we would settle in the undergrowth, probably using the two big hydrangeas as cover, and just observe and listen for a while. I was looking forward to hearing if my name got mentioned. But not only was the deck empty, everyone inside, the sliding doors were shut and the drapes pulled across. We could neither see, nor hear, anyone. There were a couple of chinks where the drapes weren't quite fully drawn and from where light spilt out onto the deck, but nothing that would allow us to properly observe what was happening.

'Aww, fuck,' I said. 'What a crock.' I said it aloud, making no attempt to hide my disappointment.

'Shhh,' Kit said. 'Someone'll hear us.'

I cast about. 'Who? They're all inside.'

'I don't know,' she said, continuing to whisper. 'Someone might come out for a smoke or something.'

For a minute or so I stood there, wondering what to do, looking up at the house and deck, feeling foolish. Having talked Kit into signing up for the trip, I suspected that right now she was seeing me for a loon, incapable of foreseeing the possibility they might all be inside, in which case the whole thing was a complete waste of time.

'Fuck,' I said again, stamping a foot. Beneath my boot, something - a twig or small branch - snapped and spun off into the bushes. Across the other side of the garden, a rustle marked something being disturbed.

'What was that?' Kit said, sounding a little scared.

'Just wildlife,' I said. 'It's nothing.'

'What sort of wildlife?' She hesitated. 'You don't mean rats do you? I hate rats.'

I knew that rats are common in most urban gardens at night, but could tell Kit was unnerved at the prospect one may be lurking close. I sighed. Our little 'adventure' was on the verge of becoming a complete disaster.

'Probably not rats,' I lied. 'More like a chipmunk, or maybe a cat. There're lots of cats round here.'

'Ahh... I love chipmunks.' Turning to peer through the dark where the rustle had sounded, she held out a hand. 'Gimme your flashlight. Let me go see.'

Grabbing her wrist, I pulled her back around. 'We're not here to look for chipmunks. And if we go flashing lights around someone'll see us.'

'In that case, we may as well go back to your house. There's nothing to see here.'

About to agree - *bummer* - I turned to head back to the fence. I'd only taken a couple of steps when I stopped suddenly, causing Kit to bump into my back.

'What's wrong?' she said, sounding scared again. 'It's not a rat is it?'

'No,' I said. 'It's just…' I knew my answer right then should be to reassure her I had not seen any rats. But that would mean having to explain why I'd stopped so suddenly, which right then, I didn't feel like doing.

Ever since that afternoon, an image, conjured from what I'd seen, experienced, had been playing around my head, surfacing at unexpected moments, shining bright, then receding as the reality presented by Kit's presence forced me to push it back under. Now, there in the darkness at the back of Miriam's garden, it had come to me again, fuelling my sense of disappointment, causing me to think again about giving up too quickly.

I turned to look back at the house, took a step past Kit, gauging.

'What?' she said.

I took a couple more steps. She grabbed my arm. 'Where are you going?'

I turned to her, torn now between getting her out of there and away from 'the rats', and the image drawing me back.

'Wait a minute,' I said.

I retraced our steps back to the hydrangeas. The deck was still clear, drapes drawn. But the chinks were still there, light spilling. *A quick look won't hurt, long as we're quiet.* I turned to look for Kit, jumped to find her right

167

beside me. I caught my breath.

'What are you *doing?*' she whispered, urgently. It was too dark to see her face, but I suspect she already knew the answer to her own question.

'We're here now,' I said. 'May as well take a quick look before we go.'

She turned to look at the house, came back to me. 'Are you *crazy?* You can't see anything. You'll get caught.'

I pointed to where the light was spilling. 'There's a gap. We'll be able to see *something.*'

I started to move forward. She grabbed my shirt, held on, tight.

'Don't Brandon, *please.* Let's just go. I don't like this.'

I could hear panic in her voice. She was really scared. I hesitated. The image came again. *Miriam. The black dress.* I turned to her, whispered, close. 'Thirty seconds, that's all. Then we'll go.'

As I pulled from her grasp and stepped out towards the deck, I heard her pleading behind me.

'No Brandon. *Please.*'

Then I was mounting the steps, moving slowly, watching where I was putting my feet. Nearer the house there was more light. I could see there was nothing in my way, nothing to trip over and cause a clatter. I closed on the sliding doors, the chinks in the drapes. I crouched down, stopped, listened. I was surprised how quiet it was. None of the party sounds I was expecting. No signs of people enjoying themselves. No chinking of glasses. No bursts of light-hearted conversation. There *were* voices, but subdued; earnest, rather than lighthearted. Someone laughed. It was a woman's laugh, though it seemed somehow more mocking than humorous. For a party, it all sounded very un-party like. I leaned forward, about to peer through the gap, then jumped as something pushed up against me. I turned. It was Kit. The escaping light lit her face. I could see she was wired - scared, but resigned. I opened my mouth to say something but she clamped a hand over it. She looked deep into my eyes.

In a fierce whisper she said, 'This better be worth it.'

I nodded, gave her a reassuring smile. *It will be.*

Together, we bent to look through the gaps in the drapes, me the upper one, she the lower.

What we saw changed our lives.

Forever.

CHAPTER 30

AS WE BURST through the door into my kitchen, my mind was still in turmoil. Shock, confusion, fear, disgust, horror, all vied for top spot - as they had been doing from the moment we fled Miriam's garden to race home as if the devil was on our tail.

I have no actual memory of that flight through the night back to my house. There was too much going through my mind at the time for it to register. I know that at one point Kit fell, and I had to stop and help her up and support her the rest of the way because she had hurt herself. It was my fault. I was holding her hand so tight as I dragged her along, I forgot she couldn't run as fast. Back at East Williamsburg, I'd run for my year. Somewhere around halfway, I felt her hand slip from mine. When I looked back, she was sprawling to the ground, arms out, legs in the air. As I helped her back to her feet, I saw blood on her chin and she struggled to walk for the first few paces, limping and yelping in pain. But she kept going, as anxious as I was to get back somewhere safe, somewhere normal. It was only when we entered the kitchen and I saw the rips in her jeans, the seeping grazes to her knees, I realised she needed seeing to.

'Sit down,' I said, pointing to a chair, still catching my breath. 'Drop your jeans. Let's see those knees.'

That she complied without comment - eyes glazed,

face vacant - told me she was in a similar state to me at that moment. Another time she'd have made some smart remark about me wanting to get into her panties. As I grabbed the first aid kit from the cupboard and started sorting out Betadine and cotton wool to clean up her knees and chin, I was glad to have something else to focus on. Had we even tried talking about it at that moment, I'm not sure we'd have been able to. I wouldn't have known what words to use, the questions to ask.

For several minutes, as I went about dabbing at Kit's grazes, cleaning out grit and tearing off fresh pieces of lint and cotton wool to replace those that were bloodied, she sat in silence, watching and wincing every now and then as the antiseptic stung. In truth, her scrapes weren't that serious and I probably made more of it than they merited. I just needed the time was all. Whenever I glanced up, I found her looking at me, rather than her knees. At first her face was blank but as the minutes passed, I could tell her focus was returning, the questions she needed to ask beginning to form. The same thing was happening in me.

Eventually, knees and chin clean, bleeding stopped, I screwed the top back on the disinfectant, packed the cleaning materials back in the first aid pouch. But as I turned away to return it to its cupboard, she reached up to grab my arm, pulling me back and round. As I looked into her face, I could see the light was back in her eyes. She was ready.

'What... What did we just see back there?' she said, still breathless.

I stared at her, trying to decide if I'd digested it enough to give an answer, worried in case if I tried to speak and couldn't, I'd look like a blubbering idiot. I settled on, 'I'm not sure. Give me a minute.'

She let me go while I put the kit back and cleaned

away the bloody waste. As she pulled her jeans up, I grabbed a couple of Red Bulls from the chiller and pulled the tabs. I didn't ask her, just gave her one. Another small act of 'normality' before we got into it.

We went upstairs and sat on my bed, slurped our cans. All the time she was watching me, waiting. I couldn't put it off any longer.

I turned to face her. 'Do you know what that was?' I said.

She hesitated, then gave a slow nod. 'Was it… was it some kind of weird sex-thing shit?'

I nodded. 'I think so.'

She gave a little gasp. Her hand went to her mouth, eyes widening. 'Oh my God. But… but it was… They were…'

I nodded again. 'I know. My parents.'

I'm not a total innocent. Like most my age, I've seen the kinds of things we're not supposed to see, visited the sites 'parental controls' are supposed to block. At school, I've sniggered with my pals while looking at Alvy Suarez's cell phone, or talking about the things we've accessed in the privacy of our bedrooms while our parents think we are doing homework or gaming. The likes of Alvy like to make out it's no big deal, like it's stuff you see every day. They like to give the impression they know what it's all about, like they're some kind of expert on that kind of stuff. I think they're full of crap. I don't have a sister, but I know enough about women's bodies that I don't have to pretend. One day adults will realise that school is a waste of time and that we'd learn more if they just leave us to surf YouTube all day. But some of the stuff you see… well, I'm not sure.

Some of it is just plain funny. I've seen a couple of vids of guys wearing diapers and sucking comforters like they're babies. What's *that* all about? But some of it, the stuff where people - women mostly - look like they're in trouble, or someone is hurting someone, or being horrible to someone in some way... I find all that quite creepy, sometimes scary. Most I know think the same, though some say it's actually normal, it's just that adults don't like to talk about it and schools don't include it in SE, they don't say why. It's all quite strange. On the one hand, whenever I've seen that sort of stuff, even though it gives me the creeps, there's something about it makes me want to keep looking. On the other, if it really is so 'normal', then why all the secrecy, parental controls and all that?

The day Kit showed me her dad's pictures of Councillor Whittingham, it reminded me of some of that stuff, but somehow different. To that point, the things I've seen and sniggered over, even if it's scary, something about it makes it somehow... not real, like some superhero movie or a graphic novel - now some of them can be *real* scary. But what happened to Councillman Whittingam - that *was* real. So real it made me sick to my stomach, which isn't what I feel when watching other vids.

Which was why, when I peeked through the drapes into Miriam's living room and saw what I saw, my head just about exploded.

Best as I could see, there must have been seven or eight people spread around the room. Most were sitting, though a couple were standing. Miriam was one of those standing. She was wearing the black dress. Most of that afternoon, I'd been looking forward to seeing her in it. Now the moment was here, I barely had time to notice. Other things grabbed my attention more. Like the fact they were all arranged in a loose circle, watching what was happening in the middle of the room. Like the fact that

173

what was happening in the middle of the room looked similar to some of the creepy videos I've mentioned. Like the fact that a couple of the women were bare above the waist. Like the fact one of those women was wearing some sort of blindfold. Like the fact she was on her knees, in the act of being tied to a post set up in the middle of the room, with her hands together in front the way Councilman Whittingham's were. Like the fact there was a chain around her neck and that a man was stood next to her, pulling on it, while Miriam was behind, doing the tying.

Like the fact the woman on her knees was my Mother, and the man holding her chain was my Father.

PART II

THE MAN WHO WATCHES

CHAPTER 31

CARVER WAS STRETCHED out on the hotel bed, wading through Curtis Whittingham investigation logs when Jess video-called. He cast it aside to give her his full attention.

Two minutes in, he said, 'Zander *who*?'

'Reed,' Jess answered. 'Zander Reed. I didn't remember him at first either.'

Carver thought on the name. Somewhere in the back of his brain, something sparked, but it was from way back. 'Remind me.'

'Think baseball. Around the same time as all the hoo-ha around Michael Jackson, and the kids' parties he used to host at that ranch of his.'

Carver closed his eyes, dug deep. *Reed, Reed, Reed. Baseball...* A memory flashed. 'Was he the commentator guy who liked kids?'

'That's him,' Jess said. 'He started off as a player, then became a commentator. Later on he took over running the National Junior Baseball Academy. Mr Baseball, they called him.'

'Didn't some mothers try to take him to court? Allegations he'd been interfering with their children?'

'More than tried. And 'interfered' doesn't cover the half of it. They claimed he'd been assaulting them for years. Everything from 'bedtime tickling games' to buggery.'

'But if I remember right, the judge threw the case out didn't he?'

'He did, but according to what's online, that was all part of it. It looks like there were suggestions after that a niece of the judge may have worked for Reed at the Academy and could have been involved in procuring kids for him. That was never proved either, but it was all enough to destroy his reputation and ruin his career.'

'So what happened to him?'

'Hard to say. It looks like he's keeping a low profile these days. No social media. Nothing listed in public company records. The last mention of him I can find is a New York Times article from two years ago, reporting the mothers' latest attempts to get the case back into court. At that time he was, "living quietly in the Hamptons", supposedly.'

Carver nodded, thoughtfully. 'And Tracy reckons he was one of Hart's cronies, and had a thing for Megan?'

'Obsessed, was how Tracy put it. Apparently he met Megan not long after she and Hart got together. He used to spend a lot of time at Hart's apartment whenever they were in New York. From what Tracy says, he was pretty much into anything and everything, not just kids.'

'And Tracy's scared of him?'

'Terrified. You should have seen her Jamie. She was shaking like a leaf. I couldn't believe she's never mentioned him before. It was me who debriefed her after we rescued her from Megan if you remember. She was bad enough then. Reluctant to talk, worried Megan may escape and come after her. But the way she was talking about Reed, I'd say that in her mind, he's as bad, if not worse.'

'Is she thinking Megan and him may have got back together?'

'Only after I told her what you were doing over there and showed her the photographs. She's always been happy to believe Megan died in Paris. She's never had any reason to believe otherwise, until now.'

'So what did she say about Whittingham? Sounds like they were all pretty close at one time.'

'She couldn't say much about him, other than he was an occasional visitor at Hart's gatherings. But she doesn't think he and Reed had much to do with each other. She reckons that most of those who were at these gatherings had no time for Reed either. They all thought he was just too weird and gave him a wide berth. And this was even *before* the Academy scandal. The only one who ever had any time for him it seems was Hart himself, but then we know what he was like as well. Brothers in arms, it seems.'

'Sounds like it,' Carver said, before slipping into thoughtful silence.

Jess waited. Eventually she said, 'So what do you think? Does any of this have any bearing on anything?'

Carver came out if it, shifting to ease the stiffness his stillness had brought on. 'It may do. It's certainly something I need to go back and put to Betty.'

'Do you think she knows about his connection with Hart?'

'Not sure. She knows something, but how much…? We'll see.'

'And what about Zander Reed?'

'He's interesting. He could be the sort of guy Megan would turn to for help if she wanted to settle in the vicinity of New York. A bit like that judge in France who let her use his house. But the fact he's a fan of Megan, means there's someone else, besides her, who could be familiar with the whole Worshipper MO and the way Whittingham died. The tying, the superglue, all that stuff. The only thing is-'

'What?'

'None of it helps explain the photographs, or why someone might want to make out she's still alive.'

'*IF* she's still alive.'

'Right. *IF* she's still alive.'

Ten minutes later, after promising to keep Jess updated and bidding her goodnight, Carver felt himself cramping up again. Swinging himself off the bed he stood up, stretching the stiffness away. Without Rosanna's encouragement, his morning exercise routine had dwindled.

As he poured himself another JD, he thought about what Jess had given him. In particular, he thought about Zander Reed. Who was he, and what was he into these days? Could he be involved in anything that might shed light on Curtis Whittingham's murder? The trouble was, he could be *someone*, or he could be *no-one*. What he needed was up-to-date intelligence. Jess had said there was little about him on-line. Which meant he needed another source. If he had been investigated for possible offences against children, there had to be a file somewhere. Like the FBI, maybe. He had a couple of connections with the FBI. One had helped him put out the poster that had resulted in Matt Lynch contacting him. But what he needed right now was someone with access to sensitive *intelligence*. He heaved a sigh.

Carver had had no contact with Rachel Hilts since they bid farewell following Aaron Lockwood's second trial. A key witness alongside Jonathan Kradesh, her analytical expertise had played a part in seeing the infamous 'mind manipulator' convicted and given the life sentences he deserved. Since then, he knew, she had accepted a temporary position working at Quantico's renowned Behavioural Sciences Division, the unit established by her grandfather. He had thought about her now and again since, but had resisted emailing the way he used to, worried not just how it may be interpreted, but scared to think too deeply about whether his reasons for doing so stood up to scrutiny. Right now, she didn't even know he was in the US. On the flight coming over, he had wondered how long it might be before some valid-sounding reason arose which would justify him contacting the young woman who now had full access to all the Bureau's most sensitive databases. That reason had just arisen.

Taking up his mobile, he brought up her number. Staring at it, he hesitated. It was coming on ten-thirty. But Rachel was a night owl.

He pressed 'call'.

It rang for something close to a minute. He was on the point of hanging up when she answered and the voice with the mid-west twang that always made him smile said, 'It's about time. What's taken you so long?'

CHAPTER 32

AS WE SAT on my bed, acknowledging to each other for the first time the truth of what we'd seen, Kit reached across to squeeze my hand.

'I can't even imagine how you must feel, seeing all that.'

I shook my head. 'To be honest, I'm not sure what I feel. I'm not even convinced it really happened. It feels a bit like it was some dream and I'm stuck in it.'

'It wasn't a dream Brandon. I saw it too.'

I looked at her. 'You saw who it was, right? The woman in the middle of-'

She nodded, quickly. 'I saw. Your Mom.'

'And the man holding the-'

'-Chain. Yeah, I know. Your father.'

I shook my head, put my hands to my face. '*Fuuuck*! I looked at her again. 'My Mom and Dad, Kit. It was my Mom and Dad.'

She squeezed my hand again.

For a couple more minutes I sat there shaking my head, cussing and repeating the fact it was them, as if maybe if I kept saying it, I'd suddenly realise I was mistaken and it wasn't them after all. During this time Kit said nothing but just sat quietly, her hand over mine. Sometimes it's best to just listen. What I should have been, I guess, was embarrassed. Kit too. What can be more embarrassing than seeing your parents, or friends' parents, engaging in the sort of thing you might see on one of those sites parental controls are supposed to block. I experienced a sudden panic. What if someone had filmed it? What if they put it up on some social platform? Everyone would see it. The kids in School, My friends back in Brooklyn. Afrid. Other members of my family. The likes of Aunt Katherine and Uncle-

I sat up. 'FUCK.'

Kit jumped. 'WHAT?'

I turned to her, the full realisation of what I'd suddenly remembered taking hold.

'The, the.. others,' I gabbled, reeling from this latest shock.

'What about them?' Kit said.

'They were there.'

'Who was there?'

'My Aunt Katherine and Uncle Hector. I saw them.'

'Your Aunt and Uncle? Oh my God Brandon, what the *fuck*…?'

I went quiet as I replayed the images I was already sure would remain burned in my memory for the rest of my life, checking in case my brain was playing tricks, making me remember things that hadn't actually happened.

The woman doing the tying. Definitely Miriam - the black dress was exactly as I remembered it. The woman in the middle of the room, and the man holding the chain - definitely… *them*. I moved on, quickly. Several other people sat around, singly or together. A man standing by the doorway, leaning against the jamb. My mind's eye zeroed in on him. Tall, bearded, longish hair. The languid look I always thought made him look half-asleep. It *was* him. My Uncle Hector. And the woman in the chair next to him, her hand in his. Short, dark hair. quite attractive I guess. Showing lots of leg in the strange dress-thing that might not have been a dress at all but some sort of long undergarment. Whatever it was, it fitted her well enough it showed her bulges. 'Nicely rounded,' she always used to laugh about herself. Aunt Katherine, no mistake. I tuned in to what memory I had of the others. None of them seemed familiar. I went round again, to be sure. No, just Aunt Katherine and Uncle Hector - and my parents.

I stood up, paced the floor. Kit waited. I stopped, looked at her, realisation finally dawning.

'They know her.'

'Who knows who?'

'My parents, Katherine and Hector. They know Miriam.'

Kit started. 'Well obviously. They were there.'

'No, I mean *before* we came to Brackers Lake. They knew her when we lived in Brooklyn. They've *always* known her.

Kit looked puzzled. 'Why do you say that? How do you know they knew her?'

I thought back to all the partying I'd witnessed over the years. The comings and goings at our house as I was growing up. The amount of time Aunt Katherine and Uncle Hector spent at our house. All the sleep-overs. I'd always seen them as just close friends of the family. Katherine and Mom were at college together. Later on they nursed in the same hospital. They were together when they met Dad and Hector at some party. That was the story I'd heard. Just good friends.

Wrong. They were more than good friends. A lot more.

So where did Miriam fit in? I racked my brain. I'd definitely never seen her before we arrived in Brackers Lake. But that doesn't mean she wasn't around. I never got to meet many of their friends.

I thought back to when we first came to Brackers

Lake. I never understood exactly where or how my father had come to meet Miriam. I just heard him and Mom talking about her one day. Not asking questions or making comments the way you do when you first meet someone. Things like, '*I wonder what she's like*' or '*She seems nice*'. No comments about getting to know the neighbours. Come to think about it, apart from the odd 'Good morning' or 'Have a nice day', we don't interact with other neighbors. Just Miriam. Like she was already a friend. Like they had known her a long time.

I though about us coming to Brackers Lake in the first place.

'Because of my work,' my father had said the first time they told me. 'A new position, with a new company.'

'And it'll get us away from Brooklyn,' my Mom had added. 'Somewhere nice. Somewhere we can start again.'

Start again.

I'd never thought about it before. Why did they need to start again? What was it about Brooklyn they needed to get away from?' Or was it that at all? Was it actually *not* so much about leaving Brooklyn, but going somewhere else? Somewhere they already knew? Somewhere there were *people* they already knew. Or maybe just one person. Someone they were already close to. Someone they'd partied with before. It triggered another realisation. *Tonight wasn't the first time.* They've done it before, lots of times. I remembered the couple who burst into my bedroom that time. The ones not wearing all their clothes, what they did before they realised I was there. It was not just some 'social'.

In that moment, all the perceptions I'd ever had of my parents changed. The same with 'Aunt' Katherine and 'Uncle' Hector, my life before Brackers Lake, everything about our life in Brooklyn.

They would never change back.

CHAPTER 33

IN THE DARKNESS under the trees across from the house, the man observes and waits. Every now and again a shadow crosses the blind of the upstairs window - the boy's room, he assumes. He smiles as he imagines what is passing between them, the conversation they are having. He would love to be a fly on the wall, witnessing their attempts to make sense of what they saw.

He stays another hour, waiting until he is satisfied the pair are there for the night, before deciding it is safe to move. He would be surprised if they dared venture out again. The way they reacted to what they saw, the speed with which they fled the garden to make their way back here, it was clear they never expected to see what they did. Which is a good thing. It meant that whatever the kid may have gleaned during his couple of weeks 'working' for her - he doubts the boy considers it 'work' at all; he's seen the way he looks at her - it probably doesn't include anything that, mentioned to the wrong people, like the girl's father, may pose a threat.

But that situation has now changed.

In the minutes before their noisy arrival, before he retreated to the cover of the bushes from where he observed the whole episode, he had been using the gaps in the drapes as they did a few minutes later. He'd seen what was happening inside, the equipment being made ready, the kid's mother being prepared. It was a shame his

185

planned viewing experience was ruined at that point. He was making ready to enjoy the spectacle when the whispers and roaming flashlight alerted him to their coming. No matter. There would be further opportunities no doubt. Maybe even, in light of tonight's developments, soon to involve pleasures of a very different kind. But the kids had seen what they did. They may not understand it - how would they? - but they saw it. Which meant that even if they did not present a threat before, they certainly do now. In which case the question is, what to do about it?

If the girl, particularly, goes running off back to her father, blowing her mouth off, or if either starts blabbing about what they saw and word gets back to him via some other route, he will be bound to investigate. For all the care he has taken in setting things up, the efforts he has gone to to make sure there are no more weak links in the chain, things are not so secure they can stand that sort of close scrutiny. So the question isn't so much what to do - that is pretty obvious - it is around how urgently it needs doing, and how.

Okay the kids have witnessed something that, for them, is a big deal. But the likelihood is, they won't understand the significance of what they've seen. Sure the girl's father is sheriff. But he can't see him sharing details of the Councilman's death with her. No responsible parent would. And as none of it ever hit the news, there is no reason she should ever make the connection. As far as the kids are concerned, it is just some embarrassing - *highly* embarrassing - event involving the boy's parents. And they are hardly likely to go around telling everyone. Hell, the more he thinks about it, the more he thinks it unlikely the kid will say anything to anyone, least of all his parents. What would he say? *Hey Mom and Dad, enjoy your little SM session with Miriam last night? Cool, what's for dinner?* And the girl? *Hey Dad, you'll never guess what we saw*

186

Brandon's Mom and Dad getting up to last night.'

No. The chances are, they will both keep their mouths shut. At least for a little while. The risk remains of course. Something could still happen that would result in them seeing it all in a different light, and deciding to tell someone. Which is why that risk must be removed. But having spent the past hour thinking it through, his conclusion is, it isn't so urgent it needs to happen right away. Which means he has time to plan what is needed, weighing the risks that will no doubt need to be overcome. Certainly, he needs to be careful. The way *She* reacted to his last intervention, he doesn't want a repeat, thank you very much. He is sure that when she sits down and thinks about it, she will soon realise he is acting in her - *their* - best interests. And she will be grateful. It is just that, being the sort of person she is, she doesn't always find it easy to show it. It doesn't worry him. He knows how she really feels. In time she will, he is sure, learn to show it more.

But until that time comes, he needs to avoid doing anything that might set her off. He knows what she is capable of. He's seen it often enough, even been party to it on occasion, though not for a long time. What he needs, is to get her on side. Make her realise how precarious the situation is. If he can get her to see things the way he does, she'll realise she has no choice but to go along with whatever plan of action he comes up with. At the end of the day, she knows that, despite the things she sometimes says, the way she behaves when others are around - *like that fucking kid* - she can depend on him. She knows he will always do the right thing, even if the right thing isn't always as clear to her as it is to him. But that's what comes when two people love each other, but one of them hasn't yet got to the point of fully realising it. She will get there eventually, he is sure. But until then…

187

The first thing is to tell her. She needs to know what's happened. Then he can begin the process of getting her to accept what needs to be done. And that needs to happen sooner rather than later. Not tonight, maybe. But tomorrow, or the day after. Tonight she's got other things on her mind. Which reminds him.

The night is still young, relatively. They'll all still be there, oblivious to what has happened. By now, he imagines, things will have progressed. How far, he wonders? The night is warm. Unless they've finished early - which would be unusual - they will still be inside. The chinks in the drapes will still be there. He thinks about it.

Why not? No point letting a little disruption spoil the evening entirely.

Taking one last look up at the window - there has been no movement for a good ten minutes or more. Probably humping each other, or she's giving him a blow-job - he steps out of the shadows, turns, and starts to head back to where he was before he was so rudely interrupted.

CHAPTER 34

AS I REALISED the effect of what I'd witnessed that night, and that everything about my life to that point was suddenly changed, I sank down onto the bed, drained.

But Kit was just getting going. 'Right,' she said, coming over all impatient. 'That's it. Tell me what's going on, what's in your mind.'

I told her. About my growing up in Brooklyn. About how my parents, while pretty liberal in their attitudes to some things - like weed - were also quite strict when it came to others. How my father's word was law - he was always the dominant presence in our house. And how my mother always seemed to be more subservient to him than I thought she needed to be. It was pretty much the same with Katherine and Hector, though they didn't have children to worry about.

'They're not your real Aunt and Uncle? Not blood, then?'

I shook my head. 'Just family friends.'

'You can say that again.'

Despite what I was feeling, it drew half a smile.

I laid it out just the way it had come to me as I'd replayed everything in my head, fitting it all together with what we'd seen. Suddenly a lot of things seemed to make sense. Like the way my father acted towards Miriam that first day he introduced us. Not going against her word.

'So what are you going to do?' Kit said, when I'd

finished.

'What can I do? If my parents want to go to these sort of parties, I guess it's none of my business.'

'And what about Miriam? Are you going to say anything to her?'

'What, tell her we sneaked into her garden, peeked through her drapes and saw her running some sort of porno session with my parents? No way. Best just let it go, forget about it. I wish now we'd stayed home and played Fortnite.' I closed my eyes, tipped my head back, opened them, looked at the ceiling. '*Christ* what a *fuck* up.' I took a deep breath, turned to Kit. She was calm now, over the immediate shock of our encounter, but she was looking at me in a way I couldn't figure.

'What?' I said.

'We can't,' she said.

'Can't what?'

'Forget about it.

'Believe me, I can and I will. I don't want to be thinking about-' I threw out a gesture. '*All that*, every time I speak with my parents or see Miriam.'

'That's not what I mean. I understand you *want* to be able to forget about it, I would too if it was my parents. What I mean is, we *can't*. We have to *do* something.'

'Like what?' I said. 'I'm not getting you.'

She breathed deep. 'You saw it Brandon. What they were doing? With your Mom I mean?'

'So?'

'So, like, where have we seen it before? Don't tell me you didn't notice 'cause I know you did. You were thinking it just like me.'

At that moment, the penny dropped. Suddenly I saw exactly what she was talking about. My stomach flipped another somersault.

'Councilman Whittingham.'

'Right. It was just like those pictures we saw in my Dad's computer files. They were doing to your Mom, what someone did to him.'

I stared at her. I think I must have turned pale or something because she looked worried, like she maybe thought I was about to faint. I tried to look for the flaw.

'But it's *not* the same. Someone killed him. It didn't look like anyone was trying to *hurt* my Mom. They were just playing some sort of weird game. *Weren't they?*'

That was when the horrible thought came. What if I was wrong? What if it wasn't a game? What if my Mom didn't come home and I never saw her again? What if they really were-'

'Relax,' Kit said. She must have read my mind. 'Don't worry, you're right. What we saw was just some game. Your Mom will be fine. I'm sure of it. But that's not the point. The point is, how do your parents, Miriam, the others, know about it? The details of how he died were never made public.'

'That's crazy, it would have been in the news, all over the media. Anyone could have-' She was shaking her head.

'No, they couldn't. My Dad told me about this kind of stuff. When someone's murdered, the police don't release all the details of the case. They keep some of it back so that if a suspect confesses, they can check if they know details only the killer would know. In Councilman Whittingham's case, all they gave out was, he died from asphyxiation. The details we saw in the file images, like what we saw tonight? None of that has ever been released. None of those people at Miriam's could have known about it, unless…'

I waited. My stomach started up again. 'Unless… what?' It couldn't be. It was just too ridiculous.

'Unless someone there was involved in Councilman

Whittingham's death. Or at least involved enough to know how he was killed.'

My head started pounding. 'But you're talking about my parents, my Aunt Katherine and Uncle Hector. Miriam. They're not *killers* for Chrissakes.'

'Then you explain it,' she said. 'You explain how they came to be playing some weird game, which just happens to match exactly what someone did to the Councilman. You saw it Brandon. The post, the rope, the way your Mom's hands were tied. It was the *same.*'

I shook my head, over and over. Just thinking about it was making me feel like I wanted to throw up. 'No, no, no. There's something wrong. There has to be.' I spotted my laptop. 'Wait a minute.' Grabbing it, I started searching.

I searched everywhere. Local news, national, state sites, police department. There was no shortage of information about Councilman Whittingham's death. It was all over the media during the weeks after, and that was several months before we arrived in Brackers Lake. Updates on the police investigation where still appearing on the local e-editions, and social media sites at the rate of one a week. They all covered his death and the efforts of Sheriff Lynch and his team in quite some detail. But nowhere was there any description of the circumstances in which his body was found. What photographs there were of the scene at the time, were all taken after the body had been moved. A couple showed a bag, presumably containing the body before they took it off to the morgue, or wherever they take bodies these days. But none showed him 'in situ' as they say in detective dramas. Kit was right. None of the details that only we two and the investigators had seen, appeared anywhere.

By now it felt like a vice was gripping my heart, and squeezing. Not only was I having difficulty breathing, I was having to work at not bursting into tears. Mom? Dad? Aunt Kate and Uncle Hector? Miriam? What could it all mean? I voiced the questions to Kit.

She gave me a long look, like she was debating whether to say what she was going to say.

'I don't know what it means,' she said. 'But I know what we should do.'

'What?' I said.

'We should tell my Dad what we saw.'

'No way,' I said. 'He'll want to talk to them, and they'll find out what we did.'

'But if someone there, not your Mom or Dad obviously, is the killer, or knows something about the killer, my Dad *has* to talk to them. Don't you see that?'

She was right, of course. But at that moment all I could think about was protecting my parents from everything that would follow if the world learned about their 'secret'. And I didn't even dare think about how Miriam would react if she learned we'd snooped, then gone to the police.

We talked it over for a good while longer. For Kit, it was clear what we had to do. We had to tell her Dad what we'd seen. For me, nothing was clear - apart from not doing anything unless we absolutely had to. Eventually I said, 'I need to think it through. Give me a couple of days to think about it. You never know, if someone gets arrested, we won't have to tell anyone anything.'

The way she looked at me, I knew exactly what she was thinking. *That's a cop-out.* But what she said was, 'Okay. Two days. But if nothing happens, or you can't come up with a better plan, then we go to my Dad, agreed?'

'Agreed.'

We talked some more but no new ideas came and we ran out of things to talk about. We went to bed, shortly after midnight, exhausted by the day's events, what we'd experienced, and all the talking. Kit was sleeping in the spare room - earlier, I'd made a half-hearted bid to my parents she could maybe sleep over in my room, but my Mom would have none of it. She's always been a bit prim about such things. So much for that. As I made sure Kit had everything she needed and bid her goodnight, she reached up, put her hand on my shoulder and kissed my cheek. 'Don't worry,' she said. 'It'll all be alright. You'll see.'

I gave her a smile, just to show I appreciated her attempt to gee me up and thought about returning the kiss, but decided against. 'Thanks,' I said. But I couldn't bring myself to agree it would 'all be alright'. If there was some means by which everything would turn out that way, I couldn't see it.

I barely slept that night. First I lay awake waiting to hear my parents come in, which they did sometime around two. My Mom was giggling and my Dad 'shushing' her, the way I remembered from times long gone. I heard them stop outside my door, listening to hear if I was still awake. I lay stock still, not breathing, hoping to God they hadn't drunk so much they'd come in and wake me up and start being stupid, asking questions about Kit, what we'd got up to, whether I liked her, that sort of thing. Thankfully, they didn't. Eventually, things quietened down and I knew they'd fallen asleep. My Mom doesn't take long when she's had a drink. After that I tossed and turned, trying not to think about what had happened, or what might happen in the future. I didn't succeed. All night the images kept coming. Mom, Dad, Aunt Katherine, Uncle Hector, Miriam, Councilman Whittingham. In particular I kept thinking about what would happen in the morning, when I had to face them, what I would say, worrying how I'd stop myself turning a deep shade of red.

It was probably the worst night of my life to that point. As it happened, it wouldn't hold that record long.

CHAPTER 35

MY PARENTS ARE usually early risers. Most days, by the time I make it downstairs they are finishing up breakfast and getting ready for the day ahead. But when we lived in Brooklyn, and after one of their parties, my Mom would often sleep late. Knowing this, I roused Kit intending we'd grab an early breakfast and head out so I wouldn't have to spend too much time in their company, feeling embarrassed as hell.

As it happened, it took me longer to cajole Kit into getting up and dressed than I expected. I had thought, wrongly, she was the sort would bound out of bed soon as she heard the birds twittering. As I waited for her to emerge from the bathroom, I could hear my dad downstairs, already up. When we finally made it to the kitchen, he was at the table, finishing his coffee and toast. There was no sign of Mom, *thank God.*

'You two are up early,' he said, cheerily. Unlike Mom, late nights never seem to affect him. 'I wasn't expecting to see you 'til coffee time.'

I waved out the window, 'It's a nice day, so we thought we'd cycle up to the lake before I see Kit home.'

My father made an, *'I'm impressed'* kind of face. 'Wow. That's a first.' He turned to Kit. 'You'll have to come again Kit. You're obviously a good influence.'

He offered to make us breakfast, but I told him cereal and juice was fine. As I filled our bowls, he asked about our night. 'What did you get up to? Gaming? Movies?'

'Gaming, mostly.' I said. 'And jawing. The usual stuff, you know.'

'Not too much excitement, huh?'

My immediate thought was he knew something and was probing. But when I looked up, his face told me it was just a 'dad' remark. I breathed a silent sigh of relief. Then, because I knew he would be expecting me to, I asked, 'How was your night at Miriam's?'

He didn't bat an eyelid. 'Yeah, we had a nice time. She made us feel very welcome.'

For no reason other than I was interested in what he would say, I asked, 'What was it, just eating and drinking, or did you play party games?'

He was smooth as silk., 'There was a bit of drinking, but not too much. And yes, she laid on a bit of supper. But it was just chat mainly. We met a few people.'

'Anyone you knew?'

'Just some of her friends. No one we'd met before. They were nice. Your mom enjoyed herself.'

I'm sure. But I didn't delve deeper in case he became suspicious.

We were halfway through our cereal when Mom came down. I don't know what I was expecting, but she didn't look much different to normal. A bit the worse for wear maybe, but not as bad as I've seen her. Still waking up, she didn't pay us much attention other than we re-ran most of the conversation I'd had with my father. But I could see Kit was growing uncomfortable. In particular, I could see she was having trouble looking at my Mom, as was I, truth be told.

Soon as we finished eating, I grabbed some slices of bread and ham, along with bags of chips and drink cans to take on our bike ride. As we were filling our backpacks, my Mom said. 'I hope you've had a nice weekend Kit. Give our regards to your father.'

'I will, and it's been great, Mrs Sawyer. Thank you for having me. You too, Mr Sawyer.'

I dragged Kit away before we got drawn into further conversation. As we hopped onto our bikes, I said, 'I'm sorry. That was so embarrassing,' but she waved it away.

'More for you than me I think. It's no big deal.'

'Even so, I'm sorry.'

About to pedal off, she paused to grab my handlebars, look me in the face. 'Hey. I said it's no big deal and I meant it. It's not like I'm going to stop speaking to you or anything.' It was what I needed to hear, and threw her a smile to show I was grateful. 'Now let's just forget about it and enjoy our ride, agreed?'

'Agreed.'

The rest of that morning we spent exploring some of the bike routes heading up to and around the lake. Kit had lived near the lake most of her life and knew her way round like it was her backyard. Bit by bit as the morning wore on, and listening to her like she was one of those country-park audio-guides - *The route marked in red takes you to… If you follow the green route you will come to…'* - the memories of the previous night began to recede. By the time we reached the shores of the lake - around lunchtime - it was like they belonged to a different world, a different time.

We found a quiet little strip of beach where we could rest and eat. It being a Sunday, there were lots of boats on the water - sail mainly, but some motors as well. Most were from Harper's Jetty Marina which is further around the east side from where we were, though every now and then a family in a cruiser came past, doing the rounds of the lake. At one stage we sent a couple of pics, just to let our parents know where we were so they wouldn't bother us. Afterwards, as we lay on the sand, listening to the waves gently lapping, enjoying the sun, eating our sandwiches and looking out across at the boaters enjoying themselves, I came to the conclusion it was one of the most enjoyable experiences I'd had in a long time. Eventually, finished our bit of lunch, I was about ready to pack up and move on, but Kit had other ideas.

'Time for a dip,' she said.

'You must be joking. The water's freezing.'

'Wassup? You some kind of wuss?' She was already pulling her top off. She did it so naturally - no bra - I wasn't embarrassed, even as she stripped down to her panties, though I couldn't help smile. 'Brazen' my Grandma would have called her.

'Last one in's a sissy,' she called, though her having a head start, it was obvious who that would be.

Turning, she skipped across the short strip of sand, waded out a few feet, then plunged forward, disappearing right under before coming up, gasping, flicking her head and whooping. I was already half-intoxicated by the surroundings, but seeing her enjoying herself without a care in the world, I almost fell out of my clothes in my eagerness to join her, though I also kept my boxers on, naturally.

The water was even colder than I'd expected. I gritted my teeth and threw everything into swimming as hard and fast as I could so I wouldn't feel the shock so much. I swam out thirty yards or so then stopped and turned. I tried, but couldn't touch bottom. Kit was looking at me, a mile-wide grin on her face.

'You're fucking *CRAZY*, Kit Lynch,' I yelled.

'So are you Brandon Sawyer,' and she launched herself towards me.

For the next few minutes we played tic-chase around that part of the shore. I've always been a strong swimmer and she looked like she was too, but there was no way she could catch me. We didn't stray out too far. Our first day at school, our whole fresher year had had to sit through the Lake Superintendent's safety briefing about how the cold can catch you unawares and the number of drownings there are every year.

When we were both too exhausted - and cold - to continue, we dragged ourselves out of the water and collapsed, laughing, on the sand. I'd lain there for only seconds, catching my breath and squinting at the sun through the overhanging branches, when Kit suddenly rolled into me and I felt her lips press hard onto mine. I could only lie there, wide-eyed and frozen as I waited for her to complete the kiss. Then as suddenly as it came, she rolled off and lay next to me. She didn't say a word. Nor did I. But as our hands brushed against each other in the sand, our fingers entwined.

Not too much, but enough it meant something.

CHAPTER 36

ROSANNA'S RESPONSE TO Carver's update on Betty Whittingham and Zander Reed was a cautious, 'So you think what happened to that councilman *is* connected with *Her?'*

Carver wasn't sure if she was hopeful, wary, or just tired of the whole thing. The weeks before he flew out, the signs were clear. Rosanna just wanted Megan Crane out of their lives - forever. It was hardly surprising. Three years is a long time to live under a shadow like hers.

'If I'm honest, I'm not sure what to think,' Carver said. 'I guess there must be *some* sort of connection, though it could just be historical. There's still nothing to say she is here, or even alive.'

The long sigh, followed by silence, was something he'd experienced before. Her next words didn't surprise him.

'Will this ever be over, Jamie?'

Something tightened in his gut. 'It will Ros. If I keep digging, one way or another I'll get to the truth.'

'You've been saying that for eighteen months. All those nights at your computer, looking at-'

'That was different,' he cut in. The hours he spent surfing video sites wasn't something he cared to dwell on, however justifiable it seemed at the time. 'I didn't have the photographs then. What I'm doing now isn't just random searching. These are solid leads I'm following up. If it was happening at home and I was SIO, I'd have teams following it all up. Bear with me a little longer Ros. There's *something* here, I can *feel* it.'

The sigh before she moved on made him wonder how much she believed. 'Have you spoken to Sue since you've been there, or thought anymore about Jason?'

'I think about him all the time. But no, I've not spoken to Sue. I'm not sure what to say.'

'Are you having second thoughts?'

Carver hesitated. Two months had passed since his decision to leave Jason in the care of his grandmother rather than pursue custody/adoption further. His reasoning was complex, and nothing to do with not wanting the boy. Whoever his father was, Angie was his mother, and that was good enough for him. But pushing for custody would raise all sorts of questions, not least around the circumstances of Jason's conception. Almost certainly, a custody process would involve DNA tests. Even for him, and certainly for Jason's grandparents, Sue and Paul, just the process, never mind the result, would be tortuous. Paul's heart problems had worsened the past year. There had even been talk of a transplant. Now was not the time to start something that would put him under more pressure. When he told Sue and Paul of his decision, they were grateful, relieved and happy. But since then he had questioned it, several times. The boy was not yet ten. His grandparents were in their seventies. His long-term future still remained uncertain. How fair was that?

'I have second thoughts all the time,' Carver answered Rosanna's question. 'But that's my problem. I can't put it on Sue. That's probably why I've not spoken to her. I need to wait until we see how Paul is.'

'And what about the The Duke?' Ros said. Any more news about him?'

'No,' he said, feeling more guilt swoop in. The night before, talking to Jess, he hadn't even thought to ask if she had witnessed any more 'episodes'. After confessing the lapse to Rosanna he said, 'I'll message Jess and let you know what she says.'

'You should ring her,' Ros said. 'The Duke is like a father to you. He's worth more than a message.'

It made him feel even worse. But she was right. 'I will,' he said. He looked to move the conversation on. 'Is the Bridgewater Hall gig still on?' Only ten days away, he knew her first appearance on stage since things had returned to normal was a big occasion for her.

'Yes,' she said. 'Will you be back in time?'

'I can't say. I might be.' Then, realising it probably wasn't enough he added, 'I'd like to think I will, but it depends what happens the next few days.' Another sigh prompted him to voice the idea he intended to mention before leaving, but never got round to. 'Whatever happens, as soon as I'm back, we'll go away for a few days. A few months ago, before the Lockwood thing, we were talking about maybe getting down to Devon. I've spoken with Dad again and their caravan is free if we want to-'

'I DON'T WANT TO STAY IN A FUCKING CARAVAN IN DEVON, OKAY?'

The force of her response rocked him. 'WHOAAA.' He said. *Where did that come from?* 'I hear you. I just thought-'

'I am sorry,' she said, calming herself. 'But if you want to take me somewhere, take me to Lisbon. We haven't been back there together since we first met. I would love us to go back to Barco Negro, it was such a lovely time...'

'Hey, Lisbon's fine with me. And yes, it would be great to go to Barco Negro. I'm sure they would love to see you back there. You could even sing a set.' Just talking about it, he found himself transported back to the club where they first met. The memory of her sultry performance that night - his first experience of Fado - remained as strong as ever.

'Maybe,' she said. 'I would certainly love to sing there again.'

'Right. Let's do it. Soon as I'm back.'

It had the desired effect. Her mood lightened. 'So tell me. What are you doing when you have some spare time?'

Spare time? What's that? 'Not a lot. It's all pretty boring really.'

'Are you sleeping? You sound tired.'

'Yeah, I had a bit of a late night last night.'

'Doing what?'

'I watched a movie on the cable service.'

'What was it?'

'One of those superhero flicks. I can't remember which one. They're pretty much all the same.' She laughed, low and gravelly. It reminded him of what he was missing. 'And I'm at the sheriff's house for lunch again later this afternoon. That'll take up a few hours.'

'It sounds like you and him are getting along?'

'Yeah, I think we are. His daughter's nice as well. You'd like her, and she'd *love* you, being Portuguese.

They talked several minutes more before he hung up, promising to ring every other day at the very least. At least she sounded brighter than when she answered. And he hadn't actually lied about watching a late movie. It was on in the background while he talked. It seemed Rachel was even more of a night-owl than he thought.

Before turning to review the Whittingham Investigation Log Files that was his task for the morning, he set himself a mental reminder. The next time he spoke with or messaged his parents, he needed to let them know. He would not be needing the caravan after all.

CHAPTER 37

AS WE LAY there - two adolescents trying to work out what was happening - I remember thinking how, despite the previous night's events, I felt pretty much at ease with the world. More than I had in a long time in fact - including that memorable night at Afrid's. And whatever happened in the future, I looked forward to re-living the experience, maybe several times, before the summer ended.

Had I known then that what we had together that morning was never to be repeated, I'd have lingered longer, stayed all afternoon and through the evening. But Kit's Dad had invited the English detective over for lunch again and she had promised she would not be late. We waited while the sun dried us off, then set off again, heading in the general direction of Kit's house.

After more exploring - the geographical sort - we found ourselves close enough to her home, I felt okay about leaving her to make the rest of the way on her own. After making our goodbyes, I turned round and started to head back.

I'd gone less than fifty yards when I heard, 'HEY.' I braked, and twisted round to look back. She was standing next to her bike, smiling broadly, yet at the same time looking somehow a little sad. 'GOOD WEEKEND. THANKS.'

I waved to her and called back. 'WE'LL DO IT AGAIN NEXT WEEK.'

'YOU BET.' Then she turned, mounted up and rode away.

I watched until she disappeared around a bend in the track. For some reason I couldn't explain, I stayed looking towards where I'd last seen her for a while, before remounting and getting going again.

All the way home, I kept seeing her. Towelling her hair in my room the day before. Taking her top off. Diving into the water. Lying next to me on the sand. Pressing her lips to mine. It wasn't until I was within a few minutes of home I started thinking about the reason we took off in the first place. But while I was still unsure about seeing my parents - we would also be lunching soon - it didn't seem as big a deal as I remembered from that morning.

Whatever passed between Kit and I that day, the effect was, other things didn't seem as important as they were before. And as I parked my bike in the garage I realised, I'd barely thought about Miriam all day.

Things continued that way over dinner. To begin with, I was a little uncomfortable, in my Mom and Dad's presence. But as I answered their questions about where we'd been, what we'd been doing, I began to relax. When I told them about us swimming in the lake, they both laughed, though my Mom felt the need to urge caution. 'You be careful, especially with Kit. Don't be doing anything dangerous. You need to look after her.' When I told her I would never do anything to endanger her, she looked at me in a way I couldn't read, before exchanging a glance with my Father, I'm not sure why.

But while I felt better than I had that morning, I didn't hang around, scooting up to my room soon as dinner was finished. There, I spent a couple of hours messaging Kit and catching up on posts from some of my Brooklyn friends, including Afrid. I'd heard less and less from Afrid the past couple of weeks. I knew that since I left, she'd been getting attention from some of the other boys, particularly Bobby Wienstock, who I never particularly liked, but would never dream of telling her. I also had some math homework to finish before school the next day, but I couldn't get into it and decided to leave it until the morning.

Eventually I lay back, put on my headphones, tuned in to my Sixties Play-list, and let the events of the weekend turn through my mind. I was conscious that the next couple of days, I would have to decide what to do about what we'd seen. I hadn't forgotten Kit's determination to mention it to her father, and while I was conscious of the difficulties that might bring to my parents and Miriam, I was coming to accept I probably had little choice in the matter.

But that was all for tomorrow, or the day after. Right now, I preferred to think about other things. Like my day out with Kit, and the enjoyment we'd shared, especially the swimming, and what happened right after. I was on the point of dropping off when my cell beeped with a notification. My first thought was a message from Kit, but when I checked, I came instantly wide awake and sat up. It was from Miriam.

Hi Brandon. Would you be able to come over tomorrow some time after school? Something I need to talk to you about. Bring Kit with you if you like, but no need to mention it to your parents. Just something private, between us. See you tomorrow. X.

I stared at it for a good ten minutes or more, reading it over and over, trying to work out if the words contained some clue as to why she wanted to see me, but which I was missing. After reading it twenty times or more, I decided it didn't. Had it arrived any other time, I'd have assumed it was something to do with her garden, maybe looking for an opinion about some idea she'd had. But coming so close to last night's events, and with the riders that I was not to tell my parents, and it was 'private, between us', it could only be to do with one thing - our visit to her garden the night before.

Suddenly, all the concerns, doubts, fears, and confusions I'd manged to ditch over the course of the day came back in a rush. Thoughts of the pleasant day I'd had with Kit disappeared, replaced by concerns about what was going to happen, why Miriam needed to see us. I almost panicked as I thought about possible scenarios. Had she somehow found out about our visit? Was she angry? Would I have to give up working for her? Was I going to learn something even more awful about my parents than I'd learned last night? Was she going to report us to the police for, what was it Kit had called it, *Tomming*?

All these thoughts and others tumbled around my brain as I turned to pacing my bedroom again, just as I had done after our return from Miriam's. The only thing that seemed clear was, whatever Miriam wanted to talk to us about, my parents were not party to it. Had they been, I would have sensed it over dinner. Eventually I remembered I needed to reply to her message, when I spent another ten minutes typing and deleting as I swung between a simple, 'OK', and trying to extract further information without reflecting the panic I was feeling. Eventually I settled on. 'Sure. No problem. See you tomorrow.' I gritted my teeth as I hit hit 'send', then waited, hardly daring to breathe, to see what might come next, if anything. Five minutes later my cell beeped in my hand. It was a simple, *Thnx'* with a smiley face.

My mind turned now to whether to let Kit know. Her mentioning Kit told me she wanted her there, in which case maybe I ought to give her some warning. But it was coming on nine o'clock. If I told her now, we would end up talking about it through the rest of the night. Neither of us would get any sleep. In the end I decided against. I would tell Kit at school and if she wasn't able to come with me - or didn't want to - I would see Miriam on my own.

For the second night in a row I slept badly, worrying about what tomorrow would bring.

CHAPTER 38

I WAS MAKING my way up the steps into school next morning when Kit appeared at my shoulder.

'Hey you,' she said, smiling. 'Recovered from yesterday?'

Seeing her good humour, I immediately felt guilty. Whatever happy mood she was in, I knew I was about to shatter it. Sure enough, the smile vanished soon as I told her about Miriam's summons.

'Oh crap,' she said. 'What does she want?'

We spent the rest of that morning, whenever the chance arose, speculating about why Miriam wanted to see us, what it may be about. On the way to school on the bus, I had held onto the hope that, being so bright, Kit would immediately come up with some plausible and free-from-worry reason for Miriam wanting to see us that I had completely overlooked. She didn't. Kit had no more of an idea than I did. And as the morning wore on I could see she was as anxious as I was, maybe more so. She mentioned that the English Detective had been for lunch the day before. But unlike last time, she didn't talk much about him. Other things on her mind I guess.

But she was clear on one thing. She would come with me to see Miriam. As if to prove it, she messaged her father to let him know she would be stopping at my house on the way home, asking him to pick her up from there later, though she didn't give a time. He messaged her back ten minutes later to say that was fine.

I don't think I've ever known an afternoon drag as slowly as it did that day, with both of us checking the time every few minutes, casting glances at each other, rolling our eyes in frustration while we pretended to pay attention to what our teachers were saying, when all our focus was on waiting for the end of school bell.

When it finally rang, Kit and I could not get out of there fast enough, not that it made any difference as we had to wait for the school bus to fill up. Then we had to sit in anxious silence as it meandered its way along its homeward route. After the bus dropped us off, we went to my house to drop our bags. Mom was in the kitchen, baking, so we grabbed a couple of cans of cola and some chips, then went up to my room. I messaged Miriam from there to say we were home and could come over anytime. While we waited for a reply, we drank the cola and ate the chips. Ten minutes later, my phone beeped with Miriam's reply - 'Whenever you like' - along with a smiley that did nothing to make me think our meeting would be in any way light-hearted.

We left the house telling my mom we were going to the Mall to hang out for a while, but headed straight across to Miriam's. We found her waiting for us out on the deck, along with a pitcher of iced lemon and a plate of black-bread-cake - not that either of was in the mood for further refreshment at that moment. Whilst she seemed her normal self - amiable, at ease - I sensed something lurking just below the surface, though that could have been my imagination.

'Sit yourselves down,' she said, indicating the chairs we had sat in the previous Saturday morning. We did as asked. 'Would you like some iced lemon?' We both declined. 'Cake?' We shook our heads. I can't speak for Kit, but I know that as I sat there, waiting to hear what

Miriam had to say, my lips were dry and my heart was pounding in my chest. It was like sitting in the Headmistress's office at school, waiting to hear what our punishment was to be for committing some grave breach of school discipline.

Miriam poured herself some lemon, took a sip, then sat back in her chair, regarding us both separately, as if weighing what we might be thinking and how it affected what she was going to say.

I'm not sure what I was expecting as I sat there alongside Kit, waiting to learn the reason we were there, but I've seen plenty of cop shows where the detective interviewing a suspect skirts around the subject for a while, before popping the vital question, 'Did you kill....?' I thought Miriam might do the same and talk first about where I was up to with the gardening, how school had gone that day, that sort of thing. So she pretty much took my breath away when she leaned forward, pinned us with a stare that was suddenly stern and said, 'I want to know what you were doing in my garden on Saturday night, and what you saw?'

CHAPTER 39

CARVER COULD SEE the change in Betty Whittingham the moment she opened the door. His last visit, she had managed to put on a brave enough front to make him feel he was welcome, *and* that she appreciated any assistance he may lend to the hunt for her husband's killer. That willingness to cooperate stayed reflected in her face more or less throughout. The only time it slipped was at the end, when he popped the 'Megan question'. This time, there was no sign of it.

This time there was a hardness about her features of the sort Carver was used to seeing in those harbouring secrets they hoped not to share. Their last meeting was five days ago. Since then, he suspected she would have reflected long and hard on it, wondering when he would return to probe further.

The hardened look also reflected, probably, the fact that as he was alone, there was no point maintaining the front she'd kept up through all her dealings with Matt Lynch. It was why he had suggested that he stay out of this one. 'If the time comes she has to back-track on anything she has told you, it'll be easier if you aren't there.' Eventually Lynch agreed, though reluctantly, and only after some discussion.

But whatever was coursing through Betty's mind as she opened the door to him that Monday morning, she remembered her manners.

Inviting him in with a cordial, 'Good-day to you, Mr Carver. I trust your investigation is progressing?' - *I 'll let you know in half-an hour,* was his unspoken thought.

Showing him through to the comfortable day-room overlooking the back garden.

Offering him tea. 'I have Yorkshire Tea. I believe it's the best.' He stuck with coffee.

Asking how he was coping with the late-summer heat, which he answered by mentioning how temperatures in England are on the rise, as they are in many places.

Courtesies concluded, he got down to it. He wasn't as brutal as he could have been - he still didn't see her as a criminal, and certainly not a suspect, but he was direct enough.

'Thank you for agreeing to see me again Betty. I can imagine you've pretty much had enough of having to answer all these questions.'

'Whatever it takes, *Chief Inspector,* is it? I just want to see whoever killed my husband brought to justice.'

It was the response he needed. 'I'm glad you feel that way. And please, call me Jamie.' As he said it, he passed a wan smile. It would be the last he would deploy that day.

'The last time we spoke, I didn't say much about the reasons I'm here.'

'No, you just said something about a possible connection between Curtis's death, and a case you once dealt with in England?'

Carver nodded. 'I need to give you the full story.'

'Please do.'

Over the next twenty-or-so minutes, Betty Whittingham drank her Yorkshire Tea as Carver told the story that began with the brutal murder of a Preston Escort Girl, Francesca Yap - real name, Soo Lin, followed by the seven further murders for which a man called

Edmund Hart was eventually arrested and convicted. It continued through another series of murders some eighteen months later. This time the victims were all dominatrices, and they were committed by a woman called Megan Crane. She was also arrested, convicted, and sent to prison. Later she escaped and fled to France where, after a fall from height into a lake with a knife buried in her stomach, she was believed to have died. During the story's telling, Carver disclosed some of the details of how the victims died - Hart's, *and* Megan Crane's. He also alluded to the fact that, like Betty, he had also lost people who were close when they fell victim to Megan Crane, and that he and his girlfriend only narrowly escaped becoming victims themselves.

Hearing this, Betty was suitably sympathetic. 'It sounds like you have been through something similar to what I am going through.'

'I did,' he said. 'I still am.' He made sure they had eye contact when he added, 'It never fully goes away, Betty. It never will.' The contact stayed for several seconds.

He concluded his account by telling how, several months ago, he received information suggesting that Megan Crane may not be dead after all, but could be alive and living somewhere in the New York State area, though he refrained from saying what that information was, or the form it took. At this point, he paid close attention to Betty's reaction to this potentially startling news. There wasn't one. She remained, frozen in her chair, her face a blank mask. *And that says it all,* he thought.

His story concluded, Betty took the opportunity to refresh her tea. He declined more coffee. When she returned, he was ready.

'The thing is Betty, the information that brought me here, coupled with what I have learned since, leads me to some conclusions, you may not like to hear.'

'What sort of conclusions?'

Carver noticed her fists balling in her lap.

'I will tell you,' he said. 'But first, let me say this. I know what it is like to carry a secret you are ashamed of. You worry that others will discover it. What they will say, what they will think. You go to great lengths to cover it up, including lying to those close to you. It rarely does any good. Secrets have a way of leaking out. And when they do, you wish then you had been honest from the start. That is especially true when the secret is the sort that could put people's lives in danger. I think you are carrying such a secret Betty. I have dealt with cases in which people were killed the way Curtis was killed. I know that the sort of people who do such things almost always kill again. Which is why I would like you to tell me your secret, before others die, like Curtis.' Finished, Carver sat back, waiting.

As he had spoken Betty's eyes had closed, her lips drawing into a thin line. She stayed that way for long seconds after he stopped. Eventually, she opened her eyes, looked straight at him.

'What sort of secret do you think I am keeping?'

As gently as he could, Carver said, 'I believe Curtis once knew both Edmund Hart *and* Megan Crane. In some way I don't yet understand, I believe his death is connected with the fact he knew them.' He paused as he saw her starting to pale. For a moment, he thought she may be about to faint, but then she recovered herself. He continued. 'I believe you know some of these things already.'

'Tell me,' she said, fighting to stop the shaking Carver could see in her arms from spreading to the rest of her body. 'What leads you to these conclusions?'

'I will tell you,' Carver said, but then I want to you promise me something?'

217

'What promise is that?'

'That you will tell me everything you know about Curtis's involvement with the people I have mentioned-' Carver reached into his document case. '-And this.'

He placed in front of her the photograph showing the group of people sitting in her garden, drinking and laughing. The one in which someone had drawn a ring, in red ink, around a blond-haired woman who to Carver's eyes, bore more than a passing similarity to Megan Crane.

Betty Whittingham stared at the photograph for long seconds. And when she looked up, her eyes were wet with tears.

CHAPTER 40

FOR THE MOST part, Carver stayed quiet as Betty Whittingham delved into her memory banks to recount her story. He didn't want to interrupt the flow with too many questions, so those he asked he kept brief, confined to clarifying details - dates, places, names. Some of the picture she painted fitted with the outline he had begun sketching for himself following his conversation with Jess. But without Betty filling in the blank spaces, he could never have guessed the overall shape. It wasn't clear yet where it would take him, or Lynch's investigation. But it proved he had been on the right path all along. If nothing else, it justified his trip over.

Betty first met Curtis when they were living in New York. At the time he was already making a name for himself as a lawyer, while she was working as a publicist for a publishing company. The way she told it, it didn't take long for them both to fall in love and begin working on building the life they would live together. It was Curtis's open-minded outlook on life as much as his looks and playful character that attracted her. Though he was a New Yorker through and through - he didn't even possess a passport at that time - he had an adventurous spirit that, in later years, would fuel their trips around the Americas, Europe, and other parts of the world. What she wasn't aware of - at least not until after they were married - was what she would come to refer to as his 'dark side'.

In those days, they were both fairly 'uninhibited' as Betty put it, when it came to sex. It was one of the things that drew them together. But Curtis's interests in that direction extended to areas that were not to her taste. 'Kinky sex' was how Betty described them. He even once suggested they sample the 'swinging' lifestyle with some couples they knew. But Betty had been brought up as a good Catholic girl and such things were not for her.

From an early stage in her marriage, Betty suspected that at least some of the many late nights Curtis spent working in his Manhattan law firm's offices were cover for his involvement in activities that enabled him to explore a side of himself Betty had no interest in discovering. What those activities were, exactly, Betty never knew. She was aware that within the firm, there was a group - singles and couples - who shared his interests, and suspected that the late nights included gatherings where those interests were more fully explored. Strangely, she never saw Curtis's involvement in these gatherings as him being unfaithful, not in the sense of having an affair. Curtis was open about what he described as his 'need to explore' and 'to find an outlet for his interests', but he never tried to bully or persuade her to engage in anything she found distasteful. As the years passed and family arrived, they fell into what Betty described as 'something of an understanding'. Every so often Curtis and his work buddies would arrange a night or weekend away, either to watch a baseball game or play golf. When he returned, he would be relaxed and keen to show how much he loved her and valued their life together. She even came to look forward to the little gifts he would bring her - items of jewellery, fashion accessories, stylish lingerie.

But every now and then Betty would fall across something that gave some insight into what his occasional trips away involved. A pornographic magazine, usually

BDSM related. A DVD. 'A Beginners guide to…' book. This was all in the days before everything went online. Curtis owned a camcorder. They used it for family gatherings, holidays, weekends away. One day, soon after one of his 'trips', while looking for the tape of a recent family birthday party, she dug the recorder out and pressed 'play'. The tape inside was not the one she was looking for. It showed a group of people in someone's apartment. A dark-haired woman dressed in a figure-hugging corset and high boots was flogging a blond woman, tied to a cross. Betty switched it off as a soon as she realised what it was. She did not wish to know more. Betty accepted this situation throughout her marriage. None of their family or wide circle of mutual friends ever got to know of it - 'Not even the slightest hint.'

But 'Around four years ago,' something happened that caused Curtis to withdraw from such activities. The trips away stopped, as did the the furtive telephone calls that Betty had come to recognise as precursors to them. At the same time Curtis began to suffer with ongoing anxiety. His blood pressure rose and he started experiencing panic attacks. His doctor prescribed RediCalm. One day Betty went to use their home computer and discovered the browser pointing to the news channel of the UK's BBC website, a feature about the conviction of a British man, Edmund Hart, for the murders of several escort girls. For weeks afterwards, Curtis's anxiety levels remained high, but eventually the crisis seemed to pass and things returned to normal. Betty never knew if Curtis resumed his 'dark side'. If he did he was a great deal more discreet about it than before. But eighteen months later, a similar thing happened. By this time she had learned how to check a browser's history. Curtis had started following the trial in England of a woman called Megan Crane, again charged with several murders. After several weeks, this second crisis also passed. When Betty conducted her own research, she discovered that Megan Crane had been convicted and sentenced to life imprisonment. Neither she, nor Curtis ever spoke of the matter. The next couple of years, Curtis seemed more devoted than ever to his life with Betty. But then, 'around nine months ago,' the furtive telephone calls resumed. Curtis started to get called to attend 'urgent meetings' which he stated were connected to his work as a councilman, but which Betty quickly saw through. But unlike the times when he used to clearly enjoy his 'secret life', this period saw Curtis's anxieties return.

'In the weeks before his death, Curtis was worried to death about something,' Betty said. 'What it was he wouldn't say, but it kept him awake nights.' She tried asking him, several times, what was wrong, but he would never say. The nearest he ever came was, 'Just a problem I'm trying to sort out.' He would not say what the problem was. Around this time, Betty and some of her girlfriends took a weekend shopping trip to New York. When she returned, there were signs that during her absence, Curtis had entertained visitors. Empty wine and beer bottles in the trash. Discarded cigarette butts in the garden. A discreet enquiry with their neighbour revealed that Curtis had, indeed, had 'people round.' 'Men *and* women,' Betty said.

At this point, Carver tapped on the photograph. 'Is that when this was taken?'

She nodded. 'I assume so. There was no other occasion they could have been here.'

'Do you know any of these people?' Carver said.

She took a deep breath, pointed to the man with his back to the camera. 'I think I did meet this man once. If it is the man I'm thinking of, he called on Curtis one day.

They spoke in the garden. I recognised him from old news reports. I think it's a man called Zander Reed. You probably won't know him-'

'I do,' Carver said. 'The baseball coach.'

She looked surprised. 'You *do* know him? Did he have anything to do with Curtis's death?'

'I'm not aware of anything that points to it, but I would like to know what his involvement with Curtis was.'

But Betty knew no more. Curtis's 'garden party' marked the end of her story. A few weeks later he disappeared, only for his body to be discovered after. Carver spent a further few minutes checking there were no other details Betty was keeping back. During a tearful 'mea culpa' that lasted a good five minutes, Betty apologised for not speaking of these matters previously.

'I was trying to protect Curtis's reputation,' she explained. ' Our children, the girls especially, would be devastated to learn their father was ever involved in such things. I was thinking of them.'

Carver reached out, placed a hand over hers. 'I understand Betty. A mother's first duty is always to her children.'

'What will happen now?' Betty said. 'Will all this have to come out?'

Carver mused on it, took a breath 'I don't know. If we can possibly avoid it, believe me, I'll do my best.'

'Thank you,' she said.

'One last thing,' he said. He flipped the photograph over. The first time he had shown her the other side, with the words, 'IT'S HER' written on it. 'Does this mean anything to you?'

He saw it in her face before she said anything.

'I can't be sure. But it looks like Curtis's writing.'

CHAPTER 41

I SWALLOWED, OPENED my mouth to say something. I think my lips might even have moved. But no words came out and as I sat there I realised. I had no idea what to say, or if I did, I was too scared to. It certainly never entered my mind to deny we were in Miriam's garden that night. However she had learned of it, the fact of our visit was not up for debate.

'I'm sorry, Miriam. It was my fault.'

The words came not from me, but Kit. Spinning round, I looked at her, astonished. She was sitting upright, staring at Miriam in a way that reminded me of that time twelve-year old Alvey Suarez squared off against Mr Bateman, the Year Head back in Brooklyn. Before I could say anything, she continued.

'I had this stupid idea we should drop into your party and see what you were all-'

She stopped as she felt my squeeze on her arm. She turned to me. I shook my head, *Don't.*

I turned back to Miriam. 'That's not true. It was my idea. I'm sorry. It *was* stupid, but I didn't mean any harm. Kit didn't even want to come. I made her.'

Miriam nodded, slowly, eased herself back in her chair. 'Alright, so we know who is responsible. What I would like to know is, why?'

I glanced at Kit, looked sheepish, turned back to Miriam. 'Like Kit said, I just wanted to see what was

224

happening at your party, what you were all up to. We didn't mean anything by it.'

Miriam didn't look convinced. 'That's it? You wanted to see what was happening? Do you often go spying on people, "just to see what is happening", Brandon?'

Her words stung. Now she really did sound like a headmistress telling off a naughty student.

'No, of course not.'

'So why this time?'

'Well, I... just...'

'What?'

'I just...'

'*What?*'

'He just wanted to *see* you,' Kit said.

I turned to her, horrified. She shrugged her shoulders, like in, *Well it's true. Let's just say it.*

'What do you mean, *see* me?' Miriam said. 'Why would you want to see me? You see me whenever you come here.'

Right then, I wished a hole would open up and swallow me. I glared at Kit. *How could you?*

'Brandon?'

I turned to meet Miriam's gaze. She looked genuinely puzzled. I felt my face, glowing.

'He *likes* to see you.' It was Kit again.

Oh My God...

'What do you mean, *likes* to see me? Of course he *likes* to see me. I like to see him. We both like to-'

She stopped with her mouth half-open. Just for a moment, her eyes flared wide, like something had just registered. For long seconds, she stared right at me, as if frozen in her chair. I waited to see what would happen, hoping to God it would all end soon. Since first receiving Miriam's message, I had imagined all sorts of possible scenarios as to how things might go when we met. This was worse than any of them. I felt exposed, like I was sitting there naked.

I can't say how long we stayed that way, she staring at me like I was some stranger who had suddenly appeared on her deck and she was seeing me for the first time, me waiting to discover where things would go next, what my fate would be.

But then, as suddenly as when she stopped mid-sentence, her whole demeanour changed.

The stern look disappeared as her features softened, bringing back the Miriam I was more used to seeing. The stiffness in her bearing also disappeared, her shoulders sagging as she fell back in her chair. Her eyes closed and for a few seconds I wondered if she had fallen asleep, or even had some sort of heart attack. When she opened them again, they were looking straight at me. Only this time, the look in her face was different to any I had seen before. There was kindness there, along with understanding and maybe, I thought, forgiveness, though that last may have been wishful thinking. But there was something else there also. Looking back, I find it hard to describe exactly, what that "something else" was. I can only say it was similar to the way my mother sometimes looked at me as I was growing up, usually when I was doing something and I looked up to find her watching me. Eventually Miriam said, 'Oh *Brandon*.' At the same time she gave a kindly half-smile, before closing her eyes a second time, lowering her head and shaking it, slowly and deliberately, from side to side, the way people do sometimes when they realise they've made a mess of something.

Next thing, she took a long, deep breath, raised herself up again, and came back to us. But when she spoke, she spoke quietly and in a way made it sound like she was speaking not to us, but someone else.

'Oh, Brandon, Brandon. Whatever have I done?'

I cocked my head to the side. 'What do you mean? You haven't done anything. It was us who-' I stopped as her hand came up.

There was another pause. I have to say I had no idea what was going on right at that moment. *Something* was, for sure, but whatever it was, it was beyond me. Then she said, 'Never mind. That wasn't a question for you. Let's just go back to Saturday night.' It was like she was resetting herself, after going missing a few minutes.

She cleared her throat. 'Let's leave the *why*. Tell me, *what* did you see?'

To that point in our conversation I had said little. Kit and Miriam had done most of the talking. Now we were at the difficult part, and it was my turn.

'There was a gap in the drapes. We looked through and saw you all... playing some sort of game.'

Another pause, then, 'What sort of game?'

I took a deep breath. 'You were... doing something... with my Mom. She was kneeling in the middle of the floor. My father was... helping.'

She lifted a hand to her forehead, shielding her face a moment. 'I see. And how long were you there... watching?'

I shook my head. 'Not long. Just a couple of seconds. Soon as we saw what was happening, we lit out, ran back to my place.'

'Did what you saw scare you?' She looked almost in pain.

'A little,' I said.

'A lot,' Kit said.

I glanced to my right. *Sorry.*

But if Miriam was angry, or upset, she wasn't showing it. It seemed she was more interested in exactly what we'd seen.

227

'I have to ask…'

'What?' I said.

'Do you, either of you, know what it is you saw?'

'I *think* so,' I said. Kit said nothing. Miriam looked at her before carrying on.

'And what do you *think* it was, Brandon?'

'I think it's maybe something grown ups do when they…' I gestured in a way that was probably pretty meaningless. 'You know.'

She took another long breath. 'You mean something to do with sex?'

'Yeah,' I said, nodding quickly. 'I've seen stuff online that-'

Her hand came up again. 'Yes, I'm sure you have. I understand. And I'm sorry. I'm *really* sorry, Brandon. I'm sure this isn't easy for you to talk about. But there's a reason I need to know exactly what you saw, or what you *think* you saw. You do know, I wasn't hurting your Mom, don't you? It was just a silly game that, as you say, some grown-ups like to play.'

'Yes. I know that.'

'Good. And… have you said anything to your parents about what you saw? Anything at all?'

I shook my head. 'I was going to, but then I thought…'

'Thought what?'

'I thought I'd wait and speak with you first.'

She nodded. 'Good. And I'm glad we've had this conversation. It makes things a little clearer.' She turned to Kit. 'What about you Kit?' Have you said anything to anyone? Your father? Anyone else?'

She shook her head.

'No… but-'

I nudged her. She stopped.

Miriam saw it. 'But… what? You were going to say

228

something?'

Kit and I looked at each other.

'Kit?'

Seeing Kit looking at me, waiting, I realised. We were there now. Whatever it might mean, we were at the point where we had no choice but to carry on. We would find out where it would take us in due course. In that moment I decided I wasn't going to lie about anything. I especially didn't want to make a liar of Kit. The way she was looking at me, I knew she would go with my lead. She was that sort of person. Holding her gaze I nodded. *Okay*. We both turned back to Miriam.

'We wondered whether we ought to say something to Kit's father about what we saw.'

I saw Miriam swallow. 'Why would you think about mentioning it to him? What has he got to do with it?'

We checked each other out again. This time it was Kit who nodded, giving me permission.

'Because.. what we saw here on Saturday night? We've seen something like it, before.'

Miriam seemed to lose a little colour. '*Where* have you seen something like it?'

'In my father's computer files. The ones on Councilman Whittingham's death out in the forest.'

Miriam stared at her, like she was seeing a ghost. 'You've... *seen them*?'

Kit nodded. I did the same.

'Pictures?'

We nodded.

'Videos?'

We nodded.

'And it was similar to... what you saw... here?'

We nodded. I said, 'He was kneeling down. There was a post-thing in the ground. His hands were like this.' I put them, palms together, and held them up and out in front of me.

Like before, Miriam stared at me long, and hard. Eventually she tipped her head right back, sank back in her chair, and let out a long sigh. She stayed that way for what seemed minutes. Again, it looked like she was sleeping. Kit and I looked at each other. At one stage she mouthed to me, *'What's she doing?'*

'I don't know,' I mouthed back. *'Wait.'*

Eventually, Miriam woke up again. To begin with, it seemed like she was stuck in some sort of dream. Slowly, without really looking at us, she rose from her seat to take a few steps past us. She looked half asleep. She stopped at the edge of the deck, looking out over the garden. Her back was to us, but I heard another long sigh escape her.

I don't mind saying, in that moment I was scared, really scared. Not for Kit and I, but for Miriam. Everything about her, everything I was seeing was telling me, something important had just happened. I had no idea what it was, but I had the feeling Miriam was realising it. And that it was going to impact upon her, greatly.

'Miriam?' I said. She turned, but gazing at us like she was half-hypnotised. 'Are you okay?' She didn't answer, but I swear, I saw a tear in her eye. In fact I know there was a tear in her eye because she lifted the back of her hand to brush it away.

What's she thinking?, I thought.

Turning, Miriam came back past us to stare through the windows into the house, like she was taking stock of something. It was a bit like the way people look at something for the last time, they way they do on the last day of a vacation… saying 'goodbye'… I don't know how, but seeing her like that, it seemed like she had suddenly shrunk a couple of inches. Her back was to us again now. We couldn't see her face. I was about to repeat my question about if she was okay, but then it happened again. She changed.

Even as I watched, the lost couple of inches returned as she suddenly stood, tall and straight. She ran her hands down her sides, through her hair, tipping her head back, shaking out whatever was in there.

'RIGHT.'

When she turned back to us, it was the old Miriam again. Confident, in control. I was glad. She returned to her chair, poured herself another glass of lemon, drank it down. Kit and I waited in silence. When the lemon was gone, she turned to us. And when she spoke, she was clear in her words but also firm, and *very* serious.

'I need you to listen very carefully to what I am about to tell you. It may help to explain some things. But then I am going to ask you to do exactly as I say. Can you do that?'

Kit and I looked at each other. I could tell what she was thinking. The same as me. *Depends what you ask*. But before I could voice it, Miriam continued.

'Let me rephrase that. You *must* do exactly as I say.'

Her forcefulness surprised me. 'If we can, Miriam, we will. But... well, what's the big deal? You make it sound like a matter of life or death.'

Miriam stared right at me. 'I'm afraid that's exactly what it could be Brandon. A matter of life and death. Yours, and Kit's.'

I think that moment is the closest I ever came to shitting myself.

CHAPTER 42

MIRIAM WAS TALKING, but I was hearing only half of it. Either that or it simply wasn't registering. My mind was too occupied trying to work out how a bit of juvenile mischief could end up putting our lives in danger. The last few days, I'd had to reappraise several aspects of my life - my parents, Aunt Katherine and Uncle Hector, our life in Brooklyn, my relationship with Kit - now I was having to do the same with Miriam. Who was she? How had those who were there on Saturday night, managed to recreate what happened to poor Councilman Whittingham? And what sort of woman plays those sorts of games in her own home, with others present? As regards the last, my occasional, adolescent, bedroom research did provide me with some ideas, though right now I preferred not to engage with them too much. Miriam wasn't *that* sort of woman. She couldn't be.

She had started off talking about how sorry she was for what we'd seen, and how people our age shouldn't be exposed to such things- 'Especially when it involves your parents,' I remember her saying. She spoke about not blaming us. That we had done nothing wrong or to be ashamed of. The same with my parents. They were good people. I shouldn't judge them. She took pains to tell me I must never do or say anything to make them feel bad about what happened, and that when we were older, we would understand more about 'these sorts of things.' She also went out of her way to make sure we understood that no one had forced my Mom to do anything she didn't want to do. That it was all just a 'silly game'. At this point she must have realised I was only half-listening as she leaned forward to grab my attention.

'You do understand that Brandon? Your Mom wasn't hurt, and she was never in any danger. It was just... a game?'

I nodded. 'I understand,' though I wasn't entirely sure I did. She turned to Kit.

'Kit?'

'Yes Ma'am.'

Next she spoke about what we saw having nothing, directly, to do with what had happened to Councilman Whittingham.

'I promise you,' she said. 'No one who was present in that room had anything to do with his death. Please believe me, I wouldn't lie to you. Can you believe me?'

'Yes Miriam,' we echoed each other.

For myself - I couldn't speak for Kit - I desperately *wanted* to believe her. Given my parents were there, I *needed* to believe her. But I couldn't escape the feeling there was something we either didn't know, or she wasn't telling us. Something that made what she was saying *technically* true, but with an escape clause.

'But you saw what you saw,' she continued. 'We can't get away from that. And I know you think that in view of what you saw in your father's files, Kit, you should tell him. I understand that. And we can't get away from that either, can we?'

'No, Miriam,' we both said. I remember thinking, *Something's coming...*

'There are things happening, right now, I can't tell you about, though I wish I could. They have a bearing on what you saw, and they are to do with the reasons why

233

your lives could be in danger. This is all my fault, so it is up to me to deal with that danger. Believe me, I will never allow any harm to come to you-' She looked at us both. 'Either of you.'

I was about to say something but she carried on.

'But in order to deal with these matters, I need time. Which is why I must ask you Kit, to hold off saying anything to your father yet. I'm not asking you to lie to him. I would never do that. But I do need you to wait until I've done what I have to do before you speak to him. Can you do that?'

I turned to Kit. I could see the conflict in her face. I had seen the sort of relationship she had with her father, could imagine what she was thinking. I had no idea what the 'matters' were that Miriam had spoken of, but, right or wrong, I hoped Kit would agree the time she said she needed. She looked at me. I thought about saying something, decided against. *Her call.*

'How long?' Kit said to Miriam.

Miriam thought on it. 'Wednesday. Evening. Give me to Wednesday evening, then you can, in fact you *must,* tell your father.' As she said it, she looked at me in a way I thought seemed a little sad. As if when Wednesday came, it would affect me - us - in a way I could not yet even begin to understand.

'Okay,' Kit said. She threw me a confirming look. 'Wednesday.' And though I hadn't tried to influence her, I smiled a 'thank you'.

'One more thing,' Miriam said. We both sat up. 'Like I say, I need to deal with certain matters. Hopefully, I will have done that by Wednesday. But until then, you must be careful. Watch out for each other. Don't go anywhere alone, and if you see anything, *or anyone,* strange, stay away from them.' She turned to me. 'The man you saw here last week, the one who spoke to you?' I nodded. 'His name is Reed, Zander Reed. If you see him, stay away from him. Run away if necessary, call 911, but just don't go near him, understand?'

Finally I found my voice. 'Is it him we are in danger from?'

'I can't say any more right now,' she said. 'Just promise you'll do as I say.'

Kit and I exchanged another look. 'Okay Miriam,' we said together.

'Thank you.'

'One thing I don't understand,' I said.

'Yes?'

'How did you know we were here that night? You were all inside.'

She smiled a strange half-smile, shook her head. 'Someone saw you.'

'*Saw us?* But there was no-one-' Suddenly, I remembered. The noise in the bushes. 'So was someone else-'

'That's all I'll say. And it doesn't matter.' She stood up.

I took it as meaning our meeting was over. We both rose. As we did so, Kit's cell beeped.

As she checked it, Miriam stepped into me. Taking my hand in both of hers, she held it to her chest. 'I know there's a lot you don't understand right now, Brandon. But you will one day. Trust me.'

The next thing, she put her arms round me and pulled me in close, hugging me to her, long and hard. I wasn't sure what it was for, or if I was supposed to return it, so I did nothing. In those few seconds, as I stood there, smelling her perfume, feeling her body pressing against mine in a way that made my head swim, I felt a bit of a panic coming on. The way she was holding me, it was like when someone says goodbye. Letting go, she

235

eased back, hands on my shoulders looking at me. Her eyes bore into mine, but in a kindly way. For a split second, I imagined I saw a kind of love there. And despite knowing I was being ridiculous, I felt the same. I was still feeling confused over everything that had happened, the matters we had discussed, but in that moment one thing was certain. Miriam Cole was the loveliest woman I'd ever known.

'My Dad's here, 'Kit said. 'He's come to pick me up.'

CHAPTER 43

WHEN LYNCH FIRST picked Carver up from Betty Whittingham's, he couldn't wait to hear if her story had changed. Carver tried deflecting it until they got back, but Lynch would have none of it. 'Tell me now. What else we gonna talk about? The weather?' Now, ten minutes into his report, Carver was thinking he should have stuck to his guns. Each time Lynch turned towards him, eyes widening on hearing the latest revelation, the SUV wandered from the straight. On hearing that Betty had confirmed the writing on Carver's photographs was her husband's, Lynch seemed to forget about steering altogether.

'*Curtis* sent you the photographs?' he said, incredulous. 'But why?' This time his gaze stayed on Carver.

As the car started to drift again towards the opposing lane, Carver straightened in his seat, gesturing at the road ahead. 'MATT,' he called.

Waking to the danger, Lynch yanked the wheel back. As the car slewed from side to side before steadying, Carver breathed out. For a second, he'd thought he'd lost it. It made him wonder what level of driver-training County Sheriff Officers receive. *Not much,* was his guess. 'Maybe we'd better wait 'til we're back,' he said.

But Lynch still wasn't having it. Rankled, it seemed, that Betty had withheld so much, he needed to hear it all.

'Just carry on. I'll watch the road, promise.'

Carver sent him a last, wary glance, before turning to stare out at the landscape flashing by. Still within the town boundaries, they were driving through a section of forest. Both sides of the road, trees seemed to stretch, endlessly. He used the lull to ponder Lynch's question as to why Curtis Whittingham may have sent the photographs. It was a good one. It had been in his mind since the moment Betty first mentioned the writing looked like her husband's, confirming it when Carver showed her the second photo. So far, he had only one theory.

'From what Betty says, Curtis's interest in the sort of games he used to play with Hart and his friends ended when he learned they were killing people. When he heard Megan had died, supposedly, he probably thought that part of his life was over for good. But if she'd suddenly reappeared here, he may have worried about getting caught up in it all again. If he did, and it ever became known, his life here would be ruined. My guess is he was trying to signal she was back, so someone might come and take her away.'

'So why not just make an anonymous phone call, or send a letter telling you exactly where she is?'

'Not sure. Maybe he thought if he was too direct or gave too many details, someone might work out it had come from him. He could still end up being exposed.'

'So he sent just enough you could track him down?'

'Right.'

The two men exchanged glances. Carver thought Lynch looked doubtful, which was fair enough. It was only a theory. There was still time for others.

'One thing for sure,' Carver said. 'It's brought our friend Reed right into things.'

Lynch's response was to exhale, loudly. At the same time he shook his head, long and slow, still digesting it.

During his lunch visit the day before, Carver had told Lynch what Jess had teased from Tracy about Reed's supposed involvement with Hart and Megan. Not for the first time, Lynch had been sceptical. 'Sounds all a bit too fantastic to me. You sure your partner didn't just fall for a line?' Carver didn't mind Lynch questioning Jess's judgement. There was much about Hart and Megan's world people struggled to get their heads around. But now Betty had confirmed Tracy's story.

'Whatever Reed's involvement is, we've now got a definite connection between Curtis and Megan.'

Lynch nodded. 'But not between her and his death.'

'True,' Carver said. But at least we know we're on the right track.'

'So where next?'

Carver thought on it. He turned to Lynch. 'Tell me again about Curtis's digital records?'

'We never found his cell,' Lynch said. 'But we traced all the numbers in his phone records and eliminated all the subscribers except one. Whoever it was, they called several times in the weeks before Curtis was killed. The number belonged to an over-the-counter burner phone. We tried it again after his body was found, but by then it had stopped working. It was bought for cash in New York. No information on who bought it. It's not been used since.

'So what're the chances that cell belonged to either Megan, or Zander Reed?' Carver said.

Lynch threw him a glance, quicker this time. 'Evens?'

Carver nodded. 'I'd say so.'

'So I say again, where next?' Lynch said. 'Sounds like Betty told you all she knows, but it doesn't take us that much further.'

Carver thought on it. 'I think we need to take a closer look at Zander Reed.'

'That could be a problem,' Lynch said. 'Right now, we've no grounds that would give just cause to arrest him, or even apply for a search warrant.'

'True, but there's nothing to stop us talking to him, is there?'

'I guess not. You want me to find out where we can find him?'

'Yes, but we won't do anything until I hear back from Rachel.'

'Who's Rachel?'

Carver stared out the window. 'Rachel is the granddaughter of the man who helped set up the FBI's Behavioural Sciences Division at Quantico. She's a Forensic Psychologist and right now she's doing research there. I asked her to do some digging on Reed.'

Lynch did a double-take. 'And you *know* her?' Carver nodded. 'Where from?'

Carver kept his voice even. 'We bumped into each other somewhere. She's helped me out on a couple of cases.'

The silence told Carver Lynch was waiting for further details. An English detective knowing a Quantico-based Forensic Psychologist well enough to ask her to do some digging would sound intriguing. *He'll have to wait.*

About to switch subject, he became suddenly aware that the landscape outside had changed. They were no longer passing trees, but had reached a residential area. Forest had given way to expansive grassed lawns fronting sizable houses. It wasn't a route he recognised. At that moment he realised, Lynch was following directions on the car's SatNav. Turning in his seat, he checked-out the houses, the surroundings.

'Where're we going?'

'Sorry, I should have mentioned. We're picking Kit up. She stopped off at a friend's house on the way back from school. He's only just moved here and I've only been here once so she messaged me the location.'

As if on cue the voice said. 'In fifty yards, your destination will be on the left.' Seconds later, as Lynch pulled up in front of a neatly-painted boarded house, elevated, slightly, above the road, it sounded again. 'You have reached your destination.' The screen map showed an address on "Henry Street". At the bottom of the sloping drive was a dumpster full of what looked like garden refuse.

Lynch checked the house against the map, before twisting in his seat to look back over his shoulder. 'Strange, I thought her friend's house was further back. I'd better call her, make sure it's the right place.'

Taking out his mobile, he made the call. When she didn't answer he tried again, same result. 'Damn it' he said, 'It's not connecting.'

The house was on Carver's side. Reaching for the handle he said. 'No problem. I'll go give a knock, see if she's here.'

'Okay,' Lynch said, at the same time typing into his phone. 'I'm sending her a message as well.'

At the bottom of the driveway Carver paused, looking up at the house which seemed quite big with plenty of garden. It wasn't neglected, exactly, but something about it gave the impression it hadn't been kept as well as some of its neighbours in recent times. He recalled Lynch mentioning Kit's friend only just moving there.

Still needs work, he thought, as he set off up the drive.

CHAPTER 44

AT THE TOP of the sloping driveway, Carver found himself level with the downstairs windows where he could see through into a living area. No signs of anyone, he was about to ring the bell when approaching voices sounded from round the far corner. Seconds later, Kit Lynch appeared, together with a boy Carver guessed was her friend. Tall for his age, he had striking black hair and the sporty look of someone who keeps himself in shape. As he took the youth in, Carver tried to remember if he'd maybe seen him somewhere.

Seeing Carver, Kit stopped in surprise. 'Oh, Mr Carver- Jamie. What are you doing here?'

Carver jerked a thumb behind. 'I'm here with your Dad. We weren't sure it's the right house. I was coming to check.'

Remembering her friend, Kit turned to him. 'Brandon, this is Detective Carver, the English detective I told you about? Jamie, this is Brandon.'

'Pleased to meet you, Sir,' Brandon said.

'And you, young man.'

Turning round Kit said, 'And this is Mrs Co-' Seeing no one there, she peered around the corner. 'Miriam…?' She spoke to Brandon. 'She must have gone. She was right behind us a moment ago.'

Brandon shrugged, like it was no big deal, but Kit persisted. 'Should you go tell her Mr Carver is here? She did say she would love to meet him?'

Carver raised a staying hand. Some he'd met since his arrival had tended to 'gush' when they learned who he was, where he was from. He and Lynch still had things to discuss. 'Maybe another time, if that's okay?'

'Oh,' Kit said, a little deflated. 'Okay.'

As they made their way down the drive together, Carver said, 'So this isn't your house Brandon?'

'No Sir, I'm just helping the lady who lives here with her garden. Kit's been helping me out.' He pointed down the road. 'I live across the street.'

As they passed the dumpster, Carver said, 'This is all yours then? Looks like a lot of work.'

Brandon nodded. 'The house was empty for a while before she moved in. The garden's a bit of a mess.'

'I can imagine,' Carver said.

At the bottom of the drive, Lynch, was hanging out the SUV's window. Brandon waved at him. 'Hi Sheriff Lynch.'

Lynch raised a hand. 'Hey Brandon.'

The youngsters turned to each other, speaking in low but earnest tones as they made their goodbyes. As he waited, Carver looked back over his shoulder, half-expecting to see Brandon's employer hurrying down, eager to meet her 'English Detective.' As he did so, a movement at an upstairs window caught his eye, a woman's figure, taking a step back from where she must have been standing, watching. Too far away to make out detail, Carver caught a glimpse of blondish hair framing a pair of sunglasses. Even as he saw her, she stepped back further. *Not that interested then.*

'Let's go Kit,' Lynch called.

''Kay, Dad. Speak to you later Brandon.'

As Kit's friend crossed behind the SUV to the other side of the street, Carver got back into the car, Kit climbing in behind. 'Seems a nice lad,' he said.

'He's okay,' Kit said.

'She's sweet on him,' Lynch said, smirking.

'*DAD*.'

As they pulled away, Carver smiled to himself. Right now, a ray of brightness in the gloom was most welcome. But even as Lynch launched into interrogating his daughter over her day, Carver's thoughts returned to matters he and Lynch were still to discuss. Top of the list was Zander Reed.

And as his mind turned inward, and the world outside shrank, he paid no attention to the bronze SUV they passed parked further down Henry Street. Nor did it register when, after they had travelled some distance along, it pulled away from the kerb, and followed in their wake.

After taking Kit home, Carver and Lynch planned to resume pulling apart what Carver had learned from Betty. But a call from a City Hall official complaining about a mis-handled fraud allegation involving a local alderman and demanding Lynch look into it as a matter of urgency forced a postponement. Diverting to drop Carver at his hotel, they arranged to meet again early next morning. It actually suited Carver. He had calls to make, and besides, an evening's reflection would help lend some perspective to their deliberating.

Back in his room, Carver showered, then rang room service and put in an order for the Rib-Eye steak he'd seen on the room menu, at the same time hoping the reality would match the picture. Then he poured himself a generous Macallan which he enjoyed while waiting for his meal to arrive and mulling over what his visit to the States had brought so far.

Some progress, but nothing concrete, was his conclusion. .

After eating, he rang Jess to let her know that with

244

Tracy's help he had cracked Betty Whittingham's story, and at least now had a firm connection between Megan Crane and Bracker's Lake. Jess was eager for details, insisting he re-hash much of what he'd recounted to Lynch on the journey back. She was particularly interested to hear Betty's revelation concerning Zander Reed.

'Hell,' Jess said. 'So Tracy was right about him?'

'Maybe,' Carver said. 'I'll talk to Matt tomorrow about what we do about him. Like I told him, if nothing else, it shows a connection between Megan and this area. I just need to figure out what it is.'

They spent a while, speculating over Reed's involvement, if any, but getting nowhere, Carver switched tack to ask how her 'Six' enquiry was going. She sat up.

'Couple of interesting developments,' she said. 'We've found a spot of blood on a victim's bracelet that was missed first time. We're checking for DNA, see where it takes us. Also, it turns out two of the victims were both treated for mild psychotic conditions in the past. Separate hospitals, doctors, etc., but it's a connection, of sorts. We're looking at the others' medical histories, but so far it's just those two.'

'It's progress, Jess. By the time I'm back, I'm sure there'll be more.'

About to ask after The Duke, a 'caller waiting' notification flashed onto his screen.

'I've just remembered I'm supposed to call Rosanna. I'll ring again tomorrow, see how The Duke is, catch up on other things.'

'I thought you said you spoke to her yesterday?'

'I did, but she's got a gig coming up. She's hoping I'll be back in time for it. I promised to keep her updated.'

'Hmm, well given your past form, that's probably no bad idea.'

'Exactly.'

After ringing off, he clicked the 'missed video-call' notification. Rachel answered immediately. She was in her apartment, wine glass in hand and wearing what he'd have described as pyjamas before someone invented 'lounge-wear'.

'I was talking to Jess,' he apologised. 'Any news?'

'Lots,' she said. 'Have you got a drink, and are you sitting comfortably?

The previous Saturday they had spent half an hour catching up before Carver moved on to explain the reasons he was stateside. Initially, she was scolding he hadn't let her know about his trip, but soon reverted to default mode - piss-taking. But when he eventually got round to mentioning Zander Reed, her mood changed. Sitting up, she turned serious. 'If there's the slightest chance he's involved, that would be Big News for some people.' She rang off soon after, promising to do some digging and get back to him.

Now, it sounded like she had made good on that promise. 'Hang on,' he said. After pouring himself a refill, he settled back on the bed. 'What you got?'

'A soon-to-retire FBI Special Agent by the name of Amos Wells.'

'Never heard of him. Who is he?'

'He's the guy who was tasked with looking into Reed's past activities and involvements, especially with kids, after his trial collapsed. He's spent a good part of the past four years in a basement room here at Quantico compiling dossiers on him. There're rumours it involves sex-trafficking, amongst other things. I'm meeting him tomorrow, but from what I've heard so far, I suspect you'll want to talk with him so if he's agreeable, I'll set up a video call for Wednesday morning.'

'You mention 'other things'. Any idea what they are?'

'I won't know until tomorrow, but I suspect it'll involve all those nice, creative pastimes you seem to like to get involved in. You know, BDSM, snuff, on-line porn, that sort of thing.'

'Thanks. Nice to know that's how you see me.'

'Hey, it's your case history, not mine.'

Carver shook his head. Her face gave nothing away. He still couldn't tell when she was winding him up.

'What else have you heard, *so far*?'

'How long have you got?'

He turned his screen, showing her the empty room.

'Wow. Best-Western? You Brits certainly know how to push the boat out.'

He shook his head again, gave a wry look. 'Just get on with it.'

A sly smile broke. 'You're gonna love this.'

He did, though 'love' was hardly the right word.

CHAPTER 45

I SPENT THE best part of that evening either messaging, or video-chatting with Kit. We were both unnerved by Miriam's warnings and couldn't understand how what we had seen might put our lives in danger. The only thing either of us could come up with - I think it was more Kit than me - was that for all Miriam's assurances that none of her 'friends' were involved in Councilman Whittingham's death, there had to be *some* sort of connection. What it might be, we could not imagine. But her warning about keeping away from the man called Reed I met on her deck kept coming back to me. I'd taken against him from the start, but that was more to do with hearing him back-talk Miriam. He didn't look to me like any sort of crazed killer. But then, what did I know?

As we talked, going over what we saw through the gap in Miriam's drapes, pulling apart all she had told us, I worried Kit might change her mind about delaying speaking to her father. But when we decided there was no point talking about it further - it was close to ten o'clock and we'd run out of questions to throw at each other - she said, 'I guess we'll just have to wait and see what Wednesday brings,' which made me feel easier.

By then I was feeling pretty exhausted by it all - made worse by two bad nights' sleep - so we agreed to call it a night. But about to bid 'goodnight', she hit me with,

'What's with you and Miriam then?'

'What do you mean?' I said.

'That hug. It seemed pretty full-on. I thought you were about to start kissing, or something.'

As I spluttered over what to say - *No, it wasn't-*' - *There was nothing-*' - *It was just a hug that's all,*' I felt myself turning red again. In truth, I didn't know what it was. But the memory of it was still right there in the forefront of my brain. And I was grateful when Kit let me off the hook.

Shaking her head, she gave a wry smile. 'Just remember, Brandon Sawyer. She's twice, maybe three times your age.'

'I know that,' I said.

'Right, well don't you forget it. See you tomorrow.'

After she'd gone, I spent some more time thinking about Miriam's hug, trying to work out how I felt about it, what it meant - and why Kit had felt it necessary to remind me how old she was. When I eventually settled down to sleep, two images kept coming to me.

One was Miriam, holding me in her arms, her eyes boring into mine.

The other was poor Councilman Whittingham, tied to the post out in the forest.

CHAPTER 46

DESPITE OUR VIDEO-chatting the night before, when we met up again next morning, it was like it had never happened. All the questions we'd tossed around re-surfaced, and through the rest of the day we kept going over it all, particularly the bit about our lives being in danger. Several times during lessons, our teachers broke off to ask what we were whispering about. We also kept getting lots of smirks from the other kids in class. I got the impression they could tell there was something wrong, and were enjoying seeing us pair of 'outlaws' all on edge. A couple of times I found myself wishing I could tell them what it was all about, just for the pleasure of watching them freak out.

It was after lunch-break Kit told me she was having doubts about not telling her Dad about what we'd seen, and was regretting her promise to Miriam to hold off doing so until after Wednesday.

'I'm worried it could be important,' she said, 'And that not telling him, might hold back the investigation some way.'

'I get that,' I said. 'And I feel the same. But don't forget, Miriam said she needs time to deal with whatever this danger is she thinks we are facing. I think we should let her do that before we do or say anything to anyone.'

'I've been thinking about that,' Kit said. 'It doesn't make a whole lot of sense. If our lives are in danger, then wouldn't the best thing be to tell my Dad? He's Sheriff after all. If we need protecting from something, or someone, then isn't he the exact person we *should* speak to? I don't understand what it is she thinks she's going to do? She's not a cop or anything so what *can* she do?'

I shook my head. They were all good questions, and I couldn't answer any of them. Nor could I fault her logic. All I knew was, we had promised Miriam. 'It's just one more day,' I said. 'Give her the time she needs, Kit, please, just for me.'

The look she gave me, I could see she was struggling with it. But eventually she sighed and shook her head. 'You better be right about this Brandon Sawyer. I have this horrible feeling we're making a big mistake, and that your precious Miriam Cole isn't quite the person you think she is.'

I was tempted to object to the 'precious' comment, but seeing she had given in to my request, I let it go. I wish now I hadn't. It may be that had we talked it through some more then maybe, just maybe, I'd have come to realise that Kit's instincts were dead right, and mine were all wrong.

That afternoon, we travelled home together on the school bus. As it drove away after dropping me off, I stood at the stop, watching her waving to me through the back window.

I'll always remember that wave.

Especially in light of what happened next.

251

CHAPTER 47

CARVER'S EARLY MORNING meet with Lynch didn't work out. As Lynch told him later, his delving into the City Hall official's 'mishandled' fraud enquiry had uncovered a catalogue of 'procedural errors' which kept him in his office through the morning and into the afternoon. Over that time, a procession of deputies paraded in and out, each giving an account of the part they played in what Lynch soon realised was a potential 'shit-storm' in the making. If he didn't get a grip on it, and quickly, his chances of re-election the following year might suffer.

Carver understood when Lynch rang to apologise for missing their meet. 'Do what you got to do, Matt. Let me know when you're ready.'

It meant he was free to call Jess. It was good timing. Alec Duncan was with her. And they were talking about the subject he'd called to discuss - The Duke.

'There's been another episode,' Jess said.

'What's happened?' Carver said.

'I'll put you on speaker. Alec will tell you.'

For the next few minutes Carver listened as the Scottish DS he'd worked with even longer than Jess recounted the story he'd been relating when Carver called. The day before, Alec had driven The Duke to a meeting at Manchester Police Headquarters. Coming away, they passed the Old Trafford Stadium, the internationally famous home of Manchester United Football Club.

'The Duke was in the back,' Alec said. 'I saw him looking at it, but a bit strange. I said to him, "Always impressive, eh?" or something like that. He just said, "Who plays there then?" like he'd never seen it before. I thought he was joking, but then realised. He didn't have a clue.'

'Ahh, Christ,' Carver said. He felt his stomach flip. A life-long United supporter, up to a couple of years ago, The Duke had held a season ticket. 'And what happened? Did you tell him?'

'Aye. At first I tried to make a joke of it, and made out we was seeing it from a difficult angle. I said, "Well it's not City is it?" but when that didn't click, I just said, "Man. United" straight off. I was watching him so hard through the mirror I nearly crashed the bloody car, but best I could tell, it took a good while for it to register. Then he just went, "Course it is," then sat back and didn't say another word all the way back. He went straight up to his office and stayed there an hour with the door shut. When he came out he seemed normal again. I tell yer, it creeped me out. The guy's jus' not right, you ken?'

'We know Alec,' Carver said. 'Jess and I have seen a few things the past weeks. Jess will fill you in. Soon as I'm back, I'm going to speak with his daughter then, depending what she says, with him. In the meantime all we can do is watch his back. We don't want anyone spreading any rumours until we know what's going on.'

'I'll watch him,' Alec said. 'But I wi'dna be too long getting back. I dunno what you and the lassie seen, but I heard a couple of the team the other day, talking about him forgetting someone's name. They were just taking the piss and no one made anything of it. But if there's a problem, you can bet your arse it won't be long before they spot it. You know what they're like.'

'Message received Alec. I'll try and speed things up here best I can, starting today, though I'm not sure how easy that'll be.'

Jess chipped in. 'On that subject, any more on our friend Reed?'

Carver brought her up to date with Rachel's information and his scheduled call with Agent Wells the following day.

'Sounds interesting. Let's hope whatever he's got on Reed can help you unlock a few doors.'

'That's what I'm hoping.'

Ten minutes later, Carver stared out of his hotel room window, seeing nothing. The news about The Duke was worrying, to say the least. And being three thousand miles away from the man who had mentored him through a good part of his CID career right at the time he might need him, weighed on him. But right now there was nothing he could do. The investigation logs he was still wading through were on the table next to him. Turning, he did his best to lose himself in them.

It was heading into evening when the two men got back together. Carver found Lynch wound tight as a drum, his internal-affairs-type investigation and the fall-out taking its toll. His enquiry into the suspected fraud case had ended only late that afternoon, with him having to suspend a long-serving deputy, Natalie McGrath, for not properly recording the original complaint in what he judged was a 'misguided' - for which read, *corrupt* - attempt to shield the suspected fraudster. The man in question, it turned out, was her husband's uncle.

Carver spent the first half-hour talking him down, at the same time commiserating over his having to suspend a colleague. Carver's empathy wasn't just show. He'd had to do the same on three occasions in the past. He fully expected there would be more. Eventually, after two coffees, both laced with something from a bottle from Lynch's bottom desk drawer, they returned to the subject of Curtis Whittingham, his involvement with Edmund Hart and Megan Crane's former New York City circle, and Zander Reed. When Carver shared with him some of what he had learned from Rachel the night before, Lynch seemed glad to have something else to focus on, other than departmental cock-ups. On hearing of Special Agent Wells's ongoing investigation, he said, 'Reed's still being investigated by the FBI? What for?'

'A number of things by the sounds of it,' Carver said. 'His involvement with kids for one. Possible sex-trafficking for another. I'll know more after my video call with Agent Wells tomorrow. All we can say right now is, if Reed knew Curtis the way it seems he did, it might just put him in the 'possible suspect' category. If nothing else, we can show he has first hand knowledge of the killer's MO through his past involvement with Megan.'

Lynch rubbed his chin. 'Enough for a search warrant at least... Do we know where he is yet? I raised an enquiry after you first mentioned his name, but I've not had anything back yet.'

Carver shook his head. 'I'm guessing that'll come tomorrow as well. As far as I know he's still operating out of his apartment in New York City.'

Before getting into it - it was close to seven o'clock now - Lynch checked with Carver if he liked Chinese food. Then he rang 'The Lakeside Wok' and doubled up on his regular late-working order. 'You'll love it,' Lynch said. 'The Wok's the best Chinese in the state.'

It arrived thirty minutes later, delivered by a freckle-faced youngster whose ginger hair stuck out at all angles under his backwards-facing "YANKEES" baseball cap. Whoever the youth was, he was familiar enough with

Lynch's ordering habits to remark on the extra portions as he handed them over.

'Guessed you had a visitor tonight Sheriff. Either that, or you bin' workin' extra hard and worked up one helluva appetite.'

'Hey, Chad Davis,' Lynch said, smiling. 'You'll make detective one day.' But he made no attempt to introduce him to Carver. Nor did Carver see any money change hands.

'Friend of yours?', Carver said, after the boy had gone.

Lynch looked to the door, before turning a wry face. 'Chad's okay. He's gotten himself into the odd scrape over the years, but nothing too serious. But it's a sad story. He lost his younger sister out at the Lake some years ago. Since then I've had to deal with his parents a few times. His dad's borderline alcoholic with a vicious temper, while his mom's a full-time stoner who does nothing but watch TV 24/7. They were managing not too bad until their daughter disappeared. Since then, they've really struggled.'

'What happened to her?'

'Never found out, not for certain anyways. She was seen paddling the day she disappeared, but she couldn't swim so the likely theory is she got out of her depth and drowned. But as her body never came up, the case is still open.

'Do you get many of those?' Carver said. 'Drownings, but no body?'

Lynch nodded. 'Some. Kids mainly. Maybe one every couple of years? The schools are forever warning the kids how dangerous the lake is, but you know what kids are like. The Lake Stewards say it's not unusual for bodies to stay under and never come up-'

'Tell me about it,' Carver said.

'Oh yeah,' Lynch said, realising. 'I forgot. Your lady friend. But anyways, we do our best to look for them, but it's a big water out there.'

Carver nodded. 'That's what my French Lake Superintendent friend always says.'

'You still checking with him?'

'Every six months,' Carver said.

'Jeez. I never realised.'

'Let's eat,' Carver said.

As they grazed the contents of what Carver thought was a ridiculous number of food cartons - courtesy of Chad - they set-to identifying as many of the what-ifs and maybes that flowed from Betty Whittingham's reveals as they could come up with. By the time they finished eating, around nine, the list was long enough for Lynch to draw attention, apologetically, to his in-tray. Neglected all day, it was spilling over with reports and case-dockets.

'It's been a long day and there're some things I need to attend to before I finish. You mind if we leave all this until tomorrow then go at it again fresh? I promise I won't bail this time.'

Having started late, Carver would have preferred to work on, eager to know his next step. But he knew what Lynch was feeling. 'No problem. I'll give it some thought while you catch up.'

Lynch called up the late-shift Deputy, Arlan Taylor, to run Carver back to his hotel. When he got there, and reluctant to return to his room - it was beginning to take on cell-like attributes - he grabbed a Macallan from the bar. Finding a quiet corner in the hotel's lounge, he turned to reflecting on his conversation earlier with Jess and Alec about The Duke. He was still doing so twenty minutes later - and on his second Macallan - when his mobile clicked an alert. It was a message from Rachel.

Just come away from meeting Amos. VERY interesting. He's

looking forward to speaking to you. Seeing someone tonight so can't call. Emailed you the video link for tomorrow. Speak then. Have a good night. Xx.

It left him disappointed. He'd been expecting she may call with an update. He wondered about who it was she was seeing, then scolded himself. *None of your damn business.* He ordered up another Macallan before returning to the subject he'd been stewing over when Rachel's message arrived - the same one that had been lurking in his brain most of the day.

It had been his decision to come to the US at this time. No one pressurised him into it. Not The Duke, not Jess and certainly not Rosanna. Just him. And he had taken that decision knowing something wasn't right with The Duke. *Selfish*, he thought. That's what it was. Fucking selfish. And now he was stuck here for a few days more at the very least as far as he could foresee. While the man to whom he owed so much might be in trouble - in all sorts of ways.

'Fuck,' he muttered, and threw back his drink.

Rising from the chair, he made his way to the lift. As he did so, he thought on the factors that had swayed his decision to come. In reality, there was only one.

The word 'obsession' had cropped up in conversation several times during the weeks leading up to his flight. Mainly, but not always, they were with Rosanna. But whoever else had used the word, he knew now they were right. He *was* obsessed. Obsessed to discover if his fears were justified. If the woman whose shadow had hung over him these past three years was alive somewhere. Hiding, shielded, but alive. He'd been obsessed to discover if the photographs that came to him through the post actually meant something, or were someone's twisted attempt to unsettle him, an act of revenge maybe, for her death. It could even just be a stupid hoax, simple as that. Sent by someone whose warped sense of humour ran to imagining his face when he opened the envelopes and studied the contents. The puzzlement. The shock. The *fear*.

'Well ho-fucking-ho, to you,' he said as he pressed the 'Call lift' button, then coughed with embarrassment as he realised the couple already waiting were looking at him, strangely. As they stood there, a whisper passed between them. He just caught the word, 'British…'

Talk about making a bad impression…

Getting ready for bed, he thought about messaging Rachel, out seeing someone, somewhere. He thought about it for almost a minute, He decided against. He didn't need any more mistakes.

He slept badly.

Again.

CHAPTER 48

ARRIVING HOME I tried to avoid thinking about everything that was going on, for a little while at least. I knew that at some point I would have to message Kit, else she would think something was wrong, but I aimed to wait until at least after supper.

My father was still at work, Mom in the office working on her study-thesis, so I went straight up to my room where I logged onto Call to War and played a couple of campaigns against 'West Coast Viper'. The Viper is a regular opponent. Online, he profiles like a kid my age, though I've a sneaking suspicion he's some fifty-year old Chinese playing out of a Bitcoin Mining-sweat shop in Kowloon or somewhere.

My father arrived home around six and we all ate supper together in the kitchen. Things were pretty normal. There was no mention of the weekend. All the talk was around school, how Kit and I were getting on, what was new on Netflix, the usual. At one point my mom mentioned a new Sci-Fi series my Aunt Katherine had recommended, but when I asked, casually, when she had seen her, she became flustered before saying they had 'talked on the phone'. As she spoke, I saw a look pass between her and my father, though they wouldn't have known I saw it.

After supper I went back up to my room, checked my media, glanced at the homework assignments I knew I would not even attempt - I'd think of an excuse later - then decided I ought to message Kit.

'U eaten yet? Wot u up 2?'

I gave it a couple of minutes - she was usually pretty quick - then sent another.

Done any HWork? My hedz not up 2 it.'

Five minutes later I sent, *WRU?*

Thirty seconds later she replied. It sent my head spinning.

BIG PROBLEM Need to CU ASAP. Pop still at work. Can u come NOW? Dont say anything to M+P. Will explain when I C U.

I stared at it for what seemed an age but was probably only a minute. My first instinct was to call her right back and ask what had happened. But I knew Kit well enough to know that a message like that meant that whatever the problem was, it was too important to talk about on a video call. She needed me there so she could explain it face to face, when we could decide what needed to be done. At that point I could not begin to imagine what it was. Her Dad was still at work, so I couldn't see it being anything to do with us hacking his computer files, which was the only thing we'd done that came close. All I knew was, I had to get there, fast, and not waste time asking stupid questions. I messaged her back.

B there 20 mins.

I stuffed a flashlight, my cell, and and some other bits in my backpack, then went and looked out the bathroom window into the yard. Most evenings after supper, my parents mooch around the back yard. Sure enough, Mom was there doing some weeding, while Dad was tinkering with the barbecue he bought when we moved in. I made my way downstairs, then through the kitchen into the garage. I grabbed my bike and left through the side door, where my parents would not see me. As I rode away, I didn't even think about how I'd explain my sneaking away when I got back. All I could think of was getting to Kit and finding out what the problem was.

The sun was going down when I arrived at Kit's. Lights were on upstairs and down, but there was no immediate sign of her. Her Dad's SUV wasn't there, which I was pleased about as it meant we'd be able to talk. I dropped my cycle out front and mounted the steps up to the porch. The screen door was shut but not locked, the door behind, open.

As I pulled open the screen, I called out, 'IT'S ME KIT.'

When nothing came back, I stepped inside. 'KIT?' I stopped, listening, but everything seemed quiet. I hesitated, then went through to the kitchen - no sign - then checked out back in case she was there. Still nothing. Puzzled, I headed back inside and stopped at the bottom of the stairs. I shouted up, 'KIT? YOU THERE?'

The silence threw me. From her message, I'd expected she would be watching for me and come running soon as I showed. Then I remembered her mentioning about wearing her Beats while doing her homework. If she was lying on her bed, plugged in, she wouldn't have heard me. I started up the stairs, but still calling, 'KIT?' as I went. I didn't want to scare her by walking in on her without warning. I stopped at the top of the stairs. Still no sound, but her bedroom door was wide open, the light on. I turned towards it. As I passed her Dad's study on my right, the room was in darkness, the door pulled to, but not fully closed. Stepping through into her bedroom, I said, 'Kit?' then stopped.

I'd expected to see her on the bed. She wasn't there. *What the fuck?*

'KIT?' I shouted, louder this time. 'WHERE ARE

YOU?'

I waited. Nothing. 'Weird,' I said.

I turned to go - she had to be outside - then stopped again.

Scanning the room as I'd walked in, something had caught my eye that my brain was still processing. I turned back to check I wasn't misreading what I thought I'd seen. Crossing over to the dresser, I looked down. On top of all the bits and pieces I remembered from last time was the item I was having difficulty placing. It was a broad-bladed kitchen knife, the blade smeared with bright red, wet, fresh blood.

As I stared down at it, my stomach started doing somersaults. I tried to think of a reason why it might be there that didn't involve something horrible. I couldn't. I started to panic. Turning, I headed out the door to retrace my steps towards the stairs. I didn't have a clear idea where I was going or why, other than maybe checking downstairs again. But as I passed her Dad's office I had the sense something had changed. I was already past the doorway when I realised what it was.

The door was open wider than before.

I slowed, probably thinking I ought to check it out. But before I could even turn, I caught a fleeting glimpse of movement over my left shoulder. The next thing, something connected with the back of my head with enough force to cause me to sprawl forward and down.

The strange thing was, I didn't experience any pain at that moment so much as a sick feeling in my belly and everything starting to spin. I tried to raise myself one more time, but it was no good and I collapsed back down on to my front.

Even before I hit the floor, my eyes closed, everything went black, and I saw and heard no more.

PART III

THE ENGLISH DETECTIVE

CHAPTER 49

CARVER WOKE TO his mobile ringing on the table next to the bed. As he reached for it, he read "Matt Lynch", the time, *06:01*.

'Sorry for the early shout,' Lynch said. 'I wanted to let you know.'

'About what?'

He heard Lynch draw breath and there was catch in his voice when he said, 'Kit's missing.'

'What?' Carver swung himself out of bed, instantly awake. 'What do you mean, "missing"?'

'Just that. I don't know where she is. That kid you met yesterday, Brandon? He's missing as well.'

'Are they with each other?'

'I don't know, but I think they must be. I've been up all night trying to piece it together. She wasn't in when I got home last night, which is unusual. I tried calling her but her cell is off. I thought she might be at Brandon's house so I drove there. When I arrived, they'd just discovered him missing as well. His bicycle has gone, so I'm thinking he rode out to meet Kit somewhere. His cell's also off.'

Carver's mind raced. 'You mentioned she's sweet on him. Could they just be doing what kids sometimes do?' Even as he said it, he knew what the response would be.

'You met her, Jamie. She wouldn't do something like

that. Nor would he, according to his parents.'

'What's your theory?

'Right now I haven't got one. That's what's throwing me. I don't mind saying Jamie, I'm worried as Hell.'

'Where are you?'

'My office.'

'I'm coming in.' He stood up. 'Can you-'

'I'm ahead of you. Arlan's on his way. Should be with you in twenty minutes.' He hung up.

Carver stared at the print on the wall showing a herd of bison roaming on the plains. He could see his face reflected in the glass. Outside, the sun was coming up, early light filtering in. He appeared ashen.

'Bloody Hell,' he said.

The Sheriff's Department was like a hive when Carver arrived. Two deputies were on telephones. A third, Cora he remembered, was on the radio, giving someone directions. He was alarmed to hear mention of search-grids. *Already? Jesus.* Paula Gale was pouring coffee into mugs. She was without makeup, and the hair which Carver had only ever seen elegantly styled, was hanging about her face. He wondered what time she'd got the call. Seeing him, she showed the coffee pot. He nodded. 'Where's-'

She jerked a thumb towards Lynch's office, thrust a mug into his hand as he passed but held onto it, making him turn. As he met her searching gaze she said, 'I hope you're the detective they say you are.' He said nothing, just took his coffee and headed in.

As he came through, Lynch was standing in front of the large scale map on the wall, talking to someone on his office phone.

'I don't know what sort of bike. You need to ask his parents. Hang on, I'll give you their number.' As he turned to rummage amongst papers on his desk, he saw

Carver, nodded a greeting. Carver returned it, waited. Lynch retrieved the phone, read a number off a piece of paper. After a pause he said, 'Foster and Annie... Sawyer. .. No, they said they'll stay at the house... Yes. 461 Henry Street... Get back to me with the bike description. We need it for the search teams.' He hung up.

For several seconds Lynch stayed hunched over, staring down at the the phone, arms locked straight, knuckles bearing his weight. Carver felt his pain. *A missing child. None greater.*

He lifted his head, fixed Carver with a look, started to shake his head. But Carver wasn't about to waste time commiserating.

'Tell me what you know, and where are you up to.'

Lynch straightened, took a deep breath.

Carver listened without interrupting, sipping his coffee as Lynch added to what he'd told him on the phone.

After Carver left the night before, he'd rung Kit about nine o'clock. She was at home, doing homework assignments. She was fine. He told her he would be home around ten-thirty. She said she would wait up for him, as she usually does when he works late. When he arrived home, all the doors were closed and the lights were on, but she wasn't there. He searched the house - everything seemed in good order - then rang her cell, but it was switched off. He'd been trying regularly since, same result. He gave it until eleven, then drove to her friend, Brandon's house on Henry Street in case she was there, though God knows why she would be. He found the boy's parents going frantic. Not long before they had discovered their son was not in his room and his bike was missing. Same story when they tried ringing his cell. His thought at the time was it was a bit soon for them to be panicking. He was still expecting there would be some innocent explanation, like in nearly all missing kid cases. The Sawyers' only thought was their son had gone out to meet up with Kit. She was about the only kid he'd become friendly with since they moved here from New York during the summer. Lynch spent the next three hours scouring the town and likely hang-out places with the night deputy and another he called in, but there was no sign. Around half-two he decided something had to be wrong, and hit the red button. Since then he and his team had been ringing round Kit's school friends - he'd called the school Dean to dig out their details. So far, no one was admitting to seeing them, or had any clue as to where they might be, though one of Lynch's deputies was out checking on a report that both Kit and Brandon seemed on edge yesterday, like they were worrying over something.

'Any idea what?' Carver said.

Lynch shook his head. 'Kit seemed pretty much normal when she went to school. And she sounded fine when I spoke to her on the phone.'

Carver cast his mind back. 'The day we picked them up from that lady's house-'

'Monday. What about it?'

Only Monday? Christ. 'I thought they looked pretty intense as they were saying goodbye. I wondered at the time if something might be wrong, but not knowing them, didn't say anything.'

Lynch checked himself. 'Now you mention it, you may be right. Kit *was* quieter than usual driving home.'

'Might be worth checking with the lady at the house. Could be she saw or heard something.'

'Good idea,' Lynch said. Looking up he called, 'PAULA?' Seconds later, her head appeared round the door.

'I need someone to run an enquiry on Henry Street.

Who've we got?'

Paula pulled a face, looked conflicted. She ran Lynch through what everyone was doing. Arlan was liaising with the school. Cora was ringing round Kit's friends. Chuck was manning the radio, while Dan was fending off the day stuff that was starting to come in. More staff would start arriving after eight, but Arlan and Chuck had worked through the night and would need relieving sometime.

Carver saw where things were going. He'd been there many times. At the beginning of an enquiry like this you need hands.

'If you give me a car, I'll go see her. There's nothing I can do here.'

Lynch checked him. 'You sure? It would be a help. She might just know something. Take the pool car. Paula will give you the keys.'

'Right,' Carver said. About to leave, he hesitated. He hated having to say it, but he knew he had to.

'What's happening at your house?'

'Nothing,' Lynch said. 'No one's there.'

'That's what I thought,' Carver said. 'Someone should be.'

Lynch looked puzzled. 'Who? What for?'

Carver took a breath. *A good Sheriff, but he's not a detective.* He gave Lynch a long look. *Don't make me say it.*

For a moment, Lynch looked blank. Then, slowly, his face started to change, colour draining away. 'Oh Christ.'

Carver nodded, but it was Lynch who put the words to it. 'It could be a crime scene?'

Carver nodded again, reluctant, but firm. 'Get a team out there. Tell them I'll meet them there after I've seen the woman on Henry Street. I'll let you know if she says anything.'

As he left, Lynch was looking grey, glassy-eyed. And as Carver grabbed the keys off Paula and headed out, he remembered how he'd felt the night an out-of-the-blue text made him realise Megan Crane, newly escaped from custody, had Kayleigh Lee's home address. Right now, Lynch would be feeling the same as he did then.

Terrified.

CHAPTER 50

IT TOOK CARVER longer than expected to find his way back to Henry Street. Part of it was morning traffic - same the world over this time of day. Not knowing how the car's SatNav worked didn't help. Eventually he realised his mobile app worked fine, so used that. By the time he pulled up at the house with the skip at the bottom of the drive, traffic had thinned to mainly parents returning from the school run.

Stepping out onto the kerb, he checked his bearings. The Sawyer's house was further down - 461 he remembered hearing the number. Depending what he learned here, he might call there after. No particular reason, but you never know when a knock on a door may bring something. He headed up the drive.

Approaching the front door, there was no sign of anyone. No car on the drive, the detached garage door shut. He rang the bell. After waiting a minute he rang again. Getting no answer, he checked down the side, listening out for anyone in the back garden. Hearing nothing, he carried on down, ready to explain himself should someone appear.

The garden was empty, though he could see where the boy, Brandon, had been doing his chopping and clearing. A raised deck ran around the back half of the house, two sets of sliding doors, both closed, giving access inside. Mounting the steps, he approached to peer through the glass. He was conscious he was now risking giving someone a hell of a fright, but finding Kit and her friend was more important.

The kitchen and living area were empty, like at the front, no signs of life. *Out early*, he thought. About to turn away, something caught his eye. On the wall opposite were two pictures. One was an aerial photograph of a large house in its own grounds, surrounded by tall trees. It could be anywhere, but the house had an English quality about it, though it was too far away to make out detail. The thought came he had seen it, or something similar, somewhere. The other picture was a more modern print-impression of a Paris street scene on a rainy day, the Eiffel Tower looming in the background. *European connections maybe?* Possible, but unlikely. He remembered reading somewhere that less than fifty-percent of Americans even have a passport.

Retracing his steps, he returned to the front of the house. Seeing a side window to the garage, he crossed to it. The glass was covered by grime and dust, but he could see enough to make out the shape of a dark coloured convertible. He couldn't be sure - he couldn't see the marque or any badges - but it had the lines of a Mercedes. But if the car was there, then where was its owner?

For the moment stymied, he decided to try the Sawyers. They may have some idea what, if anything, was on the kids' minds. But as he reached the pavement, another thought came and instead of turning right, he turned left.

It had been a long time since Carver had made house-to-house enquiries. As he turned up next door's drive, memories of days when he did so more regularly flooded back. These days, with so much focus on digital evidence gathering - CCTV, data trails, phone records -

checking with the neighbours doesn't always get the attention it merits. In fact, it's still the easiest and most productive source for an investigator. This time he barely had to wait before the door opened.

The woman looked to be in her seventies. Slightly built, grey, wispy hair that was pinned up in places. The drawn features, deep-set eyes and hawked nose gave her something of a 'wild' look. But the gaze that settled on Carver as she opened the door was razor-sharp, full of scrutiny. His hopes rose. *The sort who sees everything.* Impeccable politeness had to be the favoured course.

'Good morning Ma'am.' He did his best to not sound like he was selling something. 'Sorry to disturb you, but I'm trying to contact the lady next door-' He nodded across the boundary. 'But I can't raise an answer. Would you know where she might be this time of day? Working? Shopping?'

Suspicion clouded her sharp features. 'You a relative?'

He smiled, 'No Ma'am, I'm not a-' He stopped. 'What makes you ask if I'm a relative?'

'You sound like a Brit. Leastways, you sound like her.'

He stared at her. 'She's British?'

The suspicious look deepened. 'Well she's not from round here, that's for sure. But you would know that if you knew her. Who are you? You selling something?'

He shook his head. Suddenly no longer a casual enquiry, he needed to make sure she didn't slam the door. She looked the sort who might watch daytime TV. He'd heard Midsomer Murders was hugely popular in the US. He reached for his warrant card, showed it to her, introduced himself as, 'Detective Chief Inspector Carver.' Her face stayed blank. He continued. 'I'm working with your Sheriff Lynch. We're trying to find the young man who's been helping the lady with her garden. You haven't seen him by any chance?'

Suspicion gave way to wariness. 'Why you looking for him? He done something?'

He shook his head again, played it down. 'Not at all. It's just-' *Bollocks to it.* 'It seems he's gone missing. We're anxious to find him.'

Despite her lack of stature, she drew herself up, as if the news was sustenance to her. *'Missing?* What sort of missing? Something happened to him?'

'We are not sure Mrs... I'm sorry, I don't know your name.'

'Summersby. Henrietta Summersby. And I told that boy to be careful. Now look. Shoulda listened to me.'

Carver started . 'Why would you tell him to be careful? Was there a problem?'

She drew back, as if she'd suddenly realised she was in danger of saying too much. She mumbled something - the only word Carver could make out was "weirdos" - before adding, 'Some people you're best staying away from is all. Like I told him, "cats look beautiful, until they scratch".'

Carver hesitated. *Is she rambling, or is there a story?* 'You're talking about the lady next door? Is there something makes you think she might be connected with him being missing?'

Shaking her head, she started to withdraw back inside, making ready to close the door. 'I don't know. I don't know anything about her. I don't *want* to know anything about her. Maybe you shouldn't either.' The door started to close.

'Mrs Summersby, can I just-'

'That's all I'm saying. I gotta live here. You just go find the boy, detective. You save him.'

The door slammed.

Carver stared at it. *What the..?* He thought about

ringing the bell, trying to draw her back. *What did she know?* But he had seen people like her - old, scared - shut down like that before. Getting them to open up again can take time, and effort. For some reason he couldn't right now explain, his encounter with Henrietta Summersby had left him feeling that time was something he should avoid wasting. Turning, he retreated back down the driveway.

As he crossed the street - the odd numbers were over the other side - Carver was conscious of feelings that had not been there only a few short minutes before. One was a growing sense of urgency. The other was a sense of getting close to something, but not sure what that something was.

CHAPTER 51

LYNCH HAD DESCRIBED the Sawyers as 'frantic' when he called on them, late the previous evening. It wasn't how Carver found them. Their son had been missing for some twelve hours. He expected that by now they would be climbing walls, racking their brains for explanations and theories, full of questions, demanding answers.

They weren't.

If anything, they seemed strangely detached from the fact of their son's and Kit's sudden disappearance. It was, Carver thought as he spoke with them, almost as if they were observing the whole thing from a distance. Anxious to see their son returned to them safely of course - how could they not be? But not so much that they felt the need to influence the course of the investigation, or its eventual outcome. No questioning, no criticism, no seeking of explanations over anything that was happening, just mute acceptance. *No news yet? Okay, but would you mind letting us know when there is?*

He noticed it more or less right from the start, when they seemed content to talk to him at the front door, rather than inviting him in, eager for details of the investigation, how the search was going, what the police were doing - as most parents would be. He even detected what he read as some hesitancy in their responses to his questioning, almost as if they were reluctant to provide any more than the specific information he asked for. Parents of missing children usually fall over themselves to volunteer information - most of it irrelevant - in their eagerness to do anything they can to help in the search for their missing child. The Sawyers weren't like that.

Eventually, discomfited, and a little irked at being made to stand at the door, while dragging information from the pair that might help find their son, he broke off to ask, pointedly, 'Maybe I should come inside while we talk? I wouldn't want to cause any gossip amongst your neighbours?'

Even then, there was a moment when he thought they were about to resist to the point of refusing his request, exchanging concerned glances and turning to look back inside, before eventually inviting him in with a, 'Yes, of course, please, come in.' like it was what they had intended to do all along. As he followed the boy's mother through the house to the kitchen, father following behind, he wondered what lay behind the Sawyers' strange behaviour. *Growing marijuana in the kitchen? Urban terrorists and it's a bomb factory?* But from what he could see, everything was as he would expect in the home of a middle class professional couple. Everything in good order, the house reasonably clean and tidy. No distinctive odours. No signs of weapons.

As Annie Sawyer cleared coffee mugs off the kitchen table and gestured him to a chair, he returned to where they were before he suggested moving inside.

'So you didn't sense Brandon worrying about something yesterday?' As Mother shook her head and Father repeated his, 'No, nothing at all,' Carver checked their faces. He waited for one of them to ask, *Who says he was worried?* Nothing came.

'Everything alright at home?' Carver said. 'No arguments or fall outs recently?

'No, everything's been good,' Father said.

'Problems at school?'

'No,' from Mother.

'Drugs? Drinking? Gangs?'

They both registered shock - more than was needed, Carver felt.

'Good God no,' Father said. Mother nodded to signify agreement. 'Brandon is quite level-headed. He likes sport, works hard at school. He would never get involved in anything like that.'

Carver's thought was they were either born optimists, or just naive. But he didn't challenge it. 'That's good to hear,' he said. So let me ask you this. What do you think has happened to your son?'

Carver didn't intend it as a trick question. He'd asked it of countless victims and witnesses over the years, trying to get a feel for their perspective. But the Sawyers' response was different to what he was used to seeing. Without looking at each other, they both shook their heads before echoing each others', 'I've no idea.'

Had the response come from each independently, at separate times, he may have thought nothing of it. But under the circumstances, both of them present, the natural thing - he had seen it many times - would be to check each other before answering. Just to make sure they weren't contradicting each other, even in an innocent way. That they chose to answer without doing so struck Carver as unusual enough to make him wonder about it. Either, the Sawyers were not as close as he had thus far assumed, being sufficiently independent of each other they saw no need to adopt a 'joint' position on the matter of their son's disappearance. Or they were following some script in which their responses to certain questions were pre-ordained, thus rendering the need for consultation redundant. If that were so, it would point to factors not known to the investigators, and which the Sawyers were, for some reason, not prepared to disclose.

Carver's instincts told him that of the two options, the latter was favourite. *So what's going on?* he thought.

'Does anyone else live here apart from yourselves and Brandon?' he said.

'No, it's just the three of us,' Father said.

'And have you seen or spoken with anyone apart from Sheriff Lynch since you discovered Brandon missing?'

They both shook their heads. 'No one at all.'

Carver nodded, pondering on it. 'The lady whose garden Brandon is working on-'

'What about her?' Father was doing all the talking now.

'I just called there, but she isn't at home. Would you know where she may be?'

The answer from both, again without checking, was a curt, 'No,'

'Have you had any conversation with her about Brandon being missing?'

'No.'

For several seconds Carver just sat, staring at the couple. They neither moved, nor said anything, just waited. Eventually he stood up.

'Okay, I don't think there's any more I can learn here. I'd better get going.'

They followed him to the front door. About to leave, he turned to them. 'You're sure there's nothing else you can tell us? Anything at all?'

'No,' Father said.

'Nothing,' from Mother.

He stepped out. 'We'll keep you posted of any developments,' he said.

'Thank you Detective... Carver, was it?'

Carver nodded, gave a wry smile, then turned and headed down the drive.

He heard the door close, firmly, before he was halfway down the path.

Back in the car, Carver dug out his mobile. Towards the end of his conversation with the Sawyers, such as it was, he'd felt it vibrate in his pocket. He had two messages. The first was from Rachel, confirming the link for his video-call with Special Agent Wells, scheduled for midday. He checked the time. It was coming on ten fifteen. The second was an update from Matt Lynch. *'Meeting Crime Scene Team at my house ten-thirty.'*

Taking one last look back at the Sawyers' house, he started the engine. Lynch's house was off the main road out to the lake. The two times he'd visited, Lynch had driven him there, though he thought he could remember the turn. At least he should have less trouble getting there than he did finding Henry Street.

But as he pulled away from the Sawyers', his mind wasn't so much on finding the route, as who had been drinking from the third coffee cup he saw Annie Sawyer clear away as he entered her kitchen.

CHAPTER 52

WHEN CARVER GOT there, Lynch was out front, talking to a man dressed from head to toe in crime scene gear. Parking behind Lynch's Chevy Tahoe - two black, Ford SUVs in front - he approached the pair. Lynch turned to him as he arrived. Carver could see from his face something was wrong. He recognised the other man as Eduardo Varas, the head of County CSI Services he'd met in Lynch's office. They exchanged nods.

'Eduardo's just briefing me. It doesn't sound good. Tell him Eduardo.'

Varas turned to Carver. 'I've just done an inside sweep so we can plan our examination. There's what looks like blood spotting on a dresser in the front bedroom.' He turned to point up at the window.

'Kit's room,' Lynch said. He was trying to stay in control. Beneath the surface, Carver could sense the panic, waiting to break out.

'There's also some staining, could be blood, on the first floor landing close to an office door-'.

'My office,' Lynch chipped in again. Varas continued.

'There's also a knife in the kitchen sink. It looks like it's been wiped or washed, but there is what I think may also turn out to be spotting on the handle.'

Lynch said, 'Far as I know, Kit didn't do any cooking last night. Besides, she's obsessive about keeping the kitchen tidy and putting things away after she's used them.

She wouldn't leave a knife in the sink.'

Christ, Carver thought. Seeing Lynch struggling to hold it together, he turned to Varas. 'But no signs of major blood spillage, right?' It was the best he could come up with in the moment.

Varas shook his head. 'But we don't know yet if anyone has done any cleaning. If someone's wiped the knife, then-'

'Okay,' Carver interrupted before he added to Lynch's anguish. 'Why don't you just carry on doing what you've got to do, Eduardo? I'll stay here, with Matt.'

Varas got the message. 'Right.' Turning, he headed back into the house. Carver could see more suited figures moving around inside. He turned to Lynch.

'Don't jump to conclusions, Matt. It could be anything at this stage. Let them do their job, then we can assess what may have happened.'

Lynch nodded, gravely, gulped air. 'Yeah. I know the drill, still...'

Carver rested a hand on Lynch's shoulder, gave it a squeeze. Lynch nodded an acknowledgement.

Turning, Carver surveyed the area in front of the house. The ground to the right of the front door, across to the wooden garage and outbuildings, was close-packed hard-core. To the left, closer to the surrounding forest, was a mix of rough grass and bare earth. What looked like a track emerged there from amongst the trees. He wandered closer, scanning the area. He stopped, dropped to his haunches, studying what he'd seen. He called to Lynch, still staring up at the house.

'Did it rain here last night?'

Lynch started towards him. 'I drove through some coming home. Just a shower. Nothing too heavy. Why?'

Carver indicated the patch of ground, the earth softer than elsewhere. In its centre was a patterned impression. 'Did Kit use her bike last night?'

'Not that I know of. She was last on it Sunday, I think.'

Carver checked further, noting the rounded depression near to the pattern. He pointed to it. 'This looks to me like where someone dropped their bike. Did the description of the Sawyer boy's bike come back?'

Lynch nodded. 'Something called a Colorado. Mountain-bike type of thing.'

They checked the tyre impression again. It was wide enough.

'Come to think of it,' Lynch said, 'When he visited here a couple of weeks ago, I'm pretty sure he dropped his bike around here somewhere.'

Carver stood up. 'The CSIs need to mask this off and lift it. It may show Brandon was here.'

'Then where is he now? And where's his bike? Kit's is in the out-building. I checked. So they didn't go off on their bikes together.'

About to respond, Carver felt his mobile vibrate again. Another message. Remembering his scheduled video call, though it was still too early, he checked it. The number - a cell phone - wasn't in his contacts. But when he read the message, he nearly gasped aloud, but just managed to contain it.

If you want to know what has happened to the kids go back to your hotel RIGHT NOW. Wait there. I will contact you. Do not tell anyone. Including the Sheriff. Don't fuck this up.'

He stared at it. Re-read it once, twice, three times.

…Don't fuck this up….

'Something important?'

Lynch's voice jolted Carver out of it. He looked up. Lynch was waiting, curiosity mixing with anxiety. In that moment, Carver was keen to do whatever he could to help the man he had grown to like this past couple of weeks, was even beginning to regard as a friend. He looked back at the screen. The message was still there. It was real.

'It's, er- from my FBI contact I was telling you about,' he said.

'This Rachel?'

'Yes. I'm supposed to video-call her. About Reed. Later today.'

'And?'

'And there's been a change of plan. Something's come up. She wants to do it as soon as possible.'

Lynch nodded. Carver got the impression he was masking disappointment. 'You'd better call her then. It may be important.'

Carver looked at the house, the activity taking place inside, conflicted. 'Yes, but right now this is more important.' *But not if the message is genuine.*

'You can't do any more here until Eduardo and his team have finished. Neither can I. You go see to your call and join me when you're done.'

Carver hesitated, before giving in. 'I'm sorry Matt. I'll be back soon as I can. Remember to tell them to lift that impression.'

'I will, don't worry.' Carver was walking away when Lynch called after him. 'JAMIE.' He turned. 'I meant to ask. How'd you get on at Henry Street? Find anything?'

'Actually, I-' He stopped. *Not now.* 'I'll tell you later. Nothing that's any immediate help.'

'Right,' Lynch said. Turning, he headed back towards the house.

All the way back to his hotel, Carver fretted over whether he was doing the right thing, leaving Lynch at such a critical moment. For all he knew, the message could just be someone jerking his chain. Then again, he'd thought the same of the photographs, and now they were starting to look genuine. And if it *was* genuine, then he needed to know what lay behind it.

Either way, I'll know soon enough.

CHAPTER 53

HAVING MISSED BREAKFAST - bagels and coffee barely count - the first thing Carver did when he arrived back at his hotel was call room service and order a sandwich with fries, with a bottle of Bud to wash it down. He checked the time - eleven forty-five. He had no idea how long he may have to wait for whoever it was to contact so he booted up his notebook and clicked on the link in Rachel's email.

May as well see what this Amos has to say in the meantime.

He found her already logged on, working away on her laptop.

'Glad you could make it,' she said when he connected.

'I nearly didn't.' Before she even asked, he brought her up to date with what had happened. As he spoke, her eyes widened.

'Heck Jamie. Zander Reed's name comes up, then the next thing two kids disappear? That's one hell of a coincidence.'

'That's what I'm thinking,' he said. 'And that's not all. I visited the boy's parents earlier. Something about them seems off. I'm not sure what it is, but the boy does gardening work for some woman nearby. Apparently she-' He paused as a third video feed bearing the name 'Amos' joined. A moment later, a balding, black man with a huge 'walrus' moustache showed on screen.

'Hi Amos,' Rachel said. 'Let me introduce you to Jamie Carver. Jamie, this is Amos Wells.'

They both raised a hand.

'Nice to meet you Detective,' Wells said. 'I've heard a lot about you.'

'Don't believe everything Rachel may have told you,' Carver said. 'She's an Anglophile, and biased.'

'Actually, it's not Rachel I'm talking about. Some of the people here remember when you visited. Seems you made an impression, especially your O'Sullivan Score.'

Carver showed surprise. Six years had passed since his Quantico visit, though he still remembered almost every detail, including the assessment Wells had referred to. Based on Maureen O'Sullivan's pioneering work into lie-detection and the ability of some gifted individuals - 'wizards' - to tell when a person is lying, his high score had caused some excitement, though he didn't think it was *that* special. He said so.

'Don't do yourself down, Mr Carver. There's a much wider understanding of the behavioral aspects of lying nowadays, especially since that cop show, Don't Lie To Me, a few years back. But it's still rare to get as close to the wizard threshold as you did. That was pretty impressive.'

Carver gave a rueful look. 'If that's true Amos, I hope you'll let me use it as an endorsement when I write up my memoirs.'

The FBI Agent guffawed, causing a momentary blitz of static. 'Now that's a book I'll definitely read.'

Eager to move the focus to where it needed to be, Carver said, 'I think Rachel's filled you in why I'm here Amos?' Wells nodded, the smile vanishing in a second. 'So let me bring you right up to date.' As Wells leaned forward, listening, Carver re-ran the update he'd given Rachel. By the time he got to the blood spots found in

Kit's room and the knife in the sink, both Rachel and Wells were showing concern. Carver concluded with, 'I don't know where this is all going, Amos, but right now, I need you to tell me what I need to know about Zander Reed.'

Wells paused, gathering his thoughts. 'Okay, I was going to give you chapter and verse, but in view of what's happened, this is the abridged version.'

Wells spoke for five minutes. Carver was relieved that he stuck to known facts. Brief and to the point, he avoided the kind of embellishments Carver knew some FBI people are prone to. Nor did Wells talk up his own investigatory credentials - another common trait. But despite its brevity, Wells's account was enough to underscore the seriousness of the morning's events.

According to Wells, after Reed's trial on charges of sexually abusing minors collapsed, an FBI review of the case revealed that not only was it badly investigated and prepared, but information appearing to point to a wider historical problem had either been ignored or, in Wells's words, 'swept under the carpet.'. How that had happened was now subject of an internal investigation, the outcome of which, Wells said, was likely to see corruption charges brought against some of those involved in the initial investigation - both police officers and at least one Special Agent, possibly more. Internal, neglect-of-duty proceedings were likely against others. That investigation notwithstanding, Amos, a twenty-year served Special Agent retained for his investigative skills following a partially-disabling gun-shot injury, was tasked with re-investigating every aspect of Zander Reed's activities. His brief was twofold. One, re-examine the matters that had led to the original trial. Two, widen the scope of the investigation to cover those aspects, information and intelligence that had come to the notice of the original investigators, but which appeared to have been ignored, neglected or covered up.

Amos's work was into its second year. Over that time, his team had dug deep into Reed's background as a baseball player, and media pundit. The trouble was, as Amos was quick to declare, the more they dug, the more they uncovered evidence that was not just worrying, but horrifying. It showed that Reed was a sex-addict who followed a perverse, hedonistic lifestyle which included frequenting private sex clubs, organising wild parties, and consorting with prostitutes. As, if not more serious, was the fact it pointed to Reed being a serial child sex abuser, implicated in an expansive network of criminal activity, including sex trafficking - women, men and children. Worse, circumstantial evidence appeared to link him to the disappearances of several children, both in the United States and elsewhere, notably Greece, Albania, and a handful of other northern Mediterranean countries where the recording and handling of such matters is not always as rigorous as it might be. A separate investigation was also underway looking into Reed's business dealings involving well-known TV Sports streaming services and on-line gambling organisations. His connections with high-placed individuals in India and China were of interest to both investigations, particularly the regular gatherings he hosted at his ranch in Virginia, his New York penthouse apartment, and a yacht, presently moored in Boston harbour.

'We're in the process of getting ready to move on him,' Wells said as he drew the threads together. 'There's a meeting next week with the DA's office when we'll be talking strike tactics, warrants and indictments. Our director wants to make sure everything is done right, so that when we finally get him to court, he doesn't walk again.' He summed up. 'As you see, Jamie, Zander Reed is one bad man.'

Carver shook his head, still digesting all he had heard. 'Sounds like it.' He thought about the timing of the DA's meeting Wells had mentioned. 'The trouble is, right now we've got two missing kids. And while there's nothing to show Reed is or may be involved, in view of what you've said about children disappearing, we can't afford to wait until next week. We need to move now. Have you got anything on his recent movements? Do you know where he is right now?'

'Far as I know, he's in New York,' Wells said. 'We've run several surveillance ops on him the past eighteen months, but he knows we're looking at him and he's one crafty bastard. He has security, a big guy he uses for protection, as well as other things. He keeps an eye out and generally makes things difficult. We've plenty of information on Reed's movements, but we've not caught him doing anything we can pick him up for yet.'

'What about visits to the Brackers Lake area? Does that mean anything?'

Wells nodded. 'He ranges all over New York State. He owns a couple of properties around and has friends out that way. I don't know how much you know about New York State Jamie-'

'Not much,' Carver said,

'Well if you did, you'd know it has a reputation for attracting fringe elements who migrate there out of the city. Cultists, fantasists, spiritualist communities, New Age thinkers. The sort we used to call weirdos and whackos, if you get my drift?'

'Right. So he has plenty of contacts hereabouts?'

'Exactly.'

'Would you have anything on his movements over the past forty-eight hours?'

Wells looked doubtful. 'We've not run anything the

past week or so, but I can have a word with my team and see-'

A knock at the door pulled Carver's attention.

'Hang on Amos. I ordered food and it's just arrived. Let me get the door.'

Leaving Rachel and Amos talking to each other, he rose and crossed the room. Digging in his pocket for change while wondering how much to tip, he opened the door.

'Hello Jamie,' Megan Crane said. 'Long time, no see.'

CHAPTER 54

CARVER'S FIRST INSTINCT was to put distance between them. He stepped back two paces, and at the same time brought his hands to waist height, ready - though for what, he wasn't sure. The next thing he did was check her hands. The left was up, hanging on the strap of her shoulder bag. The other was at her side, poking out the sleeve of her tan leather jacket. No signs of a weapon. He switched his gaze back to her face. No wild-eyed stare. No unhinged grin. Nothing suggesting an imminent attack. What was there, was the knowing half-smile he knew so well. He eased down a notch - not entirely, that would be stupid - but enough he could start trying to make sense of what he was seeing.

That it *was* her, he was in no doubt, though there were differences.

The hair was blond, but the style was as he remembered. The line of her mouth had changed slightly, lips not quite as full, nose slightly smaller, forehead a bit higher. But the cheekbones and facial structure were the same. And the eyes... The eyes clinched it. They were, undoubtedly, *Her* eyes. As he marked the changes, he made a mental note to congratulate her saviour, should they ever meet. Former Harley Street surgeon, Sir Richard Hayhurst - it could be no other - had done an excellent job reversing the bloody devastation wrought on her in Paris by the mad priest, Father Alonso. Less than six feet away, he detected no scarring, though make-up could be playing its part. If Hayhurst ever got his licence back and decided to start up again, she would make a great testimonial.

For long seconds, Carver stood like a statue, staring at her.

Eventually she said, 'You could at least say "Hello"? Or, come on in…? Nice to see you, maybe?'

The sarcasm lost on him, he opened his mouth to speak. No words came out.

'Oh for *fuck's* sake.' She stepped forward, causing him to jump back. She saw it, gave a pitying look. 'Get a grip Jamie, I'm not a ghost.'

As she turned to close the door, he dodged around her to grab at it. Leaning out, he checked the corridor both ways. No one. He shut the door, turned to her. Now in the space she'd just vacated, the fragrance he could never forget hit him. *Shalimar…* Memories stirred. He pushed them away.

As if reading his mind, her mouth twisted into a sly smile. 'Ahh… you remember? I don't wear it as much these days, but I thought I would today, just for you.'

In that moment, the familiar, teasing tone combined with the surfacing memories acted like a trigger. Suddenly, the stupor that was on him drained away, the real world rushing back to fill the void. In the room behind, Rachel and Amos were continuing their conversation. 'I'm not sure,' Rachel was saying. 'I'll ask him when he comes back…' Carver reacted at once. *If they mention something and she hears…*

'Is someone here?' Megan said, looking into the room. She seemed more curious than alarmed.

'NO', he said, too loudly, conscious it was the first he'd uttered since opening the door. Sliding round her, but still keeping her in view, he darted back through. His notebook was on the table by the window. Crossing to it, he showed himself to camera.

'Something's come up. I've got to go. I'll call you later Rachel. Sorry Amos.' He closed the lid before either of them could reply. No doubt Rachel would call him out for his rudeness next time they spoke. But that was for later. Right now... He turned around.

She was in the middle of the room, casting her gaze around his home of the past two weeks. The socks and boxers he'd washed while showering the day before, still lined the window sill. Grabbing them, he stuffed them away in the dresser drawer.

'You don't have to clear up on my account, Jamie,' she said. 'I know what you men are like when you have to fend for yourselves.'

Carver could barely believe what he was hearing. The admonishing tone. The haughty manner. The flippant sarcasm. They were as he remembered during those first weeks they 'worked' together, before everything changed. Looking at her now, it was as if everything that came after - Angie's murder, her attempt to kill him and Rosanna, the night she escaped from prison, the horrors of Paris - had never happened.

He straightened, gathering himself, took a breath. 'What...?' His first attempt hoarse, he tried again. 'How did...?' *Still no good.* 'Why are you..?'

'AH,' she jumped on it. 'Finally. He speaks. Why am I here? Is that what you were about to ask? That's a very good question. And one I will be happy to answer. But first, what is there to drink around here? How about we toast our happy reunion, then we'll get into it?' She looked where to sit, chose the end of the bed.

As she made herself comfortable, Carver could not take his eyes off her. The past year and more he had thought often on what might happen when and if they

295

ever met again. He had imagined all sorts of dramatic scenarios. Unexpected confrontations. Hectic chases. Violent struggles. Hate-filled caterwauling as she was hauled off to custody somewhere. What he had never imagined, *could* never have imagined, was them sharing drinks in some hotel room, while he worried about his laundry on show. About to say something, he changed his mind.

He crossed to the mini bar. *I don't believe I'm doing this.*

As he opened it, she twisted round to peer in. 'No Cointreau? *Humph.* Never mind, Bombay Sapphire will do. And slimline tonic if there is one. I have to watch my figure these days.' She patted the stomach that, to Carver, looked no different. 'Not as mobile as I used to be since… well, you know.'

As he poured their drinks - Macallan for him - his eyes stayed on her as she appeared to check out the room, the view from the window. All the while a teasing smile played about her lips and she kept glancing his way, as if making sure he was watching.

How long has she planned this?

Handing her her drink, he crossed to the chair where, a few moments before, he had talked with Rachel and Amos about her friend, Zander Reed. Over the initial shock now, his reasoning abilities were starting to return. It had taken this long as he needed to satisfy himself she wasn't there to kill him. Another day, maybe, but not today. Nor was she there to surrender herself to him, of that he was certain. If it were to ever happen, however unlikely, it wouldn't be like this, quietly, in some come-day-go-day hotel room. It would be somewhere special, somewhere that *meant* something. The top of the Empire State Building. The steps of the Capitol Building. The Eiffel Tower. But not here, not now.

So if not to kill him, or give herself up, then why *was*

she here?

He drank his whiskey, letting its soothing warmth settle him. As calmly as he could he said. 'Right. So tell me. Why?'

She smiled, still in mischievous mood. 'Before I do, *you* tell *me*.' She struck a coquettish pose, lifting her head, angling it, like she was some model and he was the photographer. 'What do you think?' Turning her head, this way, then that, she pressed a finger to the skin at the base of each cheek.

Inside, Carver squirmed - *this is ridiculous* - but tried not to show it. 'Very good,' he said, 'Your friend Richard did an excellent job.' As he said it, he tried to let go his first thought. *Still beautiful...* But his attempt to wring something from her came to nought, her response giving nothing away.

'It *is* good isn't it? I have to say, I was really pleased.'

Carver shook his head. She could have been asking his opinion of a new dress.

She switched tack. 'But enough about me. How are you Jamie? Are you over me yet?'

He shook his head again, sipped his whiskey. 'Don't,' he said.

She feigned innocence. 'Don't what? I'm just asking how you are.'

He breathed deep. 'Just... don't. I'm fine. Thank you for asking.' All the time he was thinking. *What's her agenda? Where's this heading?*

'And Rosanna? How is she doing? Is she still singing?'

He stared at her, saying nothing, wondering how long he would have to wait. He had seen her like this before. Playful, mischievous. She would keep it up all afternoon if he let her. But after watching his silence a few moments more, her face changed, the levity disappearing.

'Oh, you're no fun. Whatever happened to the Jamie Carver I used to know?'

'You killed him, remember?'

She nodded, almost regretful. 'Ah yes… that.'

'That,' he repeated. He was in no mood for games, had no time for them. She needed to know it.

She lowered her head, looked at him through her lashes. 'That was just business Jamie, You do understand that, don't you?'

I understand you tried to kill me and the woman I love, you crazy…

'Yes Megan. I understand.' He paused, drawing it out. 'Now, playtime's over. Just tell me. Why are you here?'

For seconds more, she continued to pout her displeasure, though he had no idea how much was real, and how much was for effect. *Ever the actress.*

Eventually she said, 'Oh alright then,' and stood up, so fast he panicked, thinking the attack was coming and rose with her, surprising her to make a, 'what's with you?' face.

Feeling foolish, he sank back in his seat, took another drink. *This is doing my nerves no good.*

She stood in the middle of the room, hands on hips, turning on a heel, like she was thinking on what to say. It surprised him. She wasn't usually so hesitant. Finally, she turned to him, fixed him with a look.

'I need your help-' He started. It was the last thing he expected. 'And you need mine,' she finished.

Carver's brow furrowed. 'What help? What are you talking about?'

She took a deep breath.

Was that emotion?

'Your two missing kids.'

'What about them?' Before she could answer,

realisation hit him. '*You* sent me that message?'

She looked at him. 'Well who do you think?' The question was rhetorical. She carried on. 'Their lives are in danger and you need to find them, quickly. I can help you do that.'

He eyed her suspiciously, remembering her liking for subterfuge and surprises. 'How do you know they're in danger? Were you involved in their disappearance?'

She shook her head - *Is that a tear?* - 'But I know who was.'

He hesitated, unsure if he should say it. He let his instincts guide him. 'Does this involve Zander Reed?'

She rocked back, surprised, but recovered quickly. 'How did you know?'

He hesitated. *Ah, fuck it.* 'Tracy.'

Her head went back. 'Of course. The lovely Tracy. I'd forgotten... Is she well?' He nodded. 'I'm glad. I do miss her...'

Seeing her starting to drift, he pulled her back. 'Tell me about Reed.'

She refocused. 'What do you know about him?'

'Not much. I was about to learn more when you knocked on my door.'

She spotted his notebook. 'Of course. Your friends in the FBI?' He nodded. 'You know he... likes young people?'

'So I believe. He sounds one sick bastard.'

'Believe me, he is. But if you already know about him, that's good. It saves a lot of time.'

'In what way?'

'It means I don't have to waste time convincing you I'm telling you the truth. And also that we can get on and do what we have to do?'

'And what's that?'

She looked at him as if he was being thick. 'Why

save them of course. But to do that we need to move fast. And by fast, I mean right now. My car's parked outside. We can-'

'Whoaaa!' He rocked back in his chair. 'You'll have to give me more than that. You can't just suddenly turn up and expect me to accept what you tell me and forget about why I'm here. What's to stop me arresting you and taking you in, right now?'

'Nothing at all.' Suddenly, she was the old Megan again. Strong, determined - scary. 'But if you do, you'll never see those kids alive again.'

If she intended her words should chill him, it worked. Carver stared back at her, mind racing, weighing what he'd heard. Through all their dealings, he'd come to know one thing. She didn't do bull-shit. If she said something, she meant it.

'I don't understand,' he said. 'What's your stake in all this? Whatever happens, you know I can't let you go afterwards?'

She nodded, never so serious. 'I know.'

'Then… why?'

There was the briefest hesitation, then she said, 'Because Brandon Sawyer is my son.'

CHAPTER 55

CARVER STARED AT her.

'Your... *SON?*'

She nodded.

'You're his... *Mother?*'

She gave him a look. 'That's usually how it works.'

'Good... God...' Carver didn't so much say the words as breathe them. Too much to take in sitting down, he rose, started pacing. 'Does he know you're... his mother?' Even just saying it seemed somehow wrong.

'No, and I intend it will stay that way.'

In his wildest dreams, Carver would never, *could* never have imagined *she* was someone's mother. Had she declared her intention to join a convent and become a nun, the surprise could not have been greater. He shook his head, re-stating the fact as if to embed it in his consciousness. 'You've a *son.*'

Impatience started to show. 'Oh, come *on* Jamie, it's not *that* difficult. YES. I've a son. A child. I'm his MUMMY. Is it so hard to believe?'

He looked at her. *Fuck, YES.* But he just shook his head, still reeling from the successive surprises. Answers would help.

He started with, 'If you're his mother, then who are the couple purporting to be his parents?'

'The Sawyers are not *purporting* anything. They *are* his parents. Just not his *natural* parents.'

301

'But why would you-'

She raised a hand, as if sensing what was coming. 'Look. It's complicated. I know you've probably got a thousand-and-one questions right now, but none of them will take us to where we need to be. Just take it from me. I'm his mother, and I'm not about to let anyone hurt him, or his friend.'

But Carver's mind was still racing. He needed firm ground to start rebuilding his understanding. If she is Brandon Sawyer's mother, and the lad is fourteen.... He worked it out. Back then she was... He read the timescale. His gut crawled.

'His father...'

'Ye-es?' She read his face.

'His father must be...' He couldn't bring himself to say it.

She nodded, regretfully. 'Edmund.'.

Carver couldn't help himself. 'Fu-cking *HELL*.'

An image of the boy he had met only the day before came to him. A pleasant looking lad. Jet black hair - *of course it is*. Polite, smiling. Hard working by the look of it. The spawn of two serial killers. *My God*. He could even be Jason's step-brother.

Another thought came. The house where he and the boy met. The one he'd revisited just that morning. The one with the neighbour who thought the woman living there spoke like him. He remembered when the kids appeared around the corner. Kit had turned to address the owner but she had gone. What was it she'd said? 'Mrs Co-something?' followed by, 'Miriam?' Dominoes in a line.

The woman at the window.

The *Mercedes* in the garage.

The house just down the road from her son.

The aerial picture on the wall showing a house

302

surrounded by trees. Of course it looked familiar. He'd been there. Just never seen it from above.

You slow, stupid bastard.

'Brandon's working on *your* garden.'

Another nod, resigned now, but still impatient. 'Look this isn't helping. We need to-' This time it was his hand came up.

'Just give me a moment. This is… a lot to take in.'

She waited, hands on hips, foot tapping. She sat on the end of the bed again, watching him digest it all.

He thought about what he knew. She came here because there were people she was once close to. The likes of Curtis, presumably the Sawyers, and of course, her son. Somewhere in all of this, there was Zander Reed. Then Curtis is killed. By whom, her? Unlikely, too obvious. So who? Reed? He needed more. He turned to her.

'Right. I know things may be urgent-'

'*Are* urgent.'

'*Are* urgent. But I need you to… You need to just tell me what's going on. What's the background to all this? What's happened to the kids, and how is Reed involved?'

For a moment it looked like she was about to resist, but then the change in her face signalled acceptance. He wasn't going to do anything until he knew more. She took a long breath, gathering thoughts, then began.

'You know about what happened to Curtis, right?' He nodded. 'A few nights ago, I had some friends round to my house. We were playing some… games.' She paused, as if waiting for him to ask. He didn't. He could guess. She continued. 'Apparently, Brandon and Kit had sneaked into my garden. It seems they managed to see us.'

'*What*? Ahh, *Jesus...*'

'What they saw… If Kit ever told her father, it would draw attention. He would start asking questions…

303

about Curtis.'

'Stop there. What *did* happen to Curtis?'

She looked conflicted. *Whether to tell?* But again, no choice. 'Zander Reed killed him.'

Carver looked at her, still unsure. He hesitated to ask, but had to. 'Were you involved?'

The denial was swift and vehement. 'Absolutely not. He was my friend. I was horrified when I heard about it.'

'So why did Reed kill him?'

She gave another long sigh, everything loaded with regret now. 'I need to explain about Reed.'

'Go on.'

'I take it Tracy told you about Reed being involved with Edmund and I, years ago?'

Carver nodded. 'She told Jess.'

At mention of Jess's name her face lit up for a second, but she carried on. 'I always knew Zander had a 'thing' for me. I assumed it was just a fetishistic crush, you know? The way some people are?'

Carver nodded again. If it was aimed at anyone in particular, he ignored it.

'I was wrong. It wasn't a crush. It's a full blown infatuation, obsession more like. Reed thinks he's in love with me. What's worse, he's convinced himself the feeling's mutual.'

'Is it?'

'Are you crazy? The man's unhinged. He's a complete creep. A dangerous paedophile, and a whole lot of other things I could tell you about, only we haven't time.'

'I get the picture. So why did he kill Curtis?'

'I came here to be near Brandon, and people like Curtis, and the Sawyers, all friends from years ago. They all helped me settle here. So did Reed, truth be told. I wish now he'd never found out I was back. He thinks I returned because of him. He's completely delusional. I didn't know at the time, but after I arrived, Curtis started to worry I would draw him back into the sorts of things he gave up years ago. He said something to Reed about wishing I had stayed away. Whatever it was, Reed thought he was considering giving me away to the police, even you. You need to understand, Jamie. Reed sees himself as my self-appointed guardian angel, there to protect me against all threats. He decided Curtis was a threat that needed removing. So he killed him.'

'But why that way? It was bound to draw attention.'

'I guess he thought it would send a signal to others. Deter anyone else from betraying me.'

'Like who?'

'I've no idea. Like I said, he's crazy.'

'You sure you didn't tell Reed to kill him?'

'Are you listening? If I'd known about it, I'd have stopped him. I'd have spoken with Curtis and sorted it out. None of this would have happened.'

Carver shook his head, beginning to see the picture emerging. He thought about Curtis, hesitated. *What the hell. It makes no difference now.* Reaching for his jacket, he produced the images that had brought him, showed them to her. It brought a gasp.

'Curtis sent you these?' Carver nodded. Her surprise gave way to sadness. 'Poor Curtis. So it was all for nothing. Reed was too late, the bastard.'

Carver touched the garden photo. 'I can see this is Curtis, but who are the other couple?'

'Old friends of the Sawyers. Katherine and Hector Bauer. I met them years ago. So did Curtis.'

'When you were with Edmund?'

She nodded.

Another question answered, Carver paused, letting what he'd heard so far settle. He was conscious he only had her word for any of it, yet it rang true. Once more, he let his instincts dictate.

'Okay, that's Reed and Curtis. What about the kids?'

'It's the same thing. Reed knows they saw us that night. He thinks Kit will tell her father, he'll put two and two together and I'll be discovered. Reed's taken them to stop it happening.'

'How did he know the kids saw you?'

'Turns out he was doing what they were doing, spying on me, only he calls it 'watching out for me.' He only told me all this on Monday, but I could see what was already in his mind. I knew at once the kids could be in danger, so I got him to promise to hold off doing anything until I spoke with them. That was why they were at my house when you called there on Monday.'

'What happened after you spoke with them?'

'I had hoped that if they hadn't seen too much, we might still be okay. Unfortunately that wasn't the case. They know enough about what happened to Curtis, they'd already spotted the connection. I knew Kit would have to tell her father eventually, so I just asked her for a bit of time while I planned what to do next.' As Carver sighed and shook his head - *what a mess*- a guilty look came into her face - the first he'd ever seen. She carried on.

'I realised after, I could never get Reed to agree to leave them alone, especially after he told me he'd seen you coming away from my house with the girl and her father. It left me with only one option.'

'Which was?'

'Well it's obvious isn't it? I have to kill him.'

The matter-of-fact way she said it sent a shiver up Carver's spine. *But that's what she does...*

'So why didn't you?'

'I didn't get the chance. We were supposed to meet later today to talk about it, but he must have already made his plans and put them into effect last night. I only heard when the Sawyers rang me after the Sheriff called there looking for Kit. I've been calling Reed's mobile all day, but it's switched off.'

Carver's mind went back to the Sawyer's kitchen. The third coffee cup. 'You were there. When I called there earlier.'

She nodded. 'We were talking about what we should do. I hid out the back while you spoke with them. After you left, I realised what I needed to do, so here I am.' She breathed deep, as if strengthening her resolve. 'Reed's taken them Jamie, and I've no doubt he plans to kill them, if he hasn't already. Our only hope is, knowing him, he will want to have his fun with them first. They've been gone less than a day. There may still be time, provided we move fast.'

Even as she spelt it out, Carver felt the responsibility for saving Brandon and Kit's lives settling on his shoulders. It was not where he expected to find himself when Lynch rang early that morning. His mind went to the youngsters, stashed away somewhere. He thought about Matt Lynch, what he was going through, and the Sawyers. He understood now her rush to do what needed doing.

'Right, first question. Do you know where he'll have taken them?'

'I think so. He has a cabin out in the forest. I stayed there a while when I first arrived here, while they were sorting me a house.' Her voice lowered. 'I think he took Curtis there, before he killed him.' She paused, hesitant again. 'Also... I think he's had other people... kids, there before...'

He stared at her. 'Does that mean what I think it means?'

She nodded, grimly. 'I've heard all sorts of stories

307

over the years. I understand now why he and Edmund always got on so well.'

He looked about, searching for his mobile. 'I need to speak with the Sheriff. He'll have to jack up a trace and-strike op. I take it you can show us this cabin? Or at least tell us…' The words dried as he saw her shaking her head, slowly and deliberately.

'What…? I thought this is what you wanted? To save the kids?'

'It is, but not that way. We can't involve the Sheriff.'

'What are you talking about? We have to. Why wouldn't we?'

The way she sighed, shook her head again, Carver sensed she had foreseen the problem.

'If we involve the Sheriff, it all becomes 'official'. The story will come out, all of it.'

'So what?'

'So then Brandon will get to know who his real mother and father are. I can't allow that. Can you imagine what it would do to him, having to live knowing his parents were Edmund Hart and Megan Crane? Do you see Jamie? This isn't *just* about saving Brandon's life. It's about saving the *rest* of his life as well.'

He took a moment, then, 'I understand, but if we are to save the kids, I don't see any other options, do you?'

'Actually, I do.'

'What?'

She reached into her bag, drew out a black, short-barrelled .38 revolver, like the one Carver learned to use during his early firearms training. She brandished it before him.

'I am going to take you to his cabin. If the kids are there, we will get them out. Then, while you take them away somewhere safe, I'm going to kill him.'

CHAPTER 56

CARVER HAD BEEN party to discussion around killing people three times in his life. They were all during the course of Chief Officer-approved Tactical Firearms Operations. In each case circumstances made it necessary to include within the operation planning a 'Stop Contingency' - a euphemism for, 'a plan to take the bastard out' in the event things do not go as intended. But he had never come close to talking about killing a suspect in cold blood. He wasn't about to do so now. Which is why he imbued his next words with as much of the authority that comes with twenty-years adhering, broadly, to the rule of law and running 'strike' operations as he could muster.

'Slow down Megan. and put the gun away. This may be America, but it isn't the Wild West. Let's just think things through before we start talking about killing people.'

Her response was an almost patronising smile. The .38 stayed pointing, roughly, in his direction.

'I thought you might take that line,' she said, her tone as measured as his. 'So let me just say this. We don't have time to sit here debating the pros and cons. Unlike you, I've had a few hours to think this through, and I'm clear about what needs to happen. Someone has to get to those kids in the next few hours, or they are dead. So that is what I am going to do. I'm not stupid, I know it will be dangerous. I also know there's a fair chance I may need backup. Right now, the only person I can call on for that is you. I would feel a whole lot better if you are with me, but if you choose not to, or feel you can't, then I'll do it on my own.' At this point she held the gun steady, pointing square at him. 'And I'm not about to let you, or anyone else, stop me.'

Carver looked from her to the gun, and back again. He was in no doubt she meant every word. 'Fair enough. But the two of us rushing off into some forest isn't the way to-' The jerk of the barrel stopped him.

'This is exactly what I wanted to avoid,' she said, focusing her gaze on him. 'So here's what's going to happen. I'm going to tell you why we have to do it my way. When I've finished, you're either going to tell me where I've got things wrong, and I mean *exactly* where I've got it wrong *and* what your alternative plan for saving those kids is, or you will leave here with me, no further arguments. Agreed?'

He hesitated, but knew he had little choice. 'Agreed.'

'Sit down-' she waved the gun at the chair. He did so. '-And listen.' She perched herself on the end of the bed again. He heard the 'swish' of her stockings as she crossed her leg. 'My only aim in this is to see Brandon and Kit safe. Everything else, me, you, Reed, the legal stuff, is secondary. When they are safe, then I'll worry about all that, understand?'

'Right.'

'You're a good detective Jamie, but being a good detective means playing by the rules. The circumstances we find ourselves in mean we don't have time to follow rules. For a start, it would take at least a couple of hours, probably more, just to assemble one of those, what did you call it, 'Trace and Strike' Operations? This is Brackers Lake, not New York City. I don't know much about how county sheriff departments work, but I suspect they don't have SWAT teams hanging around just waiting for a call. Second, as I said, Brandon must *not* find out who his mother is, so whatever happens, it has to stay under the radar. Third, Zander Reed is a dangerous, psychotic and unpredictable animal. Look what he did to Curtis. Any attempt to reason with him the way your negotiators always seem to want to do could easily tip him into harming one or both kids before anyone gets near. Four and finally, the way I see it, to save them someone has to get close enough to take some action. There's only one person Reed trusts enough to allow that, and that is me. Which means I have to be involved. I don't see some SWAT commander allowing that, do you?'

She stood up. 'That's it. Time's pressing, so I'll give you thirty seconds, then I'm out of here, either with or without you.'

Carver's gaze stayed on the barrel pointing at him. When she started talking, he'd weighed the chances of being able to knock it aside and make a grab at her before she pulled the trigger. He chose to listen. During his early training he'd once sat through a lecture given by a retired Detective Superintendent who had carved a niche second career as a 'consultant', advising on emergency response to Major Incidents - disaster, fire, terrorist attack, etcetera. A good part of it focused on a concept then new to Carver - 'Appreciation of a Situation' - which the ex DS insisted on shortening, horribly, to "App-Of-Sit." Devised by the Military to aid commanders in making life and death decisions in the heat of battle, an App-Of-Sit requires that decision makers identify, at as early a stage as is possible, the key objective in challenging circumstances. Having done so, all subsequent options are assessed against that key objective. It the matter under discussion helps achieve it, fine. If not, move on.

Carver thought at the time that the ex-Superintendent was being paid good money to point out that in a crisis, clarity of thought is no bad thing. Nevertheless, there was a core running through it that stuck. Carver had even applied the principle a couple of times he'd found himself under pressure and facing options that seemed to conflict. It boiled down to, *Be clear about what is important from the start. Forget the rest.* Not as impressive as the Det-Supt's 'App-Of-Sit', but close enough.

All this turned in Carver's mind as he reflected on Megan's own 'App-of-Sit' assessment. On-the-hoof, crude, and somewhat light on the 'due diligence' everyone puts so much store by these days, it nevertheless ticked the boxes. And it took him no more than ten seconds, to conclude that her 'key objective' - the safe return of the kids - was, unarguably, the right one. He also concluded that her views on other matters - time constraints, the likely problems around involving others and what some might deem 'acceptable' - were also pretty much spot on. Taken together, it was, he thought, as succinct an 'Appreciation of a Situation' as he had come across. In which case...

He switched his gaze from the gun's barrel, to her. Halfway through the allotted thirty seconds, she was already getting ready to move.

Ahh, bollocks.

'How far is this cabin?' he said.

CHAPTER 57

STARING OUT THE passenger window, Carver was conscious of a feeling he was being pulled in several directions at once.

Foremost was the question that kept coming when he turned his mind from the other 'pulls'. *What the fuck do you think you are doing?* Each time, it prompted the inner-monologue that had played several times since leaving the hotel. *Where do you think you are going? You're a bloody policeman. What do you think you are going to do?* And, *what in God's name made you set out with an illegally-at-large killer on some ill-thought-through rescue mission that could end with someone, possibly you, ending up dead?*

An hour into their journey and despite all the thought he had given to these and other such questions, he was no nearer answers than when they set out. Which brought him to the second 'pull'.

What the *HELL* was he going to do when they got to wherever she was taking them?

Even before they left the hotel - after taking her advice and changing out of his suit into something more suitable for where they were going - he was clear on one thing. Regardless of what Megan's "App Of Sit" told her was the most expedient means of guaranteeing the kids' safety, he was not going to be party to killing anyone unless it was absolutely necessary and there was no other viable option. And by absolutely necessary, he meant circumstances that a court would recognise as providing a defence to a charge of murder. Under English law, that boils down to saving life. He wasn't certain what the American equivalent was, but he was sure there would be one. Certainly he wasn't going to allow her to kill someone just to stop her son learning who his parents were. It may be tough on the lad if he had to find out, but with proper support and maybe a bit of counselling, he would learn to live with it. And while she had, briefly, sketched the broad outline of her 'rescue plan' soon after setting out, key aspects of it remained, by her own admission, 'hazy'. When he sought to pin her down, she kept falling back on, 'Let's see what we find when we get there. We can finalise things then.' It wasn't the sort of planning he was used to, and left him feeling exposed.

Apart from doubts about the wisdom as well as the legality of the enterprise they were embarked upon, there was one other set of 'pulls'. They were very different to the others, and though he was doing his best to resist them, he was finding it increasingly hard.

They concerned the woman driving.

After Paris, it took Carver a good eighteen months to accept Megan Crane was dead - probably. After receiving Curtis's pictures, he spent a further six wondering if she could be alive after all. Over that period, he'd often found himself imagining how she may look if it turned out she had survived. Right now, he was resisting the temptation to compare the face of the woman next to him with the one in his memory. It wasn't easy. Three times since they had set out, he had woken to the fact he was staring at her, the way a student of fine art might study a Goya, or a Renoir, marvelling at the artist's skill. She caught him each time. The knowing look it triggered stirred memories, and left him feeling like the worst kind of lech.

And now I'm doing it again.

314

Turning away before she could catch him, he returned to staring out the passenger window. He couldn't remember at what point he had succumbed to her 'pull'. Outside, the blur of greens, greys and browns that had been the staple of the past hour was still rushing past. Every so often, it broke to reveal an isolated scree slope or water course wending its way down towards the lakes. But the higher they ascended, heading deeper into the forest, the less they featured. Now it was mainly trees, so tightly packed, it brought to mind the forest of Endor, the planet-moon setting for much of Return of the Jedi, one of his earliest cinema memories. He wondered what sort of resident population might live this far out - or was it just cabin-owning 'crazies'? The last he'd seen of any sort of habitation was a store-cum-service station, thirty miles back. "Clanton's Service and Provisions" he remembered the sign. Since then, nothing. It served to show just how big this country was.

And Megan catching him looking, wasn't his only source of discomfort. The car was suffused with her perfume. The cream leather seats were soft and comfortable. The Merc's spec was several steps up from his Golf. If he wasn't careful, the combination could easily seduce him to imagining they were enjoying a pleasant drive in the country. He had to keep reminding himself why they were there, where they were going.

The uniform landscape was also a stark reminder of how isolated he was from the sort of backup that was never usually more than a quick phone call away. Firearms teams, paramedics, comms links, hospitals. The sort of things you hope you won't need, but like to know they are there, just in case. Bad enough he was alone, miles from anywhere, in the company of someone who had once sworn to kill him - and had come close twice.

The reason he was here bore even less thinking

about. True, the ultimate aim - saving Kit and Brandon - was, without question, valid and in line with everything he stood for. But for him, their mission was potentially life-changing in other respects. For starters, he was struggling to think how he might ever convince someone his decisions and actions were justifiable. He had already imagined how his interview with the Professional Standards Investigators may go.

'So tell me Mr Carver, what was in your mind when you, effectively a civilian with no US police jurisdiction, and without reference to any local policing authority, agreed to accompany the convicted and unlawfully at large murderer, Megan Crane, to hunt down and kill a man against whom you had not one shred of evidence he had done anything wrong, apart from third-hand rumour and conjecture?

Worse, if things transpired the way she intended, and Reed did end up dead, then the consequences, for him especially, bore even less thinking about. He wasn't that well up on US homicide law, other than knowing its first, second and third degree categorisations made it less straightforward than Britain's relatively simple murder-manslaughter distinction. But the basic principles were broadly similar. Set out to kill someone, or put yourself on a path where that outcome is a foreseeable possibility and death occurs - expect to do time. For a serving officer, how much time is immaterial. More important is the loss of career, respect, reputation - not to mention pension - and the ensuing disgrace. Apart from anything else, it would probably kill his ex-Chief Constable father.

He hadn't even ruled out it could all just be an elaborate set-up, aimed at finally bringing about what she had long craved - his death. Her story, her reasoning, her 'App-of-Sit', all *seemed* to hang together. Certainly it fitted with the trail he had followed from Curtis Whittingham's death, to her house on Henry Street, the connection with

Reed, and the youngsters' disappearance. But he knew her capacity for deviousness. If she had learned he was close to discovering her and wanted to remove that danger, a bogus kidnapping and threat to the lives of two innocent kids, was just the sort of bait that would lure him to some isolated spot where, alone or aided by someone like Reed, she might finally achieve her objective. It made him think what Jess or The Duke might say if they were there to whisper in his ear.

Stop the car.

Get out, now.

Leave her.

Don't do it.

But then they weren't the ones on whose shoulders the lives of two young people rested. It wasn't them who may have to live with the knowledge they had a chance to save those lives, but chose not to. It was still making his head spin.

Sensing the loop that would ensnare him if he let it, he reached into his pocket, feeling for the new smartphone she had handed him before they left. Already set-up and with her number saved as the only 'contact', it was another example of clear thinking on her part, even before she got as far as knocking on his door.

'Take this,' she had said. 'Leave yours here.'

He didn't need her to explain. Depending what the next few hours brought, there could come a time when it may be useful to show that according to mobile location data at least, he had remained in his room for a period of several hours that day. It was the ploy adopted as routine by even lower tiers of criminals nowadays. *Make your mobile your alibi.* He blamed it on all the TV police dramas, particularly writers' obsessions with showing how up-to-date they are in current investigative techniques. *God help me,* he thought as he opened up the mapping app. to

317

check for a data connection and see where the nearest point of civilisation might be. *Has it really come to this?*

It prompted another thought.

What if it all *was* genuine, and he *did* end up needing backup? What if he *did* need to call Matt Lynch, Rachel, or someone else? The lack of contingencies left him feeling like a tightrope walker with no safety net. Like everyone he knew, Carver relied on his mobile when it came to others' contact details. But his was back in his room. The only number he knew off the top of his head was Jess's, not that he could ever admit that to Rosanna.

As the phone's screen showed the road in front winding through forest, Carver was relieved. At least there was a mobile data signal.

'What are you doing?' she said, glancing across.

'Seeing if there's a signal,' he said, navigating screens, fingering icons.

'And?'

'Looks like there is.' He touched 'send'. A second later a tone sounded from her bag on the console between them.

'What's that?' she said.

'I've sent you a location link as a test. I'd rather know in advance if there's going to be a communication problem.'

She gave a half-smile. 'I see you haven't changed. You were like this the night I met with William Cosworth.'

His response was a quiet, 'Hmmm.' The night she fooled them all - not least Cosworth himself - and left Carver feeling he'd failed her, was one he preferred not to dwell on. If he ever came to write his memoirs, it would not get much copy. Finished playing with the device, he put it away.

'How much further?' he said. Early evening now, the light was beginning to fade, the sun below the hills to their left.

'Not far,' she said. 'Just a few more miles.'

'Great,' he said, easing himself in his seat. 'Can't wait.'

She shot him an amused glance. 'It'll be fine,' she said. She even giggled. 'Don't worry.'

Carver was surprised how relaxed she was. No trace of concern showed in the face that, for all she had been through, still retained much of the beauty that was once her stock-in-trade. Looking at her, he could be some new man she was taking to meet her parents for the first time. He turned back to the window.

What the fuck have I got myself into?

Ten minutes later she slowed, checking the forest to their right. Fifty yards ahead, Carver spied a gap where a road joined. Slowing further, she turned into it, smooth tarmac giving way to unmade track of hard-packed stone and earth. As they bumped along it - it seemed little used - Carver's stomach tightened. *Here we go,* he thought.

He didn't see the small device fixed high up the trunk of one of the trees to his right as they passed. Had he done, and were it darker, he might have noticed the red stand-by light to the side, turn green as they approached, denoting it had woken to do its job.

CHAPTER 58

BREATHING HARD, THE man stepped back from the bed to stare down at the girl's now, limp body. Seeing the bruises and scratches to her skin, he wondered how they compared with his. He could barely wait to see himself in the mirror, when he would enjoy re-living it all.

God, she'd been a fighter. He loved fighters, rare though they were in kids her age, even the boys. Most often, in his experience, they sought safety in compliance. That worked for him as well, but not as much as good old, teeth-bared, no-holds-barred, scratch-your-eyes-out resistance - provided he came out on top of course. Which he always did. His years of training saw to that. Even now, long since stopping the daily regime of weights, aerobics and stretches that helped take him to the top of his chosen profession, his biceps, especially the right, were still exceptional. In that regard, they continued to serve him well. And though he enjoyed it when they did resist, he was yet to meet one that caused him any real problem, until this one.

Surprising her in her bedroom, he assumed the sight of him would terrify her into whimpering submission. That was the usual reaction on seeing the full-face balaclava, the gloves, the all black garb. And this time there was even the knife, though he still wasn't sure what had made him pick it up as he came through the kitchen - some sort of reflex-thing he assumed. As it turned out, it was probably as well. It was only by brandishing it in her face, threatening to slit her throat there and then if she didn't stop, she finally quietened down enough he could cuff her. Luckily, the cuts to her shoulder, hand and arm - accidental as far as he was concerned - weren't too deep, so that by the time he got her wrapped up to carry out, the only spillage was on the bedside rug, which he took with him anyway.

It was also lucky the house was isolated. Her screams must have carried far. Fuck, even he jumped when she let out the first. He guessed it was probably something drummed into her by her father. *If it ever happens to you, holler til your lungs burst,* or some such. Well she certainly did that. In which case, Thank You, Sheriff. The tussle that followed would live long in his memory. Her attempts to break free his grip. Her pressing her lips together to resist the cloth gag. Having to twist her arm right up her back almost to breaking *and* show her the knife to assert control. His only regret was he hadn't been able to record it. Now *that* would have been something. As good as the one of the Greek boy all those years ago, maybe. Or the dark-haired girl from last year, the one with the pretty eyes. She was special too.

Looking at her now - still, quiet, and yes, almost *peaceful* - he felt a pang of regret. It was a shame circumstances didn't allow for the prolonged enjoyment his trophies usually brought. True, she wasn't as much a looker as some. Not in the conventional sense at least. Her hair was too short for a start, though for him, that was not a problem. Most of the boys had short hair as well. But there was something about her - maybe it *was* the boyishness - certainly her feistiness, that would, he was sure, have stood him in good stead in the days, maybe even weeks to come. Never mind, he thought. It was good while it lasted.

But even as he made to turn away, something about the image she presented, the curves of her not-quite-adult body, the way she was lying - arms spread out to the sides, palms showing - worked on him. He stopped, thinking about it. *Fuck it*, he thought. Why not? It wasn't as if she was going to resist again.

About to remount the bed, a vibration in his back pocket stopped him. At the same time a flashing red glow leaked into the room. He knew what it was at once. Turning, he crossed to the half-open door. Sure enough, the alarm-lamp on the wall opposite was flashing its steady rhythm.

Uh-oh. Trouble. Fuck.

His heart started to beat even faster. Which was okay. A little adrenalin might just come in useful.

Taking one last look back at her - *Ah well...* he left the room, shut the door and turned the key, though he left the padlock and chain for later. She was going nowhere now anyway.

Reaching across, he flicked the switch to turn off the lamp before taking out his mobile and checking the screen. As he expected, the Video Door-Bell app was showing the view from the camera out near the road. The stretch it covered was empty now, no sign of any cars or people. Nor could he see any animals, though the adjustments he had made to the settings the week before seemed to have removed that particular glitch. He did not panic to check what had caused it to activate. There was no need. The turn off the main road was a fifteen-minute drive away. He had plenty of time. He touched the 'back' arrow, then waited while the recorded video rewound. At minus two-minutes-thirty-four seconds a car 'reversed' into view, backing to the point where it first came within range of the camera's sensor. Pressing 'play', he studied its approach.

He recognised the Merc at once of course. And though the light was going, the camera's low-light setting meant he had no difficulty seeing it was her. The thought of her coming here after all this time, especially now, brought a smile to his face. He had wondered if she might show sometime, though he hadn't expected it would be so soon. She must have worked out what he had done, and he was in no doubt he would have a job making her see it was for the best. But he was certain that once he explained-

He stopped as the car came close enough for him to realise. There was someone in the passenger seat. A man.

'What the-?'

As it disappeared out of shot, he touched the rewind arrow again. In the seconds he waited, the sinking feeling in his stomach and his thumping heart echoed his first thought. He hoped to God he was mistaken. He pressed play again, but this time waited until the car was right under the camera before hitting 'pause', and zooming in. What he saw caused the elation of a few seconds before, vanish. In its place rose mystified fury.

'*JAMIE-FUCKING-CARVER?*'

He stared at the image for nearly half a minute, trying to make sense of it.

Carver? Here? And with Her?

That it *was* the detective about whom he had heard and read so much he was in no doubt. He had seen enough pictures, watched enough videos, he would know him anywhere, even under these less-than-ideal conditions. As the seconds ticked, his mind worked to reassemble what he knew into some narrative that fitted with what he was seeing. Her on her own, he would understand. But her and Carver together? It could mean only one thing. They had formed an alliance. And he could think of only one reason for them doing so. They were there to stop him. Which led to another conclusion. Whatever she had tricked him into believing about their relationship, their prospects for the future, it must all have been lies. If she really did love him - she had never said the words, but it fitted with everything she had said and done over the years - she would never bring the police here. And as the inevitable conclusions fell into place, like tumblers in a lock, he found words to sum up his disappointment.

'You *traitorous* fucking *BITCH.*'

Turning, he raced back up the steps, cursing and swearing as the realisation of it all continued to settle. By the time he slammed the trap shut, he was almost reeling from the shock of her betrayal, of sensing all his hopes and dreams, crumbling around him. Over the years, the choices he had made concerning the lifestyle he craved had led him to know both the heights of ecstasy, and the depths of despair. But what he was feeling right now - the pain, the devastation - was as visceral as anything he had ever experienced.

For several moments, he stood stock still, gathering himself as he thought on what he must do. From outside, the sound of chopping wood reminded him of options, spurring him to action. Snapping himself out of it, he checked the clock on the wall. Five minutes had passed since the 'Video Door-Bell' had activated. It meant he had another ten or so to prepare. More than enough.

Crossing to the kitchen drawer, he took out the broad-bladed knife that always felt so good in his hand. Crossing to the window, he pulled the drapes aside to look out to where the road emerged into the clearing.

'Right, *Mistress. And* your fucking lap-dog. Come and get it.'

CHAPTER 59

AS THE MERCEDES bounced and rocked along the track, Carver hung onto the grab handle. Coming on a quarter hour or so had passed since they'd turned off the main road. The potholes were becoming harder to avoid - and deeper. As Megan picked her way along in the semi-dark, the occasional 'clunk' from below testified to the car's low suspension being not well suited to this sort of terrain.

'OUCH,' Carver cried as another sudden dip and a thumping 'clank' heralded the latest unseen hazard.

'Sorry,' Megan said. 'I missed that one.'

Carver said nothing. Given the conditions, he was sure he would do no better. But with the light fading, he hoped there wasn't much further to go. Their safe return depended upon an intact sump.

A moment later, as if having heard his prayer, she eased the car to a stop. Fifty yards ahead, the road curved round to the left. She turned to him. Her face was set. She looked determined but, for the first time, there was also trepidation.

'It's another hundred yards around that bend,' she said. 'You better get out here.'

He stared at her. His doubts and fears still remained, but having got this far with no better alternative coming to him, he had little option but to go with her plan.

'You're sure about this?'

She nodded.

He brandished the mobile. 'If this doesn't work, if something goes wrong and you need me, scream like Hell.'

'Nothing will go wrong,' she said. 'I'll be okay. Zander would never dream of hurting me.'

Carver wished he shared her confidence. In other circumstances, he would have spoken of the danger of trusting those whose habits diverge from what most consider 'normal'. But he knew it would do no good. Besides, she would probably assume he was having a dig. He let it go. Still, he thought to check with her one last time.

'You'll let me know me the moment you know the kids are there?'

'I've already written the message. All I have to do is hit send.'

'And you're not going to do anything until I've-'

'JAMIE.'

He stopped.

'We've been over this. We're here. Just get out the car.'

He looked at her, trying to read her mind. But it was no good. When she'd first outlined her plan, he thought he had got her to agree she would not harm Reed unless absolutely necessary, and in any case not until they had the kids safe and he'd spoken to her after. On reflection he'd realised that what he heard was maybe not so much agreement, as her acknowledging his point of view. Out of things to say, he reached for the door handle.

'Wait.'

He looked round to see her opening the glove box under the steering wheel. She drew out a black, semi-automatic pistol, the grip marked with the distinctive Glock logo. She held it out to him.

'Take this. Just in case.'

He raised his hands in refusal. 'I told you, I don't do guns. And I'm not about to let this turn into a shoot-out.'

She thrust the weapon towards him. 'Don't be a prick, you may not have a choice. And this is no time to play the principled English detective. I don't know if Zander is armed, but I wouldn't be surprised. I'm the one going in there. If he does have guns, and something does go wrong, I'd rather my backup isn't handicapped from the start.'

He stared from her, to the Glock, and back to her. Shaking his head, he took it, thrust it down his waistband. 'If I have to use this, I suggest you hit the floor or take cover. My firearms permit ran out years ago. Only saying.'

It drew a smirk. 'Keep the end with the hole pointed at the other guy, you'll be fine.'

'Can I go now?'

She nodded.

He started to turn.

'Jamie.' He felt her hand grab onto his. He looked round.

The determined look was no longer there. In its place was something more complex. Her eyes bore into his.

'In case something does go wrong, and I don't get the chance to say it later… Thank you.'

As they stared at each other, Carver felt the roles they had played thus far suddenly reversing. For all the assured manner, her determined independence, right now she needed him. He squeezed her hand. 'Stick to the plan, it'll be fine.'

She nodded, gave a weak smile. After a few seconds more, he turned to look for the handle again.

'Jamie.'

Now what?

He turned back just in time to meet her mouth as she clamped her lips to his, her tongue delving, deep. Her hands cupped his face as she leaned across, pulling him to her.

The kiss was as ferocious as it was passionate. Her perfume was around him. He felt her hair brushing his face. Memories of a previous time - another life maybe - where something similar had happened rose to distract him. That time, thoughts of Rosanna saved him. He was about to deploy the same tactic, when another thought came. If something *did* go wrong, and the worst happened, this would be the last time... Slipping his arm through the gap between her neck and shoulder, he pulled her to him, returning the kiss with all the fierceness she was putting into it.

For several seconds - he would never know how many - Jamie Carver let himself fall into the abyss he had always imagined was there, but never allowed himself to dwell on too long, or too deeply. For that brief stretch of time, a kind of darkness engulfed him, one in which only two people existed - him and her. All thoughts of the world beyond vanished. Where they were, why they were there, none of it was important. All that mattered was the two of them, the moment they were in, the feelings they were arousing in each other right now, conflicting and confusing though they were. And even as it happened, Carver could not decide if it was something beautiful, or horrifying.

Suddenly, as quickly as it happened, it stopped. As if both triggered by some silent alarm, they broke apart, sitting back in their seats, breathing hard, saying nothing. He gave her one long, last look, before turning away. This time he found the handle, pulled it. He stepped out, straightened, took a deep breath of fresh, cleansing, forest air.

His hand was still on top of the door. About to lean in to say something - he had no idea what, but it seemed appropriate - he just had time to jump back and push the door shut as the car leaped forward, tyres spinning in gravel.

Alone, in the middle of the track, Jamie Carver watched as the car containing the woman who once vowed to kill him disappeared round the curve and out of sight. Only then did he let out the breath he had been holding, along with a low, *'Jesus Christ.'*

Then, remembering what he was supposed to be doing, he started jogging after her. It was only when he began to move he realised, his legs were shaking like jelly.

CHAPTER 60

LIGHTS WERE SHOWING within the cabin as the Mercedes emerged into the clearing. The big SUV was parked up over to the right. She didn't stop next to it, but swung around in a wide arc to park facing back the way she had come. As she reached for her purse, she glimpsed movement in the rear mirror. He was already out, descending the steps to come towards her.

Even as she opened the door she heard, 'Hey Megan. Great to see you. You shouldda let me know you were coming. I'd have had supper waiting.'

Stepping out, she turned a stony face on him. 'This isn't a social call Zander. You know why I'm here. Why aren't you answering your phone?'

He made a dismissive gesture. 'Ah, it's been playing up. I had to switch it off to save the battery. You been trying to reach me?'

'You know damn well I was. What have you done Zander?'

He looked innocent. 'Done? Waddya mean?'

She looked at the ground, drew a long breath, lifted her gaze. 'I'm not here to play games. I told you not to do anything about the children until you heard from me. Where are they?'

Her cold manner seemed to have its effect. Over the course of several seconds, as he met her withering gaze, his face changed, the jokey lightheartedness giving way to something more serious.

'Someone had to do something, or we'd all be blown.'

'I told you I was handling it. You agreed to wait until you heard from me. Why didn't you?'

He looked chastened. 'I decided it was too risky, and you weren't seeing things straight. If you remember, I did try to tell you you were getting too attached to the boy. It was always going to be a problem.'

In the space of a single second, she reddened, before exploding. 'HOW *DARE* YOU?' He rocked back. 'Who are you to lecture me about my relationships? I have known the Sawyers longer than I have you. And I am quite capable of making my own judgements on such things, *THANK YOU*.'

He tried to reclaim ground. 'I only meant that-'

'I know full well what you meant Zander. You've always had a jealous streak when it comes to people I care about. Well no more. It stops here, right now. Do you hear me?'

He looked at the ground, kicked a rock. 'Yes, *Ma'am*.'

As if playing the role, she sought to tighten her control. 'Don't *Ma'am* me in that tone of voice. Now, tell me. Where are they?'

About to speak, he hesitated, like he had a tale to tell and was debating how. 'It's getting cold. Let's talk inside. I'll tell you everything.' He gestured towards the cabin.

She held her ground a few seconds more, reinforcing her authority. 'Yes, you will tell me everything. But *I'll* tell *you* this. If you've so much as hurt a hair on those children's heads, you will answer to me, understand?'

His surly, 'Right,' was barely audible.

'Good. You go ahead. I'll follow.'

Head down, he started trudging back to the cabin, muttering words she could not hear. But before starting after him, she threw a look back over her shoulder, scanning the road, the surrounding trees and vegetation. There was no sign of Carver. But if he had stuck by the plan, he should have heard at least some of their exchange. Turning back, she followed in Reed's footsteps.

He waited for her at the cabin door as she mounted the steps, holding it open like he was some hotel doorman. She gave him not so much as a sideways glance, as she passed him to head inside. But as soon as she did so, a sly smile formed. *Bitch*, he thought. As sounds of sudden movement reached his ears, he turned to mirror her sweep of the clearing - *no sign yet* - before stepping in.

The noise he'd heard was not from outside, but he made sure the door was firmly closed before turning in expectation.

Megan Crane was being hoisted clear of the ground by a completely bald, heavily-built man, one arm round her waist trapping her arms, the other hand clamped, tight, over her mouth and nose, pulling her head back onto his shoulder, holding it there. Her eyes were wide, legs flailing as she fought, vainly, for air.

For almost half a minute, Reed watched as her struggles grew weaker, revelling in the cameo which, while brief, was no less enjoyable to watch. Eventually her struggles ceased and she went limp in her captor's arms. Letting go, she fell to the floor like a rag doll, where she lay still.

Reed stared down at the limp form, his face now full of regret. *Such a shame... It could have been so beautiful.* Lifting his head he smiled at his friend.

'As well I brought you Jasper. Now, we just need to get ready to welcome our next visitor.'

CHAPTER 61

CARVER SHIELDED THE mobile inside the wind-cheater she had suggested he wear, checking again for any message. Still nothing.

Fuck.

He was checking every couple of minutes now. Over the past hour, the intervals had grown shorter as his anxiety increased. Something had to be wrong.

Leaning round the trunk he was using as cover, he peered through the vegetation at the cabin, some thirty yards away. Fully dark outside now, slivers of light leaked, here and there from between gaps in the gingham curtains. Even where there were none, the material was thin enough to let some light permeate. The effect was to cast the cabin in a halo of silvery-yellow, like a beacon in the wilderness.

Since arriving in time to witness her enter, the only signs of movement Carver had seen were shadows passing across the curtains. No one had come out, and he'd heard no conversation or noise, though that was understandable given the distance. More importantly, the mobile's messaging app stayed empty.

When she first outlined her plan, she had said it could be a good half-hour before he heard from her. Depending on Reed's demeanour, his mental state, it might take that long to wheedle the children's location from him. She wanted to be sure before she messaged him. Anything shorter than thirty minutes would be a bonus. The important thing was not to alert Reed to her true purpose. She needed to make him think he was safe sharing their location, assuming there was one to share. She even mentioned the possibility it could take longer than thirty minutes - 'Forty-five maybe'. But an hour-twenty was never in the frame. And Carver was worried.

It was the scenario he had feared. An interruption to the plan - through whatever cause - and a communication failure that left him having to guess what was happening, what action to take. He had thought, several times, about approaching to within hearing distance. What was stopping him was his experience - rather, one in particular.

Years before, Carver had taken part in a surveillance operation where a major drugs target was meeting with associates to discuss an upcoming importation through Spain. The meeting was to take place in the garden of an end-terrace house on Runcorn's then notorious Murdishaw estate. The garden was enclosed by a high wooden fence, and the house's owner happened to be a Registered Police Informant. When the listening device she planted - literally, in a plant pot - stopped working, a young CID trainee took it upon himself to rescue the operation by creeping along the fence and eavesdropping on the conversation. The young DC failed to take account of next door's German Shepherd, which went ballistic the moment it detected his creeping presence, alerting the dealers, two of whom promptly grabbed him, beating him so badly he spent four weeks in hospital, two of them in a coma. Their defence in court to the charge of attempted murder was they thought he was one of a rival gang about to attack them and they were simply 'defending themselves'. The jury didn't buy it and they went down, but it was another three years before the now ultra-surveillance-conscious target was brought to book for his crimes. He later died during a prison riot which Carver always suspected was cover for a gangland 'hit'.

But Carver never forgot the lesson. Don't creep where there's a dog. He didn't know there was one in the cabin, but so far he had not been able to rule it out. To his mind, forest-cabins and dogs seemed to somehow go together. When he first thought about approaching, it triggered the Murdishaw memory. At that time still within Megan's forty-five minute time-frame, he decided to wait, reasoning that a dog would need letting out some time. Another forty-five minutes on, he was as satisfied as he could be that his caution was groundless, in which case-

He ducked down as the cabin door opened, flooding the area in front with light. Carver's Obs Point was to the right of the door, which opened towards him, meaning he had no view inside. The man he glimpsed following Megan inside - it had to be Reed - stepped out. Closing the door, he crossed to the SUV, got in, turned the engine. Carver's hopes rose. If he was going somewhere, it should leave Megan free to communicate. The car reversed, then made a three-point turn so it faced directly towards him. The headlights were full-on main beam, dazzling him to the point he could see nothing but vague shapes behind. It came forward to stop just past the cabin but still pointed towards Carver, rendering everything behind effectively invisible.

What the Hell's he doing?

For the next ten minutes, Carver watched and listened as Reed, shielded by the searing lights, undertook some activity, behind the SUV. It was accompanied by much heavy breathing and coming and going in and out the cabin. At one point Carver thought about moving to where he might see better what was going on. But he worried that with the lights pointing right at his place of concealment, any movement might be seen.

Eventually, his task seemingly complete, Reed got back in the car and started manoeuvring it to a different position, this time pointing towards the cabin. Headlights now off, and with much revving of the engine and nudging the car inches first this way, then that, he seemed to be taking pains to line the car up in a particular configuration, though for what reason, Carver could not imagine. Throughout the activity, all Carver's attention had been on the car, trying to work out what Reed was about. He had barely paid attention to the area in front of the cabin. Now, as Reed seemed finally happy with the vehicle's positioning and the revving stopped, Carver noticed, for the first time, something about the cabin's porch area seemed different, the shadowy lines not quite as they were. Then part of it moved, and he gasped. At the same time, Reed turned the car's lights back on, revealing to Carver's horror, the terrifying tableau he had spent the past ten minutes preparing.

A wooden porch ran the width of the cabin's front. It was supported by wooden posts with a rail between. The post nearest the door rose from the lowest of the wooden steps up to the porch roof. Megan Crane was on her knees on the step. Ropes around her chest, thighs and ankles held her, fast, to the post behind. Her arms were out in front, tied at the wrists, palms together as in an act of prayer, or worship. They were supported by a rope running to an anchor point somewhere above.

Carver missed the second rope on his first pass, only spotting it when, heart pounding, breath coming in gasps, he checked again to confirm he really was seeing what he thought he was seeing. It was around her neck, rising vertically to loop over a beam above from where it stretched out and down to the front of Reed's SUV. Even as Carver realised its presence, Reed demonstrated its awful purpose. With the car in reverse gear, he revved the engine against the parking brake just enough to rock the car gently back, pulling the rope taught. A muffled scream escaped the cloth gag tied between Megan's lips as the pressure on her neck bit, pulling her up momentarily, off her knees. Carver didn't know whether to be relieved she was still alive, or horrified by the possibility Reed might slip the brake altogether - which would almost certainly see her head removed from her shoulders.

Even as Carver stared at the scene in front of him, Reed stepped from round the car to come forward, looking out into the forest.

'I know you're out there Carver. You've got one minute to show yourself or I'm going to reverse back ten yards. If you don't want to see what happens when I do, you better come out.'

CHAPTER 62

CARVER JERKED BACK behind the trunk, mind spinning as he contemplated the horrific dilemma facing him. The thought of what could happen was so all-consuming it took him almost half the minute he'd been given to realise, the solution was right there, stuffed in his waistband.

Pulling out the Glock pistol, he held it in both hands, pointing it straight down, feeling its weight, checking the balance. It was two years since he'd last held a weapon, and that was on the range. Straightening, he took three calming breaths, before turning to step out, just as Reed made to move back towards the car.

'STOP RIGHT THERE REED.' He came forward, clearing the concealing bushes. Remembering his training he called, 'I'M ARMED AND CARRYING A WEAPON, AND ITS POINTING RIGHT AT YOU. MOVE AWAY FROM THE CAR.'

Even as he said it, some part of him scoffed at him complying, under these circumstances, with established 'protocol'. A voice in his head told him, *Fuck warnings, just shoot the bastard,* and for a moment he thought about it. Then he remembered. The kids were still missing.

Reed stopped, turning towards him, hands in the air, just like in the movies. With the light from behind, his face was in shadow. Nevertheless, Carver could see enough to make out the unsettling smirk that made him wonder what he might be missing. From the porch steps, a stream of muffled cries signalled Megan attempting to make herself heard.

'IT'S ALRIGHT MEGAN, STAY STILL, I'VE GOT HIM.' He edged forward, skirting to Reed's left, keeping the gun trained on him as the frantic noises coming from Megan continued.

'Well hello there,' Reed said, turning to follow Carver's movements. His calm manner fuelled Carver's uncertainty. 'Nice to meet you at last, *Jamie Carver*. I've heard a lot about you.'

Carver leaned to his right, straining to see beyond Reed and the car, looking for his best option for securing Reed so he could focus on freeing Megan.

'ON YOUR KNEES,' Carver barked, remembering again. *Give clear and firm instructions. Demonstrate that you are in control.*

Reed sank to his knees.

Good, Carver thought. Now all I need do, is to-

A noise from behind made him turn, too late, as a huge figure rushed out of the darkness to hit him in a full-on body slam. The force of the impact carried him forward and down, his attacker's arms about him as they rolled over and over towards Reed. When, eventually, they stopped, the first thing Carver realised was he was no longer holding the gun. Lifting his head, he saw Reed, now standing, brandishing it in one hand, while already covering him with what looked like Megan's .38 in the other.

Winded and still in his attacker's crushing embrace, Carver gasped as stabbing pain in his chest accompanied his attempts to breathe, making him wonder about rib fractures. Suddenly his attacker let go and rolled away, rising to reveal himself as a shaven-headed bull of a man of vaguely mixed-race heritage. Carver had never seen him before, but he remembered Amos Wells' mention of Reed having security. *'... A big guy he uses for protection, as well as other things.'* It had to be him.

'Well done, Jasper,' Reed said. 'You really are earning your corn tonight. Say hello to Jamie Carver, the famous English detective.'

Still catching his breath, not yet able to stand, Carver struggled to interpret the man's guttural, growling response. The only words he made out were, *'-fucking pussy.'*

A series of lamenting moans from the steps drew his attention. Megan was breathing hard into her gag, shaking her head.

She was trying to warn me.

'Right then,' Reed said brightly to no-one in particular, 'Now that everything's under control again, I think we better not waste time and should start clearing the decks. I can't see there being any more surprises this evening, but best not take chances. Jasper, bring Mr Carver over next to his accomplice-in-crime.' He turned to Carver. 'Or have I got that wrong I wonder? Maybe there's more to your relationship than that.' He called to Megan. 'What about it Megan? Are you and him an item, or what?' He chuckled at his humour.

Grabbing Carver by the jacket - he yelped as spasms of pain shot through his chest and ribs - 'Jasper' hauled Carver around the SUV to the front of the cabin, dropping him in the dirt in front of Megan. As their eyes met, Carver saw she was no longer trying to communicate, focusing instead on assessing the rapidly-changing situation. Considering the strains her bondage had to be imposing, she didn't look as distressed as he thought she might. *Practice*, Carver thought.

Reed appeared between them, speaking to Megan. 'I'm sorry we don't have the time to see where this little role-play might lead. In other circumstances, I'd enjoy finding out, though the ending might be a bit messy, even for my stomach. I guess we'll have to settle for something less dramatic.' Turning to his minder he said, 'It's a nice evening for a ride out into the forest, Jasper. Go get the boy. He can come too. And this time let's not leave anything for hunters to stumble across.'

'Right boss,' Jasper growled. Shuffling past them, he started to mount the steps.

'Before you go,' Reed said. He held out some nylon ties. 'Just see to Mr Carver. We don't want him getting any silly ideas.'

Taking the ties, Jasper fastened Carver's wrists together, then used another to secure them to one of the porch rails. Grunting in satisfaction, he returned inside the cabin.

Carver watched him go, relieved to hear it sounded like Brandon, at least, was still alive, but heart set pounding by Reed's reference to a 'ride out into the forest'. He needed to do something, or they were all dead. *And what about Kit? Where is she?*

Less winded now, but ribs still hurting when he breathed deeply, he checked himself. Despite the force of Jasper's impact, he seemed otherwise unhurt. He pulled at the tie holding him to the rail. There was no give. He could only hope an opportunity would show itself before their 'ride out'.

With Jasper gone, Reed settled on the step beside Megan. Placing a hand round her throat, he stared deep into her eyes. 'Such a shame, Megan. We could have been so good together.'

Sitting only feet away, Carver thought he could imagine what was going through his mind.

Unable to resist, Megan's only response was to return Reed's gaze, but with as much disdain as she could muster. It didn't deter him. Holding her still, Reed stroked his other hand around her shoulders, across her chest, down her stomach to her legs. She winced as he forced his hand between them, but didn't react further. He shuffled closer to her, as if intent on continuing his assault, but at that moment voices from within the cabin seemed to break whatever spell he had fallen into.

Jumping up, he grabbed her hair, harshly, pulling her head back. He spat once directly into her face, 'You *fucking* traitorous *bitch,*' he called, before pushing her head down. Turning his attention to the ropes securing her to the post, he began untying her.

As Reed worked at the knots, Megan gazed across, evenly, at Carver. And as he saw into her dark eyes, he was sure of one thing. If he ever thought she might spare Reed, should the now unlikely opportunity to kill him arise, that hope was gone. And as he reflected on the desperate position in which they now found themselves, he was conscious of the irony that, while he often disparaged those who seemed incapable of living unless they were 'connected', right now his own life, as well as that of Megan, Brandon and Kit - if they were still alive - could depend upon the existence of a decent data-signal.

CHAPTER 63

AS THE DIZZINESS and nausea returned, I paused again in my efforts, recognising the pattern that had established itself. The symptoms - headache, nausea, dizziness - were fairly constant, if at a low level, but once every hour or so they seemed to flare up. During those times, which lasted around ten minutes, all I could do was close my eyes and wait while it passed. It wasn't so much the headaches, as the crippling nausea that was most disabling. Trying to do anything while feeling like you are about to throw up isn't the easiest.

As I waited, I gave thanks, again, to whoever it was at the Saturday Morning Soccer League arranged the safety talk at the beginning of last season. If I hadn't learned all about concussion, how to recognise the symptoms, what to do about it, I might have panicked when I first woke up, sick as a mangy dog, to find the room spinning, and my head feeling like someone was knocking a nail in it. I remember us being told that if the symptoms are severe, or worsen over the first few hours, then hospitalisation is urgent. But if the symptoms are relatively mild, or last just minutes at a time, simple rest may be all that is needed. I hoped mine would prove to be in the 'mild' category, though any thought of rest was pretty much a non-starter, given my circumstances.

My hope was bolstered by the fact my memory seemed to be working okay. I knew who I was, remembered all my history and, as far as I could tell, wasn't suffering any black spots. That said, my memory of how I got here was sketchy, though I assumed that was because I was only semi-conscious, at best, through most of it. The last memory I had before I blacked out - I'm pretty sure it *was* a memory and not a dream - was standing in Kit's bedroom, looking at a knife. After that, I have some vague recollections of being carried up and down stairs and steps, travelling in the back, or trunk of a vehicle, being bounced around during the journey. But that was it until I woke up, wrists and ankles taped, on the stained and stinky mattress I was now lying on.

The main difficulty working out the severity of my concussion was, I had lost all sense of time. I had an idea I woke up maybe twelve hours or so ago, but having dozed again a couple of times since, I could not be sure. Same with how long ago I got banged on the head. Unless I had been out over a full day, today was Wednesday, though when on Wednesday, again, I couldn't say. The only markers I had time-wise were, first, the visit by the big, bald guy, some hours before when he brought me water and a bag of candy bars. With my wrists taped behind, I had to rely on his help with the water, after which he shoved a candy bar in my mouth then left, ignoring all my questions about Kit, where we were, who he was and what was happening.

The second time-marker was more recent, just two, maybe three hours ago. And it was a whole lot more anguishing.

It began with me waking up from one of my dozes to voices coming from the other side of the cell wall. I had worked out fairly soon after I came round that the room I was in was some sort of purpose-built cell, but that was all I knew. Hearing voices made me wonder if there was more than one, and when I recognised Kit's voice, I guessed she was next door. The other voice was a man who sounded like the one I'd met, this Zander Reed Miriam had warned us about. If so, it answered my question about why we were there, but filled me with fear as to what the future held. The worst part was when Kit started shouting and screaming. The way it echoed all around meant I could make out very few of her actual words, other than the repeated 'NO's and 'PLEASE's but it was clear enough she was being subjected to some sort of physical attack. I tried to not dwell on what sort of attack it might be, but hearing her anguished cries, it was impossible not to.

I will never forget that awful, terrible half hour. Seeing my Mom that night at Miriam's was pretty bad. But listening to Kit crying out for help and not being able to do anything will, I suspect, haunt me for the rest of my life. Through it all I could hear him shouting at her, though a good part of it seemed as much cajoling as angry. I even heard him laugh a couple of times. There was only one interruption to it, which was when he stopped to come round and burst into my cell - I recognised him as Reed at once - having decided, presumably, my screaming blue murder to leave her alone was too much of a distraction. He left after taping my mouth shut, winding the tape around my head and mouth several times until my yelling and cursing was sufficiently muffled he could return to what he was doing without being too disturbed. The period that followed - maybe twenty minutes - almost drove me crazy, and I was glad when all the noise stopped, suddenly. But then I worried myself sick over what he had done to make her go quiet. I'd heard nothing from her since.

With the latest wave of nausea and headache now beginning to ease, I returned to my task - sawing away at the tape around my wrists.

It was probably the concussion made me take so long to realise that the uncomfortable 'lump' in the bed I had been putting up with for a good part of the time I'd lain awake, not moving, was nothing to do with the mattress, but Miriam's lock-knife-gift, stuffed in the side-leg pocket of my cargoes. When I first woke up and realised my cell had gone, along with my bill-fold, I assumed I must have been thoroughly searched and my pockets emptied before I was dumped there. I never gave a thought to the fact I'd put Miriam's knife in the zip-pocket that runs down the pants' seam, and that whoever searched me may have missed it. It was only when I turned over and found the 'lump' still there I realised what it was. Getting it out wasn't easy either. For over an hour, I stretched, pulled, twisted, trying to reach the damn zip and pull it down. When I eventually managed it, I had to lift my legs in the air and jig about on the bed to get it to fall out - the pocket being deeper than I remembered. When it finally dropped out to lay on the bed next to me, I even let out a quiet, but victorious, 'Yessss!'

Opening it up was no trouble, but then I discovered something. All those scenes you see in movies where some captive uses a sliver of broken mirror or a razor to cut through their wrist bonds? They are just so much horse-shit. Trying to just keep hold of the knife while angling it up, to reach the tape was bad enough - I kept dropping it. But wielding it in a productive way that would cut, slice, or saw through the tape was, I found, near impossible. It was only after trying for quite some while I realised the reason it kept slipping out of true was because it was wet, and that the wetness was actually blood from the wounds I'd sustained during my many 'misses'. I kept having to use the blanket to mop up blood and wipe my hands, before setting to once more, hoping to God I didn't cut so deep into my wrists to slice through an artery or vein.

It was pure luck that when Reed burst in to quieten me down, he didn't bother putting the light on, concerned only to tape my mouth shut, else he'd probably have seen the mess and discovered what I was about. But after he left, and after having to listen to Kit's wails and cries, I found myself spurred to new efforts, more determined than ever to free myself and maybe give us some chance, however remote, of doing something that might get us out of there. Eventually, after settling into a steady rhythm of sawing, cutting and pulling, I realised I was getting somewhere. Bit by bit, movement was becoming easier, the tension around my wrists beginning to ease. Scraps of tape started to appear on the bed whenever I checked. I had no plan as to what I might do if and when I freed my hands, but at least it might bring options. At the very least, I would cut the tape around my ankles so I could run or kick, if the opportunity came.

It was around fifteen minutes later when the rattling of the chain at the door signalled one of those options had maybe arrived.

CHAPTER 64

AS WHOEVER IT was went about turning keys and slipping chains, I stopped my sawing. The past few minutes had brought further progress and I checked behind me to cover any tape debris with the blanket, lying still and steadying my breathing while I waited to see what was about to happen. A minute later the door opened and the big guy stood there. He was carrying a length of rope in one hand, a knife in the other, and wearing this strange-looking smile that just about creeped me out there and then.

He jerked a thumb at the ceiling. 'Get up,' he snarled. 'We's goin' on a little trip.' The chuckle that followed made me think that whatever sort of trip it was, it was not one I would find pleasurable.

Coming forward, he grabbed my ankles then used the knife to cut through the tape before bringing me to a sitting position on the edge of the bed. He looped the rope round my neck, then used it to pull me to my feet, causing me to choke and splutter as it bit tight. He pulled me in, close. His breath stank of beer and cigarettes.

'We's goin' upstairs. If you try anything stoopid, I swear to God, I'll kill ya right here.'

I swallowed and nodded, in no doubt he meant every word.

As he pulled me out through the door, I saw we were in some sort of cellar. Steps over to the right led up through some sort of trap to a room above. I had no idea what sort of place it was, but it seemed too rough and ready for the city. We stopped at the bottom of the steps while he turned his stinky breath on me again.

'I'm going up first, then I'm going to pull you up. Remember, any funny business, you're dead.'

I watched as he mounted the stairs. At the top, he turned to look down, started pulling on the rope round my neck. 'Come on you, and watch your step. Don't want you falling and hanging yourself now, do we?' The chuckle that followed turned my blood cold.

With the rope digging into my neck, I knew I had no choice but to comply, and would need to heed his advice about not falling. The steps were not much more than a ladder. Climbing them with hands behind my back would not be easy.

Putting one foot on the first step, I started up, taking one step at a time, the bald guy pulling on the rope while cajoling me to, 'Come on', and, 'Hurry it up'. I didn't resist, but I took it slow and easy. I didn't want to risk falling with the rope around my neck. Besides, I needed a couple more minutes. A voice drifted down from above.

'How you doing Jasper?' It sounded like Reed.

'Coming,' Jasper called back over his shoulder. Turning, he cursed down at me. 'Come on you slow bastard, we haven't got all night.'

Keeping to my steady pace, I ascended through the trap into a room that had the look and feel of a log cabin. Beyond Jasper, a door was standing open and I saw trees. *We're in the forest.* At once, thoughts of poor Councilman Wittingham came to me. I needed to do something. Now.

As I took the last couple of steps up, I stumbled forward. Instinctively, Jasper reached out to steady me, at the same time letting the rope go slack.

'Clumsy fucker,' he muttered.

As I stepped out to stand on the edge, Jasper looked to take up the rope again. Suddenly I swayed back, as if losing my balance and about to topple back into the hole. Alarmed, he leaned forward, stretching out both arms to grab me. Which is when I brought my arms from around my back - I'd completed my sawing halfway up the steps - grabbed both his wrists and pulled them sharply, forward and down, past me and into the hole.

Jasper was a big guy, much bigger than me. But off-balance, leaning forward and with his momentum already going in the right direction, he had nothing to grab onto for purchase. Before he could even cry out, he toppled in, nose-diving straight down into the cellar. He hit the bottom with a thud and a crack that echoed, but not so loud as would carry far. Looking down, I saw him lying in what seemed an unnatural position. He jerked, violently, just once, then lay still. A low, moan escaped his throat, then he went quiet.

My first thought right then was to go straight back down for Kit. But I knew that if I did, I would end up trapped there when Reed came to see where 'Jasper' was. A call from outside confirmed it. 'Everything alright Jasper? I heard a noise.'

As I looked round, pulling the rope from around my neck, my mind raced. There was no other door. The only way out was through the one standing open. Reed was somewhere outside. To the right of the door was a window, red and white chequered drapes pulled across. But through the gap in the middle I could see movement. It had to be him. At that moment he seemed to be facing away from the cabin, but I knew that any second he would come looking for his accomplice. My only advantage was surprise. I moved towards the door, still unsure whether I was going to try and jump him, or run off into the forest and find help.

But as I stepped out, ready to make a snap decision, I found myself confronted by a scene that stopped me in my tracks and scrambled my brain even more than it already was.

CHAPTER 65

MIRIAM WAS KNEELING on the porch steps directly in front of me. Her wrists were bound together as she finished removing a rope from around her neck. Other ropes lay about her, one still draped around her chest, another, loose around her ankles. She looked a mess, her usually well-kept hair all over the place, cheeks streaked with makeup, as if she had been crying. Straight away, I thought of Councilman Wittingham. The shock of seeing her there made me gasp.

'*MIRIAM?*'

She whirled round, as astonished by my sudden appearance it seemed, as I was seeing her. At the same time a movement to my right drew my eye. It was Reed, turning towards us. Beyond and behind him, another man - Detective Carver I realised - was rising to his feet. His wrists were also fastened together and secured by some means to the porch rail. Both looked every bit as shocked as Miriam. It's probably fair to say we were all as shocked as each other.

In that moment, a million questions exploded in my head. Why was Miriam there? And Detective Carver? How had they come to be tied up? What was going on? But I didn't let my mind dwell on them for even a split second. I didn't have time. For even as the questions started forming, all my attention focused in on something else - the gun in Reed's hand he was already bringing up to bear on me.

I acted purely on instinct.

Mounting the steps, I'd slipped my knife into my back pocket the moment I felt the tape cut through, knowing I would need both hands free should things go to plan, which, thankfully, they did. But as I crossed to the door, knowing Reed was there, I'd taken it out, though why, I wasn't sure. Ever since the day Warren Vincent stabbed Julio Degas in the school playground, just the thought of stabbing someone makes me feel sick. But now, seeing the gun coming up to where it would point at my chest, the hours I'd practised on Miriam's old beech trunk and in my back yard these past weeks triggered my response.

I threw it. At the same time, the gun went off.

Time froze.

I have this mental picture of us all standing there, variously wearing expressions ranging between fear, surprise, and horror. For one, two, three long seconds, no one moved.

Reed was the first to do so, looking down at the knife sticking out of his chest, blood already beginning to ooze into his blue shirt. Then his head came up, slowly, looking first at me, then Miriam. His expression seemed one of utter puzzlement, as in, *how the fuck could this happen?* The gun was still pointing in my direction, but even as his mouth opened and he attempted a strangled, gurgling, '*Whhaaaa??*' his grip on it loosened and it slipped from his hand, hitting the porch with a loud clatter before bouncing off into the dirt opposite the front door. A second later, Reed himself began to topple sideways. He took one step out to his right in a final attempt to stay upright, before collapsing to the ground with a heavy, 'Ugghhh.'

He lay where he fell, face down, not moving, blood

already starting to pool under his chest.

For a moment, I could only stare in horror at what I had done.

'Oh my God. I've killed him.'

I don't know if I actually spoke the words, or just kept repeating them in my head. But then someone called, 'BRANDON,' and broke me out of it.

The shout came from Detective Carver. I snapped to him. He was holding his wrists up, showing me the nylon ties holding them to the rail. He seemed calm, though his expression was grim.

'Get a knife. Cut me loose. Then help Megan. Not the knife in his chest. Get one from inside.'

Before moving, I turned to look for Miriam. She was still on the step, staring across at Reed. But as I turned to her, her face came up and round to meet my gaze. My thought was she looked shocked, but otherwise okay.

'Are you alright?' I said.

She nodded. 'I am now.' Her eyes checked me over. 'What about you? Are you okay?'

I nodded. 'Yes.'

'But the shot..?'

'It's okay,' I said. 'He missed.'

'No. He didn't.'

It was Detective Carver again. I looked across at him. He was pointing at my right side. I looked down, following the line. Only then did I see the hole in my shirt. At the same time, I started to become aware of a dull, hot pain, coming from that area. I pulled my shirt up. There was a neat, black-red hole, blood seeping from it. Miriam grabbed me, turning me round so she could see.

'OH MY GOD BRANDON. YOU'RE HIT.'

I don't know whether it was the shock of just seeing the hole and realising I'd been shot, or a delayed physical reaction, maybe due to adrenalin or something, or the concussion returning, but suddenly I started feeling dizzy, my legs starting to buckle.

As I slid to the floor, Miriam screamed. 'BRANDON.'

She rushed to my side, checking my wound, holding my head up, beginning to panic. She turned to Detective Carver. 'HE'S BLEEDING JAMIE. WHAT CAN WE-'

He shook his wrists. 'Get me out of this, quickly.'

She looked around, came back to me, stared deep into my eyes. 'You hold on. I'll be right back.'

She disappeared back into the cabin, came out seconds later with a knife. Crossing to Detective Carver, she cut the ties on his wrists, then he did the same for her before she came straight back to me, Carver alongside her.

'Let me see,' Carver said.

Miriam made space while he examined my wound.

'There's a hole the other side. Looks like it went right through.'

'Is... Is that good?' I said.

He frowned. 'Let's hope so.' He stood up. 'We need to get him to a hospital.'

'Kit...' I said.

'Where is she?' Carver said.

'She's...' As another wave of nausea and dizziness hit me, I lifted a hand to try to point.

'In the cellar?' Miriam said. I nodded. She turned to Carver 'There's an open hatch She must be down there.'

'I'll get her,' he said. But about to rise, he stopped, suddenly, as a shadow fell across the porch. I looked up and round.

Jasper was framed in the doorway, holding Kit up in front of him like a rag-doll shield. Bleeding from a gash to his head, he was pressing a knife-blade to the side of her neck. Kit seemed floppy in his arms and I could see she was only half-conscious. But at that moment, I was just glad to see she was alive.

When I first saw him, Jasper was looking at us, but as he saw Reed, lying there, he called out. 'WHAT HAVE YOU DONE?' He shouted across to him. 'ZANDER? ZANDER!'

Getting no response, he turned back to us, an anguished look in his face. Then it twisted into anger. His eyes rolled. 'You *BASTARDS.*' He spat the word out. I saw the arm holding the knife flex as he pulled Kit closer to him. I thought, *He's going to kill her.*

It all happened so fast, I only remember it as a blur.

A shot rang out. Blood spurted from Jasper's thigh. Grabbing at it, he screamed in pain. As his grip on Kit loosened, she started to slide towards the floor, revealing more of him. Another shot echoed. His head snapped back as a black spot appeared, square between the eyes. A second later he collapsed, straight down, lying in a heap half across Kit. I looked around. Miriam was kneeling on the ground opposite the front door. She was holding Reed's gun in both hands, still pointing it at Jasper as if he might suddenly get up again.

'KIT,' I shouted. Jasper's legs were across her, but as I moved to reach for her, I let out a yelp as pain, like a red-hot knife, ripped through my side, stopping me in my tracks.

'Don't move Brandon,' Miriam called.

Dropping the gun, she went to Kit's side, shoving Jasper's legs off her and pulling her away from the blood pooling from his wounds. At the same time Detective Carver went to check Jasper's vitals, though I was pretty sure he had to be dead. As Carver stepped down to check Reed, Miriam cradled Kit on one side, me the other.

Kit's eyes fluttered. She seemed out of it, but just for

a second, she must have managed to focus enough to see me. She stretched out a hand. '*Brandon?*'

I grabbed it. 'I'm here Kit. We're okay.'

Her eyes closed as her head lolled into Miriam's chest.

Suddenly a shout came from somewhere out front. 'JAMIE? ARE YOU OKAY? I HEARD SHOTS.'

Next thing, Sheriff Lynch came running out of the darkness. He was holding his gun in both hands. He stopped next to Carver, looking down at Reed.

'*Jesus-fuck.* I came as soon as I could. Jess forwarded the GPS location you sent her. But seems I'm too-' Looking round, he saw us, huddled together on the porch. 'KIT!' He bounded across, knelt next to her, grabbed her hand. 'KIT? Is she alright?'

She must have heard him as she roused herself enough to turn to him. 'Dad?' she said, as if she thought she might be dreaming. Then she drifted off again.

Frantic, Lynch looked up, first at me, then Miriam. 'Is she...?'

'She's had it rough,' Miriam said, trying to sound reassuring. 'But she's okay physically, I think. She'll be okay... in time.'

He looked over at me. 'What about you Brandon?' He spotted the hole in my shirt.

'About the same,' I said

'He's been shot,' Detective Carver said. 'Flesh wound I think. We need to get both of them to the hospital.'

The sheriff nodded. He looked around, taking stock of the bodies, Kit, me, Miriam. He looked across at Detective Carver. 'Jesus Christ Jamie. What happened here?'

'I'll tell you all about it,' he said, 'But let's get the kids inside first. It's bloody cold out here.'

Miriam made to get up. She looked up at Lynch, put

out a hand. 'Would you mind?'

'Of course,' Lynch said. Lifting Kit to cradle her in his arms, he took Miriam's outstretched hand and pulled her up. As he did, I saw him looking at her, strangely. Far as I knew, they had never met before. For some reason, his mouth seemed to gape as he stared at her. He looked across at Detective Carver, back to Miriam.

'Is this…? Are you-?'

'Miriam Cole,' Detective Carver said. 'Miriam, meet Sheriff Matt Lynch.'

He stared at her like he was seeing a ghost, before turning to carry Kit inside. As Detective Carver helped me, and with him under one arm, Miriam the other, started to guide me inside, I had the strangest feeling I was missing something, but couldn't work out what.

CHAPTER 66

PROPPED ON THE couch with Kit next to me, us both wrapped in blankets, I watched through the window at Detective Carver and Sheriff Lynch talking out front. I couldn't hear, but from the looks on the Sheriff's face - eyes wide, mouth open - I got the impression it was some tale, even before he got to the bits I'd witnessed. Watching, I was conscious of Kit's weight against me. And while I was still worried about her, it was a nice feeling. Over by the stove, Miriam was rustling up hot drinks from the cocoa and powdered milk she'd found in a cupboard.

Thumbs hooked in his belt, Lynch looked to be paying close attention as Carver talked, pointing and gesturing around like he was painting a picture of whatever had occurred before the big guy brought me up from the cellar. The gestures took in the road where Lynch had come from; the surrounding forest; Reed's Ram SUV, still parked out front; the porch roof, for some reason; the cabin - several times. Every now and then Lynch interrupted - I assumed to ask a question - because following Carver's reply he shook his head, like he was struggling to take it all in.

Observing them, I hoped I would get to hear the story myself sometime - there were a hundred questions in my head needed answering - but right now I was just grateful Kit and I were still alive. In particular, I was concerned for Kit, worried about what happened to her down in that cellar. According to her Dad and Miriam - they checked her out soon as they got her on the couch - she wasn't seriously injured in any way. But I'd heard them talk about shock and trauma and her 'mental state', which didn't sound good. And while she was still mostly out of it, every few minutes she came round, felt for my hand, found it, mumbled something I couldn't make out, then drifted off again.

Whatever Carver and Lynch were talking about, I hoped it wouldn't take much longer. It wasn't that I was worried about the hole in my side so much. According to Kit's Dad, who seemed to know about gunshot wounds, it didn't look 'serious'. But just being there was beginning to freak me out. I couldn't stop thinking about the cellar, what may have happened there. Earlier, Detective Carver and him had descended the steps to, 'check no one else is there.' When they came back, their faces were grim. The didn't speak of what they'd seen. I've seen lots of movies where crazed killers living in forest cabins do horrible things to people. I never thought I'd ever star in one. I still didn't know how Miriam and Detective Carver had come to find us, but I didn't like to think what may have happened if they hadn't.

'Take this Brandon,' Miriam said.

I turned to her as she handed me a mug of steaming hot chocolate. 'Thank you,' I said, trying a smile.

By way of a response, she stroked the back of her hand down my cheek, carried it on round to the other side, pulling me to her as she leaned forward and kissed the top of my head. It gave me a strange-but-nice feeling - tender, *loving* even, though not in the way I might have expected had it happened the week before. It left me feeling confused.

Taking the other mug, she sat next to Kit. Stroking

her hair, as tender with her as with me, she said 'Drink this sweetheart, it'll make you feel better.' Kit stirred enough to take a few sips, with Miriam's help.

Sitting there, watching her administering to Kit like a nurse born to it, I found myself wondering if she'd ever had children. During all our conversations, we had never talked much about her. She only ever seemed to want to talk about me. But seeing the way she was with Kit, I would not have been surprised.

Catching me looking, she said, 'How you feeling now? Any better?'

I nodded, tried another smile. 'A little.' I started to ask, 'How-?' but stopped, unsure if this was the time. But she cocked her head, waiting, so I tried again. 'How did you and Detective Carver find us? And why did all this happen? I thought that man Reed was your friend?'

Her face turned sad. 'He was once, I'm sorry to say. But that was a long time ago, before he started... doing horrible things to people.'

I stared at her. 'You mean he's done what he was going to do to us... before?'

Just for a moment, her eyes closed, like it was hard to talk about. She nodded. 'I'm afraid so.'

'What? Here?' I looked around the cabin.

She nodded again, hung her head. It was like she was ashamed.

'Is that how you knew where to find us? You knew about this place?'

She lifted her head, but seemed hesitant. 'I... knew about this place. But not... down there.' She nodded towards the hatch. I looked at it. There were lots of questions I could ask about what she knew, but I decided they could wait 'til another time, when we were away from here.

'But I still don't get how you and Detective Carver

came to be here on your own. Why didn't you come with Sheriff Lynch, his deputies?' It was only then I realised. There *were* no deputies. I'd watched CSI a million times. After what happened here, the place should be crawling, blue lights all over.

Miriam looked at me, as if gauging what to say. 'It's… complicated. I just thought it best we come alone… to begin with.'

It didn't make any sense, but I could see there were things she wasn't ready to share yet. I didn't know why, but I trusted her enough not to push it.

'I'm sorry, Miriam.'

She looked puzzled. 'Whatever for?'

'For whatever you went through with Detective Carver before I showed up.' I gestured around. 'For all this. It was my fault, and I'm sorry.'

She shook her head, reached out, took my hand. 'It wasn't your fault Brandon, and you must never think it was. If anyone is to blame, it's me.'

It was my turn to look puzzled. 'But you didn't do anything. It was me who sneaked into-' I stopped as her hand came up.

'This all began long before you ever thought about sneaking into my garden. You probably won't understand that right now. I'm not sure you ever will, fully. Right now, all I can say is, there are things I can't share with you just yet, and hope you will accept it, for now at least.'

The way she looked at me, I could never refuse. 'Okay Miriam. If you say so.'

'Thank you.' The look she gave me right then was about as deep, and meaningful, as any that had ever passed between us.

She looked about to say something when the door opened and Sheriff Lynch and Detective Carver came back in. Kit's Dad came and stood in front of the couch, looking down at me, then over at Miriam, still next to Kit. His gaze seemed to stay on Miriam quite some time before he spoke.

'From what Jamie says, it seems it's you two I must thank for Kit still being alive.' He looked at me. 'Thank you Brandon.' He turned to Miriam. 'And thank you... Miriam.' Again, there was something weird about the way he said her name which I didn't understand.

Miriam stood up, sent him an equally weird smile before nodding at me. 'It's this brave young man here, we should all thank Sheriff. If he hadn't managed to do what he did, everything might have turned out very different.'

The Sheriff took a long breath. 'That may be so, but thank you anyway.'

As he said it, he held his hand out to her. She looked at it, then across at Detective Carver standing by the door, watching, then back at him, before taking it. As they shook, their gazes stayed locked on each other. It made me wonder what the fuck was going on. Eventually, Kit's Dad turned to Detective Carver.

'I need to get these kids to a hospital.' He looked like he was about to turn back to Miriam, but stopped himself. 'Are you...?'

Carver nodded. 'We're okay. We'll sort things out here.'

He nodded, firmly. 'I'll get my car.'

He left the cabin, leaving me to watch as Detective Carver and Miriam just stood there, staring across at each other just like she and Sheriff Lynch had done. By then, I'd had enough.

Oh, for fuck's sake, I thought.

While Sheriff Lynch was gone, Miriam rang my parents on her cell and I spoke with them. They were almost hysterical to learn I was safe, and Kit as well -

apart from me being shot, which Miriam had told them was 'not serious.' Like me, they had a million questions, but Detective Carver and Miriam had warned me not to say too much yet about what had happened, so I just stuck to lots of, 'See you soons', and 'Yes. I'm fine, I promise.'

After the call, Miriam took back the phone and went outside with Detective Carver where they carried on speaking - about what I don't know, but it looked pretty serious. By then I was starting to flake out and had given up trying to work out what was going on between them all. I just wanted to get home, see my parents, and make sure Kit was okay.

A couple of minutes later, as Sheriff Lynch arrived back, Miriam came back inside. 'Time to get you two gone,' she said.

Sheriff Lynch came in, picked Kit up in his arms and carried her out to the car. Detective Carver and Miriam helped me up - by now my side was giving me hell - and more or less carried me out to the car between them. Sheriff Lynch had dropped the passenger seat for Kit to lie on and was making sure she was covered and strapped in as they put me down so I could slide onto the back seat.

Before I got in, Carver offered me his hand, which I took. 'You did a good job back there son,' he said. 'Well done, and thank you again.' Then he stepped back, leaving me alone with Miriam.

Before I could say anything, she came forward to wrap me in her arms, hugging me tight, like she was reluctant to let go. When she eventually did, we stood there, looking at each other. I said, 'Will you come and see me in hospital?' Sheriff Lynch had mentioned taking us to the Thomas Memorial Hospital. He reckoned I'd maybe be there a couple of days. When Miriam didn't reply but looked down, reluctant to speak, it seemed, I started to worry. Eventually she lifted her head, gave me a straight look. Her eyes were moist.

'I'm not sure when you'll see me again, Brandon. I… I have to go away for a while. I'm not sure when I'll be back.'

I started to panic. 'Go away? What do you mean? Where to? Why-' I stopped as she pressed a finger to my lips. She shook her head. A tear trickled down her cheek.

'Right now, the important thing is for you to get to hospital and get seen to.'

'Fuck that,' I said. 'Where are you going? Why do you have to go away?' I felt anger starting to rise. *What's with all the fucking mystery?* But she just shook her head. More tears appeared.

'I'm sorry, I can't say anymore right now. I'll maybe ring you in a couple of days… if I can.'

It didn't help. 'What do you mean, "If I can"? What's to stop you?'

Suddenly she bowed her head, 'Oh *Brandon.'* She buried her face in her hands. Her shoulders shook.

It was then I realised. Whatever was going on, it wasn't her choice. And my being angry wasn't helping. Taking hold of her again, I hugged her to me. 'It's okay, Miriam. I'm sorry. If I have to wait to hear from you, then I'll wait.' We stayed like that while she gathered herself. When we stopped hugging, the tears had gone and she seemed more like the old Miriam, though I could see she was still upset.

She lifted a hand. Her fingers stroked my face. 'Just know this. Whatever happens, you'll always be special to me. Wherever you are, wherever I am, you'll always be my Brandon, my beautiful, wonderful, Brandon.' Leaning forward, she kissed me, softly, on my cheek.

I'll always remember that kiss. The softness of her

lips. The tickle of her hair on my face. Her fragrance.

She held the door as I slid into the backseat, buckled my seat belt.

Sheriff Lynch called from in front. 'We good back there?'

I caught his eye in the mirror, nodded. 'Yes Sir.'

'Okay then.'

I gave her one last look, 'Would you like me to carry on looking after your garden while you're away?'

She chuckled. 'That would be nice. Though I don't know how I'll pay you.'

'Don't worry,' I said. 'I'll do it for free.'

She threw me one last smile. It was the most beautiful smile I ever saw. Then, as the car started moving, she closed the door. 'Stay safe', I heard her call, followed a second later by, 'I love you Brandon.' Then we were heading down the road away from the cabin.

Before we reached the bend, and biting back the pain, I managed to turn round and look back. She was just standing there, silhouetted against the light from the cabin, watching me go, Detective Carver next to her. Just before they disappeared from my view, I thought I saw her slip an arm through his. Then they were gone.

I never saw her again.

CHAPTER 67

THE FIRST THING Megan did when they returned to the cabin was go to a cupboard and pull out a bottle of Jack Daniels. She showed it to Carver. He shook his head. She poured herself a generous measure, then threw it straight down. As she tipped her head back, her hair swung about her shoulders. Behind her, Carver watched, remembering a similar scene the first time they met. Her hair was glossy-black then. It had shimmered in the sun. He also remembered the tight, white leggings that nearly made him spill his coffee.

Putting the glass down, Megan leaned on the counter, as if composing herself before turning to him.

'So what now?' Her face was a blank mask.

'Are you okay?' he said, conscious of the parting he'd just witnessed.

She took a quick breath, stifling something, before straightening. She nodded. 'I will be.' She took another, then said, 'Where do we go from here?'

He gave it a second. Outside, the dawn was not far away.

'We leave, but there's a couple of things I need to do first. I'll need your help.'

It took them close to an hour to attend to the things Carver and Lynch had discussed. The important thing was it stand scrutiny when the FBI Forensic Team went over the place. It involved moving Reed and Jasper's bodies, some wiping and cleaning, and setting the scene so that when the FBI did, eventually, arrive, the evidence would fit the narrative Carver had agreed with Lynch. In truth, Carver wasn't certain it would work. Good Forensics is hard to fool. Time would tell.

The sun was showing through the trees when they got into Megan's Mercedes to head back. Carver was conscious he could do nothing about tyre tracks. An observant CSI may even manage to lift a cast. But without a suspect car to match it to, it wouldn't lead anywhere.

The return journey was mainly silent. Carver imagined her head full of thoughts of the son she would, in all likelihood never see again. For him, there was no shortage of things to think about. They revolved around the mental picture he was trying to compose of what the coming days would look like. It should have been clear, It wasn't.

He came here intending to find out if Megan Crane was alive and, if she was, detain her and see her returned to where she belonged - prison. Well he *had* found her. And right now there was nothing to stop him putting her into custody and completing his mission. Apart from one thing. She had just saved his life, not too mention those of two innocent kids.

It shouldn't matter. She was still Megan Crane, the serial killer who had killed more people than even he yet knew, including the woman he once loved. That she had saved him, Kit and Brandon, didn't change anything.

Only in his mind, it did. He wasn't sure why. The facts were all pretty straight forward. There was no reason he should be confused. Only he was. And the more he thought about it, the more confused he became. He wondered if it was to do with the fact he hadn't slept for twenty-four hours, and with everything that had happened, his brain wasn't working properly. He hoped that *was* the case, because if it was something else, he was in trouble.

He was still thinking about it when they reached the town limits, having made two stops for coffee then a light lunch on the way, neither of which did much by way of breaking the silence that had fallen between them. Easing the car to a stop at the sign proclaiming, 'Welcome To Brackers Lake - Where People Make Progress', she turned to him.

'You need to tell me where we're going,' she said.

He looked at her. The seconds ticked.

'Listen,' she said. 'If it's any help, I'm not intending to go anywhere. Brandon and Kit are safe. That was all I wanted. I'm tired now and I've had enough of running. I'll do whatever you want me to do.'

For several seconds longer he stared at her, nodding, slowly. Eventually he said, 'You better call at your house. I assume you'll need some things.'

She stared at him, said nothing, then set off again.

It was around five in the afternoon when they pulled up her drive. Carver accompanied her inside where she filled a bag with the things she would need, then checked the house was secure. Standing in the kitchen, she spent some time staring out at the garden. *Remembering, no doubt,* Carver thought.

'Ready,' she declared.

They left through the front door, setting the alarm and making sure it was double-locked, before getting back in the Merc, and heading back to Carver's hotel.

As they made their way to his room, Carver was conscious he was flying blind now. He had no idea what he was doing, why, or where it would lead. All he knew was he needed time to work things out, when the answers to his own questions would be clear - he hoped.

While Megan showered and changed, he rang room service. He didn't ask her what she wanted, but ordered a mix of various food items and a bottle of wine. She liked Pinot Noir he remembered. After finishing in the bathroom, she appeared wearing a white cotton robe that looked a lot more comfortable than those that came with the room and reminded him of the first time he laid eyes on her. His turn, he spent half-an-hour showering and washing away the smells that come with death and cellars. As he donned his robe and made to come out, he wondered if he would find her still there. She was, having laid out the food that had arrived five minutes earlier, and was now pouring wine. They ate as they had driven, mostly in silence. They didn't speak of what had happened over the previous twenty four hours, or talk about the future. Nevertheless, Carver didn't find it as unsettling as he thought it might be. Whether through exhaustion or something else, he felt at ease in her company. He put it down to just being glad he was alive. And while she seemed similarly relaxed, he didn't delve into her thoughts or feelings. She didn't ask what the coming days would bring, or what his plan was. And certainly not what he intended to, 'do with her'. He doubted Megan Crane would ever see herself as being at any man's 'disposal', whatever the circumstances.

By nine o'clock, having eaten and drunk enough, including a second bottle - 'Make it Rioja this time,' she said - he was as close to sleeping on his feet as in a long time.

They turned in together, she taking the second bed. As he turned out his light, he said, 'We'll talk tomorrow. Good night.'

'Good night Jamie,' she answered. Then followed it with, 'And thank you.'

For once, he slept soundly.

He woke at seven to find her gone. Reaching across, he felt the sheets. They were cold. He lay back, thinking on how he felt about her not being there. He knew he should have been feeling something, but didn't know what. *Stupid? Disappointed? Angry with himself for not doing what he knew he should have done?*

After lying there a while, he got up and went into the bathroom. While he was there he heard a noise. When he came out, she was there. Dressed casually and with her hair brushed rather than styled and wearing only light makeup, she looked fresh, bright, and different to how he'd ever seen her. On the table by the window were Starbucks' coffees and an assortment of bagels, pastries and doughnuts.

He switched his gaze from the table, to her.

'I thought you were taking care of your figure?'

She smiled the sly smile he knew so well. 'Today's my day off.'

CHAPTER 68

I WOKE TO discover I'd slept three days and was on a drip. It seemed the day after I was admitted to Thomas Memorial, I developed a blood infection the doctors thought was sufficiently serious they put me out while they fed me antibiotics and stuff. When I opened my eyes, the first thing I saw was my Mom, sitting in the chair next to the bed. I learned later she'd been there throughout.

'Hey you,' she said, squeezing my hand.

I smiled at her. 'Kit?', I said.

'She's doing okay,' Mom said.

I went back to sleep.

They let me out the next day, Monday. The infection had cleared and I was feeling much better but the medical advice was I needed ten days recuperation - which meant no school - and suited me fine. When I got home, I sat down with my parents and we talked about what had happened. It was a weird conversation.

Driving to the hospital, Sheriff Lynch had told me not to say anything to anyone about what had happened until he had, 'seen to some things'. He said he would let me know what, and how much to say. I guessed it was all part of the 'mystery' and didn't argue. But while my parents didn't push me on some of the details - like my killing Reed - I got the impression they knew most of it anyway, just didn't want to say. I asked what was happening about what went on at the cabin. 'Will I have to speak to the police about it?' They shook their heads and told me Sheriff Lynch would explain. I asked if they had seen Miriam, and wasn't that surprised when they glanced at each other like it was a hard question. I was coming round to realising there was something about Miriam I wasn't supposed to know.

'Miriam will be gone a while,' my father said. 'Maybe a long while. But she said to tell you she'll miss you and will always remember you.'

'Is she... will she come back?' I said.

Another look passed. 'We don't know. One day, maybe. We'll have to wait and see.'

I didn't like the sound of it, but didn't kick back. I assumed that at some stage, everything everyone seemed to not want to talk about would become clear.

Sheriff Lynch came in the afternoon. He brought my bicycle with him.

'We found it out in the forest around the cabin. We're searching the whole area. We've found others as well.'

I never asked who the others belonged to.

After reassuring me Kit was doing okay and looking forward to seeing me, we talked out in the garden, alone.

'You probably want to know what'll happen over what took place up there?' he said.

I nodded, wondering if he'd spoken to my parents.

'Well I can tell you. Nothing.'

'Nothing?' I said, as surprised as I was puzzled. 'But I killed someone. Don't I have to explain-?' His head was shaking, slowly, side to side. He became even more serious than he was already.

'What you did out there, Brandon... It was pretty incredible. If it wasn't for you, it's likely you might all be dead. You, Kit, Detective Carver and Mrs Cole. Yes, you killed someone, but you only did what had to be done. As far as the law is concerned, it all comes under self-defence.'

'I understand that,' I said, interrupting. 'So why won't-'

His hand was up. 'What you experienced was pretty horrible, and you need to know. What Kit went through? Well, that was especially horrible. Do you know what I'm talking about?'

I swallowed, nodded. I'd thought about it a lot. As long as I live, I'll never forget her screams.

'Kit is strong, Brandon. She'll be okay, in time, but she'll need help getting there. I'd like to think you will contribute to that?'

I nodded, 'Of course. Any way I can.'

He nodded. 'Good.' He continued. 'Kit will have to live with what happened to her for the rest of her life. The sooner she can come to terms with it, the better. The man who hurt her is dead. So is his accomplice. It'll do her no good, or you for that matter, having to go over it all with some detective just for the purposes of a police investigation that will achieve nothing anyway. So my thinking is, it would be better for all concerned if the record shows that neither you, nor Kit, were ever there.' He paused before adding, 'But only if you agree, of course.' He paused again, letting the implications of what he was telling me sink in. 'So I need to ask you this. Are you prepared to agree to what I am suggesting, bearing in mind it will mean never talking about it again to anyone, ever, other than me, your parents, and Kit?'

I barely had to think about it. I'd heard stories about how hard it is for victims, particularly girls, when they have to re-live their experiences in court or for some police investigation. I knew it might do Kit some good to talk about it to someone one day, but not a cop, and not so soon. So I said, 'Absolutely. If it'll help Kit then...

Fuck, if anyone asks, we just went swimming.'

He smiled at me. Offered me his hand. We shook,

'Thank you, Brandon.' He stood up. 'She's at home if you want to call round. I think she'd like to see you, if you feel up to it?'

I nodded. 'Just something I gotta do first, then I'll bike round?'

'Good. I'll let her know you are coming.'

We went back inside where I left him talking with my parents while I went up to my room and grabbed my back pack and some things. When I came down, they were sitting at the kitchen table, drinking coffee.

'You sure you're okay Brandon?' my Mom said. She still looked concerned.

'I'm good Mom,' I said. 'Is it okay if I-' Her nod and smile told me I didn't need to finish.

'Don't be too late, though. I don't want you out after dark.'

'Okay Mom. 'Bye Sheriff Lynch. Thanks for bringing my bike back.'

'No problem. Tell Kit I won't be late. Just sorting some things out.'

'Will do.'

Retrieving my bike from the garage where my father had put it away, I rode out. I went via Miriam's house, cycling up the drive and dropping my bike at the side gate. Her car wasn't there and I saw through the window the garage was empty. The gate was bolted, but I knew to reach over and just slide it back. I walked down the side to the back and up the steps onto the deck. The drapes were drawn across the windows with just one gap I could see through. There was no sign of anyone. The house looked deserted. Without her, it seemed dead, like a graveyard.

I turned to look out over the garden. It was as I'd left

it the last time I worked there - that Saturday. A bunch of my gardening tools still lay where I'd left them under a plastic sheet, ready for when I returned after school on the Wednesday. I thought about putting them away, but didn't want to delay getting to Kit's. *Another time,* I thought. Then I remembered. I'd promised Miriam I'd finish her garden. It might even do Kit good, helping me. If nothing else it may help take her mind off other things.

I surveyed the garden, the deck, the house one last time. I'd spent a good deal of time there that late summer. An image came of me sitting there, talking to Miriam, drinking iced lemon and enjoying her black-bread cake. I never did discover where it came from. I remembered the first time my father brought me round to meet her, the effect she had on me. It seemed a lifetime ago. It was probably just my imagination, but to my mind, the Brandon Sawyer I was remembering, was a different person to the one standing here now. I wondered if, were she there, she would have agreed?

I turned to go, stepping down off the deck to walk back up the side. At the corner I stopped, took one last look back.

''Bye Miriam,' I said, then turned and left.

When I got to Kit's house, there was a woman in the kitchen I'd never seen before.

'Hi,' she said, as she let me in through the screen-door. 'You must be Brandon. I'm Paula, Kit's upstairs. She's expecting you.'

'Thanks Paula,' I said. 'Nice to meet you.' I didn't know who she was, but she seemed at home, cutting up vegetables with a pot boiling on the range. I thought she had a nice smile, quite attractive, in an older-woman kind of way. She smelled nice too. I went upstairs.

I hesitated at her door before entering, but could see

her reflection in the mirror across the room. She was on her bed, plugged into her Beats. And as I looked at her, I was shocked to see a different Kit to the one I had come to know. I wasn't sure what it was about her that had changed - that knowledge would only come over time - but there was a darkness clouding her features I had never seen before. But before I could give it further thought she suddenly looked up and saw me. Her face lit up and, just like that, she was the old Kit again. But as she sat up, pulling the headphones off, she affected an annoyed expression.

'About time. I've been waiting for you. Can we go swimming?'

CHAPTER 69

VIDEO CALLING JESS, Carver braced himself. Her reaction was as he'd anticipated.

'Another *week*?' Why the delay? I thought it was all done and dusted and she'd agreed to come back voluntarily?'

Carver shifted in his chair, keeping the camera tight on him. 'Thing's *are* done and dusted, pretty much. But Matt's still waiting on advice from the DA's office. He wants to be sure the Sheriff's Department won't be getting sued by some Human Rights lawyer claiming we tricked her into returning just to cut out extradition.'

Jess gave a disappointed sigh. 'I thought your Sheriff friend was the sort who doesn't worry much about red-tape and legalities. Sounds like I was wrong.'

'Matt's okay Jess. He's just being careful.'

'If you say so. But if we're not extraditing her, what are you holding her on? I thought you said she's not broken any laws over there.'

'She hasn't,' Carver said. 'She's in voluntary detention.'

'*Voluntary detention*? What the Hell's that? Is there such a thing?'

Carver quashed a smile. Her 'sceptical face' always amused him. 'There is here. Don't worry, she isn't going anywhere.'

'I should bloody hope not,' she said. 'I'll just be glad

when it's over and and she's back in Stigwood.' She paused, thinking. '*Will* she go back there, or somewhere else?'

'That's up to the prison service. But being an escaper, I'd guess they'll put her somewhere more secure.'

'That's what I thought,' Jess said. 'It's why I can't get my head around it.'

'Can't you get your head around what?'

'Her surrendering herself like that when she heard you were over there looking for her. She must know she'll never enjoy a regime as liberal as Stigwood again.'

Carver shrugged. 'Maybe she's finally realised that given her history, no matter where she goes, there'll always be a risk someone might turn her in. Don't forget, a lot of her former circle are still scared their association may become known. Like Curtis Whittingham was.'

Jess didn't look convinced. 'Did she tell you that?'

'Not in so many words. But it's one explanation. Three years on the run is a long time. Maybe she's just had enough.'

Jess snorted. 'What? Megan Crane had enough of freedom to come back to a life of sewing mailbags and laundry, or whatever it is they do inside these days? You must be joking.' She thought a moment. 'Are we sure she hasn't got something up her sleeve?'

'Like what?'

Jess thought. 'Was she ever involved with someone from the Security Service, MI5 or MI6?'

'Not that I know of, why?'

'Because if she was, it wouldn't surprise me if she comes back, serves six months then is quietly let out under cover of some story she met with a fatal accident inside. It has happened you know.'

Carver shook his head. 'You've been watching too many films. I'm sure it's nothing like that.'

'No? Well okay, but I tell you this. If we ever hear she's died in prison, I'll want to see her body *and* take my own DNA sample. Just saying.'

'I'll remember that,' he said.

'Good. But talking of your late Councilman Whittingham, how's the FBI investigation going. Have they linked his murder to Reed yet?'

Carver shook his head. 'They're focusing first on identifying the bodies they are still digging up in the forest, but they'll get to Curtis eventually. It's just a matter of time.'

'What's the tally so far?' Jess said.

'Eight,' Carver said, grimly. But they are expecting more. According to Rachel's mate Amos, they think there could be as many as another dozen still to be found. They've lost some kids around the lake over recent years. They've already provisionally identified one of the bodies as one of them. It isn't looking good.'

Jess blew out her cheeks. 'Twenty is a lot of missing kids, especially in one state. Didn't anyone ever spot a pattern?'

'Reed operated out of several bases, remember. The thinking is, he picked up most of his victims in New York city, lured them to his apartment or his house on the Hamptons, then drugged them and carted them off to his forest hideaway.'

Jess winced, shook her head. *Jesus*. Those poor kids…'

Carver gave it a moment, conscious other matters were pressing, before asking. 'I gotta go in a minute. Tell me, how's the Six Enquiry going? Where are you up to?'

She roused herself. 'Alec and his teams are still trawling for other cold cases, and the HOLMES people are just finishing uploading the six we started with onto the system. I'm hoping that when we run them all together, it'll throw up some links we've never spotted before.'

'When will that be?' Carver said

'Towards the end of next week, provided there are no technical problems. Why do you ask?'

He kept his face blank. 'Just curious. What about Kradesh? How involved is he?'

'Funny you should ask,' she said. 'Seeing how his role, supposedly, is to interpret and advise on behavioural aspects, he seems to want to be involved in everything. He's becoming a bit of a pain to be honest.'

'I warned you. He'll be thinking about his next best seller. The more involved he is, the better he'll look when it gets published.'

'Only if we're right and it turns out all the murders *are* the work of the same killer.'

'It's a good theory Jess. Stick with it.'

'I intend to.'

She hesitated. Carver sensed what was coming. He was right.

'By the way. Have you spoken to Rosanna?'

He nodded. 'Last night. Why?'

'She rang me yesterday. She was worried she hadn't heard from you for a few days and was getting no reply on your mobile.'

He nodded. 'Yeah, I saw yesterday I'd missed some calls. I think it was a glitch with my mobile registering on the network over here.'

'How is she? Looking forward to you getting back I expect?'

'You could say that. Any more on The Duke?'

'Not since Alec told us about the Old Trafford incident. But then I haven't seen much of him since, so I-'

'Well at least you're there to keep an eye on him. I

have to go Jess. Matt Lynch is trying to call me. I'll let you know about flights when they're booked.'

'Okay. I was going to ask-'

'Bye Jess.'

He ended the call.

Jess Greylake stared at her mobile. She'd been about to ask if he'd managed any contact with Jason and his grandmother since flying out there, aware it was one of his concerns before he left. But his abrupt cut-off stopped the question mid-flow. She understood he was working closely with Sheriff Lynch, and the time-difference meant their calls were sometimes stilted. But she was conscious she had not heard the 'beep' that signals another call waiting.

Reflecting on it, her brow furrowed. All in all, it had been a strange conversation. Jamie had sounded not quite his normal self, though she wasn't sure she could put a finger on why. Had he sounded distracted? She was conscious he'd avoided going into detail about any of the subjects they'd touched on -Megan, Reed, the bodies in the forest, his flight home. Not even Rosanna or The Duke come to that. And to not even mention Jason.... Considering he must be looking forward to seeing him soon, it was puzzling.

He'd mentioned talking to Rosanna the night before. She wondered if that might have something to do with it. Rosanna had rung her several times the past twelve months or so, confiding her struggles over Jamie's determination to answer the 'Is she alive or dead?' question. She was aware it had strained their relationship, almost to breaking point. Now, the question answered, the strains should start to ease.

At that moment an image formed. It was of the three of them, together in Megan's living room. They were talking about how best to lure the so-called

Worshipper Killer - even now, looking back, she cringed at their naivety. Megan and Jamie were on Macallan. Jess was on water. She was driving. She remembered the jokey-banter between them, the occasional innuendo that, had it carried on, would have led to her saying something afterwards. Thankfully it never went quite that far. It was the first time she got a close look at the chemistry between them. Right now, two thousand miles of ocean lay between Jamie and Rosanna. But Megan was there, on his doorstep, albeit in 'voluntary custody', whatever that is.

It made her wonder.

She was still wondering when Jonathan Kradesh knocked on the door and poked his head round. Unable to think of a reason not to, she beckoned him in.

'Thanks Jess,' he said, parking himself in the chair to the side of her desk. 'I've just been looking at some of these other cold cases you've got Alec chasing up. I was wondering if it might not be better if...'

Here we go, Jess thought.

CHAPTER 70

CARVER PUT HIS mobile down and breathed out. His call to Jess was never going to be easy, but he hadn't expected to feel quite so uncomfortable. But while the problem he now faced was still there, at least he had bought himself time. All he had to do now was work out how to use it.

Turning, he stared out over the hotel's parking area, the green park next to it and the fields beyond. Where fields ended, trees stretched to the hills on the horizon. Somewhere out there, Amos Wells and his team of FBI forensic anthropologists were uncovering bodies. He was glad it wasn't his case. He'd done his bit, making the call to the sheriff's department the day following their return, putting on what was probably the weirdest accent the operator had ever heard while getting her to repeat the GPS coordinates he'd given her. His claim to be a passing hunter who didn't want to get further involved and refused his details, wouldn't have washed with any police operator he'd known, but they needed some means to get the FBI out there. It sufficed.

He was conscious that Jess had sounded less and less convinced the longer the call went on. He wasn't surprised. She was good at spotting evasion. It was what made her such a skilled detective. She always looked for the full story. Right now she would know that his contained gaps. She would be wondering what they were.

Carver, on the other hand, didn't have to wonder. He knew. The gaps were the things he hadn't yet shared with her. He was still thinking on how best to frame it all. Even when he did, he still wasn't sure he would show it to her. Some of it, he thought she would probably get. But some, she might struggle with. It was why he had tried to not say too much. Better a stilted conversation than trying to explain things that may not make a lot of sense. Hell, some of it still didn't make a lot of sense to him, which was why he was still working on it. That all said, Jess was probably the one person who, if he took time to explain, might just understand. She had been involved in it all from the beginning. She knew Megan, and him - better than Rosanna he sometimes thought. But right now it was good she had other things to think about. It would stop her thinking too much about what he was doing - maybe - which might help him buy time. .

The voice came from behind.

'I'm glad I was here, or my ears would have burned.'

He turned.

Megan Crane was sitting at the dresser, glancing at him through the mirror while applying the finishing touches to her makeup. While speaking to Jess, she had finished doing her hair. Restored to its natural glossy-black, and coiffured as if she'd just come from the stylist, it reminded him of how she looked that first day, when she appeared, framed in her kitchen doorway. It brought to mind other images of her, the ones he only got to see later, once trust had been established - illusion though it was. None of it helped resolve his present dilemma.

He still wasn't sure what, exactly, was in his mind when he brought her back to the hotel, rather than hand her over to the Deputy US Marshal's Office to be detained pending extradition. The fact she had contributed, along with her son, to saving their lives had something to do with it, that much was clear. Matt Lynch even raised it when they spoke, outside the cabin, trying to work out how they might repay at least some of the debt they owed by keeping Brandon from the truth he didn't deserve to learn. The only way, they decided, was to keep him - and Kit - out of it altogether, which had the added benefit of sparing Kit from the ordeal of having to relive her experiences for the benefit of police, FBI, Coroner's officials, et al. The problem was, it meant keeping them *all* out of it. Despite trying, they could not devise a credible enough version of events involving him and Megan but without the kids, that might stand the sort of scrutiny it would attract. And if a cobbled-together script did fall apart, as Carver suspected it almost certainly would, it could all lead back to Brandon and Kit anyway. Their disappearance was well documented. In the face of an account with holes, even a half-decent investigator would soon put two and two together. Which was why they opted for the 'scorched earth' solution, removing all traces they - any of them - were ever there, and arranging things so that while a fall-out between partners-in-crime leading to them killing each other might seem a stretch, it was still, at the very least, plausible.

Carver's original thought - mightily generous, the likes of Jess, certainly Rosanna, would no doubt say - was to grant Megan a last few days of freedom. Apart from saving the kids, and himself, she had helped remove a pair of killers who might otherwise have carried on their horrific work. It seemed reasonable. Even Matt seemed keen on it, grateful to just have his daughter back, scarred maybe, but alive.

For two days, holed up in his room and out of sight, everything was fine. They used the time to recover from the mental and physical trials they had endured. To Carver's amazement, Megan stuck by her promise not to run. She even offered to return with him to the UK, voluntarily.

'You helped save my son's life, Jamie. He's the only thing important to me now. That and him never discovering who, what, his mother is. If I run, sooner or later you will want to know if I've tried to contact him, and he'll want to know why. The only way that won't happen is if I come back with you.'

He was sceptical at first, doubtful he would get her on a plane without a warrant of extradition. But by the end of the second day, with no signs of any change of heart on her part, he was beginning to wonder if he might not need one after all. Two days on, he was even more firmly of that view, helped by the fact that the other problem he had foreseen had also never materialised.

To begin with, he'd worried that sharing a room between them, even one with two large double beds, might throw up the kind of problem some might see as inevitable, given their - rather unique - personal history. To his surprise, it didn't. Respectful of each other's privacy, careful it seemed, to avoid anything that might trigger a change, they both quickly settled into a routine based on a kind of polite formality that, in other circumstances, might have been comical. When he spoke with Rosanna, Megan took herself off to the bathroom, staying there until he'd finished. During his 'work' calls - Jess mainly, but The Duke and Rachel also - Megan stayed out of sight, plugged into her iPad, paying no attention. It was only when he spoke with Matt Lynch, she popped up to show herself, accepting his friendly wave and somewhat inappropriate, 'Hope you two are getting along,' with a diverting, 'We are managing. I hope Kit's recovering okay?'

Throughout, they managed to not talk about anything that might acknowledge the history that lay between them. All mention of France, Paris, or what went on during the Worshipper Investigation, was studiously avoided.

This state of so-far-okay equilibrium persisted for three days.

Then everything changed.

CHAPTER 71

ON THE THIRD DAY day Carver woke in the early hours to what sounded like her stifling sobs.

'You okay?' he whispered across.

The noises stopped. He waited a while. They did not return.

Over breakfast, he noticed her mood was subdued compared to the days previous, almost sombre. Mid-morning, they walked out to nearby Alexandra Park for some fresh air. Part of their daily routine from Day One, it allowed them to relax in a way the room did not allow for. As they sat on their favoured bench, Starbucks in hand, she was distant and withdrawn, paying no attention to those passing, the joggers, kids playing. Eventually, he felt he had to say something.

'Apart from the obvious, is something wrong? You're very quiet.'

It took a couple more prompts to get her to speak. When she did, she was hesitant, the words interspersed with sighs.

'It's just... These last few days... Thinking of Brandon, and what might have happened... Being here with you, seeing a little into your life... It's made me realise some things.'

'Like what?'

She lifted her head, stared into the distance. 'Like what a vile, evil person I am. Like how I deserve whatever awaits me when I get to wherever they put me. Like how, if I had my time over again, I would avoid the mistakes that led to me becoming what I am.'

Wary about breaking their unspoken pact, he hesitated to respond. Curiosity drove him. 'And what's that?'

Turning to him, she met his gaze for the first time since waking. 'I think we both know the answer to that question, Jamie. Let's not go there.'

Happy to comply - what was he supposed to say? - he lapsed into silence.

The rest of the morning and afternoon she stayed mainly silent as he found things he needed to do on his notebook - drafting emails and long-overdue log-reports - and made calls to Matt Lynch, Rachel, Rosanna. Meanwhile she busied herself on her iPad and watched a movie - some nondescript thriller - on the hotel video channel. Later, when she went along with his suggestion for a pre-dinner drink out on the hotel terrace, overlooking the neatly-laid-out garden, he thought maybe she was coming out of it. But as the waiter brought their second drinks, she skirted back to the conversation she'd begun earlier.

'Can I just say something?'

'Sure,' he said.

'I just want to say, I'm sorry.' She turned to him. 'Sorry for everything I've done to you, and to those you ever cared for. I know how much you must hate me. I mean *really, really* hate me. In fact I'm surprised you haven't taken the opportunity to strangle me in my sleep. I know I would, if someone had done to me, the things I've done to you.'

Surprised to hear such an outpouring of mea-culpa - and from *Her* of all people - it took him a while to find words. His first thought was to respond in the affirmative.

Tell her yes, she was absolutely right, he *did* hate her. And yes, he *had* thought about sneaking from his bed at night, taking one of her black silk stockings, entwining it about his fingers, slipping it round her throat and pulling until her face turned blue, her eyes bulged and bits of tongue protruded between her teeth.

But then he realised, that would simply be spite. Sure, the past couple of years, he had entertained all kinds of thoughts about what he might do to her - including physical harm - if the opportunity ever arose. But he had had no such thoughts now for some while, certainly not since the day she knocked on his hotel room door. And while the scenario with the stocking did pass through his mind that very first night they were together, as he looked across at her, sleeping in the bed next to his, it never got close to any sort of intent, being more of *'I could if I wanted, but I don't, so I won't'* kind of reflection.

Which is why his response to her *mea culpa* was a deliberately low-key, 'We all make mistakes Megan. I've made plenty myself in my time.'

'Not like mine, you haven't.'

'True,' he said. 'They weren't like yours. But my mistakes hang over me, just the same as yours are hanging over you right now. When they do, we feel bad about it.'

Doubt showed in her face. 'Are you saying that just to make me feel better?'

He shook his head. 'I'm saying it because it's true.'

Still not convinced, she said, 'I can't imagine you ever making that bad a mistake, Jamie. You always come across as the sort who knows exactly what to do, whatever the circumstances.'

He gave a self-deprecating snort. 'That's where you are wrong. I know you once read that Sunday Times article that made me out to be the best thing since sliced bread, but let me tell you, it was way off.'

Her eyes narrowed, subjecting him to mock-scrutiny. 'What? So you're not the world's greatest detective after all?'

'No,' he said, 'That would be Batman.'

It triggered a smile that turned into a chuckle, then a throaty laugh. Not a throw-your-head-back-and-guffaw kind of laugh, but a laugh all the same. And as it came, her eyes sparkled and her hair swung about her shoulders. When it passed, the smile remained though it was tentative. 'So tell me… *do* you hate me?'

Carver picked up his glass, threw down what remained of his second whiskey.

'Let's get dinner,' he said.

Wherever her bout of depression had come from, their mutual soul-bearing seemed to have the effect of dispelling it. Over dinner, and as the evening wore on, her mood started to lift. She started to relax. So did he. Wine helped. By the time they finished the meal and returned to the room, something had changed between them.

Lying on their respective beds, conversation flowed like it had not done before. They still picked their way to begin with, treading carefully to avoid anything that might reverse the thaw. But bit by bit, they delved. She was interested in hearing about his early years, growing up in Liverpool. He wanted to know what Cheltenham Ladies' College was like, how she got into modelling. That took them to Paris, but by then it didn't seem to matter. Time passed. They ordered another bottle of wine. As she talked more, he spoke less. Soon he was just listening, fascinated as she told the story he had never heard, until now.

The trouble was, he had no way of knowing how much to believe.

CHAPTER 72

IT WAS MEGAN'S boyfriend-photographer, a Frenchman, who introduced her to the world that would become her lifestyle. It was him with whom she watched, for the first time, a video of Just Jaeckin's 1975 *Histoire d'O* - The Story Of O. She was nineteen. As she told Carver, it would prove influential. Certain famous clubs around Montmartre, Montserrat and later, London's Soho, gave her opportunities to explore and discover, both about herself, and the wider human condition. It was in one such club she met Edmund Hart. At this point, the light in the room seemed to wane. She still talked, freely, but they both knew they were now in territory that did not lend itself to even dark humour, let alone some of the breezy point-scoring of earlier.

It had always puzzled Carver how someone like her - educated, independent, *beautiful* -allowed herself to be seduced into taking up with a monster like Hart. As Carver only learned after his capture, Hart's tastes for depravity - *real* depravity, not the sort of consensual, fantasy role-play kind that many otherwise-respectable professional couples pay a monthly on-line subscription for these days - knew no bounds. Okay, the Probation Service reports quoted by the Judge when passing sentence at the end of her trial, painted Megan as someone with few, if any, redeeming qualities. On the other hand, Carver had met many - all decent, all law-abiding - who seemed, genuinely to hold her in high regard, describing her as a loving and, when not in role, caring friend. According to them, she was the kind of person they would happily invite to dine with family - before she was convicted of murdering people that is. 'Misunderstood' was a word Carver heard often when, following her conviction, he set out to determine the full extent of her network. It was why, for him, she had always presented a conundrum.

Now, as he listened to her describing how Hart, twelve years her senior, played on her youth, her eagerness to learn and her naivety - 'Hard to believe, but BDSM doesn't feature much on the Cheltenham Ladies' College curriculum' - he began to see how it could have happened. During their early time together, Hart managed to keep hidden from her his involvement in things he knew she would find so shocking, she would run, like any sane, well-balanced individual. The way she told it, it put Carver in mind of the Boiling Frog Theory beloved by behaviourists. Put a frog in tepid water, gradually turn the heat up, and it will stay there, never perceiving danger until it cooks to death. Megan's story sounded similar. Hart's gradual, 'turning the heat up' enabled him to manipulate her perceptions of 'normal', persuading her to cross boundaries into territory that was not just dangerous, but immoral, unethical and, in due course, illegal.

An 'experiment' here. A 'stretch' there. A carefully coordinated succession of 'Why don't we try...?', together with the occasional, 'Here take some of this, It will heighten the experience'. Such were the methods Hart used on her, over several years. All the time painting himself as a free- thinking, liberal-minded force for good, whose only mission was to free those caught in the bonds of convention, and expose the hypocrisy by which society condemns those whose interests and behaviour it deems 'unacceptable', while gorging on a daily diet of cultural representations - books, movies, games, websites - comprised, largely, of the very things it condemns.

By the time Hart's 'mission' extended to murdering high-class escorts who were helping 'those who condemn' camouflage their worst hypocrisies under the cloak of 'professional, business-based personal services', Megan could no longer distinguish between 'moral hypocrisy' and cold, bloody, murder of the most depraved kind. In her eyes, Hart was a Crusader, his victims, peddlers of a deadly virus infecting those vulnerable to its particular pathogen. Even after Hart's capture, her blindness, and his influence, continued.

'During his trial and even after,' Megan said. 'We kept in contact, secretly, through his lawyer. He managed to convince me that, in his absence, my mission was to exact vengeance on those responsible for his downfall. Which meant you... and... Angie.' Carver felt a stab to his heart, but said nothing. 'Even those I killed...' she paused, shaking her head, wiping away tears. 'God help me, what sort of monster was I? Even those, I convinced myself, were necessary, simply collateral damage along the road that would take me to you, as they eventually did.' She shook her head again, as if struggling to believe her own story.

At this point she paused, as if needing time, while she swung herself off the bed and took herself off to the bathroom. While she was there, Carver stayed stretched out on the bed - he was on the whiskey by now - staring up at the ceiling, reflecting on what he was hearing.

When she returned she seemed calmer, more together again. But instead of returning to her bed, she sat on the edge of his. Leaning towards him, she stared at him with an intensity greater than he had ever known.

'I've done some terrible, terrible, things, Jamie. I'm not looking for forgiveness or anything. It's too late for that. But I do want you to know. The Megan Crane I've been describing is gone. I'm not entirely sure when she went away, but I know this. She's never coming back.'

Her story told - or as much of it as she was prepared to share right now - she fell silent.

For a long time, they stayed like that, silent, attending to their own thoughts, staring into each others' faces. During it, Carver thought about what to say, or not say, by way of response. There was so much in all he had heard, part of him - the detective - yearned to dig for more, especially concerning Hart. He had often wondered about the period he lived in New York, what he got up to, what he may have done. She would know, he was sure. But the other part, of him, the Jamie Carver part, had heard enough, for now at least. So much of what she had talked about, struck at the very heart of who he now was, what he had become these past years, he needed time to digest it all, let it sink in before trying to put words to thoughts.

In the end he settled for nodding and saying simply, 'Okay.'

Her face told him she understood his brevity. She didn't push him to comment further on what he had heard. Reaching out, she found his hand, squeezed it, just once and only briefly.

'Thank you for listening,' she said.

Then she rose, and returned to her 'side' of the room. Out of his view, she undressed, before slipping under the duvet. 'Goodnight Jamie,' she said.

'Goodnight Megan,' he replied.

Carver never knew how long he stayed, listening as her breathing settled to a soft, rhythmic purr. He couldn't say how much wine and whiskey he'd had. Enough that, normally, he would have had no trouble falling into a deep, alcohol-fuelled sleep. But right now his mind seemed clear, and it was so full of thoughts, ideas, what-ifs, he doubted he would sleep at all. Through it all, one question stood out.

What happens next?

Carver came awake with a start. The light was still on next to his bed. Somehow - God knows how - he *had* managed to fall asleep. Megan Crane, dressed only in her silky black nightdress, was staring down at him from the side of the bed. His first instinct was to look for the knife in her hand, but then her face told him he was in no danger. He raised himself onto his elbows.

'What?' he said.

'I can't sleep,' she said, before moving.

For a split-second, he thought she was about to lie down next to him, which would have tested him, but she simply sat where she had earlier. Sitting straight, like a teacher about to have a difficult conversation with a student, she paused a moment, dipping her head to look down at her hands, playing in her lap. Carver sensed conflict in her.

She looked up, searching for, then holding his gaze.

'I didn't finish my story,' she said. 'There's something I left out.'

'It's alright,' he said. 'We can talk more in the morning.'

'NO,' she said, firmly. 'I need to tell you now. If I wait until morning, I may change my mind.'

Curious to discover what could possibly be so important, he sat up.

'What is it?' he said.

Suddenly nervous to the point of shaking, she grappled with it for several seconds longer. Then she told him. And when she did, Carver knew, for certain this time, he would not sleep again that night or, possibly, many more to come.

It was that last, early-hours of the morning conversation that was still whizzing round Carver's head as he came off the phone to Jess - having broken the news he would not be home for another week at least - to meet Megan's gaze in the mirror as she carried on applying her make up. Having not slept since he woke to find her standing over him, still reeling from her final, devastating revelation, he was beginning to feel like he was losing focus.

As it happened, she still managed to come up with something that made sure he didn't, and it would lead to a great deal more talking through the rest of that day.

'Did I hear you mention someone by the name of "Kradesh"?' she said.

CHAPTER 73

AS ALWAYS, THE approach roads into JFK airport were heavy with traffic, those through the airport itself clogged with buses, taxis drop-offs and service vehicles. As Lynch threaded his County Sheriff Department SUV through the gaps that opened, mysteriously, in front, he turned to Carver next to him.

'I think you may be right. I maybe just better drop you at the gate entrance and let you walk in from there. It could take me a while to get parked, and-'

'Hey, that's fine Matt,' Carver said. 'We can manage if you just drop us off. I've been through here before. I'm sure I'll remember it once we're inside.'

Checking his mirror, Lynch said, 'Is that okay with you, Megan?'

'Of course,' she smiled from the back. 'I'm sure Jamie won't get us lost.'

'Right then… so let me see…'

As Lynch started checking signs and gate numbers, looking for theirs, Carver twisted round in his seat to see how she was doing. Poised and elegant in the black and cream trouser suit combination that gave her the air of a business traveller, she seemed calm and very much in control. *Remarkable*, he thought, though he was not altogether surprised.

'You okay?' he asked.

She nodded, threw him a smile.

He held her gaze, making sure, before turning back. The last few days had been hectic, filled with making plans, arranging things that needed arranging, settling matters that needed settling. Through it all, she had stayed calm and composed, exhibiting the sort of control those that knew her would expect. But beneath it all, Carver knew she was nervous. Understandably. Her life was about to change, again.

'This is it,' Lynch said.

Swinging left, he pulled up outside an entrance marked "Gates 23-42". An Airport Security Officer, automatic rifle cradled across his chest, was standing outside. He raised a hand and nodded the acknowledgement that passes between law and security officers the world over where parking is restricted. As Megan stepped from the back, Lynch offered her a hand, which she accepted. Then she waited as he helped Carver retrieve their cases.

'Well this is it, I guess,' Lynch said as they came together. His voice was a mix of cheery- 'off-you-go', and regret. He knew what awaited Megan the other side.

He put his hand out. 'Thanks for everything, Jamie. I hope we'll meet again some time.'

As they shook, Carver said, 'Me too Matt. Give me a call if you ever come over.'

'Don't worry, I will. Kit's desperate to see England. She's hoping you'll use your pull to fix a meet with Royalty, or something.'

Carver chuckled, 'Tell her I'd love to.'

Lynch turned to Megan. There was moment's awkwardness, then he leaned over, - 'Oh come here, you,' - and hugged her tight. Surprised, Megan looked at Carver over Lynch's shoulder. A wry smile formed. Letting go, Lynch hung onto her hand. He turned serious, as Carver knew he would.

'Kit and I owe you more than we can ever repay Megan. Whatever the future holds for you, please, take with you our blessing.'

'I will Matt, thank you. And please, tell Kit I'll never forget her.' Reaching up, she kissed him, lightly on his cheek before holding his gaze for a further moment. Looking slightly uncomfortable, he broke from it.

'Right, ' he said. 'One last thing.' Taking out his mobile, he held it up, pointed it at them. Seeing the looks on their faces he said, 'It's for Kit.'

No option but to give in to the blackmail, Carver stood close to Megan, feeling hugely self-conscious and trying not to smile.

Lynch counted them down. 'One, two, *THREE.'* He checked the shot. 'That's great. I'll send it you Jamie.'

'Do that,' Carver said.

'Right, I better go before this guy gives me a ticket.' Lynch nodded at the man with the carbine.

After one last round of 'Goodbyes', they trundled their cases towards the door.

'Remember me to Jess,' Lynch called, as they passed inside.

Stopping, they turned to give him one last wave, then they were off, looking for the information boards showing their flight.

As he watched them disappear inside, Lynch shook his head, experiencing the mood down-swing partings often bring. At the back of his mind was the thought he may never see either of them - certainly not Megan - again. He brought up his phone, checking the picture. It was a good one, he thought. It showed a not-too-bad looking guy, his hand resting, lightly, on the waist of his very good-looking travelling companion. Anyone meeting them would probably assume they were a couple returning from holiday, or business colleagues on their way back from some high-powered meeting. They would never guess he was a detective, returning a convicted multiple murderer to serve out the rest of her sentence.

Just goes to show, he thought. You never know who you are dealing with these days.

Climbing back into his SUV, Lynch waved a 'thanks' to the security guy, indicated right, then swung out into the gap left for him by the car behind. Flashing his lights, he followed the signs for "EXIT - ALL ROUTES."

As he weaved his way through the traffic, he was looking forward to getting home and seeing what Kit had prepared for dinner.

****

As the Airbus A330 accelerated down the runway, part of Carver's mind was already focused on the issues he needed to address over the coming days, seeking to put them in some order or priority. The other part was musing on what else may arise he had not yet even thought about. He was certain they would arise - given the circumstances, what has about to happen, it was almost inevitable - he just hoped that whatever came up, his experience and ability to think on his feet would see him through. If it didn't, the consequences would be... well, right now, he didn't care to think on it.

Normally a relaxed flier, he was conscious his heart was beating a littler faster than usual. Nothing to do with the stresses some feel on take-off, or the three cups of coffee he'd downed while waiting for their flight to be announced, rather it was the natural consequence of knowing what awaited them when they landed. At that moment, a mental picture of Jess, waiting at the barrier in the Manchester Airport arrivals hall came to him. It made his heart beat even faster. Suddenly uncomfortable, he tried to force his mind elsewhere. As luck would have it, a diversion from an unexpected source came to his rescue.

A hand gripped his, squeezing it tight.

Turning, he was surprised to see the woman next to him staring, rigidly, at the seat back in front. Without moving her head, her eyes flicked in his direction, before snapping back.

'Don't laugh,' she said, 'I'm okay once we're up. It's just take-offs and landings I'm not keen on.'

Given who she was, the things he knew she was capable of, several responses sprang to mind in that moment. Most were the sort he might give to another detective who had suddenly revealed a surprising nervousness about flying. Low on genuine sympathy, high on teasing sarcasm. But under the circumstances he knew it would be neither appreciated, nor appropriate. For that reason he let her hand stay there until the 'Keep Belts Fastened' symbol switched off and the changed engine tone signalled they were at cruising height. As her grip eased, he turned to check how she was doing.

Her eyes were closed, lips apart, breathing low and steady. Even as he gazed on her - striking as ever - her head lolled to rest on his shoulder and a lock of hair fell across her cheek. Reaching across, he tucked it back, conscious of the casual intimacy anyone observing may read into it.

Soon, he knew, he should turn his thoughts back to where they were when she gripped his hand. But for now…

He looked up, searching for cabin crew, wondering when the drinks service may start.

CHAPTER 74

JESS LEANED ON the barrier, watching the steady stream of bodies emerging from Passport Control. The arrivals board showed the flight landing thirty-five minutes ago. They could appear in the next ten minutes, though she knew the vagaries of Manchester Airport baggage-handling made it unlikely. She'd knew some who had taken two hours. *God, I hope not...* If only Jamie would remember to switch his mobile back on, or even just reply to the message she'd sent ten minutes before, he might give her some idea. But she imagined his mobile languishing wherever he put it after enabling flight-safe mode prior to take-off. She was already resigned to having to be patient.

Turning, she looked across to where Alec was talking with the two prison officers, a man and a woman. Catching Jess's glance, he paused to return her a hopeful look. He pointed to his wrist. She spread her hands. *Who knows?* He shook his head, resumed his conversation. She went back to leaning on the barrier.

She was looking forward to seeing Jamie again. She had missed him these past weeks, both as colleague and friend. And with her Six Enquiry beginning to throw up some interesting aspects, she was keen to get his perspective on some of the emerging issues. But meeting Megan again after all this time was a different matter, even if it would only last as long as it took the POs to confirm her identity, inform her that, having escaped from lawful imprisonment, she was now in their custody, and cart her off to HMP Stigwood. Earlier, the senior PO - the woman - had mentioned how she would only be held there temporarily pending re-allocation. Jess knew their reunion would last no more than a minute, two at most. But knowing Megan - more to the point, what *Megan* knew about *her* - it was long enough for Megan to get inside her head, if she was in that sort of mood. At the very least, it may prove uncomfortable.

What the Hell, she thought. If she's still into playing those sorts of games, I'll just have to ride it out and take it. Taking out her mobile - still no reply from Jamie - she started checking her notifications and socials while she waited.

She was still doing so an hour and ten later when Alec slid into the seat next to the one she had finally sought out after deciding fifty minutes standing around was enough for anyone, particularly in heels.

'What d'ye reckon?' he said. His burr was full of boredom. 'D'ye want me to go check what the problem is?'

Quarter-of-an-hour before, they had spoken of contacting the Airport Police and pulling strings to find out what the delay was, but agreed to give it a while longer. She was aware some Border Force officers like to flex their considerable powers over entry when presented with a traveller whom their screen pings as, 'Of Interest'. Megan was flagged on the Police National Computer as a Prison Escapee. Border Force use a different system, but Jess knew steps had been taken recently to make the two 'speak' to each other. Megan's new, British Embassy-issued emergency passport would, undoubtedly, lead to questions. And while Carver's police warrant card would normally be enough to steer passage through most bureaucracy, Jess could well imagine someone rubbing their hands on realising they had an escaped murderer *and* a senior police officer in their grasp. Not for the first time she wished she had held out longer when Jamie insisted there was no point giving Airport Special Branch advance warning of their scheduled arrival. 'It'll take as long as it takes,' he'd said.

'You better go check Alec,' Jess said. 'We could be here all night at this rate.'

'Aye,' he said, then murmured, 'An' them POs are getting antsy. They're due off at midnight and reckon they're not authorised for overtime.'

'Oh, for God's sake,' Jess said. 'See what you can find out. I'm going to grab another coffee. Want one?' He nodded, before setting off towards the Terminal One Police Office.

He was gone some twenty minutes, during which time Jess experienced a growing sense of unease. Surely a delay this long would have prompted Jamie to ring her, at the very least check his phone and see her message? Then again, it could just be a dead battery.

But as she saw Alec returning through the terminal, his face like stone, her unease deepened.

'The duty Inspector walked me through the baggage hall,' he said. 'There's no sign of them. He's just rung the airline. They have no record of them being on the flight.'

'*What?*'

'There was no booking in their name for this flight, and they're not coming up on any others either.'

As Jess stared at him, something started squeezing her stomach. 'That's crazy. Jamie messaged me the flight details.' She re-checked her mobile, read the message again, cross-checked the flight number against the information boards, though she knew she had not misread. 'And he replied to a message I sent last night wishing him a safe flight. He says, "See you tomorrow".'

'So what's going on?' Alec said. 'It either has to be a mistake, or something's wrong.'

Jess's feeling of unease surged again. She knew how easy it was to forget that Megan Crane was a dangerous, duplicitous killer. Jamie would know that too. But there had been occasions when she'd wondered if he might not have a blind spot. She hoped to God he wasn't lying in some airport toilet or storage area with a knife in his gut. She checked the time. Just after one am. Early evening in New York.

She rang Matt Lynch.

He was in his office. When he heard what was happening, he was surprised, and concerned.

'Everything seemed okay when I dropped them off,' he said. 'They were in good time for the flight so I can't see how they'd miss it.'

'They didn't *miss* it Matt. They were never booked *on* it.'

She relayed Alec's discovery. Lynch's confusion matched her own.

'But where could they... What could have happened to them? I don't understand.'

'Neither do I,' Jess said. 'But *something's* happened. I need to work out what.' Her mind clicked into gear. 'The last time I spoke with Jamie, I wasn't sure I was getting the full story. Talk me through it. What's been happening since Megan surrendered herself and you found the kids out at the cabin?'

'Not much,' Lynch said. 'Most of the time they've been recovering from what happened while Jamie's been waiting to confirm flight bookings and things.'

'You said recovering. Recovering from what?'

'What happened out at the cabin.'

'What happened at the cabin?'

407

'You know, Reed taking them prisoner, Brandon killing him, the shoot-out. All that stuff.'

'I have no idea what you're talking about Matt. I thought Megan surrendered herself, told you about the cabin, you went there, found the kids safe and Reed and his accomplice dead.'

There was a pause on Lynch's end. 'Is that what Jamie told you?'

'More or less. Why, is that not what happened.'

'Not exactly.'

'You better tell me Matt. I'm getting a bad feeling about this.'

Over the following minutes, Jess kept her mobile clamped to her ear, listening with a growing sense of disbelief as Lynch told a story very different from the version Jamie had given her. He hadn't lied to her. It was just that he'd left so much unsaid.

In retrospect, Jess understood now why the times she had spoken to Jamie the past week, she had come away with the feeling she was missing something. Words such as, 'I'll tell you more when I see you,' and 'It's complicated,' rang in her ears, several times. She assumed they referred to extraneous details that didn't add up to much. She was wrong. The details he had left out were by no means extraneous. Far from Megan's 'surrender', the youngsters' rescue, and the deaths of the two kidnappers being the result of a fortuitous string of events that happened to see the kids safe and justice served, Jess now saw it for what it was - a daring and dangerous rescue that, were it not for the actions of the boy, Brandon, and Megan herself, could have turned out very differently. The way Lynch told it, Jamie owed them, and maybe even her, his life. When Lynch mentioned something about "her son," Jess thought she had misheard.

'I missed that. What was it you said about "her son"?

Whose son?'

'Megan's.'

'What do you mean, "Megan's"? She hasn't got a son.'

'Yes she has. That's what I'm talking about. Brandon is Megan's son. Didn't Jamie tell you that either?'

Stunned to silence, Jess could only stare into space, mouth agape. *Oh. My. God.* And as the seconds ticked, the fog that so far seemed to have shrouded the whole sequence of events began to lift. As it did so she realised. The picture Jamie had painted for her, and which she thought she had a rough idea what it looked like, was not just different in the detail, but a whole different shape to the reality. But the real kicker was still to come.

As she sought to put what Lynch was telling her into a framework that might make some sort of sense, a thought occurred that, even as it arrived, made her unease worse. Lynch was still talking, having moved on to something about Megan giving her son up when he was young.

'Hang on Matt,' she said. Lynch stopped. 'Since all this happened, Jamie's been talking about Megan being under some sort of 'voluntary detention'?'

'Well, ye-es, I guess that's right.'

Something in the way Lynch drew it out, alerted her. 'What do you mean. "you guess". It either was, or it wasn't. You're the Sheriff. You must know. What sort of voluntary detention are we talking about?'

Lynch's silence was telling.

'Matt? What sort of voluntary detention was Megan under?'

'Well… I'd have to say it wasn't any sort of real detention at all. More like… an arrangement, I suppose.'

'What sort of "arrangement."?' Jess was having to work at not becoming annoyed. Suddenly it felt like she was interrogating a suspect, trying to zero in on the truth.

'She agreed to stay under Jamie's personal supervision, 24/7, until they returned to the UK.'

'Where?'

'Where what?'

'Where was this 'supervision'? Some sort of detention centre? A hostel of some kind?'

'No. His hotel.'

Jess froze. 'His hotel?'

'Where else? It had to be somewhere he could keep an eye on her. His hotel was as good as anywhere.'

'But not for some sort of voluntary supervision. Putting her in a hotel room is hardly what you'd call personal, 24/7 supervision.'

There was another pause. 'He didn't put her in a room as such. It was his room.'

'You mean he took another room and gave her his?'

'No. I mean they shared his room.'

Jess fought to stop her head spinning. Her heart was pounding now. A chill ran up her spine. When she spoke, she did so slowly, softly and deliberately.

'Are you telling me that since all this happened, Jamie and her have been sharing a hotel room?'

'Yes.'

Later, Jess would struggle to recall her own reaction to the news. She wasn't sure she did react. For several seconds, it was as if her mind went blank, unable to comprehend what she had heard.

Jamie, and Megan?

Sharing a room?

For a week and more?

And as everything Lynch had told her, combined with thoughts of the two of them confined that way - where it could lead; where it *had* led - started to form into something that could, eventually offer some sort of

410

explanation for their non-appearance, one question, clear, sharp, and utterly terrifying in its implication stood out from the many that were swirling around her brain that moment.

Oh Jamie... Jamie... Whatever have you done?

Epilogue

HE STARES UP at the whirring ceiling fan, not sure it is doing much good. The third night in a row he has witnessed it emerge from the darkness, he has already decided to revert to air-con this coming night. Bugger her blocked sinuses. Not that it will make much difference sleep-wise. There is too much going on his head for that. Still too many things to work out, plan for, resolve.

In that regard, his thoughts fall into two broad categories. Some things he knows he *ought* to be thinking about. Others, he *needs* to think about. The former comprise everything he has left behind. They include those who, right now, will be missing him most. And while he regards them as important, he knows that the only way he can continue to function, to avoid the guilt that will otherwise consume him, is to consign them, in his head, to the box marked, 'past.' By this means, he frees himself to focus on the '*needs*' category. It covers those things he must now do, the plans he must put in place and which will, he hopes, turn 'past', back into 'future'.

The two are not unrelated.

For close to five years he has lived under the shadow of one individual. The shadow comprises guilt, regret, shame - and fear. Up to a short time ago, he believed that individual to be dead. It led him to believe that escaping the shadow was not just difficult, but nigh-on impossible.

He has tried of course - *God how he has tried* - but the best he ever came up with was 'learning to live with it.' Which means the shadow never, ever, really went away.

But he knows now he was wrong. The shadow's

owner is *not* dead, which means there may yet be a chance - slim perhaps, but still a chance - by which he can remove it, permanently. How he will achieve that is not yet clear, though if he thinks on it hard and long enough, he hopes it will become so - hence the sleepless nights. The good news - if it can be called that - is that it boils down, essentially, to an exercise in problem-solving. And as experience shows, he is good at that.

But as well as how to remove the shadow, several other things remain unclear. One, perhaps the most important, is how much of what he has been told can he believe? That comes down to trust, and that is one of the confusions.

Over the years, he has learnt to rely on instinct and feelings - his so-called 'wizarding' abilities - to help him decide on whom and how far, he can place his trust. Those instincts have let him down only once. The trouble is, the person about whom he is presently confused is that very one.

As the room starts to lighten, heralding the dawn of what will be another hot, sultry day - one he has decided must bring some decisions - he turns on his side, letting his thoughts dwell on another, though related, 'confusion'.

On the face of it, there is nothing to be confused about at all. The spill of glossy-black hair on the pillow. The gentle curves of the naked form lying next to him. The still-beautiful face that seems so peaceful, so *harmless* in repose. The exposed throat with its rhythmic pulse. The fragrance he has concluded must emanate from her very pores. They are all such as would trigger - as they now are - feelings that are both natural, and understandable.

The confusion, however, lies in whether those feeling are, can ever be, *forgivable*.

As his hand lifts, driven by those feelings, his thought is, *Time will tell.*

He reaches across, keeping the hand an inch above her body as he traces her outline, shoulder to thigh, and back again. Withdrawing it, he lies next to her, watching, waiting, trying to decide whether, maybe, he can afford just one more day 'recuperating', as they have been the past week.

He could, he thinks, justify such a decision by telling himself that one more day may just help him become clearer in his mind as to whether her last, explosive revelation is based on some sort of truth, or is simply another strand in one of the complex webs of deceit she likes to weave and in which he already finds himself, partially, trapped - and could soon, if he is not careful, find himself more permanently cocooned.

The alternative of course - if he is only strong enough - would be to extricate himself, right now, and get on with accomplishing the task he has set himself and for which he is now risking so much. Tracking down the man who, up to a few short days ago, he also believed was dead.

The man who started it all.

The man he knew as Edmund Hart.

Even as he dwells on the name, her eyes open, slowly, and he finds himself staring into two dark pools. If he is not careful, he knows, they will draw him in, as they do every time. And now, even as he is thinking about it, he can feel it starting to happen. And as it does, he thinks that maybe, just maybe he *should* just give it another day.

After all, what difference can just one more day make?

Nine Years Later -
Extract From Brandon's Journal.

THIS ACCOUNT OF what happened that eventful summer being now, finally, complete, I am still not sure why I took so long to record it all. That the events I describe had a huge impact on my life is, to me at least, fairly obvious. Over the years I have thought often about writing it all up. At one time I imagined it might prove therapeutic, maybe even cathartic. But as time passed, the urge to do so dwindled, the thought of revisiting and reliving the events becoming in my mind less a satisfying trawl through memories of a formative period of my adolescence, and more a deep, possibly disturbing, delve into something that may prove darker than even I remembered.

But now it's finished I'm glad I've written it, though I'm still not sure what purpose it may serve in the longer term - if any. It's not like anyone else is ever likely to read it, other than Kit maybe, who is already badgering to get her hands on it. But at least it is there now, recorded 'for posterity' as they say. And just the act of getting it all down, in proper order and with the benefit of a more adult perspective on my then, youthful thoughts, feelings and experiences, has, I think, helped me better understand what was going on all those years ago.

Though not *quite* everything.

It goes without saying my adolescent infatuation with Miriam Cole over that summer was just that - the over-excited, fantasising of a fast-growing, pre-pubescent fourteen-year old taking his first steps towards learning about that strange creature called, in most cases still at least, 'Woman'.

And yet... sometimes, even now, I still find myself wondering - usually when I'm alone, reflecting maybe on what was actually in my head when I wrote the latest chapter of my current novel-in-progress - if it might, just might, have been something more than plain, teenage infatuation.

Given the passage of time - coming up nine years now - I would have thought that sort of infatuation would have receded more in my memory than it has. Even now, when I think of her, I can see her clearly, exactly how she was the day my father walked me over to her house, knocked on her door and introduced us. If I'm honest, I remember the black dress she wore *that* night just as if not more vividly. But hey, I'm a guy, what more can I say? And of course it is true that other, more dramatic, even life-changing aspects were also part of the story, so that might explain why the memories remain so strong.

But still, when my thoughts do turn to her - not every day, but often enough - I can't help wondering if maybe there *was* more to our relationship than I ever realised, but just never got around to recognising.

I sometimes think Kit has a better feel for it all than I do.

I never did see Miriam again after our parting that night in the forest. Nor did I ever hear from her, or Detective Carver again. For a long time, neither Kit, nor I, nor anyone else I know, ever spoke to me about Miriam, what happened to us, or anything associated with it. For several weeks after, there was a lot of stuff on the news and showing up all over social media about the FBI investigation centring on a cabin out in the forest. It involved missing teenagers and the disgraced former baseball star, Zander Reed, whose body was discovered there, along with another guy, following an anonymous tip off by some passing hunter to the Brackers Lake County Sheriff's Department. At the time, Kit and I kept well away from it all, even walking away when our fellow students started engaging in wild, 'what-if'-type conjecturing. By then, our 'embarrassing' two-day long - *ahem* - 'fling' that caused a brief panic while everyone looked for us, was all but forgotten. But I also know Kit was someway more curious than I to fill in the gaps in our understanding, despite what she went through.

I know she worked on her dad quite a bit, when they were alone. It would surprise me if she didn't get more out of him than she ever shared with me. She isn't shaping up to be the best investigative journalist The NY State Bugle has ever had for nothing, though the bump in her belly - our first - may just mean she'll have to give more attention to things other than corrupt politicians and 'celebrities with closeted skeletons' for a while. Maybe.

I also know she trawled on-line quite a bit once she finished all the counselling to see what she could find that might fill out what we/she already knew. She certainly dug deep into Reed and his background, though for why, I never really understood. I'd have thought he was the last person she would want to know more about. She also researched the English detective, Jamie Carver, to see if she could discover how he came to be involved in it all. I remember her once saying something about him being an 'interesting character' though she never expanded on it and never sought to tempt me into looking at whatever it was she discovered. And while my curiosity was aroused, I managed to stop myself following in her virtual footsteps, wary, I think, as to where they may lead.

I guess it was her dad's last visit prompted me to finally put virtual pen to virtual paper. Now retired from sheriffing, he and Paula are soon to embark on a state-to-state road-trip in the camper-home they invested half their savings in - once his chemo is finished and provided everything is looking the way we hope it will. Kit is desperate he gets to meet his grandson before he goes anywhere, whether travelling or, God forbid, somewhere else.

The weekend Matt and Paula visited, he and I spent a couple of nights out on the porch, sharing beers. I remember the last night in particular. His treatment was due to start that week and he was in reflective mood. Beer must have loosened his tongue, because he's never spoken to me about that night in the forest since we talked in my parents' garden, cementing our oath of secrecy. And it was only when, with a catch in his voice, he mentioned how he was so looking forward to meeting his grandson, and how, if things had gone differently, that would never even have been an option, he pointed to the irony of having to thank, *'that woman'*, for the fact he would soon be a grandfather. I didn't understand who he meant to begin with.

'What woman?' I said. 'Who are you talking about?'

He swigged his beer, 'You know,' he said. *'Her.'*

I must have looked blank because he looked at me like I was an idiot. 'Come on Bran, you know. That woman you had the hots for back when it all… happened. The one you did all that, "gardening" for.'

I didn't much like the way he made 'gardening' sound like something else, but I let it go. 'Oh, *her*,' I said, like I'd not thought of her in years. 'You mean, Miriam.'

'Yes,' he said. *'Her.'* He shook his head, swigged more beer 'God, she was something, wasn't she?'

I began to feel a tad uncomfortable. This was my father-in-law talking. And his wife, and mine, were just inside. 'Yes,' I said. 'I guess you're right. She was special.'

'Special?' He almost spat a mouthful of beer. 'I'm not

418

sure *special* is how I'd put it. More... extraordinary, I'd say.' He shook his head again, looked out over our garden, like he was remembering. 'Yeah...' Another swig. '*Damned* extraordinary...Tch.' He shook his head again. More beer.

Keen to move the conversation on, I remembered I wanted to ask about their van.

'Tell me,' I said. 'How much-'

'You know, Bran,' he said, not even listening. 'I said to that Brit detective one time, what was his name...? Carver?'

'Jamie,' I said, a little surprised his memory was unclear. 'Jamie Carver.'

'That's him. I remember now. "Jamie" I said to him. "Jamie, that Megan is some woman. If I didn't know about her, if I met her somewhere, a bar say, or some hotel, Hell, I'd be in there like a shot. *Like a shot*, God help me." That's what I told him. Can you imagine that?' He shook his head, swigged beer, chuckled at his reminiscence.

'Miriam,' I said.

'What?'

'Her name was Miriam.'

'That's what I said, Miriam.'

'No,' I said. 'You said, "Megan".'

He went still, looking right at me. 'No, I'm sure I said "Miriam".'

I smiled, shook my head. 'No, you called her Megan.'

He fidgeted, swigged from his bottle. I think he even started to color. 'I er... I meant Miriam,' he stumbled. 'Just a slip of the tongue.' He looked at his bottle. 'Too much of this,' he laughed.

I laughed with him.

We turned in shortly afterwards.

In bed that night, I replayed the conversation that had started something in my head. A memory of

419

something I thought I'd forgotten. It's amazing how memory works, even years later.

It was soon after our conversation, I started working on this account.

And though it is now finished, I've still not looked further into what prompted it. I'm not sure I ever will. I'm not sure I'll ever want to. But it's there if I, or even my son, one day, decides to do so.

I'm pretty sure I'd find something if I looked hard enough. Kit found Jamie Carver easy enough, so there's a fair chance there'll be something there, even if it's only a quick reference. For while slips of the tongue - *genuine* slips of the tongue - are meaningless and therefore impossible to track down, names are not.

If I'd had more beer that night, I might easily have put Matt's 'slip of the tongue' down to what he claimed it as - too much Bud - were it not for the memory that stirred the moment he said her name wrong.

It was the night it all happened, out in the forest. We were all on the porch outside the cabin. I'd just thrown the knife into Reed's chest, and we were all standing there, looking down at his body, in shock I guess. Detective Carver was the one who broke us out of it, calling to me to go get a knife and cut the ties securing him to the rail. Even now I can remember him standing there, holding up his wrists. I also remember his words, pretty much exactly.

'Get a knife. Cut me loose. Then help Megan… Not the knife in his chest. Get one from inside…'

It didn't register at the time. There was too much going on. Besides, why worry about him getting Miriam's name wrong? It wasn't like he knew her well. I assumed they'd only met during the twenty-four hours previous. A slip like that was understandable, particularly given the circumstances.

But *two* slips of the tongue? And by different people - both law officers - nine years apart? Aren't cops supposed to be hot on details like names and stuff? Okay, Matt has been retired three years, *and* he'd had beer, *and* had other things on his mind at the time - his impending trip, the cancer, his grandson...

But for them both to come out with the same 'wrong' name - Megan?

It's got to mean something. Hasn't it?

Especially when it was that same name I remember hearing all those years ago during my parents' 'partying' phase.

Megan isn't *that* common a name. If 'Jamie Carver' is on-line, then perhaps there's a reference to someone he once knew called Megan. I have to admit to thinking that, one day, it may be interesting to find out.

But until that day comes, if it ever does, I'll just continue to remember her the way I have these past nine years.

As simply, Miriam Cole, the woman across the street.

THE END

Enjoyed reading? Please consider posting a review. Reviews are the lifeblood of authors as they help to keep our books visible to new readers, and give us a better understanding of what you like in a story. You can post a review on Amazon by visiting the Breathe Again book page - ***here*** - then click on *"xxx customer reviews"*, next to the star rating. Thank you. For a glimpse of what's next, read on....

Coming Next.... 'BREATHE FREE'

Has Jamie Carver lost the plot?

Jamie Carver is missing, as is the woman from whose shadow he has spent the last three years trying to escape. Has his one big weakness finally claimed him - or is something else going on?

Jess Greylake has always stood by her boss, one hundred percent. But, struggling to contain the fallout caused by Carver's disappearance - emotional, personal *and* professional - she is finding it hard to refute those who claim it proves they were right about him all along. It isn't her only problem. The major investigation she lobbied for and is now running is at a critical stage. If she doesn't get a grip, her theory that a serial killer is avoiding detection by repeatedly changing his 'signature', will never see daylight again. In the meantime, the victim tally is mounting....

Fifteen hundred miles away, Detective Inspector Vasilis Stefanou of the Cyprus CID is under pressure from his bosses to declare the deaths of the two backpackers whose remains were recently unearthed, 'Accidental'. With no direct evidence of foul play, they could be right. But with three similar cases in as many years, Stefanou is open to other possibilities. When he is approached by a man claiming to be an English detective with an improbable story about a well-connected serial killer, thought to have died in prison but who may be living on the island, he wonders if there's a connection....

Book Seven in the DCI Jamie Carver Series, *'BREATHE FREE'* sees the chain of events that began in *LAST*

GASP -with the arrest of a serial killer by the name of Edmund Hart - come full circle. In this latest novel of murder, cover-up and conspiratorial intrigue, Carver is forced to reassess everything that has happened to him these past four years. At the same time, he must find the answer to a chilling question. Did a corrupt establishment let a serial killer walk free in order to preserve reputations and ensure secrets stay secret?

In the end it comes down to one thing. Can he - *dare he* - trust the dangerous dominatrix who now claims to love him, but has already twice tried to kill him?

Find out in 'BREATHE FREE', next in the DCI Jamie Carver Series

FREE DOWNLOAD

OTHER BOOKS BY Robert F Barker

The DCI JAMIE CARVER SERIES

LAST GASP (The Worshipper Trilogy Book #1)

The last time Jamie Carver let a would-be victim as bait for a serial killer, it ended badly. Now they want him to do it again, only this time the 'victim' is a dominatrix.

FINAL BREATH (The Worshipper Trilogy Book #2)

A monstrous killer, safe behind bars, but just how safe is 'safe'? An archive of debauchery and murder, poised to ruin reputations, carers, lives. A detective, running out of time to find what he seeks

OUT OF AIR (The Worshipper Trilogy Book #3)

One City; Paris. Two killers, one in hiding, the other stalking the streets. An innocent young couple, bewitched into the deadliest danger. The detective who must find them before the worst happens.

FAMILY REUNION

How do you save a family from slaughter when you don't know who they are, and you're not allowed to find out? A killer is coming, and Jamie Carver has to to stop him. But how?

DEATH IN MIND

"Five minutes before she killed herself, Sarah Brooke had never had a suicidal thought in her life."
A mind-bending psychological thriller with a terrific twist. 'A treat for all Derren Brown fans.'

BREATHE AGAIN

Grainy photographs showing a woman whose features recall someone who died two years ago. A murder in upstate New York bearing signatures with which Jamie Carver is all too familiar. Dare he even ask the question…??

OTHER TITLES

MIDNIGHT'S DOOR

A novel of nightclub bouncers, Russian mobsters, and serial killing. Introducing Danny Norton, the man who runs the door at Midnight's, the hottest nightspot around. When it all kicks off, you'll want him by your side.

A KILLING PLACE IN THE SUN

His 'Place In The Sun' is simply a house. But to this Englishman, it's his castle, and he wants it back. "An action-packed international thriller that grips from the start, and ends with a gut-punch that pulls at the heart."

Robert F Barker was born in Liverpool, England. During a thirty-year police career, he worked in and around some of the North West's grittiest towns and cities. As a senior detective, he led investigations into all kinds of major crime including, murder, armed robbery, serious sex crime and people/drug trafficking. Whilst commanding firearms and disorder incidents, he learned what it means to have to make life-and-death decisions in the heat of live operations. His stories are grounded in the reality of police work, but remain exciting, suspenseful, and with the sort of twists and turns crime-fiction readers love.

For updates about new releases, as well as information about promotions and special offers, visit the author's website and sign up for the VIP Mailing List at:-

http://robertfbarker.co.uk/

Made in the USA
Las Vegas, NV
22 November 2021

34995522R00252